Kate Furnivall was born in Wales and studied English at London University. She worked in publishing and then moved to TV advertising, where she met her husband.

In 2000, Kate decided to write her mother's extraordinary story of growing up in Russia, China and India, and this became *The Russian Concubine*, which was a *New York Times* bestseller. All her books since then have had an exotic setting and Kate has travelled widely for her research. She now has two sons and lives with her husband by the sea in Devon.

Visit Kate's website at www.katefurnivall.com

The
SURVIVORS

Kate Furnivall

**SIMON &
SCHUSTER**

London · New York · Sydney · Toronto · New Delhi

A CBS COMPANY

First published in Great Britain by Simon & Schuster UK Ltd, 2018
A CBS COMPANY

1 3 5 7 9 10 8 6 4 2

Simon & Schuster UK Ltd
1st Floor
222 Gray's Inn Road
London WC1X 8HB

Simon & Schuster Australia, Sydney
Simon & Schuster India, New Delhi

www.simonandschuster.co.uk
www.simonandschuster.com.au
www.simonandschuster.co.in

A CIP catalogue record for this book
is available from the British Library

Hardback ISBN: 978-1-4711-7227-4
Trade Paperback ISBN: 978-1-4711-7228-1
Paperback ISBN: 978-1-4711-7230-4
eBook ISBN: 978-1-4711-7229-8
Audio ISBN: 978-1-4711-7624-1

Typeset in Bembo by M Rules
Printed and bound by CPI Group (UK) Ltd, Croydon, CR0 4YY

MIX
Paper from
responsible sources
FSC® C020471

Simon & Schuster UK Ltd are committed to sourcing paper
that is made from wood grown in sustainable forests and support the Forest
Stewardship Council, the leading international forest certification organisation.
Our books displaying the FSC logo are printed on FSC certified paper.

To Marian
with all my thanks

SURVIVORS

CHAPTER ONE

Poland, Spring 1945

A hand closed over my mouth. I didn't move. I didn't make
a sound. Didn't breathe.

It was dark. I opened my eyes and I could make out the
first knifepoints of dawn spiking through the trees. It left
golden markers on the forest's black trunks in a direct trail
towards me. I was lying at the base of an oak, wrapped
in my skirts for warmth in the chill night air. The hand
pinned me there.

'They are coming.'

The voice was so close to my ear I thought it came from
inside my head, but it belonged to a young girl. I blinked to
show her I understood. Her hand lifted. I rolled silently to
my feet and leaned down so that my lips were pressed hard
against her soft cheek.

'Where? Where are they?'

'There.'

She pointed off to the area of trees on our left, barely visible where the forest still clung to the last scraps of the night. Blackness swirled among them, blurring my vision, stealing any sense of what was real and what was not. Shapes shifted. I kept my lips shut tight because I feared that if I opened them, a scream would come barrelling out.

'Are you sure?' I whispered.

'I saw them.'

'How many?'

'Six.' She was breathing fast. Her cheek felt ice cold. 'Maybe more. It was dark.'

I nodded. Not that she could see it. The thought of my ten-year-old child searching out hunters on her own in the black labyrinth of the forest while I slept made my heart cut loose in my chest. I drew her to me. Placed a hand on her small chest. Her heart was thundering against her twig-like ribs. I could push her behind a tree and run, crashing through the undergrowth, smacking into branches, luring the hunters away from her.

But Alicja was not that kind of child. She wouldn't stay where I put her. She would come after me. She would yell. She would rip their eyes from their sockets if they caught and beat me. So I dragged her over to a towering beech tree off to the west where it was out of reach of the spikes of dawn. Its roots writhed up from the earth like violent serpents and I tucked her under one of them where she could not be seen. I threw an armful of leaf litter over her and concealed myself behind its ancient trunk.

They came.

How many? I didn't know for sure. Certainly six. Ten? It was hard to tell. I could hear them, their urgent whispers. Sticks were cracking underfoot. They wanted me to know they were there, they made no secret of it. Fear slid up my throat as they moved constantly in and out of the trees, grey as ghosts, brief flickers in the darkness. Circling us. Like wolves. One laughed, high-pitched and greedy. My skin crawled.

They came closer. I caught a rustling behind me, a scratching among the new leaves. I twisted my head round to confront it and found the barrel of a pistol in my face. A Polish Pistolet wz.35, semi-automatic. One of the finest. I know my handguns. My heart split wide open when I thought of Alicja in her hideout only a metre away. These people were serious about killing.

'What have you got?'

'Nothing. I keep alive by eating worms.'

'Liar.'

'No, it's the truth.' My words stuck to my teeth, welded by rage. I held out my hands, palms up. 'See? Nothing.'

They were women. No men. Only women. A dishevelled group of all ages, young and old and everything in between. A dozen of them, most in trousers, some wearing skirts, muddy and ragged, greasy hair hidden under scarves. One with scars on her face. The women looked cold and tired, and I could smell the feral odour of them.

Was I like that? Wild-eyed and dangerous? Was that what they saw in me? Was that why two of them kept a gun aimed at my head?

I tried to be reasonable but it is hard to be reasonable when people have tracked you for days, their foul breath on your neck. Hunted you down.

'We are all doing the same. Trying to survive.' I spoke calmly to the woman who stood out as their leader, dressed in a man's heavy jacket and with skin tight to the bones of her gaunt angry face. 'We are all travelling to the West, fleeing ahead of the Soviet Army.' I spat on the black earth at my feet at the mention of the brutal Soviets. 'Their troops are marching through Poland, using rape as a weapon. In Warsaw we thought the Nazis were evil, but the Russians are worse.'

The woman nodded in the gloom. 'The devil's army. Stalin's bastards.' She spat in agreement.

I nodded back at her. Conversation was my way out of this. 'How far have you travelled?'

'Not far enough.'

'The German border can't be much further,' I pointed out. 'The American and British zones will be—'

'What have you got?'

'Nothing.'

We were back where we started.

'You want us to strip you?' She showed me her strong peasant hands. 'Leave you naked?'

Ice shot through my veins. I knew I had to give them something. My fingers reached for the hem of my skirt and, with a curse that I made no attempt to hide, tore it open. Three rolled banknotes dropped into my palm. Not worthless zloty or Deutschmarks. Good American dollars that had cost me dear. I tossed them on the forest floor, startling a beetle from its hideout. A woman with death's shadow in her eyes snatched them up, kissed them as if they were holy, and handed them over to the gaunt leader.

'And the rest?' she demanded.

'I have no more.'

She thrust the notes down the inside of her boot and the eyes of each woman regarded me in a way that made the hairs rise on the back of my neck. I tasted bile in my mouth. I'd seen that look before. In a Nazi firing squad. When they shot my dear friend in Warsaw's Old Town Market Square because he had blown up a Panzer tank and decapitated its crew.

'Shoot me!' I snapped into the silence of the forest. 'I've told you, I have no more.'

'Jewels then. You must have jewels.'

I laughed, a sharp animal sound. This woman had sunk her teeth in me and was not letting go.

'Do I look as if I have jewels?' I demanded. 'Would I be here? Like this? In the forest? If I had jewels?' My words were breaking up. Jagged and disjointed. I had to fight not to lick my cracked lips.

The woman scratched at her throat with a dirty fingernail. 'Some people swallow their jewels.'

The darkness thickened around me. The trees leaned

closer and the stink of rotting matter rose from the forest floor. I clenched my teeth together to silence the tremor that shook my jaw. These were women, not animals. Not Nazis. They would not cut me open.

That's what I told myself.

'I have no jewels,' I told them.

Believe me. This once.

I turned my back on them and walked away from the beech tree roots as fast as my boneless knees would take me. Every muscle in my back tensed. Waiting for the bullet that would tear into my flesh.

'Where is the child?' the leader rasped out after me.

'What child?'

I kept walking, forcing one foot forward, then the other. I needed to draw the women with me. Branches brushed at my face as I edged deeper into a tangle of hazel trees.

'Don't take us for fools. Where have you hidden her?'

I could hear the rustle of their feet behind me coming closer. I glanced back. A young woman with chalk-white skin and deep-set blue eyes that were full of a sad sort of kindness launched herself towards me ahead of the others. A gun dangled from one hand but her arms were spread wide as if to embrace me and her smile gave me hope. I stopped walking. She slammed the gun barrel into the side of my head with a crack that split my scalp and exploded through my brain. I crumpled to the ground as if my strings had been cut.

*

I woke. Voices crawled over each other around me, twisting and turning beyond my grasp. But I could make out Alicja's among them, strong and insistent. I used it like a rope to haul myself up from the black pit I was in, hand over hand, till I could prise my eyes open.

The light. It split my mind into a thousand pieces. I could taste blood and soil on my teeth, but right in front of my nose a pair of filthy brown boots took shape, old and laced with string. I knew them. They were Alicja's. I tried to touch one but nothing moved, so I swivelled my eyes painfully upwards instead. Her back was turned towards me, her thick blond plait snaking over one shoulder and she was shouting. I could see through narrow slits that in her hand lay a stick sharpened to a point. I felt sickness rise within me. Where had that come from?

I fought to speak. But no sound emerged. I wanted to scream for her to stop shouting but could make no sense of her words, until another's words took their place. It was the woman with the angry eyes, but her voice was quiet now. As though something in Alicja's face had stolen her anger.

'Listen, child. Give us what she is hiding and we will walk away. But if you don't . . .'

The threat hung in the damp air above my head.

No! No! No! Give the bastard bitch nothing.

It took no more than five seconds to destroy all my hopes and dreams. Alicja swung around and bent over me. Her tears dripped on to my face as her penknife sliced off the tip of my coat collar and threw it into the hands of the huntress. The woman upturned the tiny pocket of material on to her palm and two diamonds slipped out. Even in the gloom of the forest they glittered and shone like fire. I rolled my head violently to one side and retched up my rage in a scalding stream of bile on to the earth beneath me. By the time I looked back, the women had vanished. My diamonds were gone.

'Alicja,' I murmured.

Through my damp lashes I saw her young face float over mine. Her huge blue eyes were filled with tears as her hand gently touched my head and came away covered in blood.

'What have you done?' I whispered. 'You have given away our future.'

'Shh,' she crooned, 'stay still.' She kissed my forehead and her lips turned scarlet. 'We'll survive.'

'No, Alicja. We will starve.'

CHAPTER TWO

Germany, Autumn 1945

The camp for displaced persons was called Graufeld. It's German for Grey Field. Exactly the right word for the grey world that swallowed us here, a twilit existence suspended somewhere between day and night, its edges blurred. We lived in a fog of hope and despair. There were 3,200 of us in Graufeld. Millions more had been crammed into holding camps throughout Germany by the Allied Military Government since the war ended. VE Day on 9 May had triggered the biggest mass migration in world history, as half of Europe struggled to find homes.

We were refugees, a costly and intractable problem that no one wanted. I couldn't blame them. I wouldn't have wanted us either. We were the dregs of Europe.

But Alicja and I didn't starve as we dragged ourselves into Germany. I'd found ways to feed us, ways I didn't care to think about now. And we'd finally crawled on empty bellies to the barbed-wire gates of Graufeld where we'd been swept up with the dirt and the sentry's cigarette butts like the post-war bomb debris that we were.

If you've always been safe, you don't know the meaning of unsafe. That it changes you. I thought I was safe. Here. In this camp. With bread on the table and a roof over our heads.

But I was wrong.

All it took was an open doorway and the world crashed around my ears. My heart cramped. I became a creature whose every breath was made up of fear. Because in the split second that it took for me to glance at the open door of one of the hundreds of barrack huts, I decided to kill a man.

Don't think of me as bad. You don't know me, not yet. You don't even know my name. It's Klara. Klara Janowska. Half Polish, half English. I've saved a man's life. That counts in my favour doesn't it?

It was the usual kind of dull morning in this camp for displaced persons. That's what they called us, the arrogant ones in their crisp British Army uniforms; they labelled us DPs for short. I am a DP. A Displaced Person. The kind of label you'd give a dog. I called the camp a hellhole, an overcrowded rats' nest, hating it. But yes. Fool that I was. I thought I was safe.

Until I saw the man in the doorway.

I'd been walking through the camp with Alicja, discussing lathe turning, when my gaze wandered to the figure in the nearby barrack hut as we passed. I immediately dropped to one knee, hid my face. Pretended to tie my bootlaces and straighten my skirt. My thin fingers were shaking but on my shoulder I felt the soft fearless weight of Alicja's young hand. We had been heading over to the metal workshop at the end of the row and Alicja was skipping at my side, eager and focused. I had finally agreed she could make a knife for herself. Which was not allowed under Camp Committee rules. The day was warm and sultry for autumn, the sky stripped bare to a blinding white that bleached our grey dispossessed world. It turned the sandy soil under my feet into false shimmering diamonds, as worthless as my false shimmering hopes.

I risked a second glance at the tall man in the doorway of Hut J. He looked ordinary. I was shocked. I'd never thought of him as ordinary.

Cruel, yes.

Evil, yes.

Powerful, yes.

Ruthless, certainly.

But never ordinary. Maybe it was his workman's shirt. Or his cracked metal-rimmed spectacles. Or his threadbare corduroy trousers. Or the string binding his shoes. Maybe. But I think it was his dirty fingernails, black as his soul. He had always been meticulous. I should know. I had sat on a stool at his side and groomed his nails. His blond hair was shaved to almost nothing. It's what they did when we first arrived, to rid the camp of head lice. It made newcomers look defenceless.

He was not defenceless.

His face was thinner. Good. He had gone hungry. His mouth and eyes had softened. Loosened. To make him look harmless.

He was not harmless.

As he stepped out of the hut and moved away without a glance in my direction, he shuffled his feet in the dirt. A good imitation of a beaten man.

But I knew better.

That's why I needed to kill him.

I seized Alicja by the wrist and ran. She tucked in beside me, asked no questions, just ran with me. She was well trained. I heard her quick breath, saw her bony legs flash, the tip of her knees honey-gold. I chose the dirt path that squirmed through the undergrowth down behind one of the endless rows of barrack huts. It took us out of sight but kept us moving parallel to the main walkway – named Churchill Way by the British Army – within the camp, so that we were tracking in the same direction that the man from Hut J had taken. I glanced to my left each time we reached the end of a hut, eyes fixed on that walkway, but I didn't spot his shuffling figure in a patched flannel shirt. That worried me. Where was he?

I speeded up. Another hut. We raced through its shadow and through a gap of white light between the huts. Then another hut, another gap. I frowned. A huddle of men had gathered on Churchill Way, their voices reaching us, raised in dispute, their heels kicking up swirls of dust. But not a patched shirt among them.

'No further,' Alicja said.

She spoke in that soft whisper of hers but it made my heart jump. I could hear the tightness in her throat. I jerked my gaze from the men to my girl at my elbow. We hid behind the corner of the hut, and I registered with a jolt the huge size of her pupils. A stark warning sign of her fear.

'We should go back,' I agreed reluctantly.

'Yes.'

I ruffled her tufty crop of blond curls that had started to regrow. To reassure her. To reassure me.

'It's dangerous in this part of the camp,' I admitted.

'Yes.'

Graufeld Camp was not a place to let your guard down. I had learned that much in the few months I'd been here. In the flat autumn light it looked innocuous enough, huts freshly daubed with battleship-grey paint, now that the Allied battleships no longer required it. But looks can be deceiving. The place didn't just smell of overcooked cabbage and leaking latrines. It reeked of desperation and need. Of sickness. Of souls gone bad. Of displaced persons made homeless – and even stateless – by war. Certain people here would steal the skin off your back if they thought they could get a price for it.

We were all dispossessed. The dregs of a devastated Europe with nothing to our names except shame. It showed in the way we walked, in the way we looked at each other, quick brief glances. Turning away our gaze. Sliding our lashes down like a portcullis, keeping others out in case they saw in us what we saw in them.

'Let's move,' I said, her wrist still in my hand. I forced myself to abandon my hunt.

Down this end of the camp it was not safe. Graufeld Camp was constructed in an L-shape and in the foot of the L were the huts where the single men were housed. Hundreds of them. They prowled the camp like lone wolves, lean and hungry for more than food. Eyes stripping female forms. Hands touching where they shouldn't touch. Drugs. Drink. Danger. Hell, what was I thinking?

I should not have brought Alicja here.

I spun around to retrace our steps. But a man was charging towards us from the far end of the barrack huts and he was big, the way a bull elephant is big. His massive shoulders were almost too wide for the narrow path and his hand was stretched out like a shovel in front of him, as if to pick me up and toss me over the three-metre-high concrete boundary wall that ran alongside us. Like other people toss an apple core.

'You!' he shouted.

I stood my ground and pushed Alicja behind me. He rumbled to a halt so close to me that I was forced to look up as he towered over us. His broad chest was only partially covered by a filthy vest, and the black stubble on his head and huge jaw glistened with sweat. I could smell him. He looked like the kind of bastard who trampled through life, fists swinging, thoughts trailing in the dirt somewhere behind him.

'What?' I demanded.

It wasn't the ferocity in his dark eyes that scared the hell out of me, it was the tattoos on his face. The image of five drops of blood spilling down one cheek. They meant five murders. My eyes flicked quickly away from them and noticed the two scrawny DPs behind his bulky figure. They were nobody. Pilot fish. I ignored them.

That was a mistake.

'What's the matter with you?' the big man growled.

'What do you mean?'

We spoke in German, the common language for all the mongrel East Europeans in the camp. But I swore at him in Polish.

'Why do you bring a child down here, you *Arschloch*?' He pushed his face closer to mine.

'I was looking for someone who—'

Alicja stepped out from behind me. I saw no fear on her face, none that she let anyone see. 'Do you know a man in a check shirt with cracked round metal glasses? He just walked down Churchill Way.'

I stared at her. She saw too much. She was only ten.

But the big man's sidekicks stared at her too. For all the wrong reasons. The one with the sulky face pushed forward to squeeze past his friend and get within touching distance, just as I started to pull her away. But the big man swung out the edge of his hand without even changing his expression. It landed effortlessly across the surly one's throat, a sledge-hammer blow that dropped the nobody to his knees. Brutal noises wheezed from his mouth. The casual violence of it shocked me.

I tried to draw Alicja back up the path but she had better manners. She detached herself from me and held out her hand to him. Very polite. Very proper.

'Thank you,' she said.

'You are welcome, little one. What's your name?'

'Alicja.'

'Well, Alicja, I'm Niks. From Latvia.'

He extended his great bear paw and shook her hand, swallowing it up as if it were a fawn, and I saw his eyes change. Their darkness lost its harsh glazed surface and the muscles around his mouth softened one by one.

'Alicja,' he crouched down in front of her, 'tell that *Dummkopf* mother of yours never to bring you down here again.' He scowled and I knew it was meant for me. 'Go now.' Reluctantly he released her hand.

Alicja stood there, smiling up at him, unaware that her smile could melt iron.

'Come,' I said sharply and marched her away.

CHAPTER THREE

Walking into the camp laundry was like entering one of the outer circles of hell. It was unbearably hot, the air too drenched to breathe. Half-naked figures thrashed with giant paddles at bed linen immersed in massive vats of boiling water. Mangles clanked, scrubbing boards rattled. Everything was blurred by steam and sweat. And everywhere the ammonic smell of lye soap, sharp as the devil's pitchfork in the huge shed.

It worked like this. The camp's maintenance was performed by the inmates who received a small payment in exchange for their work. Each one of the 3,200 DPs was treated to one clean sheet, one clean pillowcase and one clean towel every two weeks. By my reckoning, that meant an awful lot of laundry. The overseer of this mammoth task was Hanna Pamulska. She was Polish. From Lublin in the east. But she chose most of the time to speak German. She wanted to forget Poland, to put its broken heartland behind her.

Hanna was my friend. I loved her for many reasons – one was her uncanny ability to distil *sliwovica* out of thin air – but most of all because she could make Alicja gasp with delight. Hanna could juggle. Anything. Not just balls. Tin cans, plates, cups, washing tongs. I once saw her juggle a bunch of chicks that had been smuggled into the camp. Her father used to work in a circus. The first time I saw her pick up six knives and send them twirling through the air in an ever-spinning arc that made Alicja's mouth fall open with wonder, I knew I was going to love this woman.

'What the devil is chasing your fucking tail today?' she bellowed at me from across the steamy shed.

Only then did I realise I was still running. I slowed to a walk. Alicja did the same and I heard a small impatient click of her tongue, though whether it was aimed at me or at Hanna, I didn't know. My daughter was oddly prim about language. Strictly no swearing. Sure as hell she didn't get it from me. I put it down to her three years in the convent of St Mary of the Blessed Sacrament when they wouldn't let me near her.

Hanna greeted me with a hug and dropped a kiss on Alicja's head.

'So what are you two cherubs doing here?'

Hanna was a raw-boned woman, not far off forty. She went round in what looked like one of her own threadbare sheets with holes cut for her head and arms, and trimmed to an indecent mid-thigh length. Her arms were thick and muscular, five numbers tattooed on her forearm, her hands as big and capable as a man's. But there was nothing masculine about the abundance of her bosom or about the curves of her hips to which the sheet was pasted with sweat. She laboured long and hard to produce spotless linen for Graufeld Camp each week and she expected her workers to do the same. I wouldn't want to swap places with the one who failed to meet those expectations.

I slipped an arm through hers and steered her towards the open door at the back that led into the drying yard. 'I need to speak to you.'

'What about?'

She turned to me, sharp brown eyes brimming with curiosity as she grinned at me. Hanna loved secrets.

The laundry yard always made me uneasy. It was enclosed by a high wooden fence, topped by a barbed wire fringe to keep out thieves, who were the curse of the camp system. Anything that was not nailed down was fair game on the black market, but Hanna protected her sheets with the ferocity of a gamekeeper protecting his chicks.

I didn't like them myself, the sheets. Though I would never tell Hanna that. Row after row of them, stretched out on lines like the skins of dead animals under a taut white sky. I'd seen too many dead things. That's why Hanna's yard and I were never going to get along.

'So?' she demanded, hands on broad hips.

I glanced pointedly at Alicja.

Immediately Hanna raised her voice in a shout that set the nearest sheet billowing. 'Rafal!'

'Here, Mama.'

'Alicja is here to see you.'

A frown appeared on my daughter's face. She hated Rafal to think she cared for him, but Rafal had no such concerns. A wide smile shot across his handsome young face at the sight of her and he beckoned her over to where he was seated on the dusty earth with a chessboard spread out before him. Hanna's son was twelve, two years older than Alicja, but he had not yet vanquished her at chess. A small smile tilted one corner of her mouth, like a sly cat tasting cream. She could not resist the challenge.

'You can be white,' Rafal called out.

Her slight figure drifted towards the chessboard with feigned indifference. 'I'm not sure I want to play today.'

She was not yet as good a liar as her mother.

'Isn't Rafal working?' I muttered to Hanna.

She rolled her eyes. 'He's on strike.'

I laughed. A sound I hadn't expected to hear today. Rafal was Hanna's guard dog. She paid him in cigarettes – the currency of the camp – to prowl her yard with his slingshot and a pocketful of stones. Word got around. I had seen him break the skull of a fox at twenty paces with his stones. The sheets stopped disappearing.

'Why is he on strike?'

'Because he wants to be off playing poker with the men. I forbid it.'

'He knows better than that.'

'That's what I told the stupid bastard.' She paused. 'What is it?' she asked softly.

'Will you watch Alicja for me? Just for an hour. Keep an eye on her.'

'Since when did that girl need watching?'

'Since now.'

'What happened?'

'I saw someone. A man I used to know in Warsaw. Here. On Churchill Way.' I waved a hand vaguely in the direction of the main thoroughfare and was shocked to see it shaking. I snatched it back but too late. Hanna's keen eyes missed nothing.

'Not someone you want to know again,' she said shrewdly.

I gazed blindly at the sheets. 'No,' I said at last, 'I need to say goodbye to him properly.'

Hanna made no comment. 'What do you want?'

'Watch Alicja for me.'

She nodded.

I turned to her and found a smile from somewhere to stick on my face. Lopsided, I admit, but still resembling a smile. 'And a bottle, Hanna. I need a bottle.'

CHAPTER FOUR

ALICJA

Alicja watched her mother leave. She called out that she'd be back in an hour and to stay there. Where she'd been put. Like a dog. Alicja almost shouted, 'Why don't you tie me to the drainpipe with a piece of string?' The way old Novak tied his fleabag to the metal bed leg, even though dogs were not allowed in camp.

She knew where Mama had gone. After that man, the one with the eyes. He hid them behind spectacles, and so he should, because they didn't look like eyes. They looked like the points of knives, silver and sharp, so sharp they could cut you. Mama had dropped to her knee so fast when she saw him that Alicja thought she had been shot. Alicja had made no sound, just stood over her mother, shielding her from another bullet.

Now Mama had gone off after him again, into the dangerous end of the camp. Why?

Was he her lover in Warsaw?

Alicja had learned about lovers from the girls at the convent. They said that a lover makes you go hot and trembling and you want to be with them all the time. When she ran with her mother at the back of the barrack huts, Mama was hot and trembling. Her fingers had been like points of fire on Alicja's wrist, and now . . .

She has abandoned me. She has gone to be with him. It was the convent all over again. But this time it was a laundry she was abandoned in.

'Hah!'

Alicja blinked. Rafal had captured her rook. She nodded quietly to herself as if she'd intended that move and his smile of triumph changed to a downturn of worry.

'What?' he demanded. 'What are you planning?'

She moved her queen's knight, threatening his bishop. The pieces felt solid and safe in her hand and brought her mind back into the yard. Rafal had carved them himself and made the board. He was clever with his hands but not with his brain. He moved a pawn – a pawn! – out of harm's way but failed to see the two-pronged attack coming for his queen.

His baffled eyes searched hers for some clue to the point of danger.

'Rafal, do you have anything to eat?'

His dark eyes with their thick sooty lashes brightened. 'I can get you something.'

Three pigeons were strutting on the roof ridge of the laundry. Quietly Rafal rose to his feet and extracted a slingshot from his back pocket. He looked at Alicja. She nodded. Standing there, he made her think of David in the Bible. The pigeon wasn't Goliath but it came tumbling down the corrugated roof with a noisy clatter when Rafal released the stone. He fetched the bird and laid it out on the ground next to the board. Its head was bloodied but its ash-grey breast feathers were unsullied and felt like petals under her fingertips.

'I'll pluck it and cook it on a fire for you,' Rafal offered. He hitched his slingshot back in his pocket with a small pat of satisfaction. It had been a good clean shot. 'If you tell me one of your stories, Alicja.'

She nodded agreement to the deal.

'A forest one,' he added, his hand on the bird.

Alicja let her eyelids drift closed. She could see better that way.

We were in a forest. I remember that much.

I was so tired I couldn't walk straight. Branches and twigs elbowed my face and the world turned yellow because the wind was snatching leaves from the trees and throwing them at us. Does it hurt? When a leaf is torn off a tree. Do you think it feels like having your fingernails pulled out?

The Nazis used to do that. In Warsaw. I know this because I saw my teacher's hands. She had a pretty face but her fingers were ugly. Like Mama's. Pincers, that's what they used. The thought of it made my own fingers ache and I pushed them into my pocket but it didn't help. I could hear the trees whispering, nudging each other, the wind skittering through the branches.

Mama was there. Dimly I knew she was the grey shape in the ragged dress ahead of me as we walked, but all the time it drifted further away. I called to her but she didn't hear. I ran to her but she vanished. I started to cry and was ashamed.

'Alicja?' Mama asked.

I was flat on the forest floor, a worm among the yellow leaves. I hadn't called out, I hadn't run, I didn't cry. Damp moss lay under my cheek. How did that happen?

'Alicja, my darling.' Mama's face floated close like one of the leaves from the tree. I could see a vein pulsing at her temple. 'Are you all right?'

I closed my eyes. 'Yes.'

'Can you get up? We can't stop here.'

'Yes.'

My feet hurt. My stomach hurt. I could feel snakes writhing inside it. Starvation, Mama called it.

'We must find something to eat,' she urged and took hold of my arm. 'Come, Liebling.'

It was one of our German days. When she would speak only German to me. The heavy words were crushing my tongue.

'Ich komme,' I said. 'I'm coming.'

But the words stuck in my mouth and my eyes closed. I dreamed I was walking.

Alicja opened her eyes. They prickled with tears but she would rather die than cry in front of Rafal. His clever hands were busy plucking the bird, its feathers soft as snow.

'Don't stop,' he told her.

'That's all there is.'

'There *must* be more.'

'No. That's the end. Now cook me the pigeon.'

Reluctantly he took the bird, dangling it by its red spidery feet, and left. Alicja closed her eyes. It wasn't the end of the story.

I woke. I was wrapped in a blanket of forest leaves, my head warm on Mama's lap, but she smelled different. Not of the forest. I breathed in the scent of her skirt and found the stink of a farmyard in my nostrils. Of cattle. Of straw. Like the barns we used to sleep in. But no more. Mama said it was too dangerous to risk going into barns now we were in Germany. The German farmers didn't want us.

Night had crept into the forest. The darkness was solid but it was not silent. It shivered with sounds that made me bury my face in Mama's skirt. Softly she stroked my head, warm and comforting, picking leaves and knots from my long unwashed hair.

'Alicja, sit up. I have food for you.'

I didn't move. I knew she was lying. Sometimes she did that to get me on my feet. But I turned my head. I couldn't stop myself, saliva drowning my mouth. And a small knob of black bread brushed against my lips. I devoured it before it could become a dream. Then more. Tiny piece by tiny piece. Mama fed it to me in the darkness the way I'd once fed a young bird under a hedge. The young crow had a broken leg but Mama said it would mend if I could keep it alive.

Would I mend?

'Sit up, Alicja.'

I sat up and she placed the rim of a stoneware jar against my lips.

'*Drink.*'

I drank. Greedy and disgusting. It was milk, still warm from the cow, like silk on my parched throat. I was trembling with happiness, but I forced my milky lips away from the rim.

'*Mama, you must drink too.*'

It's what we'd agreed. Half each. Even if it was only a single berry.

'*No. I've had mine. Milk and bread. This is all for you.*'

I wanted so badly to believe the lie that I drank all the milk. She pulled me on to her lap, as if I was a baby, feeding me again with her fingers, skimpy morsels of cheese this time. I cried. I hated the tears that she brushed away with kisses and I tucked my head in the hollow under her jaw where I could hear her pulse beating. But as I snuggled close against her, my bones moulding perfectly with hers, I knew it was not a farm I could smell on her. It was a farmer.

CHAPTER FIVE

DAVIDE BOUVIER

Davide Bouvier stood at the window of his office in the Administration block. He kept it open at all times to draw in fresh air. His lungs were bad. Not that he was complaining. Far from it. He knew he was lucky to come away with nothing worse than shoddy lungs after two years of the tunnels at Peenemünde and Mittelwerk. Most came away in sacks.

His gaze scoured the open square in front of the building, where meetings were often held and where Colonel Whitmore liked to address the various committees from his favourite perch on top of his jeep's bonnet. Right now there was just a small male-voice choir practising Czech folk songs. The sound was pleasant and gave Davide a stab of homesickness for his own choir in Oradour-sur-Glane in western France. Not that there'd be any more singing in the church there. Not now.

He turned away sharply but the pain was still there. Like

28

an ice pick in his back. He dealt with it the only way he knew how – by working all hours of the day and night as an administrative assistant to Colonel Whitmore. The amount of paperwork involved in keeping this camp afloat could easily sink one of the Royal Navy's battleships. He studied the list of inmate questionnaires in his hand, cursed Captain Jeavons for his absence, and was about to pick up the telephone to track him down when he caught sight of a figure crossing the square. He put down his papers and watched her.

She was slender, but taller than average. She carried herself upright, as if she were wearing armour plate that wouldn't bend. Her stride was long and determined, and there was something intimidating about her, even though he knew she was quietly spoken. Something in her eyes. Something that made him tread carefully even when she laughed. She wasn't laughing now. Her expression was stern, inward looking and focused. She must have been good at her job before the war, he'd bet his last franc on that. She had worked on building a *métro* in Warsaw, an engineer, creating something out of nothing. That appealed to him. A maker of things. Whereas he had been a destroyer of things.

He watched her coming directly towards the Administration block, but just before she reached the entrance she paused. Shook herself, the way a dog shakes itself after a bath. Her limbs loosened, her jaw relaxed and a smile drew itself across her face. Davide allowed himself a chuckle. She was putting on the charm. She wanted something.

*

'*Bonjour*, Davide.'

'Hello, Klara. Come in.'

'Busy?'

'I'm always busy.'

'You shouldn't work so hard. I've seen your light on late into the night.' She frowned at him and he was amused at the way she could smile and frown at the same time.

'You'll burn yourself out, Davide.'

He laughed and waved her to the wooden seat in front of his desk. It wasn't a comfortable seat. He didn't want people to stay long, though for Klara he made an exception. She claimed to be half Polish, half English – certainly she spoke English, Polish and German fluently – but too many DPs claimed to be someone they weren't. That's part of what made his job so hard. *Merde!* Lies stacked on top of lies everywhere he looked.

But he was tempted to believe Klara. There was something of the mongrel about her, something out of step and unfettered. She wasn't one to stick to the rules. Twice she had been in serious trouble for dealing in black-market goods. The usual stuff – cigarettes, butter, sewing needles. She had her paltry wage for working as a teacher in the camp school docked to pay the fine. And they'd stuck her on latrine duty for a month. She'd smelled horrible. He'd found her extra soap.

Davide closed the manila file in front of him, added it to the ever-growing stack of them on his desk and tossed his fountain pen beside them. He tried for a deep breath but heard his lungs crackle in protest.

'What can I do for you?'

'Can you get me in to see him?'

'Colonel Whitmore is extremely busy. Sorry, Klara, but it won't be today. He doesn't have a moment free.'

'Dammit, Davide,' she always spoke in English to him, 'when does that man *ever* have a moment free?'

She laid a hand flat on his desk, as if to snatch up the telephone that would connect her to the colonel, but he saw her remember her manners and switch on a smile instead.

'Please,' she said softly. 'It's urgent.'

He could feel the tension in her. Her fingers were rigid on the desktop. The intense blue of her eyes was almost hidden by the dense black of her huge pupils, and her mouth, her lovely full mouth, pulled into a tight line that she was struggling to release. She was not one for showing her emotions, he'd learned that. Not one for showing anything of herself. Most of the time she wore a scarf wound round her cropped corn-coloured hair and a shabby blue cotton dress that came almost to her ankles. A shapeless navy cardigan covered her thin arms. He had once given her a white sleeveless blouse for the summer heat, not new but nice, and he'd never seen her in it. When he spotted another woman wearing it last week he knew she'd sold it. He'd cared more than he was willing to admit.

'What is it, Klara? What has happened?'

'I need to get Alicja away from here. Please, Davide, I have to talk to the colonel again.'

'Klara, how many times have you seen him already?'

31

She nodded slowly. 'I know. But this time it's . . .'

'It's what?'

'Different.'

She was closing down. Though her hand still lay on his desk, he could feel her withdraw, the shutters coming down as she slid away from him.

'Why is it different this time?' he asked.

'I think Alicja and I are in danger.'

It was the way she said it that made him believe her. So quiet. So controlled. The words flat. Her fear had stolen the life out of them.

'What kind of danger?'

She cast a glance at the drab olive platoon of filing cabinets that stood to attention along one wall, as if they might help.

'Someone I used to know,' she said. 'He has turned up here in this camp. I saw him just now.'

'Who is he?'

'He . . .'

She paused, the words unwilling to come, and in the middle of the pause, just when Davide could see something unlock at the back of her eyes, the door at the far end of his office opened. Colonel Jonathan Whitmore strode into the room. He had the look of a man who knew how to make things happen. Tall, brisk, efficient. Immaculate in his officer's uniform. Intelligent eyes that missed nothing. Yet there was a fullness to his mouth that gave it a soft edge that did not quite match the straight lines of his face.

Klara leaped to her feet.

'Bouvier,' Whitmore snapped out. 'I need the file on—'

The colonel noticed the silent figure of Klara at the desk. The hard military lines of his shoulders seemed to melt into those of a middle-aged man who worked too hard. Suddenly he looked bone tired.

'Good day, Mrs Janowska.'

Davide admired that in him. The way he knew their names. The way he could always find a smile for them, a word of encouragement to give them hope. So many of the military staff regarded DPs as nothing more than a major logistical headache and a drain on overstretched resources and finances. In all fairness Davide couldn't blame them. That's exactly what DPs were. But Colonel Whitmore saw them as people who needed saving, and he saw it as his duty to save them.

'Colonel Whitmore,' Klara stepped forward before Davide could stop her. 'Could I have a minute of your time, please?'

Whitmore drew his brows together, then held out his wrist ostentatiously in front of them both, displaying his watch. 'Sixty seconds, Mrs Janowska. I am counting.'

If Davide thought she would be intimidated by such military precision, he misjudged her. Her words came out neat and brief.

'Have you heard back from England whether they have found my mother's family yet?'

'No, I have not. If and when there is any information you will be informed. I have told you this before.'

'Sir, please ask again. I am desperate. For my daughter.'

'Do you know how many people say those exact words to me each day? I can't walk out that door without someone begging for help.' He drew a deep breath, like a swimmer diving into deep water, and gestured to the grey camp world outside the window. 'There are so many,' he said quietly, 'so many. All wanting to get out of here. All wanting a home and food, a family. All desperate. We are doing everything we can, Mrs Janowska, as fast as we can, as efficiently as we can. But,' he gave the smallest of very British smiles, 'there was a war on, you know. It's over now but the world is in chaos out there. We do not have enough staff. We do not have enough resources. You must be patient.'

He wiped a hand across his face to remove any trace of pity.

'I can't be patient any more, Colonel.'

Her eyes watched the officer's face intently. Davide's watched hers. It was not a beautiful face, its features too irregular, but there was beauty in its fine bones and in the still, intelligent eyes.

Abruptly Colonel Whitmore turned his head away from her. 'Your time is up.' He dropped his hand to his side. 'I am off to a meeting with our Supply Officer.'

She opened her mouth to speak, but Davide cut her off. 'I have that file for you, sir. And there is another convoy expected this afternoon.' He walked from his desk and handed over the file, enabling the colonel to break free from her gossamer-fine web.

Whitmore nodded stiffly. 'Thank you, Bouvier.' But suddenly he turned back to Klara, a twist of anger

34

darkening his expression. 'Do you know how many Polish and Czechoslovakian refugees are here in the Western Zone, Mrs Janowska?'

'No. Tell me.'

'Six and a half million. And that's not all. Another four million in the Soviet Zone. And some days it feels as if they are all in this camp. Here in Graufeld our DPs each week devour twenty-five tons of bread, thirty tons of potatoes, eight tons of meat, seven tons of vegetables and it all has to be supplied and transported by an overstretched army that is not in the business of managing hordes of refugees who are starving and frightened and suspicious of . . .'

His deep voice was filling the office, ricocheting off the wooden walls as if it would tear them down. He halted. The sudden silence seemed to suck all air from the room. Davide was acutely aware of how important self-control was to this military Englishman, how he wrapped it around his soul and how mortified he must be at losing it.

Whitmore started towards the door, but Klara's voice followed him.

'Colonel, my daughter's life is in danger. Hers and mine. From someone I knew in Warsaw. He is here now. I cannot stand aside and wait for—'

'Not you as well,' the Colonel mumbled.

'I'm sorry?'

'Claiming your life is in danger. I didn't expect you to stoop to that. It's what they all do.' He waved a hand in the direction of the window where an inmate was trundling a wheelbarrow towards the garden area. 'In the end they'll say anything and tell any lie to speed up the process of getting out of here.'

Davide walked rapidly over to the door and opened it with the brisk manner he had learned from the military. 'Sir, you will be late for your meeting.'

Without another word, just a curt nod of his head, the colonel marched out of the room.

What is life worth?

In this instance the answer turned out to be a bottle of home-made samogon.

Davide had closed the door after the colonel left, but Klara didn't move. She remained staring at the spot where Colonel Whitmore had stood, as though still seeing the man's powerful imprint in the air. A tremor shook her. Her fingers fluttered at her side.

He wanted to go to her but he knew she'd hate what she'd regard as pity, so he returned to his desk and picked up a sheet of paper with today's list of admissions to the camp infirmary. Twenty-five yesterday. *Mon Dieu*, disease was rampant. Didn't those at the top realise? SHAEF – the Supreme Headquarters Allied Expeditionary Force – might be happy to herd hundreds of thousands of DPs into camps to prevent them clogging up the roads, but you only needed one to be sick with typhus. In the cramped conditions it spread like wildfire. Each person's breath had already been through a dozen lungs. Each hand carried a million germs.

Davide kept a bowl under his desk with water and disinfectant in it. He put down the paper, dipped both hands into the bowl and dried them meticulously on a clean towel. When he straightened up, he was coughing and Klara was seated on the hard chair in front of him.

'Why did you do that?' Her manner was grave but if she was angry it didn't show. 'Why hurry the colonel away from me so fast?'

'Because the man can only take so much, Klara. You could see how he was. He doesn't sleep. He works all hours. Drives himself to the limit to keep this camp functioning. I didn't want you to damage your cause by pushing him over the edge. You must realize you need his support for your claim.'

'Thank you.' She smiled one of her rare unguarded smiles that gave him a glimpse of the person she was before the war kicked the hell out of her life. She twisted round and fixed her gaze on the bank of filing cabinets lined up along the wall.

'You can help me, Davide.'

'Klara, I am not allowed to give out private information.'

'I know.'

'So don't ask.'

With all the panache of a magician she drew a bottle of samogon from one of the deep patch pockets of her shabby dress and placed it at the very centre of his desk. The murky liquid within it swirled and settled. Tempting him. He didn't touch it. Klara leaned forward, blue eyes bright and demanding. He could feel the heat of them.

'I am looking for a certain man,' she whispered. 'A man named Oskar Scholz.'

Davide flicked through the files under 'S', his fingers fast and thorough. When he'd finished he went back to the beginning and searched again more slowly. And again. As a last resort he hunted through the 'O' files. Oskar Scholz. While he searched, Klara stood close, looking over his shoulder, her breath warm on his ear.

'He is not in this camp under that name, Klara.'

'So he is using a fake name.'

'You're sure he is here?'

'I saw him.'

'Could you have been mistaken?'

'No.'

'Who is he? This Oskar Scholz.'

'A German. I knew him in Warsaw.'

'And you believe he is a threat to your life?'

'I know he is.'

'Why?'

But it was a step too far. He could see on her pale face the struggle inside her. Whatever had happened with Oskar Scholz, she had buried it deep.

'He stole my daughter.' Her words came out flat and shapeless. 'He removed Alicja from me in Warsaw and incarcerated her in a convent for three years.'

Davide thought of his own daughter, taken when a Mauser machine gun exploded into life. No one should lose a daughter. No one. Not ever. They were still standing beside the filing cabinets and he leaned against one, shaken by sudden rage. He fought to quieten the crackle that started up in his chest as the anger speeded his breathing.

'Why did he have authority to take your daughter from you? Was he in the Wehrmacht? An officer?'

But instead of answering she turned her face from him to the metal filing cabinets and for a moment stared at them before putting out a hand to touch them. He watched her run her palm over the surface of one, soothing it, the way he'd seen his father run a hand over a skittish horse's rump.

'Davide,' she said, her gaze skimming the cabinet drawers, 'how many Germans are billeted in Hut J?'

CHAPTER SIX

Some days I felt a deep rumble running through the camp. A kind of vibration that rose up from the bare ground and rippled through me, so that my bones seemed to grate together. I didn't know what caused it. Were we perched on the top of old mining works? Or was it the camp machinery droning on – the roar of the smithy and the growl of the generator at work?

Or was the tremor triggered within myself? Something that had dislodged. I didn't know.

I heard it now, the rumble. As I hurried to Hut J. A man was seated on a low stool outside the open doorway, legs outstretched, so I would have to climb over them to enter. He was the keeper. His job was to keep people out. Most of the huts had someone on duty each day on an agreed rota to combat theft or abuse. Some liked the job more than others. This man was one of the likers. Just a little taste of power can make a man lick his lips, hungry for more.

His gaze flicked over me. He was bored and looking for amusement, and I could tell he thought I might provide it.

This was the curse of the camp. Boredom. It had a stranglehold on the inmates, at times quite literally choking them to death. Suicides were not uncommon. He was no more than my age but he had the manner of a weary old man.

I gave him a lovely big smile. 'Hello.'

Instantly he spat out the matchstick he was chewing on. He sat up straighter and returned the smile. 'You looking for something?'

'You must get to see a lot of things going on around here,' I said cheerfully.

He nodded. Eyes on my breasts.

'What's your name?' I asked.

His attention jumped to my face. 'Adomas.'

'Well, Adomas, a short while ago I saw a man leave this hut. Tall, blond hair and in a dark shirt. Wearing spectacles with a cracked lens. Know him?'

'No.'

'Do you remember him in the hut?'

'No.'

His denial sounded genuine. But I wasn't sure. 'You weren't here when I saw him, so—'

'I had to go over to the medic.' He smiled again. 'Nothing much wrong. Nothing that a bottle of whisky wouldn't shift.'

Was he offering me a deal? Was that it?

'I haven't got any whisky. But maybe I can lay my hands on some other—'

He spat. It just missed my foot. 'None of that home-made shit for me. It wrecks my gut.'

He spoke fluent German but with the spiky accent that said Lithuanian. Or Latvian. Somewhere on the Baltic. Somewhere that had been trampled by jackboots and stripped for slave labour. His expression was hopeful rather than expectant. His path hadn't crossed with Oskar Scholz, I felt sure.

'I've come to speak with Fritz Geissler. I was told he is billeted here.'

Adomas frowned and stood up. Even thinner than I was. 'He's German,' he said in a low voice.

'I realise that. Is he here?'

He nodded. 'Inside. Last bed but one at the far end. On the left. A bunch of bastards are down there.' He spat again. I couldn't blame him.

'They suffered too, the Germans, you know they did,' I said. 'Not all of them were Nazis. They are as desperate as we are now. No homes, no food, no jobs.'

'Let them go and suffer in some other camp. In some other fucking hut. You can tell them that from me.'

'Thank you, Adomas, you've been helpful.'

He found his smile once more and stepped back into the doorway. 'Fritz,' he yelled. 'You got yourself a visitor, lucky bastard.'

Adomas stood aside to let me pass with a gentlemanly wave of his hand.

Fritz Geissler was sick. I could smell it on him. Cheeks flushed the colour of plums, eyes glittering too brightly. He said he was in bed because he was a bit tired, yet he barely had the strength to raise his head from the pillow. But his young face burst into a smile when I approached his narrow bed. He was lonely.

Every pair of eyes had turned on me when I entered the hut. Normally I'd have ignored them, shrugged them off. But here in Graufield Camp nothing was normal. I walked the length of the central aisle of the barrack hut, past the rows of beds. The intimacy was overpowering. Socks and underpants hung drying on the metal bedheads, one man's pisspot stood waiting to be emptied, the odour of grease and hair oil rose from pillows. But all the blankets were neat and tidy. Whoever was boss of this hut ran it with military precision.

There were about fifty beds crammed together but most of the occupants were out. Working in the kitchens. Scrubbing the dining tables. Rewiring the new Recreation block. Kicking a ball. Betting on a cockroach race. Anything to fight off the dead weight of boredom. For those still in the hut, well, I was their entertainment today.

They stared openly. I walked with no sign of haste down that scrupulously swept aisle and inspected each face I passed. Long lazy ones, square ones, fair ones, frightened ones, angry ones, ones barely old enough to wield a razor. But none of them was the one I sought, the one with eyes as grey and sharp as a razor that could strip the layers of skin off you. With a broad flat forehead, which I had seen break a person's nose, and a bony chin that he had asked me to shave.

If I stood before him now, as I did then, with a razor poised between finger and thumb, would I lash out? Would I? Could I?

'*Guten Tag.*' The voice was soft.

'*Guten Tag*, Herr Geissler,' I said in greeting to the gaunt young figure in the bed near the far wall.

He tried to sit up but didn't make it, so I perched on the edge of his bed and prayed there were no fleas or lice.

'I'm looking for someone, Herr Geissler.'

He didn't ask for whom. Or how I knew his name. His feverish eyes looked out of focus as they smiled up at me, eager to please. He couldn't be more than eighteen or nineteen, a fine looking boy with skin as smooth as a girl's.

'I'm Fritz,' he said.

'Well, Fritz, I am told that there are four Germans billeted in this hut. Is that right?'

He blinked. Yes.

'Are the other three here now?'

He glanced across at the empty beds next to his. His eyes moved slowly as if they hurt. '*Nein*. They are not here.'

'Can you tell me their names?'

'Hans Becke, Friedrich Taube and Reinald Weiner.'

That tallied. Those were the names that Davide had given me.

'Are any of them tall with blond hair and wearing spectacles with a cracked lens?'

'No. They are blond. Like me. Not tall.'

'Did a German come here today who wore cracked spectacles?'

'Why do you ask?'

'He is someone I am looking for. I saw him leaving here earlier.'

He nodded. Just that small movement brought him out in a sweat. 'Yes, you mean Jan Blach.'

The name stunned me. I felt my jaw drop open.

'What did he want?'

'None of us know him. He said he was just checking on the Germans in the camp.' He frowned. 'He wants us all to be billeted together in huts just for Germans, so we don't get spat on.'

'Does he indeed?'

There was no question that the German nation had suffered too during the war, its people battered and bloody. I knew that. The result was clear to see in the ruins of their cities. We all knew that. But I had to keep reminding myself. They're not the ones who tore your nails out or beat you with rubber hoses, or put a bullet in your friend's throat. But sometimes the sound of their language on my tongue made me retch. They shot my husband out of the sky and he died in a ball of flames. Sometimes I think I hear his screams.

'Did this Jan Blach mention what hut he is billeted in?'

'No.' The boy's eyes were closing.

'Fritz,' I said softly, 'you are sick. I think I should report it to the Medical Officer to—'

His eyes shot open, wide and terrified. I placed a hand on the blanket where his leg underneath was suddenly shaken by tremors.

'Hush,' I murmured, 'the doctors will make you better.'

'*Nein, nein, nein.* No, don't report it.' His long pale fingers reached for me. 'I know what they do to patients in the infirmary.'

'Fritz, I promise you they will—'

'No! They will do experiments on me. They will.' The young German was shaking all over, his teeth chattering. 'I was sent to Gross-Rosen concentration camp for helping an old Jewish man who fell over in the street. Dr Mengele was there, the SS officer and physician. He performed terrible inhuman experiments.' The boy was sobbing. 'Amputating limbs and sewing twins together and . . .'

I moved further up the bed, unable to stop myself taking his hand in mine. 'You're safe here, Fritz. The British doctors here are kind. They will help you to—'

'No. Please no. Don't tell them.'

His smooth cheeks glistened with tears, his pale eyelashes spiky, his mouth convulsed.

'I'll bring you some medicine to take here instead,' I offered. Though how in hell's name I could persuade the medics to cough up tablets of some sort without them whisking him into isolation in the infirmary, I didn't know.

'I beg you,' his long desperate fingers clamped around mine, 'tell no one. No tablets.'

I knew what it was to beg. I knew what it was to plead for silence.

'Very well, Fritz. But if you're not a little better tomorrow, I will have to call in a medic.'

His mouth softened into a trusting smile. 'Thank you.' His eyelids slid closed, too heavy for him to lift.

I sat there for a long time stroking his hand.

CHAPTER SEVEN

Jan Blach. How could he bring himself to use that name? It was the name of my brother. He was killed on 25 September 1939 and Oskar Scholz knew it. Yet still he climbed into my brother's dead boots and tramped through the camp in them. He wanted me to know, I am certain. He intended me to grieve all over again.

On that September day in 1939 the skies over Warsaw had blackened with German Stuka aircraft. Five hundred tons of high explosive bombs rained down on my beloved beautiful city of Warsaw as though the devil had loosed his ravenous swarm of demons on us. Death and destruction gouged out the heart of the city and left it bleeding, while fires from incendiaries incinerated anything left standing. The flames seemed to set even the River Vistula alight as I stood on its banks, howling at the planes above me and clutching our four-year-old daughter in my arms.

My husband was up there, somewhere in that hellish battle. In his PZL P.11 fighter. A brave pilot in the Polish air force; a David against the Nazi Goliath. On the ground the earth shook under our feet and the noise ripped our eardrums apart. Explosions and screams. The frantic rattle of anti-aircraft guns and the blood-curdling shriek of dive bombers. Everywhere we heard the roar of the fires that swept the city and the rumble like thunder as buildings collapsed.

And the dust. Dear God, the choking dust. It clogged our lungs. I didn't know it then, as I spat my rage into the sky that a bomb had landed directly on my parents' house, killing them instantly, along with my brother.

Now Oskar Scholz had taken his name. *Jan Blach*. Don't think it is an accident. Or a coincidence. Because I know it is not. He is goading me.

There were four children perched like sparrows on my bed when I entered my hut. Relief spiked in tiny pinpricks along my skin when I saw that Alicja was one of them. She was laughing and for a moment I paused to listen to that sweet sound. It was rare. Or was it just around me that it was rare?

The hut was busy, humming with the voices of women gathered into groups. Knitting. Darning. Sewing. Making garments stretch through the winter ahead. One was turning a square wool headscarf into a skirt for her little girl while the child watched wide-eyed, snatching at the colourful trails. This was a hut allocated just to women with children. No men. Those with husbands were billeted in the family huts where rivalries flared like small flash fires.

Alicja once asked me why the women were always busy while the men sat around talking, scratching their bellies and smoking most of the day. I had no reply. No polite one anyway. *Because they're lazy sons of bitches.* I bit down on my tongue and shrugged in silence.

I liked these women. I liked their grit, their cussedness. Their instinct for survival. I liked the way they found smiles for their children on even the blackest of days and the ease with which they could reduce a stiff British army officer to a blushing jellyfish with their earthy teasing and suggestive hip-rolling. As I walked past the rows of metal beds, a scrawny Latvian with impatient dark eyes stepped out and clamped a hand on my wrist.

'Klara, I need . . .'

Before she had finished speaking, my ever-present notebook was out of my pocket and I was flicking through its dog-eared pages.

'Need what?' I prompted.

'Spectacles. For close work. Can you . . . ?'

'Ask at the Medical block. They provide them.'

She uttered a thin screech of disgust. 'They are taking months to get hold of any. In the meantime I can't read, can't sew, can't write my own bloody name.'

'I'll do what I can,' I promised and detached my wrist from her grip.

Two steps further and a young blond woman called out, 'I need a mirror, Klara.' She was very pretty. I could see why she would want a mirror. I nodded and jotted down a note.

Always I was pursued by the words *I need*.

*

Alicja once told me I look fierce.

Fierce? I was shocked. And hurt. Fierce? How did that happen? My husband used to tell me my face was so sunny it made him smile just to look at me. Now it is fierce. So as I approached the four children on my bed I forced it to look happy.

'Ready?' I asked cheerily.

Four wide grins shot back at me. Four young heads nodded. I loved those grins. They were bright flames on which I warmed my cold hands. My bed stood at the far end of the hut, tucked in the corner. Safe. My back covered. It had cost me a hefty bribe to gain possession of it. Privacy and safety were two things that came at a high premium in Graufeld Camp and a corner spot provided both. So I'd paid through the nose but it was worth it to have a wall at my back, and I'd wangled a bunk bed, so that Alicja slept above me. Anyone coming at her would have to come through me first.

Hanna had walked my daughter back from the laundry and set her son Rafal to guard her, but I could tell from the set of Alicja's angular little shoulders that she was not happy with such protection. She was excited about tonight, so submitted with no complaint in case I banned her from being part of our mission. It wouldn't be the first time.

That's how we termed it. Our mission. We planned it with military precision, each child playing their part. Alicja and Rafal were the seekers. The other two children, Izak and Alzbeta, were the distraction. They were all experienced. Watchful and patient beyond their tender years.

Izak was a nine-year-old German Jew from Dresden who had been hidden in a wardrobe for three years by a neighbour after his parents were dragged off to Auschwitz. The neighbour risked her life every day for him. Sharing her scanty rations with him. Such courage. Such humanity. I never knew her but I admired her. Dead now. Burned alive by the infernal firestorm created by the Allied bombing of Dresden in February this year. Izak escaped, but one side of his face was burned to a kind of molten moonscape. He spoke little but followed me like a shadow, unless Alicja shooed him away. I think sometimes she did not like the way he leaned his body against mine as though I were a wall to keep him upright.

The other child, Alzbeta, was the same age as Alicja, ten years old, a Czechoslovakian orphan, I think. I say I think, because she refused to speak about her parents. She was loud and bossy with dark bottlebrush hair that stuck up straight. She constantly bickered with the two boys but worshipped the ground Alicja walked on and I knew she would always be watching out for my daughter on the missions. She was quick-witted. She would look at me in that way of hers from under her thick smoky eyelashes and would give a little nod. We both knew I was relying on her.

All four were my fledglings. I took care of them in the camp. I bound their wounds. I fought their corners. I dried their tears, I cleaned their fingernails and I read them stories whenever I could get my hands on one of the precious books in this place. I taught them maths with an enthusiasm bordering on obsession. I love numbers. They don't lie. Not like words. I kept my fledglings safe.

Why?

I don't like that question.

I dared not use the word love. It was too dangerous. Too risky. It can blow up in your face. Too liable to bleed you dry when the loved one is taken away from you. So I used the word *need* instead. We *needed* each other.

That would suffice. Need.

I *needed* more than ever now to get myself and Alicja out of here. To do so, I *needed* the missions. For my missions I *needed* the children.

There. No mention of love.

I stroked each head, fed each child a Huntley & Palmer biscuit from the cache in a tin under my bed, and grinned back at them.

'Ready?'

The missions terrified me.

'Mama.'

Alicja twisted a fist into my cardigan, anchoring me to her, preventing me from stepping out of the hut after the other three children.

'What is it, Alicja?'

'Did you find him?'

'Find who?'

Even as I said the words, I regretted them. My daughter deserved better.

'You know who, Mama. The man in the broken spectacles, the one who came out of the hut, the one you're
frightened of.'

Her blue eyes always saw too much.

'No, I didn't find him. Not yet.'

'Was he your lover?'

My mouth fell open. Where did this come from? What
does my daughter know about lovers?

'No, sweetheart, he was never my lover. What on earth
makes you think such a thing?'

'Because . . .' a faint finger of colour slid up her cheek,
'you seemed to burst into flames when you saw him. So I
thought . . .'

'You thought wrong.'

She gazed up at me, solemn as a judge in her dreary blue
dress. I could see changes in her face during the five months
we'd been trapped in the camp, the childish softness giving
way to a firmer alignment of bones. She was beautiful. It took
my breath away when I set eyes on her each morning. If anything she was growing more beautiful, her delicate features
so exquisite, I feared for her. If I loved her enough, I would
rid her of the burden of perfection. Because it would be her
downfall. I should take a razor blade to her face, then no one
would want her. But I couldn't do it. I couldn't. Did that
mean I didn't love her enough? Or that I loved her too much?

'I was angry, Alicja. Angry with him. That's all. I used to
know him in Warsaw.'

'Did he hurt you?' She slipped her hand in mine.

I wrapped my palm around her young fingers, glanced down at my own deformed fingertips, and took a long time to find a reply.

'No, my darling, no. I hurt myself.'

CHAPTER EIGHT

ALICJA

Alicja loved the darkness.

It suited her. Soft as a fur mitten. It slid over her skin as she raced down the track through the woods, so fast that it wiped from her mind the look on her Mama's face when she left her. She didn't want to see her mother like that, white with fear.

Rafal was running through the night two steps ahead of her, able to float over tree roots and dodge branches that were invisible to the rest of them. Izak and Alzbeta, who ran behind her, smacked straight into them, uttering grunts of pain, though all had promised no noise. Alicja copied the silent movements of Rafal, determined to follow his easy shift of step, but she didn't have his eyes. He was a fox, a night animal. She could see his gingery hair flash silver when threads of moonlight trailed through the trees.

Izak was the one frightened of the dark. She could feel his breath soft as feathers on the back of her neck. But if she'd been shut in a wardrobe for three years, maybe she'd be frightened of the dark too. He kept very close. Alzbeta, at the rear, was like Alicja, happy as hell to be out. Day or night, it didn't matter.

To be free.

It meant everything.

CHAPTER NINE

I'd watched the four children go. It felt like a stake in my chest. It was always the same. I couldn't decide whether it was guilt or fear. But either way I knew I would be fit for nothing till they squeezed their boneless young bodies back up through the drain.

The narrow waste pipe ran from the back of the Laundry block down into the culvert on the other side of the perimeter wall, the one that emptied into the barren field that had once been a lush green spread of sugar beet. Stripped by desperate hands before the crop was even ripe. By day you'd be instantly spotted out there and the guards were trigger-happy. No one dared risk it. But by night you were as invisible as the owls that patrolled the nearby woods, soundless as lost souls.

Stay silent, my love, and you will not be shot.

No, no. Don't. Don't even think that. The British don't shoot kids. They are not Nazis. Nor are they the barbaric Soviet Russians who are right now ripping the heart out of my beloved Poland. The camp had imposed a ten o'clock curfew in the evening, which meant we were obliged to remain in our huts till morning because they didn't trust us in the dark. Rightly so. It was a unit of Polish soldiers in blue uniforms who patrolled our perimeter and I made a point of knowing each one of the bastards by sight. Observing how thorough – or slapdash – each one was at his job. The solid one with the permanent frown etched on his forehead was the one to watch. His name was Majewski. What was it about a uniform that twisted a man's mind?

Was it the uniform that did it for Oskar Scholz? Or did the devil already inside him climb out on the back of the swastika?

This Majewski never laughed or turned a blind eye like some of them. He snapped handcuffs on your wrists tight enough to break your bones and marched you down to the local German *Polizei* for the slightest misdemeanour. The police didn't like us. None of the locals did, because we were being fed while they starved.

In their shoes I would hate us too.

I was hunched beside the mouth of the drain in the pitch dark, the stench of it thick at the back of my throat. My eyes fixed on every shift of the blackness, as I pulled tighter the blanket wrapped around my shoulders. The night wind swept across from the harsh Russian steppes, carrying the icy fingers of the winter that lay ahead. And every moment I pictured my daughter. Running like a wild animal among people who hated her.

*

ALICJA

Alicja's eyes were huge. Snatching at every wisp of moon-light. Her heartbeat was steady, not racing. Not yet. Ears sharp for the faintest sound. She smiled in the darkness. She was good at this. They entered the village and she could smell its breath, smoky and stale like an old man's.

She moved on silent feet over the cobbles and the houses leaped out of the night at her, right on the street, no front gardens. Good. No kennels to pass. No lights, no sound. Just the wind stirring the last of the leaves. Her fear was always dogs. Every village had dogs.

'Rafal,' she whispered and pointed to the opposite side of the shabby street.

He nodded, grinned at her and slunk off into the shadows, Izak at his heels. Alicja and Alzbeta would take this side. Each pair carried a small torch and a sack. They all knew what to do. The two girls crept around the corner of the first house, Alzbeta so close that their shadows bumped each other. Even in the darkness Alicja could see that the house was small and humble, a worker's cottage, so nothing fancy. But there would be tools. Tools were good. Everyone wanted tools.

A shed. There would be a shed.

There were rules. Mama's rules. Mama always had rules. These were about sheds.

Rule 1: *Only take two items from each.*

Rule 2: *No garden spades, no garden forks.*

'How else,' Mama insisted, 'can they grow the food they need to survive? You hear me, sweetheart?'

Alicja didn't care whether they survived or not, as long as she and Mama survived. And Rafal and Izak, and Alzbeta, of course. And Rafal's mother, Hanna. That's all. The rest of the world could go hang itself.

She switched on her torch. No more than two seconds. Then off. She'd seen enough. The dim shape of a lean-to shed at the back of the house. No padlock, just a bolt. Why did they make it so easy for her? She spat on the bolt to help it slide, but as she eased it back, it still squealed into the quiet night.

Alicja froze. Alzbeta was on lookout, tucked against a wall where the shadow swallowed her so completely, she didn't exist. Alicja felt suddenly alone. Exposed to the night. Somewhere a fox barked, as if aware of her. Hairs rose on her arms in the chill air and she was up on her toes ready to flee, but there was nothing out there except her fear. No shout, no light. No dog.

She slipped inside the shed and for a moment risked the torch. Its small hoop of yellow light picked out the tools that hung in neat rows from nails on the walls. She reached out a hand. There was a billhook. Spanners, pliers, hammers, rolls of wire. A box of nails. Chisels and screwdrivers. A row of saws. She was tempted, really tempted to throw everything into the sack and run away with the lot. Mama would never know they had all belonged to one person.

Her hand darted out.

But then her sack would be full and she'd have to return to the camp.

So her fingers closed on only a hammer and one of the small handsaws. Her tongue flicked over her dry lips and she scuttled out of the shed. She didn't want to go back to camp.

CHAPTER TEN

Am I a monster? I ask myself that.

What kind of mother sends her child out to thieve for her?

I was prowling back and forth. Back and forth at the mouth of the drain, my fingers raking the skin on the back of my hands to tear it off. It fitted too tight. The blood underneath pumped too fast. Too hot. Too out of control. If I could dismantle my limbs and slide myself down the filthy outlet pipe piece by piece, I would.

No one will harm my young team of thieves. This was what I told myself again and again. Children are protected by being children. If they were caught, it could mean a beating, a blow from a peasant's callused hand, even the bite of a belt buckle, but nothing more. They would be returned to the camp, returned to me, and I would bathe their bruises, kiss their proud little cheeks, bind their war wounds.

This is my justification.

If it were me out there and I was caught, it would be the

end. I would be thrown into a German prison and left to rot. Then what?

Who would care for Alicja?

Or for Alzbeta and Izak, and even for Rafal with his slingshot and his childish swagger. Yes, he had a mother in Hanna, but she was a strange detached kind of mother. She loved her laundry more than her child, it seemed to me. She slaved over her sheets all day, took an evening nap, then battled in the laundry again alongside her night-shift crew. She would clean the filth out of these thousands of sheets if it killed her. Sometimes I wondered what the dirt was that she was so obsessed with scrubbing away.

But we all had our own dirt. We'd survived a war. You couldn't do that by keeping your hands clean.

I pushed my own hands under the blanket wrapped around my shoulders. I couldn't bear to look at them. Even in the darkness of the cold night air they shamed me. The black bulk of the Laundry block shielded me from view but a guard's footsteps sounded on the gravel and a flash of torchlight sneaked around the corner. I sank to the damp ground and flattened back against the barbed wire that lined the perimeter wall, its spikes sharp as knifepoints in my shoulder blades. The yellow beam danced towards me. Only two metres from my feet. Like the lick of a flame, I could feel its heat.

Then it was gone as suddenly as it had come. I tried to move, to rise to my feet, but my limbs were shaking. Not just a shiver. I was gripped by the kind of bone-deep tremor that cracks the bedrock of you.

'No.' The word crept from my mouth in a harsh whisper.

Because I could hear the rattle of a cage in my head bursting open, dragging me back to a Warsaw street and the last time I was pursued by the yellow beam of a torch.

Warsaw, Summer 1942

'We're fucked, Klara.'

'No. Keep running.'

'They've got us cornered.'

'We have to get to Krochmalna Street.' I dragged in breath between rapid strides. 'I know a bombed house there that has a cellar where we'll be safe.' My lungs were burning as we ran through the darkness.

At my side Tomasz shook his head. 'No, the bastards have got us this time.'

Our soft soles were silent on Warsaw's cobbles. The night air was warm as a peach on our skin, yet we wore our coats buttoned tight.

I'd lied. We'd never be safe.

The street was narrow. We raced down past the houses that were jagged from bomb damage. They had become unpredictable, leaning drunkenly as though about to fall over, some propped up by metal buttresses that glinted in the moonlight. The growl of a military vehicle sounded in the stillness somewhere close behind us and a sense of failure hit me, so acute it was a sharp pain. My feet flew faster, beating a path through the night.

Abruptly lights flared ahead of us. More behind us. Trapping us. Headlamps stripped the street of shadows and blinded our eyes. My mouth was so dry, and my jaws so tight I bit through my tongue. A *Kubelwagen* slewed across the road in front of us with its spare tyre perched on its ugly blunt nose and torches pursued us, while shouts tore through the summer night.

'Klara, hide,' Tomasz hissed. '*Szybko.*'

He tried to push me into a doorway but it was already too late. The German soldiers circled us like grey dogs, snarling and snapping. The rattle of their rifles threatened us and I could smell the stink that clung to their Wehrmacht uniforms. It was the stink of violence.

'Halt!'

That was the first word I ever heard Oskar Scholz utter. He possessed a powerful and decisive voice. A voice full of self, a commanding voice that filled the street. Moonlight slid down over tiled roofs, painting his grey eyes silver and turning his field-grey Waffen SS officer's uniform into a suit of metallic armour. He looked untouchable.

'Against the wall,' he ordered.

Rifle tips jabbed at our throats forcing us back.

'We are only on our way home,' Tomasz offered. Calm brave words. 'Here, I have my papers to show—'

'I know exactly who you are. You are Tomasz Chlebek, leader of the Resistance group that blew up the troop train to Krakow last week. And you,' he swung his flat silvery gaze on me, 'are Klara Janowska, explosives expert for these filthy traitors.'

'No,' I said quietly. 'You are mistaken, *Sturmbannführer*.'

He laughed, a sour sound that I was to become familiar with. 'Take their coats,' he commanded.

They stripped our coats from us and I felt a button tear off and heard it fall to the ground. As if it mattered now. The hand of death, cold and clammy, tightened around my heart. Terror is not something I can describe. It is like trying to describe fire. Both consume and destroy. Both reduce you to ash.

Terror seared my gut now when I watched the Nazi officer remove radio parts from a secret pocket inside Tomasz's coat and two tubes of carefully packed gelignite from inside mine. We had just collected them from our nervous supplier down on the banks of the Vistula. Someone had betrayed us. The officer regarded the courageous freedom fighter at my side with distaste for a long moment, dangling a pair of radio valves from his fingers before giving a brief nod.

The rifle at Tomasz's throat fired. The explosion roared in my ears and I screamed as Tomasz crashed to the ground. I fell to my knees beside him, cradling my friend's bloodied head in my arms. His throat was a gory mess, as black and sticky as my hatred in the twisting torchlight.

The terror vanished.

Rage roared through me in its stead and I launched myself up at the German officer, craving to rip his face off. My fingernail sliced through his cheek, drawing blood, before a rifle butt slammed into the back of my skull. My brain whitened out. My last thought was of my daughter, seven years old and able to strip down a Mauser.

66

CHAPTER ELEVEN

ALICJA

'The sack is full,' Alzbeta announced. 'Time to go home.'

'No. One more.'

'It's heavy, Alicja. It will take us ages to get all of this up through the drainage pipe into the camp. Let's go home.'

'How can you call that place *home*?'

'Because it's where we live.'

'Not, it's not where we *live*. It's where we *wait*.'

They were whispering in a fold of the pitch-black shadow of a tiny church with a stubby bell tower, but Alzbeta dropped her voice lower. She pressed her head tight against Alicja's. 'I don't want you to leave to go to England.'

But Alicja would not be sidetracked. She shouldered the sack.

'One more.'

*

Another of Mama's rules: Don't ever enter a house unless its door or window is unlocked. Never break in. Someone will hear you. The risk is too great.

The last house in the village was the best. Set back from the road up a gravel drive, it was a large timbered and red brick building with a steep pitched roof and stone dogs squatting on each side of its front door. It scared Alicja. But drew her to it like a moth.

'No,' Alzbeta whispered. 'It will have a dog.'

But Alicja shook her head. 'Wait here. Look after the sack.'

She circled the house, one more black shadow in the darkness, a faint shift of night air. Nothing more. These walls smelled different from the other houses, they breathed out the scent of polish and paint and something that smelled sweet like peaches. She let her shoulder rub against the brickwork as she passed, tucked tight under its protection. The sky was black as a stagnant pond. Lifeless and unhelpful.

There were outbuildings. But no dog.

She ignored the outbuildings. She only had eyes for the beautiful house, as she carefully fingered each studded oak door and every window she could reach, but none opened.

Never break in.

She smacked the stone hard against a glass pane. The sound was muffled by the wool of her coat but still it sounded like a gunshot to Alicja. She felt the night crack open and she shivered, then grew still once more. She waited, as motionless as one of the stone dogs. When nothing moved and no light flared within, she slid a hand through the hole in the broken glass, flipped open the window latch and climbed inside.

She meant to be fast. A split second skim with the torch, a couple of good pieces shoved under her arm and then back out and invisible in the night. Easy. A minute. Two at most. And she would be running, full of laughter, with Rafal and the others through the woods again. That was her plan.

So what went wrong?

The moment she set foot in the room on the soft silken carpet she could feel the house winding a thread around her, holding her there. She'd never been inside a house like this before.

Her first seven years she'd lived in a Warsaw apartment that she could scarcely remember. Then the convent. Three long years of plain walls, cold floors and hours each day on her knees clutching a rosary. The smell of incense made her retch. Not that the nuns were unkind. They weren't. Just indifferent. Their hearts belonged elsewhere.

She flicked on the torch. Faces jumped at her out of the darkness, making her heartbeat hammer in her ears. The walls were covered with paintings, huge bold portraits. Men with moustaches like squirrels under their noses. Women with tiny waists and children at their knee. She touched them, she couldn't help it, to feel their canvas rosy cheeks. A family held together for eternity.

She looked around and saw that the room was a dining room. A large table stood in the middle with eight chairs.

Silver candlesticks glittered in the torchlight and a bowl of fruit offered itself to her. She reached for an apple . . .

Mama's Rule: *You don't take food.*

People need food to survive.

She withdrew her hand and followed the yellow path of her torch to the door, opening it a crack. She listened hard. No sound. On tiptoe she crept across a large dark hall and held her breath as she slowly turned the handle of the door opposite.

The room welcomed her with the scent of pine logs and lavender polish. She let it seep into her nostrils. Is this what happiness smelled like? She could just make out the looming presence of a piano, as her torch beam flashed off the face of a glass cabinet and a snowy white marble mantelpiece. She jumped and cursed under her breath when an arc of torch-light flared at her off a mirror.

But it was the armchair by the fireplace that drew her. It looked loved. It looked well used, the green velvet worn as smooth as moss on a stone. She longed to sit in it, to be part of this house. But a book lay abandoned on the seat cushion and, curious, she bent closer to inspect it. It was a volume called, *Listen, Germany!* by Thomas Mann.

As she stared at it she felt her throat close with excitement. Sweat trickled, but it wasn't the book that caused it, it was what lay on top of the book inside the tight circle of torchlight.

A ring.

A ring that burned and danced with a life of its own. Alicja

70

touched the tip of her finger to it. She knew a diamond when she saw one. Hadn't she handed two of them over to her mother's attackers in the forest? It had the power to steal your soul. She had seen it happen. Mama would be in England now, not rotting in a stinking DP camp if only Alicja had not given away the diamonds. They'd have bought passports. Fake identity papers. Travel permits. Train tickets. Lodgings in London. A life of—

She snatched up the ring.

'Put it down.'

Alicja jumped violently. The sound of the German words behind her made her crash into a small side table, sending a pair of spectacles flying. She whirled around. Her torch beam leaped into the shadows.

Where?

The door?

The window seat?

The sofa?

'Put down the ring.'

The voice was liquid. Like warm water. Female but firm. It came from somewhere in the corner, where a large velvet armchair rested deep in the shadows.

Run! Get out of here!

The words screamed inside Alicja's head, but she didn't listen and instead her feet carried her across the room closer to the woman with the kind voice. She swung the torch's glare full on the chair. It revealed abundant folds of a scarlet dressing gown, waves of long dark hair and a full mouth that was curved into the beginning of a smile. A woman no older than her own mother. But the woman wore a large black eye-patch, which gave the beautiful face a lopsided strangeness. It made her look dangerous.

'Give me the ring.'

The woman held out her hand. She didn't rise from the chair but now Alicja could see why: an infant was curled up fast asleep on her lap. Her arm curled around its boneless young body protectively.

Alicja didn't move.

'What's your name?' The question was gentle.

'Alicja.'

'Are you from Graufeld Camp, Alicja?'

'Yes.'

'You know it's bad to steal.'

'I know it's bad to starve.'

'You won't starve in the camp, child. We hear that you are well looked after by the British Army there. It is the people of Germany who are starving to death in our towns and villages.' A sigh drifted through the shadows. 'For the last time, I'm asking you to give me the ring, please.'

The woman's pale hand reached out, removed the diamond ring from Alicja's palm and slipped it on her own finger.

'I need it,' Alicja whispered.

'So do I.'

Her fingers placed something bulky in Alicja's hand. She flicked the torch on it. It was a doll, her daughter's doll.

'Now go,' the woman said, the eyepatch suddenly leaning closer. 'Go and play with dolls instead of causing pain to people who have enough pain already.'

Still the voice was soft and silky, and it made Alicja feel warm somewhere deep inside, though she didn't know why. But the words hurt, like tiny nicks in her skin.

'I owe my mother two diamonds.'

'No, *Mädchen*, your mother wouldn't want you to be out stealing.'

'You don't know my mother.'

A silence stretched between them in which neither spoke, neither moved. When the door banged open with a crash they both recoiled.

'No!'

Alicja dodged away from the man's muscular hand that tried to grasp her arm. He had charged into the room, his anger brighter than the oil lamp raised in front of him.

'What the hell are you doing in my house, you thieving brat from ... ?'

Alicja was off. Ducking and weaving between chairs. Running away from the burly man whose shouts set the baby wailing, but she switched off the torch and fled into the dining room. She threw herself through the window, his curses ringing in her ears, and slithered down on to the gravel.

The night swallowed her. Her feet flew over the grass towards the ploughed field beyond, panic snapping at her heels. Still no moonlight to guide her but no moonlight to betray her either.

Where was Alzbeta? Where was she hiding? She released a low whistle as she ran.

Nothing.

Panic sank its teeth into her. Which way? Which way should she run?

'Alzbeta!'

A light flashed just ahead of her. On, off, and on again. With a whoop of relief she set off towards it, stumbling in her haste. Above her the clouds thinned to a pale veil across the face of the moon, but suddenly she could see Rafal a short way in front of her, and Alzbeta and Izak a few metres behind with the sacks on their shoulders.

Alicja was running too hard to call out again but she raised a hand. She saw her friend's mouth open wide, screaming at her. She couldn't hear the words. The thump of her pulse in her ears was deafening.

She should turn. Look behind her.

That thought was still beating a path from her mind to her limbs when she heard the explosion. Its sound was brutal in the chill dark field. Thunder? Was it thunder?

That was when the pain hit. A thousand spears in her back. They knocked the breath out of her and hurled her face-down in the dirt. She tried to crawl. Towards the white light that flooded her mind but it faded to a pinpoint speck as blackness kicked in her skull.

CHAPTER TWELVE

DAVIDE BOUVIER

Davide Bouvier was not a sleeper. His nights were long and wakeful, so it was a matter of choice – as well as necessity – that saw him in the Administration office before seven o'clock in the morning. He planned on getting two solid hours work in before the rest of the offices started to fill up, so he sat down at his desk, pen at the ready.

He was most comfortable sitting or standing. His lungs functioned better. Lying down was the worst. He allowed himself a frantic coughing fit as no one else was within earshot and then opened a thick file. It contained the constant official requests that poured in from the Russian administration of the Russian Zone of post-war Germany. An avalanche of them. Hunting down the individuals they suspected of being answerable to them, rather than to the British or American authorities.

Davide viewed it as a rather vicious game of tennis. He

75

blocked their requests, stamping the forms with a large *Unknown Here*, and batted it back to them. Only to find it slamming in return straight on to his desk with longer forms, larger signatures and on occasions a silky splat of red sealing wax with an elaborate crest impressed into it. Designed to intimidate. Some games he won, some he lost. Each one meant life or death to someone.

It was still dark outside but Davide knew that Colonel Whitmore would march in shortly, two porcelain cups of sweet tea on a tray, and he would greet Davide, as he did each day, with the same unfounded optimism.

'Morning, Davide. Today we'll knock 'em for six.'

Davide hated sweet tea. He had no idea who or what the colonel was referring to. And what the number six had to do with anything was a mystery to him. But he admired Whitmore's unquenchable determination to get the job done.

'*Oui, mon colonel.*'

Davide would give him a cheerful ironic salute. Sometimes a cup of tea went a long way towards getting things done in the unfathomable world of British etiquette. He smiled at the thought, coughed into his fresh white handkerchief – no blood on it yet – and he settled down to work.

He was deep into drafting a response letter to the latest Russian request when there was a knock at the office door. Only faint. More of a tap. And a shuffling of feet.

'Come in,' Davide said. Irritated.

The door opened slowly and a child slid round it, dark eyes bright with nerves. Davide recognised him at once, one of the urchins who ran round with Klara Janowska and her daughter. The Jewish kid with the scarred face. The child threw quick glances around the room, at the desk, at the filing cabinets, at the pot of parsley on the sill, eyes darting, checking for danger. He closed the door but kept one hand on it. Escape at his fingertips.

'What is it?' Davide asked kindly.

'I have a message.' His eyes found Davide's. 'For you.'

'What message?'

'Come.'

Davide frowned. 'Who sent this message?'

'Frau Janowska.'

Davide threw down his pen and jumped to his feet. 'Tell me the complete message.'

'*Come.* That's all.'

'*Merde!* What has happened? Is she in trouble?'

The boy snatched open the door but Davide was across the room before he could take to his heels. His lungs rumbled at the sudden exertion. 'Where is she?'

'In her hut.'

'Is she all right?'

A tear slid out of the boy's good eye. Davide stepped out into the early morning gloom, dragging the boy with him.

Whatever it was, it was bad.

Outside Hut C Davide bent double, heaving for breath. Coughing his lungs raw. His arms wrapped around his ribs, holding them together, as he stared down at the smears of blood in the dirt. The sun was rising now, spilling what looked like its own blood on to the road, rebuking Davide for being stupid enough to run through the camp at the boy's scampering speed.

The huts and dusty thoroughfares were still quiet, with lights flicking on here and there as a new day of hope began in the camp. Davide harboured no hope for himself – he had lost his wife, his daughter, his family, his friends and his home in Oradour-sur-Glane on one violent day in June 1944 – but he harboured hope for Klara Janowska and her daughter. He quietened his breathing. Whatever was going on in Hut C he needed to appear calm. Panic was always simmering just under the surface in Graufeld – it was what Colonel Whitmore referred to as the status quo.

Davide straightened up, wiped his mouth and that was when he saw a slight movement off to his left. He focused his eyes in the semi-darkness and picked out the figure of a man, leaning against the outer wall of the hut down at the far end. His outline was blurred, but his clothes looked shabby. But then everyone's clothes were shabby in this god-forsaken place.

There was something about him, a watchfulness that made Davide notice him. In his hurry to find Klara he'd have thought no more of the man in the shadows – except for one thing. He was tall and had a way of standing that betrayed a history of command, of getting things done his way. It was there in the way he held his head, in the set of his shoulders. And what was his interest in Hut C?

It made Davide think of the German who Klara had described. A man who wore spectacles, she said. This man wore spectacles. And for a moment when his lenses caught the crimson rays of the rising sun, it looked as if his eyes were full of blood.

'Come,' the young messenger boy called out from the doorway.

When Davide turned back to the man, he was gone.

CHAPTER THIRTEEN

DAVIDE BOUVIER

The girl lay in a pool of blood, face down on the bed. Her naked back was peppered with shot. There must have been more than a hundred pieces of lead buried in her paper-white skin and deep in her muscles. Davide felt his stomach turn at the sight.

Mon dieu! Who the hell would fire a shotgun at a child?

Klara Janowska was perched on the edge of the narrow bed, leaning over the motionless figure of her daughter, her concentration intent. She was wielding a knife. Its sharp tip was probing the swollen young flesh, nosing its way through the ripples of blood to extricate each piece of lead shot. But it was hopeless. It was the wrong tool. A big woman dressed in white was kneeling on the floor holding the child's hand and beside her a terrified boy stood close beside the bed holding up a candle. Vaguely Davide knew the woman from the laundry.

'Klara,' he said softly.

It took a moment. He could imagine her ears tuned to

nothing but the faintest whimper or gasp of breath from her daughter, but the girl uttered no sound. Not even when the knife-tip slipped deeper under a pellet. She was stretched out on her stomach, her face twisted to one side, her huge blue eyes so wide open you could drown in them. There were streaks of scarlet on her temple and in her hair.

'Klara?' He placed a hand on her shoulder. 'We have to move her to the infirmary at once.'

Klara lifted her face to him. Her cheeks were grey and rigid with shock. 'No, Davide. Typhus is rampant in the infirmary.' Her head was bound up in the usual drab scarf and there was a streak of Alicja's blood across her forehead but her eyes burned with such rage that he knew she would listen to no one.

'She needs a doctor, Klara. I'll fetch a stretcher to—'

'No.' She paused in her knife work. 'Would you send a daughter of yours there, Davide?'

There was no reply to that.

A spider's web of rough ropes crisscrossed the hut at head height, so that sheets and blankets could be draped over them, giving a degree of privacy around each bed. But it was no more than an illusion. He lowered his voice.

'I'll do what I can.'

She rose to her feet. 'Thank you.' Her hand caught around his for a fleeting second. 'Hurry.'

Davide had once seen a lynx in the mountains of Sweden on the trail of its prey. Its shoulders low, its head forward, its gaze fixed. Klara had the same look. The look of a huntress.

*

The colonel's office door was locked, dammit. The one time Davide needed him to be there early, Whitmore chose to be late. Davide rattled the handle as if he could summon the camp commander out of thin air.

He was breathing hard, trying to clear his mind. Klara's child was in pain, severe pain, and needed medical care. If he reported the situation to a doctor, Alicja would be forcibly admitted to the infirmary. Klara was right. Typhus had been brought into the camp and no amount of quarantine would contain it. Would he have let his daughter, his beloved Amélie, be taken to one of those wards?

The answer was no. *Non.*

He rummaged quickly in his desk drawer, pulled out the key he'd never used before and inserted it into the lock to Whitmore's office. He felt a sense of betrayal doing it but pushed it to one side. He had to acquire medical equipment and the only way was through a requisition form. He was only a DP himself, a French national who was good at administration, but he had no actual authority here.

Inside Colonel Whitmore's office he knew exactly which drawer to search. His lungs were pumping so hard, he could hear the whistle of air wheezing from his throat, but he worked fast. He removed only one requisition form, closed the desk drawer, straightened the chair to its usual exact ninety-degree angle and relocked the door behind him.

He picked up a pen from his own desk and with no hesitation signed the form: Colonel Jonathan Whitmore.

CHAPTER FOURTEEN

ALICJA

Alicja could smell the blood. She could hear Hanna's triumphant clicks of her tongue against her teeth each time a lead pellet dropped from the medical tweezers into the bucket. Worst of all, she could feel the heat in her mother's hands. As though a fire was burning in them.

Alicja wanted to run.

But her body lay as still as stone. It fought back against the pain. Against the touch of iodine. Against the certainty in her head that she was going to die.

So she let her mind run instead. Let her thoughts fly.

I remember I followed her one day in Warsaw. My mother. She didn't know. She thought I was in our neighbour's apartment playing dolls with their daughter Liljana. She was the same age as me, six, but Liljana knew nothing. Not even how to clean a K98 Mauser rifle or stitch a wound. I stitched Mama's wounds that time she came home with a long gash in her arm. She said I was brave. I can still taste her blood in my mouth where I kissed it better. Four stitches. That's what it took. Mama said I would make a good doctor. Silly Liljana knew nothing.

Liljana's mother had six other kids, so she didn't notice I was missing when I put my shoes on and crept out after Mama. I was quick and small. Like a mouse chasing a cat. She was fast in the back streets and silent. Whenever she kissed me goodbye she told me not to cling, that she had work to do.

What work, Mama, what work?

'Kocham cię,' she would say.

'I love you too, Mama.'

But it never made her stay.

It wasn't day and it wasn't night. It was that hairline crack between the two when all the colour drains from the world, that was when I followed her in Warsaw. Through the bombed-out commercial district where the smart shoppers and businessmen used to crowd on to the red trams. All gone now. Down Jerozolimskie Avenue and into the rubble behind. She met a man in a café and I stood in a doorway opposite. One of the German soldiers who marched past stopped and gave me a coin because he thought I was begging. When he was gone I spat on his zloty and threw it in the gutter. I've never told Mama that I trailed behind her and the man after they came out of the café. It was dark then. But darkness didn't scare me. What scared me was what they did.

They blew up a building.

I never found out what the building was but it had a Nazi swastika flag hanging outside. I watched Mama set the gelignite. I didn't know then that that's what it was, but I know now. The blast made my ears ring all the way home as I ran faster than a mouse. I hid in bed. She never knew.

Like she never knew about the other time. In the pitch dark, the city of Warsaw blacked out and airless. I saw the Kübelwagen *come. I saw its lights cut the darkness into pieces. I saw the rifles nip at the throats of you and your friend. The shot, I heard your scream. The German rifle butt on your skull. The Nazi who tossed you like a lifeless dog into the back of a truck.*

I thought you were dead.

They came for me next morning before it was light. The jackboots so shiny and sure of themselves. I stamped on one and they threw me against the wall.

'You're done,' Mama announced.

'*Mein Gott*, you are a brave girl,' Hanna smiled and stroked my head with her big hand, as red as strawberries from all the hot water in the laundry. 'My Rafal would have been screaming the place down.'

But it wasn't true. I knew Rafal. He would rather pull his eyes out than let me hear him scream. Mama had sent everybody else away. She and Hanna sat me up, touching me as if I were made of glass, and they wrapped the bandages – the ones her French friend had brought us – round and round me, so that in the end I looked like a mended doll.

Mama sat me on her lap, wound her arms around me, and said, 'You can cry now, sweetheart.'

But it was Mama who cried, not me.

'Tell me what happened in the village,' she whispered into my hair.

So I did. But I didn't tell her about the ring.

CHAPTER FIFTEEN

I became a guard dog.

I kept Alicja on her top bunk and parked myself on the lower one. I sat there hour after hour, day after day, listening to every sound she made and I told people she had fallen off the roof of a hut and broken her ribs. Only Hanna, Davide and the three kids knew the truth.

The inmates had their attention on other matters. Word went through Graufeld Camp like wildfire that Colonel Whitmore was to be replaced as Camp Commander. Kicked out on his arse. The army was pulling out of overseeing the Displaced Persons' camps, and UNRRA was taking over the reins. That's the United Nations Relief and Rehabilitation Administration in all its glory. God alone knows how badly we craved Rehabilitation.

But right now I didn't care a damn who did or did not oversee Graufeld Camp. I had no intention of hanging around. All I had in my sights was getting my daughter well again. Each time I changed the dressings on her back, I called down curses on the head of Oskar Scholz. If it weren't for him, she would not have been desperate enough to risk entering someone's house.

I abandoned all else. Forget teaching mathematics lessons. Forget the cleaning rota. Forget the queues at the canteen. Forget every wretched thing. Except healing my daughter, my only child. I anointed her swollen flesh with iodine and watched its yellow smears circle each pellet hole. As I watched I wanted to circle Oskar Scholz's throat with my hands, to press my thumbs down hard on his windpipe. If whoever pulled the trigger on the shotgun had been twenty metres closer, it would have blasted her lungs to bloody shreds.

'I have his name, Davide.'

He didn't even ask whose name. Just raised a dark eyebrow. 'What is it?'

'Jan Blach. That's the name he was using last week. He may have others for all I know.'

'If he's registered as Jan Blach, I'll find him for you.'

'*Merci*, Davide. I am grateful.'

I laid a hand on his arm and for several minutes neither of us moved because he had a kitten curled in the crook of his elbow. The tiny creature was grey with a white face like a miniature clown and a ridiculously fluffy tail. I patted its little pink paw pads.

'Where have you come from, little one?'

'It has taken up residence in the kitchens, it seems. Just walked into camp from outside one morning.'

'Shouldn't you teach it that the aim is to get *out* of camp, not come *in*?'

He laughed, a lovely French sort of sound and it made me ask, 'Don't you want to get out of this hellhole, Davide? To go back to France.'

He gently placed the kitten on my lap. We were sitting in a scrap of autumn sunlight, right outside the window near my bed. I would hear Alicja if she called. Was she my kitten? My little golden-haired pet to cheer me up? If I didn't have Alicja, would I even be here at all?

'You must have someone to go back home for, Davide?'

He smiled at me and tweaked my chin. 'If I left, who would bring you bandages or buy that paint stripper you make and call samogon?'

I knew he had sidestepped the question but I smiled and leaned my shoulder against his. 'Helping me may not be a wise move, *mon ami*. Have you considered that?'

But again he let the question lie unheeded. 'I don't want to know how Alicja got out of here,' he said, his finger rubbing the kitten's dusty ear, 'but I would keep her under lock and key in future, if I were you.'

'I will.'

He heard something in my voice, something I thought was buried.

'I'm not accusing you,' he said quickly.

'I know.'

He didn't need to. I was accusing myself.

*

Hut W.

Written in Davide's stylish hand.

I screwed up the piece of paper, set a match to it and watched it writhe as it turned black.

Hut W. Branded in my brain.

'What's eating you?' Hanna asked.

'Nothing.'

'If he is the man you think he is, masquerading as a homeless and helpless German refugee, when in reality he was a fucking Nazi SS officer pig who had thousands of people in Warsaw shot, then what are you fussing about?' Hanna chuckled so hard that her broad bosom rose in a tidal wave. 'You've got the bastard over a barrel.'

She slapped me on the back and I nearly brought up the ground-acorn coffee she'd poured down me. We were briefly alone in the steamy laundry. It was during one of the lulls between shifts when the exhausted night workers had staggered out, blinking like moles, in search of their beds and the morning shift had not yet arrived to start their twelve-hour day. Graufeld Camp was a noisy place, too many people crammed into too small a space, so we took advantage of the moment.

Inside the Laundry block by the far wall stood a long row of large waist-high containers that held the mountain of dirty bed linen. It always smelled unpleasant back here. I pushed my way to the one at the rear, squeezed in behind them and started to unload the dozen sheets at the top of the container.

'You after something special?' Hanna asked.

'Yes.'

'What is it this time?'

I burrowed deeper. 'Dieter Koch has broken two teeth on his saw. He needs a new one. It takes him ages to requisition a replacement.' Dieter was one of the inmates who was employed to do odd jobs around the place.

'You got one?'

'Of course.'

'One of Rafal's pickings?'

'Yes. He's good.'

Hanna snorted, pleased. 'He enjoys the missions.'

'I know.' I paused and glanced back at her over my shoulder. 'But I am calling a halt to them. I never believed anyone would shoot at a child and I'm not willing to risk your son's life any more. Or any of them.'

My hands touched metal. A pair of shears. I shifted the tools to one side. This was my secret stash. This was what was going to buy us a ticket out of here. Except it wasn't enough yet. I drew out a short, cross-cut saw, dusted it off with my skirt and slid it into a deep canvas bag on my shoulder.

'That boy loves you, you know,' Hanna commented.

It took me by surprise. I couldn't tell what she meant by it. 'I love him too.' I smiled at her.

'If anything happens to me, I want you to . . .'

'Nothing is going to happen to you,' I said briskly. 'Nor to me. We are invincible.'

We looked at each other and laughed. Suddenly she seized

my face between her rough hands and rubbed my cheeks hard, as though scrubbing one of her pillowcases.

'Klara, promise me you will be careful.' She glanced beyond the wide entrance doors to the laundry where the sunlight softened the harsh grey edges of camp internment. 'There are people out there who would give more than their right arm for the stash you have here.'

'I know, Hanna.' I removed her hands before they bored through to my teeth. 'But it's going to get both of us Polaks to England.' I kissed her round sweaty cheek.

'Hah! Not if your filthy Nazi pig has anything to do with it. He'll have us sent back to a Soviet Russia firing squad in Poland if—'

'No, Hanna. No. I will deal with him.'

From inside the container I extracted a handful of items and slipped them into my canvas bag. But not before Hanna had spotted the stubby skinning knife among them. Her eyes narrowed to slits and I thought for a moment she would wrestle me for it. We both knew she would win. And we both knew if you got caught carrying a knife in the camp it meant a month's solitary confinement.

But instead she tightened the strip of white sheet around her head and glared at the first girl who arrived early for her shift.

'I'll come with you,' she announced.

CHAPTER SIXTEEN

'Jan Blach,' I repeated. 'You know him?'

The man sitting on a stool beside the doorway of Hut W was Czech. His thick brown hair was oiled back off his face leaving it bony and naked except for a two-day stubble on his jaw. But his eyes were lazy. He did not look as if he would give me any trouble.

'Yes, lady, I know him.'

'Is he billeted here in Hut W?'

He nodded. Watching closely. 'You want to see him?'

My mouth was dry. I nodded in return.

'Go on in then.' His gaze fixed on Hanna's breasts. 'You and your friend.' He adopted a helpful smile and waved a hand towards the doorway. 'We like visitors.'

'I would no more visit inside your hut than I would a Nazi death camp,' Hanna snapped. 'Now go and get this Blach *Mensch* out here to talk to us.'

I liked having Hanna at my side. It was like having my own personal tank. Before the man could decide whether to deprive himself of the pleasure of ogling my friend's breasts, another inmate emerged from the hut, a man with broken veins on his cheeks and a freshly shaven head. He inspected us with oddly inert eyes that did nothing to hide the damage within him. Whatever he'd been through in the last five years of war, it had ripped the life out of him.

'Blach is not here right now,' he stated flatly.

I didn't like this man. I'd seen eyes like that in Warsaw. In men who took pleasure in inflicting pain. My hand slid into my bag. I glanced around to check our exit route but it wasn't looking good. Hanna and I had walked down the full length of Churchill Way to the far end of the camp where the huts of single men were huddled like the rejects many of them were. Bored, angry, suspicious and terrified. Damaged men. Deprived of comfort and the civilising influence of women.

I understood that. But it didn't mean I would tolerate their lustful stares as they gave up their card games and abandoned their arm-wrestling to drift closer in a wide circle of about twenty men around us.

'Time to leave,' I muttered and turned away.

There was a moment when I thought we'd get away with it, a kind of pause. When the pack mentality seemed to fragment. But no. I felt it surge back into life when one man clutching a bottle of beer in his hand called '*Putains*!' The atmosphere suddenly changed. Full of naked desire. Sparks leaped from one man to another. Bright. Fierce. I could feel their heat from ten paces away.

'Come,' I said to Hanna and grasped her wrist.

But the man with the cold eyes darted from the doorway right into our path and with no warning grabbed himself a handful of Hanna's abundant bosom encased in its sheet-tunic. She didn't hesitate. She threw a fist the size of a meat cleaver at his face but he smacked his elbow into the side of her head with such force that she collapsed down in the dirt. Her eyebrow spurted blood.

Instantly the bastard crouched down next to her. Both hands on her breasts now. 'I can see clearly what you like, you whore,' he yelled in her face.

Dimly I heard a cheer rise from the circle of onlookers. But there was a roaring in my ears. A spike of hatred in my heart. I dropped to one knee. Seized the back of his thick neck. It was slick with sweat. With my other hand I pushed the point of my skinning knife just under his eye where the skin was soft as putty.

'You see this clearly enough?' I hissed in his ear.

He froze.

A thin tear of scarlet oozed over his cheekbone.

'Take your hands off my friend or I will pop your eye out.'

His hands shot in the air in surrender. He was breathing hard. But I was too. I was frightened I would not be able to stop myself pushing the knife deeper.

But abruptly our tight-knit huddle on the ground burst apart. Hanna and I were yanked to our feet by a grip of iron around our upper arms while a massive boot with a metal-tip slammed into the left kidney of the man still on the ground. He screeched like a stuck pig.

I twisted my head round and found myself staring at five tattoos spilling down a man's stubbled cheek, each one in the shape of a tear. I grinned up at him.

'Niks,' I said.

'This is Niks,' I said to Hanna as I dabbed the end of my headscarf on her eyebrow, mopping up the blood. 'He's from Latvia.'

She was leaning her weight on him heavily as the big man walked us back up into the centre of the camp. I wanted to hug him tight despite the smell of him, despite the guttural growls of disapproval in a language I couldn't understand, despite the fact he was probably one of the most dangerous men in the camp. Instead I walked on the other side of Hanna, helping to support her with an arm around her waist.

Though it did occur to me to wonder if my friend was quite as groggy as she seemed. I saw the way she slid glances at our grizzly bear of a rescuer from the corner of her eye, and the innocent pressure of her pillowy breast against his massive ribcage as his arm held her on her feet as if she were thistledown. As innocent as Alicja when she denied any knowledge of the army pencils she'd been handing out to kids in the camp.

'This is the second time Niks has helped me,' I explained to Hanna. 'Thank you, Niks. I am grateful for—'

'You are a fucking *Arschloch*, I told you before. You must not go there. It is dangerous. They are no better than the rats I get rid of down this end of camp.'

Again he towered over me and again his face was hard and ferocious, hacked out of tectonic plates, but his dark eyes beneath the black undergrowth of his eyebrows were actually smiling at me. In spite of the *Arschloch* insult, Niks from Latvia was pleased to see me again.

'How is Alicja?' he rumbled, surprising me.

'Not so good at the moment, but getting better.'

'What is wrong with her?'

'She fell off a hut roof and broke some ribs.'

He glared at me, drawing his brows together. 'You should look after your daughter better.'

It was like a kick from his metal-tipped boot.

'I know,' I said softly.

Hanna intervened, pulling her arm away from the Latvian. 'She is a good mother. Don't you say otherwise.'

Without a goodbye she marched off towards her laundry, steady as a rhino. For a moment we stared after her in amazement, then both of us broke into a laugh, but it faded quickly.

'Niks, I'm still looking for the man I told you about before.'

'The one in spectacles.'

He had forgotten nothing of our encounter.

'Yes. It seems he is going under the name of Jan Blach and billeted in Hut W. Do you know him?'

He rubbed a hand back and forth over his huge black-furred jaw. 'I might.' His dark gaze focused on mine and I let him see my anger, hard as stone. 'Or I might not,' he added. 'This man will bring you nothing but grief.'

He shifted his hand from his jaw and placed it on my

shoulder. It felt like a rock. I wanted to tell him that Oskar Scholz had already brought nothing but grief into my life. Into Alicja's life. But now was not the moment. I dug into my canvas bag, burying the knife, and pulled out a sealed envelope that I stole from Davide's office. I held it out to Niks.

'I've written a note to him. Will you give it to him, please? Make sure you put it into his hands.'

The big man stood staring at it for a full minute and I thought he was going to refuse, but eventually he took it. He ran a thumb thoughtfully over the writing on the front.

'What do these words say?' he asked.

I allowed no surprise to show in my voice. 'It says *To Mr Jan Blach.*'

He nodded without the faintest trace of embarrassment. 'What's your name?'

'Klara Janowska.'

'So, Klara Janowska, give this gift to your daughter from me.'

From his baggy trouser pocket he drew out a small packet wrapped in greaseproof paper and tied with string. Suddenly he was awkward. Uncertain what to say. 'For Alicja.'

I was touched by his thoughtful gesture and said, 'Why don't you give it to her yourself?'

'No, no.' He scowled at me from under his black brows. 'She is an angel. I am the Devil's bastard son, I warn you.' Suddenly he flashed his tobacco-stained teeth at me. 'I look after the camp's vegetable garden, you know. Why don't you and your friend come and visit me there some time?' Then he lumbered off, his broad back and tattooed face forming his armour in this uncertain world.

'Thank you, Niks,' I called after him.

He raised a hand but didn't turn. I opened the packet, peeling back the layers. Inside lay a scarlet ribbon.

How long had he been carrying it in his pocket on the off chance of seeing me?

That night I woke shuddering. My whole body in spasm. In bed. In darkness. My blanket in knots. A violent throbbing between my legs and my heart thundering behind my ribs.

Had I cried out?

I clamped a hand over my mouth to silence the screams of joy that streamed through me and threatened to burst out into the sleeping barrack hut.

How long since I'd had a sex dream? Six barren years. Not since my husband had been shot out of the skies in his P.11 fighter in a ball of flames above Warsaw, but tonight he had come to me, my Dymek. My love. My breath. My joy. My reason for being on this earth. He had come to me, his naked skin like fire on mine again, his lips teasing secret places till I almost ripped the hair from his head with need. And his hands, his strong and clever hands, cupping my breast, my cheek, my buttocks as if he would devour my flesh.

I had forgotten. In the long dark nights. Forgotten how that searing moment of release strips you free of this world and hurls you into another pulsating existence. My hands reached out, desperate in the blackness, and searched in vain for Dymek. They found only vacant air. I curled over on my side, wrapping myself tight around the tiny fragile bubble of joy. Tears streaked my cheeks and my chest refused to cease shuddering.

I was losing him. I knew that. Day by day, month by month, he was abandoning me. The clean lines of his face were fading, the outline of the taut muscle on his chest where I used to lay my head, was blurring. But tonight I could smell him. The scent was fierce in my nostrils. The scent of the hollow at his neck, of his hair, of the engine oil that infused the skin of his hands. I smiled because tonight I could recall his smile; I laughed because I could remember a reason to laugh. I reached out.

'Please, Dymek,' I mouthed. Only blackness.

I could feel it leeching the last traces of goodness from me the way fleas leech the blood from a filthy gutter hound. I opened my eyes wide, staring the blackness in the face. It didn't realise what it was dealing with.

No more than Oskar Scholz did.

CHAPTER SEVENTEEN

He would come.

I was sure he would. This displaced person. This Oskar Scholz. This man who stole my brother's name. Writing *Jan Blach* on the envelope almost broke my fingers, the effort was so great, but I knew that if I wrote *Oskar Scholz*, he would not come.

I wished I could have seen his face when he opened the note and saw my name at the bottom. Did his eyes half-close in that odd way he had when seeking to hide shock? Did his mouth quiver? Did his finger rub that spot on his high pale forehead where pain seemed to stab in moments of upset? He believed he was safe here. Now he knew better. Now he would kill me.

So why tell him I am here? That's what you're thinking.

I told him because however much I want this man dead, a part of me wants to make a deal.

A deal?

I know. It sounds crazy. I knew from the moment I saw him in the doorway of Hut J that Scholz would scratch his own eyes out rather than make a deal with me. That's why I had to resolve to kill him. But the part of me that has seen enough killing and enough dying to last ten lifetimes won't shut up. It sits in the back of my skull and throws rocks at me.

I perched on a seat at one of the chessboards in the Recreation hall and waited.

My mind would not steer clear of the memory of that other chess game, however hard I tried. It was a warm summer evening in Warsaw. Oskar Scholz had brought me to his elegant apartment. But in those days he was Sturmbannführer Oskar Scholz, an officer in the Waffen SS.

He was holding up a photograph in front of me.

'So what do you think, Frau Janowska? Handsome enough for you?'

I gave it the barest of glances.

'You recognise who he is?' he pressed me.

'Yes.'

'You know his name?'

'SS Oberführer Axel Fleischer.'

'Good.'

Scholz was seated opposite me at his 18th century ebony and ivory inlaid chess table. It had been looted from the Royal Castle in Warsaw's Castle Square when the Nazis marched into Poland in 1939. But that was not all. This man was greedy. Around us in the sumptuous salon of his Warsaw apartment spread a lavish array of tapestries that dated back to King Stanislaw Augustus and royal silverware that glittered brighter than stars in the candlelight.

The spoils of war, he called them.

I called them stolen property. To his face.

He just shrugged and smiled his amusement at the anger I made no attempt to hide.

'Oberführer Fleischer is coming to play chess with you tonight,' he announced.

I couldn't stop myself. My skin crawled as I turned and spat on his nicely polished parquet floor. I tried to rise to my feet but his arm snapped out and he pinned my hand to the chess table. I refused to look at him, but I knew his eyes would be narrowed to arrow slits and a faint line of sweat would have sprung out along his hairline, his blond hair cropped so short I could see the shape of his skull.

'Klara!'

'No.'

'Do as I ask.'

Why?

Why would I do what this man asked? This enemy whose forces had shot my husband out of the sky in flames and bombed my parents and brother to pieces of raw meat. This man who had personally ordered the execution of my friend Tomasz in the street; who had stood over me in an interrogation cell hour after hour, day after day, week after week, trying to extract from me a betrayal of my comrades in the Warsaw Resistance. Who had, with his own hands on the pincers, ripped out my fingernails, slowly, so that it would hurt more.

And when I was reduced to blood and mucus and a hatred so fierce it was like a machete in my chest, he threw a silk frock at me and brought me here to his apartment.

Why?

If it was sex he wanted, he could have taken it. But he didn't touch me. Instead he took a hairbrush and slid its bristles through my matted mane, sprayed a sultry perfume on my throat and sat me here. At the chess table.

Why?

I was used to fear. Its grip on my heart was there with each beat. I was used to pain. I was used to the Totenkopf, the metal death's head insignia on his SS cap, grinning at me. I was used to his voice, the kind that can steal your thoughts from you, winding itself through my mind. What I wasn't used to was kindness.

He cupped my chin in his palm as gently as if I were a kitten. I became a chill and silent creature. His smile should have been angry; as hard and unforgiving as the iron in the German trains I had been blowing up. But his words were soft. Whispered across the table by candlelight.

'Let me explain to you,' he said gently, 'why I can persuade you to say yes.'

I waited.

The minutes ticked past as slowly as though the hands of the wall clock were wearing leaden boots. Graufeld Camp's Recreation hall was busy as always, crowded with people snatching at a moment of escape. From the boredom. From the mind-numbing despair that breathed its stale air into their faces when they opened their eyes each morning. Here they could pretend. They could be normal. They could clutch at laughter.

At one end two couples played table tennis. A circle of six women sat in the centre, scaring each other with ghost stories, their hands knitting all the time. Their wool hung in kinky twists from the needles because it was old wool, reused wool, make-do-and-mend wool.

I waited.

The card tables along one wall were occupied but everyone knew that the real card games, the ones where players staked their last Deutschmark and then their dead father's watch or even an hour with their wife, those games took place elsewhere. Behind the huts or under the oak tree. I was sitting at one of the board-game tables. I'd chosen chess. I'd laid out the pieces and wrapped a pawn in each hand, one white, one black, for him to choose, but we both knew I would win. Black or white.

If we played chess, I wouldn't have to look at him. And why would I want to look at a man I was going to kill?

He was late. Nearly an hour late. But not for one moment did I doubt that he would come. He was playing games. I looked at my hands and they were steady, no sign of shakes.

I waited.

Oskar Scholz opened the door. *Jan Blach*, as he chose to call himself – *liar, liar* – walked into the Reception hall. A cool spiteful draught slid in with him, stirring the smoke-laden air and nipping like a sly dog at our ankles.

I had three seconds to study him before his eyes searched me out. He was still in his disguise. Not tall any more but hunched and narrow, folded in on himself, his head low, his silver-grey eyes hooded and watchful. Still wearing the workman's cords and collarless shirt. The lens of his spectacles was still cracked, creating a look of helplessness. It occurred to me in that second that he had cracked it himself. If I didn't know him like I know the back of my hand, I could easily have missed him in a crowd.

He saw me.

We both knew this moment was coming, we were both prepared. Yet still, the moment our eyes fixed on each other, it felt like an act of violence. A kick in the gut. A mix of pain, shock and terror, but something else too. An overpowering desire to finish what we'd started, to put an end to . . .

To what, exactly?

An end to *this*.

The second his gaze hooked on mine, I saw him forget himself. His spine straightened, his chest swelled, his chin lifted. Before me stood the powerful SS Sturmbannführer Scholz once more, eyes cold as a rifle barrel, and his mouth hardened. I flicked a pointed glance at the chair opposite, summoning him to me.

As fast as the SS Sturmbannführer had arrived, he vanished. In his place stood the imposter, *Jan Blach,* shoulders slumped, jaw loose, hands hidden in pockets. He shuffled over to my chess table and sank down on the seat.

'Good day, Frau Janowska,' he smiled politely.

As if he'd never stolen my daughter.

'You're late,' I said sharply. 'My note said an hour ago.'

'I apologise.' He widened his smile but his eyes remained cold and suspicious. 'The note came as a surprise. I had no idea you were here in Graufeld Camp.'

That was it.

No more words. Just silence. No apology from him. No begging for an absolution, which I could no more give him than fly. Neither of us spoke and there seemed no way to open a pathway to negotiation that might save at least one of us from a bullet in the brain.

I held out both hands to him, fists closed tight. 'Choose,' I instructed.

He raised one blond eyebrow in surprise, then with a neat grim nod he tapped the knuckles of my left hand. I flicked it over and uncurled my fingers. On my palm lay a pawn. It was black.

I moved my bishop to Queen 4 and silenced my flutter of satisfaction. I was white, therefore I had the advantage. I had gained control of the centre of the board, so I sat back, studied my opponent and waited.

Chess used to be my addiction. I would use it like a drug to make me forget. You cannot play chess and think of anything else. This meant that for a brief respite each day it wiped my mind. When I sat at the board, rows of black and white squares hypnotised me and the fate of my chess king became my obsession instead of this man in metal-rimmed spectacles. For an hour, sometimes two or three, my world would begin and end at the edge of the board.

Chess is a game of war. The middle-game is always carnage. In the early days I had encouraged Alicja to play against me because it would teach her to work out strategies, to think ahead. To focus her mind.

But today my opponent was Oskar Scholz and we fought our war in silence. He was strong in defence on the board, but less skilful in attack. That fact galled him. I intended to turn the screw today. I'd opened with the queen's gambit and his position was now cramped, but I saw a flicker of a smile on his lips. I knew he was about to exchange pieces. The way he had exchanged me.

With a sudden sweep of my hand I sent the board and all the chess pieces flying off the table. Kings and bishops and castles rained through the air and crashed on to the floor. Heads turned to stare at us and a young boy came running over to pick them up, but Scholz waved him away. I gripped the sides of the table with both hands, my knuckles white as bone, and I leaned forward until my face was within spitting distance of his. I could feel blood draining from my cheeks as I fought to keep my hands off him.

'This is not about the deaths,' I said to him, my voice so low I could scarcely hear it myself. 'Not about the violence. Not about loss or about rage. It is about the removal of personal freedom by people in positions of power. That is what you Nazis did.' I made myself sit back. 'You are not in power now,' I hissed.

His eyes gleamed behind his spectacles in a way I found hard to understand. He was in danger from me every moment of the day. All I had to do was report him as a war criminal. Didn't he comprehend that?

'Klara.' He let the word linger in his mouth. It set my teeth on edge. 'We are both a constant threat to each other because of what we know about each other's past. Let's accept that, Klara.'

He rubbed his boxer's square chin thoughtfully. His features were heavy, their bones strong, no hint of weakness anywhere in his face. It would have had a certain attraction for some, had his eyes not been so deep, nor so secretive.

He smiled at me now, a cold shark smile. 'So what do you suggest?'

'I wish to make a deal.'

At the other end of the hall a man whooped with triumph and waved his table-tennis bat in the air when he won his game, but neither of us looked away for a second.

'What kind of deal?' Scholz asked softly.

'I don't report you to Colonel Whitmore who would throw you to the dogs for war crimes, and you don't report me. As simple as that.'

His chest was rising and falling faster.

'We go our separate ways,' I stated.

He folded his arms across his threadbare shirt and made no response.

'You agree to the deal?' I asked.

'I agree.'

'Then there is no need for us ever to speak to each other again.'

He didn't like it. Didn't like to be told. I saw a flash of the SS officer in the way he pulled back his wide shoulders and held out his hand to shake.

'It's a deal,' he said.

I turned away from it, rose to my feet and walked out of the hall.

Did Oskar Scholz really think I believed his word?

This had nothing to do with my personal freedom. It had everything to do with saving my daughter.

CHAPTER EIGHTEEN

I stood behind the Recreation block and vomited up the bile in me. I wiped my mouth on the back of my hand and sucked in clear air to rid my nostrils of the stench of him. But still I could not rid my head of that moment Scholz opened the door of his apartment and invited Oberführer Fleischer to walk his jackboots into my life.

I was still seated at Scholz's chess table. I must have looked a mess, a toad among the exquisite marble-carved nymphs and naiads that were draped suggestively about the room. In contrast to their perfection I was damaged. Fingers bloodied. Face bruised. My bones visible beneath my skin. I sat where I had been told to sit. Like a dog.

'Guten Abend, *Frau Janowska.*'

'*Good evening, Oberführer Fleischer.*'

Fleischer. Do you know what the surname Fleischer means in German? It means butcher. A man who butchers. I was sitting there waiting to be butchered.

Oskar Scholz greeted him warmly with an immaculate 'Heil

111

Hitler' salute. The two men in their tailored grey uniforms with oak leaf patches, shoulder boards and iron crosses at their throat looked like respectable men you would want to know. Capable officers you would want on your side, blond and strong-necked, though Fleicsher was sinewy and lithe rather than muscular like Scholz. You would not look at them and think, These men are killers.

Until you got to know them better, that is.

'What will you have to drink, Axel?' Scholz offered.

'What do you have? I fancy something special tonight.' He laughed lightly and glanced across at me, but I did not play his game.

'I have the most wonderful Polish vodka for you,' Scholz declared, throwing open the doors of his maple-wood cocktail cabinet that was designed to resemble an Egyptian temple. 'It's a Soplica.' He started to pour a silky clear liquid into two shot glasses. 'Created by that Polish genius distiller in Gniezno, Boleslaw Kesprowicz. I've brought him to Warsaw.' He raised his own glass. 'Na zdrowie. Good health.'

'Good health to you, Oskar.'

Axel Fleischer turned and studied me. I studied him right back, ignoring Scholz's pointed frown. He downed his drink in one and murmured, 'A fine vodka, Oskar. Smooth as a Fraülein's thigh.' He refused a second drink, approached the chess table and sat down opposite me. I was close enough to spot weaknesses now, the way his tongue touched his full top lip when he was nervous, but also to smell anticipation on him. An excitement. I wondered if I smelled the same.

The lights were low and a recording of classical music was playing softly in the background, something bold and Germanic. Wagner, I suspected. Fleischer picked up two pawns, beautifully carved out of marble, one white, one black, and concealed them in separate hands, which he held out in front of me. I noticed his fingernails were groomed and buffed, his nails just a fraction longer than was normal on a man. I could imagine them scratching my eyes out.

'Choose,' he ordered.

I chose. He turned over his hand. The pawn was black.

'Are you good?' he asked.

'Yes.'

A trace of a smile curved the corner of his mouth. 'Can you beat me?'

'Yes.'

He raised one sceptical eyebrow. Not for one second did he believe me. 'Let play begin.'

Axel Fleischer was good, yes, I admit it, but not as good as he thought he was. I let him win the first game. But only after I could have taken his king at least ten times. Fleischer was over-eager pushing forward at the wrong moments. Is that what he was like on the battlefield too, a commander too willing to sacrifice his troops? I didn't care to think of that.

In the second game I boxed him into a corner, forcing an exchange of queens and I saw a flicker of panic in his neat fingers, so I opened up a path for him to my king. When he won this time he made no secret of his disappointment in me. He lost interest, having expected more of a challenge. I'd underestimated him. Scholz was prowling behind me, restless as a cat. He laid a heavy hand on my shoulder.

'Enough,' Fleischer announced, pushing back his chair. 'No more chess. Danke, Frau Janowska.'

'One more,' I said.

For the first time I smiled at the Oberführer. I peeled away one of the layers of indifference that coated my eyes and I saw him hesitate. He glanced with irritation at Scholz as if he were to blame for my inadequacy. In that assumption he was right. Oskar Scholz had ordered me to lose. He had misjudged his man.

'Oberführer Fleischer,' I said, pushing back from my face a strand of long hair still stiff with blood, 'I would like a drink.'

I was given one. A shot of vodka. I drank it straight down and wondered why Fleischer was here. There must be other chess-playing women in Warsaw, ones without nail-less fingers and bruises on their skin. Why me?

I put down my glass and leaned forward, my eyes on his. 'Now let us play for something worth playing for.'

The blue of his eyes grew more intense, suddenly intrigued.

'Like what?' he demanded.

'My daughter's freedom.'

He coughed, an uneasy bark of annoyance. 'I know nothing about your daughter.'

'But Sturmbannführer Scholz does.'

Scholz's thumb dug into the side of my neck.

'Leave her alone, Oskar,' Fleischer muttered impatiently. 'Das is genug! I want her mind sharp.'

Scholz removed his hand.

'What's your first name?' Fleischer asked.

There was something different about him now, something sharper. The row of medals above his left breast pocket appeared to swell and the heavy metal insignia on his chest pulsed in the lamplight. My fingertips started to throb.

'Klara,' I said.

'Well, Klara, this is what we'll do. We'll play one more game and whoever wins gets to stay out of Sturmbannführer Scholz's blood-soaked interrogation room. How does that suit you?' He smiled playfully. His mouth was very full and wide, and I wanted to reach across the table and peel it off his face. 'Agreed?' he prompted.

'Agreed.'

As if I had a choice.

Fleischer set up the board, eager now. Why? I didn't know. The deal was meaningless to him. He lit himself a cigarette, clearly expecting a long drawn-out game.

I demolished his king in six moves.

He laughed, the loud satisfied laugh of a man who has won. Which, of course, he had. I let him lean over the decimated board and kiss me on the lips, hard and triumphant. I let him drive me in his sleek black Mercedes-Benz 170V into the warm night and through the bombed-out streets of Warsaw, its powerful head-lights picking their way over the pathetic shattered ruins of a once proud city.

I let him take my arm. Walk me through the grand archway of his fine apartment. I let him slide the straps of my borrowed finery off my chill shoulders. I let his full wide lips invade my throat and neck with their soft demanding heat.

I let him take me to his bed. Tumble me between his silk sheets and take possession of my body as brutally as I had taken possession of his king.

But didn't they know, these men? This Oberführer Axel

Kate Furnivall

Fleischer. This Sturmbannführer Oskar Scholz. Hadn't they learned? That when it came to war on a board of black and white squares, the king may be taller. But the queen was more dangerous.

CHAPTER NINETEEN

'Thank you, Klara.'

The young woman in my hut with the golden curls and the pretty doll's face beamed at her reflection in the hand mirror I had just presented to her. It had a tortoiseshell frame and a handle that fitted snugly into the palm. To the other woman who loved to sew I gave a choice of three different pairs of spectacles, two with wire frames, one with small round lenses in a black frame. She tried on each one, selected the one that helped her most, the black ones, and hugged me hard.

'Thank you, Klara.' She was weeping with relief. 'You are a magician.'

They both paid me well.

A *magician*? I wish.

I checked on my daughter. She was well enough now to be impatient with my constant hovering at her side, but whenever I left her I made certain one of the other children took my place. Today it was Alzbeta. They were seated side by side on my bunk bed, heads together while Alicja demonstrated to her friend how to do one of the maths puzzles I had set them. I sat beside her.

'Did you speak to him?' Alicja asked.

I nodded. 'Yes.'

Her solemn face was pale. Though she was mobile again, her back healing well thanks to a supply of ointment from Davide Bouvier and the resilience of her young skin, I could still see the shock lingering in her eyes. Dark smudges like fingerprints on their clear blue surface. I took her warm hand in mine but she gently removed it. She was angry at me. I knew why. I had forbidden any of the children to leave the camp ever again.

'What did he say?'

I smiled. 'Don't worry. Scholz and I agreed to just leave each other alone. Relax, sweetheart. Everything is fine.'

'Then why do you look so bad?'

'Because seeing him again brought back bad memories. But that's all they are – memories.' I lifted her hand into mine and held on to it firmly this time. 'No need for us to think of him ever again.'

Alzbeta regarded us with a baffled gaze. 'Who?'

'He's a friend of Mama's.'

'He's no friend of mine.'

Only when I saw the girls' eyes widen did I realise how sharp my tone was. I hugged them both close to me, inhaling the smell of their camp-scented hair, and I felt something bulky tucked under Alicja's jumper. I knew exactly what it was. That wretched doll.

The one given to her by the woman in the village. It was too babyish for a ten-year-old, dressed in its lacy baby clothes and with its ugly rosebud of a mouth. I confess I took an instinctive dislike to the thing, but when I saw how my daughter cradled it lovingly in her skinny little arms, well, what could I do? I patted its rosy porcelain cheeks and accepted without murmur that it must sleep tucked in beside her each night. Something for her to love. We all need that, don't we?

I released my hold on the girls, but Alicja stopped me. She lifted her hand and stroked my cheek, over and over again. Her fingers felt as soft and fragile as butterfly wings. As if she were trying to smooth away something rough and spiky that she could see lying under my skin, something I didn't know was there.

She stretched forward and whispered in my ear, 'I trust you, Mama.' She looked down at my scarred fingers hiding in a ball on her knee. 'Do whatever you have to.'

CHAPTER TWENTY

Scholz would come for me. I didn't know where or when, but I knew he would come. He didn't trust me to keep my mouth shut about his past, any more than I trusted him. I was tempted to seize my daughter's wrist and run for the hills. But that wasn't an option, so I did the next best thing, I queued.

You have to understand that queuing was a way of life in a Displaced Persons' camp. It was how we functioned. All day we stood in line. Queues for the washrooms and the lavatories; queues at the canteen for meals; queues at the post room for letters. Queues for doctors. Queues for dentists. Queues to fill out forms. Queues to hand in forms. Queues to join queues. Were the queues designed to keep us docile? Sometimes I wondered.

Outside the Permits office, that's where I queued. We called it Hell's Kitchen because we had to walk through hellfire to come out the other end with a permit that allowed us to be absent from the camp for a day, or even a few hours. It was hard to remain patient for nearly two hours while shuffling forward in the late autumn sunshine. To me the camp seemed to possess a grey carapace that not even the sun's rays could shift. It had the smell of a graveyard, the huts our wooden coffins.

But I refused to be buried here.

'Request refused.'

The soldier stamped my form with a black cross. His words slithered in my gut.

'Please,' I said. 'I need to try for a job out there. I am a good skilled worker and—'

'I'm sorry. There are no jobs out there. For anyone. I know it's hard to understand but there aren't enough jobs here in Germany for Germans, never mind for Poles and Czechs and all the other displaced persons. I'm sorry.'

The soldier was kind. He had the sort of soft English face that is gentle and unmemorable. How many times had he said *I'm sorry* today, his face creased with concern?

'I am an engineer,' I pointed out. 'I can assist with rebuilding.'

I knew it was only a few individuals with scarce specialist skills who were finding work outside the camp. A steeplejack was rebuilding a factory chimney locally. An accountant went every Friday to do a glove company's books. But the soldier's eyes remained regretful.

'I'm sorry, miss, but the British Army's Royal Engineers are looking after that job.'

He pushed the rejected form across the desk to me and I wanted to thrust it back at him and take his large capable hand between mine. I wanted to hold it tight and say, 'Please. Please sign the form. It means everything. If you don't my daughter and I will die. Just let me out for one day, that's all I'm asking. Please.'

I was willing to beg. To go down on my knees if it would help, but I knew nothing was going to change this decent young man's mind as he stuck to army rules. Already I could see his gaze flicking to the door behind which the queue was building up like water behind a dam. I was only here now because someone had yelled, 'Fight!' and ten of the men ahead of me in the line had abandoned their spots and raced off to the dusty patch behind the Washroom block where disputes were settled with fists. Always a popular spectator sport in the camp.

I rose from my hard seat because I was wasting time. He did the same, raising his pale eyebrows with encouragement.

'Maybe your transit permit will come through soon,' he smiled. 'Then you won't need a work permit, will you?'

He was right, of course. If my transit permit came through, I had no doubt I would not need a job. I would be carried out of here in a box.

'How is Alicja?' Davide asked.

'Improving.'

'I'm glad to hear it.' He examined my face from under thick lashes as if I wouldn't notice. 'Bad day?'

'They won't let me out of here.'

Davide laughed, a rich rolling sound that eased the

tightness in my throat. 'Have you only just noticed?' he asked and pulled out a battered old hip flask.

We both took a swig. God knows what was in it but it set my stomach on fire. We were seated on a bench, idly watching a bunch of children kick a ball around a square of scrubland on which goalposts had been erected. Light was fading fast and the warmth had drained out of the day, leaving the air chill as it fretted our cheeks. But the sky in the west was a sheet of fiery pink that gave us both a healthy glow. Deception came easy in Graufeld Camp.

'The only way out of here,' I told him, 'is inside a vehicle.'

'No, Klara.' He shook his head at me, indulgently. 'You're crazy.'

'No, I'm not. It's true.'

'Anyway, if you did escape, without a travel permit, a work permit, identification card or ration card, you'd die of starvation within a week. To get to England you'll need money and a passport and . . . what about Alicja?'

'Don't worry. I'd only be gone a few hours.'

'Forget it, Klara.' He threw in another laugh to convince us both that I was joking.

I knocked back a second swig from the flask and leaped to my feet to applaud when Rafal's lanky legs scored a goal. Davide rose to stand beside me, the warmth of his shoulder seeping into mine.

'I won't help you, Klara.'

'I'm not asking you to.'

'Stop staring at the repair shed.'

I allowed myself the smallest of smiles and to distract him I nudged him in the ribs, which I instantly regretted because it set him coughing.

'Do you know what I saw go into the repair shed this afternoon?' I asked.

He turned his head and regarded me warily. 'I dread to ask.'

'An ambulance.'

DAVIDE BOUVIER

The soldier, Benny, was small and chirpy. 'I'm a Cockney from Stepney. That's in London,' he claimed with pride.

Davide had no idea what that meant but it didn't seem to matter because Benny was too busy laughing and slapping his thigh to notice. It had not been difficult to track down the name of the ambulance driver – Lance Corporal Benjamin Kemp – and to turn up at the vehicle repair workshop with one of Colonel Whitmore's official-looking files under one arm and a clipboard in his hand.

'What's the problem here?' Davide asked.

Lance Corporal Benny Kemp was surprised to be answerable to a man in civvies. 'And who might you be, sir, if you don't mind me asking?'

'I am Monsieur Davide Bouvier, aide to Colonel Whitmore. It's my job to keep all the different elements of Graufeld Camp, military and civilian, running together smoothly.'

The lance corporal grinned. 'Rather you than me, mate.'

He patted the khaki canvas flank of the ambulance affectionately, the way you would an injured horse. 'This old girl is
leaking oil like a sieve. Her differential is buggered, if you'll
excuse my French, and her rear axle shaft seal is all to cock.'

It was an easy matter for Davide to share a hip flask with
this pleasant young soldier while he was waiting. It was his
first visit to Graufeld – he was based in Hanover, twenty
miles away, and needed to return to his base before nightfall.
While oil leaks and shaft seals were being attended to, it was
the most natural thing in the world to invite him to a private
viewing of a scratchy reel of a Laurel and Hardy film he'd
got his hands on, *Jitterbugs,* that sent the lance corporal into
whoops of laughter.

Davide envied him. Envied him his ease of mind. The
clarity of his pleasure in life. Whatever horrors he had seen
in the back of that military ambulance of his had not dimmed
the sheen of his smile. Why could Davide not do that himself? Let the horrors go.

When they emerged from the film, still chuckling at Stan
Laurel dolled up as a woman, Klara just *happened* to be passing and just *happened* to tempt them to join her in trying out
the new infusion of samogon.

They had him then. In the small spotless office at the rear
of the laundry where Hanna kept her ledgers and lists, and
her latest offerings from the still in her laundry yard. He
drank her home-made moonshine and he smoked his Players
cigarettes, clogging up Davide's lungs, and he laughed louder
with each different tasting.

So it came out of the blue when young Benny stretched out his long legs in their khaki serge trousers and said, 'I didn't fall off the turnip truck yesterday, you know. What is it you want from me?'

KLARA

Oh Benny. Don't let me down now. I thought we had you. Sitting in the palm of Davide's hand. I thought his easy French charm and Hanna's hooch, strong as nitro to blow the roof of your mouth off, had snared you.

And now this.

What is it you want from me?

You. With your cheeky laugh. Homesick for your Stepney and your girl, Betty, her photograph soft and dog-eared in your pocket. How do I get to you? How do I put my hand down your throat and squeeze your English heart?

'You don't have a daughter, do you, Benny?' I said.

His cheeks coloured. 'No, of course not. I'm not married.'

'Do you have a younger sister?'

'Yes, I do.'

'What's her name?'

'Ethel.'

'I bet she misses you. But you will be home soon.'

'You bet.' He was grinning at the thought.

'Benny, I want you to smuggle me out of here in your ambulance. I'd only be gone a few hours.'

'What?' He jumped to his feet and stubbed out his

cigarette in his empty glass. 'No chance. I would get done if I was bloody caught.'

'You won't get caught,' Davide said quietly. 'I'll see to that.'

'No.'

'Benny, I have a daughter.'

'Oh, well that's nice for you.'

'Her name is Alicja. She's ten. Would you like to meet her?'

What I could see he wanted was to back out of the tiny room and leap into his driving seat, safe in his khaki ambulance with its big red cross on the roof. So I slid my arm through his to prevent a dash for freedom, and marched him through the camp, along Churchill Way to Hut C.

'Alicja!' I called.

She appeared in the doorway. She was in her nightdress, so had draped a white sheet around herself, and stood there with the sun streaming down on her, her golden hair a halo around her beautiful face. She looked like an angel. Exquisite and ethereal. My heart tightened so hard in my chest that I had to fight back tears. How on earth had I produced such a child? An angel with the heart of a lioness. They may have torn off her wings, but they'd forgotten her claws. She looked at me with those intense blue eyes and she looked at Benny at my side.

Then she smiled at him.

CHAPTER TWENTY-ONE

I was out of Graufeld.

Out.

Such a tiny word for such a huge sensation. The feeling was ... it is hard to find words for it. Like something cracking wide open inside me and birds flying out. Their wings fluttering to freedom, the sounds vibrating in my ears.

No wonder Alicja was so angry when I banned her from leaving the camp again.

I was rattling along inside the ambulance, jolted and shaken as Benny drove like a bat out of hell to Hanover. The Austin K2/Y ambulance was kitted out to hold four stretchers, two each side at varying levels, without much care for comfort, I have to say. I was rolled up in a ground-sheet of green canvas and tucked away under one of the bottom stretcher beds. Not visible to a half-hearted search. Davide was calm and organised. He ensured that the search by the two guards on the gate was barely even half-hearted by bringing them a flask of tea from the canteen at the moment my ambulance rolled up for inspection. We were waved through.

Davide had wanted to come with me to Hanover, and Hanna had tried to stop me. Only Alicja urged me to go.

'Oh, Christ!' Benny cried out.

I couldn't breathe.

I hadn't expected this. A police road block. Just as we were approaching Hanover.

'Oh Christ!' he whispered this time. Panic made his voice sound young. 'What now?'

I was perched in the small doorway that led from the stretcher area to the cab of the ambulance. I'd been watching the road unspool ahead of me, as pockmarked by bomb damage as a Swiss cheese. In my head I was planning my next moves. Step by step. A chess game played out on a board slippery with blood.

'Stop here, Benny,' I said urgently. I squeezed his shoulder. His chest was heaving.

In the back of the ambulance I had with me a sack of stolen goods that I'd come to sell. We both knew that if the *Polizei* caught me, the penalty for dealing on the black market was a prison sentence. For a military man I had no idea what the punishment would be, but sure as hell neither of us was going to hang around to find out.

'Slow down when you pass those barns. Be quick!'

Ahead of us there was quite a queue of military lorries blowing out smoke and at least a dozen cars waiting to get through the police checkpoint. If I was lucky, and if I was quick, and if all eyes were focused impatiently on the police, I might get away with it.

If. If. If.

I jumped.

The road here was still rural. It passed through landscape that was flat and featureless, part of the great plain of northern Germany where even a molehill becomes a mound worth noting. The only thing of interest about the fields around me was their barrenness. They had been stripped. Scraped to bare bones. There was just naked brown earth. Desperate hands had plucked out every scrap of life in the land, even the blades of grass.

In the camp we'd all heard the rumours. We knew that beyond our barbed wire and perimeter walls, Germans were starving. Starving to death in the streets of Hanover and in the filthy gutters of Berlin. All because of their Führer's greed.

I hit the ground running.

'Thank you,' I yelled to Benny. 'Have a happy life with your Betty.'

The headlights of a car came swooping up behind me and I threw myself and my sack into the black cavern of the stone barn that hunched drunkenly at the side of the road. Its walls swallowed me instantly and I lay silent. As if I didn't exist. The car swept on past and I watched Benny's ambulance rumble unhindered through the checkpoint, vanishing in the direction of Hanover.

I was alone. The barn was empty except for the comforting smells of pig and sweet hay that lingered in the stonework. When nightfall came, I would make my next move.

My heart wept at the sight of the city. If you wanted to see somewhere where a butcher had run amok with his cleaver, Hanover was it. The city had been slaughtered. Skinned and crushed to a pulp. Even when adorned by a lacy veil of moonlight like tonight's, the city was unrecognisable as a place to live.

Whole streets were reduced to rubble and rats ran freely over my feet as I picked my way through it in the darkness. I carried a torch but used it sparingly. I wanted to draw no attention to myself or, more importantly to the sack, heavy and cumbersome, on my back. Hanover sprawled out on the banks of the river Leine and I was finding my way into its heart, into the old town, its medieval centre. There in its twisting narrow streets I would find the twisted narrow world I was seeking.

'You got something to sell, *meine Dame?*'

The man stepped out of nowhere into my path. I jumped back. Fear snatched at my heart. I hadn't heard him approach. The silence of his feet worried me more than the gauntness of his face thrust towards mine, or the stink of alcohol on his breath. You don't creep up on a woman in the dark unless you plan on doing something you're sure she isn't going to like.

'No,' I said curtly, 'nothing to sell.'

'That sack looks heavy.'

'I'm moving house.'

'At this hour of the night?' He hissed softly. 'Here, let me help you.'

He put out a tentative hand to touch the bulky hessian, but before he could lay a finger on it I slammed my torch on to the sharp bone of his right cheek. The jolt of the impact went right through me and to my astonishment he turned and ran. Blood glistened black as oil on the metal casing of the torch. I tried to feel guilt but all I felt was relief.

I found a church. When I say *church*, what I really mean is the *remains* of a church. A sad, angry shell. No roof, no altar, no stained glass, just the ruins of high pointed walls spiking up towards the moon like a row of sharp teeth, baying their rage. Aegidien Church was its name. No good to anyone tonight. Except me. I ducked inside, deep into its musty shadows, and started to dig a large hole among its rubble of stone and timbers. I tucked my sack inside it. Please don't think that I came to this city unprepared. Not just with the torch and knife in my canvas shoulder bag. No, I came ready for Hanover. I had leeched information about the place from anyone in the camp who had been there, including Benny, my generous driver. So I knew exactly where I had to go.

Hanover was an important railway junction and an essential industrial centre for the Third Reich, so no wonder the

Allies gave it a hammering. Eighty-eight air raids. Nearly a million incendiary bombs.

Imagine it. The look on the faces of the top brass of RAF Bomber Command and of the US Army Air Force when they saw the photographs of half-timbered buildings going up in flames like a haystack. The same way that, night after night, I imagine my husband's P.11 fighter over Poland shot down by a German Messerschmidt. The flames roaring towards him to burn out his eyeballs. The commanders must have been beaming with pride while children in Hanover fled their houses with their hair on fire.

The city had to go. Of course it did. It was producing a never-ending supply of tyres for Hitler's military vehicles, providing guns and tracked vehicles for his army, and an AFA factory was manufacturing batteries for his submarines and his lethal torpedoes. So the centre of the city was ninety per cent obliterated. Bombed and incinerated.

That was precisely where I was heading.

CHAPTER TWENTY-TWO

ALICJA

'Alicja, what are you doing?'

'Reading.'

'It doesn't look like reading to me.'

'I'm drawing as well.'

Hanna looked sceptical but returned to her conversation with the Berlin woman three beds away. She was Alicja's guard dog for the evening, keeping a close watch on her charge. The moment Hanna's head was turned, Alicja went back to sketching the illustration in the book she'd taken from the library. It was a book on the history of French medieval warfare, presumably scavenged for the camp from a school or university.

Rafal was peering over her shoulder, in awe.

'There,' she said after a few more minutes. 'That's the best I can do.'

He reached forward and lifted the sheet of paper as if it

were a holy relic. His dark brow pulled tight in concentration as he examined the details of the drawing. It was of a crossbow.

'They were good with crossbows, the French archers,' he muttered in her ear. 'At the Battle of Crécy.'

'You really think you can make one?'

'Yes.'

'One that works?'

'Of course.'

He blushed a rosy pink all the way to his hairline when he saw her look of admiration.

'I'm good at woodwork. With a bit of metalwork too, it's not so hard,' he muttered. 'It's working out the stirrup and the roller nut positions . . .'

He forgot her as he stared at each detail of the drawings, and she smiled at him now that he could not see. *Focus, Rafal, focus. It is the only way.*

They were seated on Mama's bed and Alicja ran a hand over the spot on the pillow where her mother's cheek would lie. If she kept her palm there all night, would it bring her mother back? For a moment she bent down and laid her own cheek on the thin pillow and breathed her own breath over Mama's pillowcase.

'Is your back hurting?' Rafal's voice was soft with concern.

'No.' She sat up immediately.

The muscles of her back still felt as though they had fishhooks caught in them, but they were healing each day and she didn't want Rafal to think she was a *girl*.

'Rafal, will you do something for me?'

He laughed, folded up her drawings and slid them into his pocket. 'You want a game of chess?'

'No.'

She stood up and removed an envelope from under her own pillow on the top bunk. She scooted close to Rafal and passed it secretly into his hand, unobserved by his mother.

'What's this?' he asked.

'A letter I'd like you to deliver.'

She watched her friend's handsome face carefully and noticed for the first time that he had soft dusky down starting to sprout along his jaw. He was twelve, nearly thirteen. She didn't want him to leave her behind. She put her hand on his bony knee as if that would hold him with her.

'Who's it for?' he asked and turned the envelope over to see the front. It was one of a handful that her mother had snaffled from Davide's office.

'Someone in Hut W.'

'That's the rough end of camp. I'm not supposed to go . . .' He stopped, embarrassed, and ran a hand through his dense dark hair to rumple his thoughts.

'Forget it,' Alicja said and snatched the letter back. 'I'll do it myself.'

'No! Don't.' He shrugged. 'I'll go. Early in the morning.'

He held out his hand. There were yellow calluses on some of his fingers from where he used his slingshot. She placed the letter on his outstretched palm and he made it disappear before she could blink. She placed her hand back on his knee. It felt warm and alive. She felt cold and half dead.

'Don't worry, Alicja,' Rafal murmured and wrapped an arm around her shoulders. 'She'll come back. Your mother would never abandon you.'

Something in his voice was all wrong but she didn't know what.

'Who is the letter for?' he asked.

'A man called Herr Jan Blach.'

'Is he a friend of your mother's?'

'I think so. Back in Warsaw. I need to talk to him. She won't tell me what happened to her after I was locked away in the convent, but I need to—'

Rafal ruffled a hand fondly through her short blond curls. 'Sometimes it's better not to know, Alicja.'

'She's here in this camp because of me. But why did she run from Poland? Why is she so frightened of going back?'

Rafal dropped his voice to a whisper, one eye on his mother's broad back. 'You know why. Because she was in the Resistance. The Soviets in Warsaw now will have her shot if she is sent back there.'

Alicja was shaken by a tremor that made her teeth rattle. 'No, there's more to it. I know there is. I have to find this Jan Blach.'

CHAPTER TWENY-THREE

Günther's Bar was long and thin. The air in it hung thick and heavy as cat fur; coils of cigarette smoke joined a fog bank on the ceiling. It was more crowded than I'd expected. But what else is there to do in a city like this, except hide in the bottom of a glass?

I found myself a table near the door and ordered a beer. Even in my drab dress and headscarf I drew glances. Of course I would. Every other woman in the place wielded a professional smile and plunging cleavage, so the men looked me up and down like I was a dusty sparrow that had hopped into a cage of gaudy lovebirds by mistake. I kept my eyes to myself and waited for my beer to arrive.

It was Hanna who had given me the name of Günther's Bar. It seemed my laundry-obsessed friend had lingered a while in Hanover before arriving at Graufeld Camp and so could pass on to me directions from Aegidien Church, down Marketstrasse, then right to Osterstrasse. Easier said than done. The old town centre used to be the happy hunting ground of criminals and prostitutes but now its destruction had left just a confusion of masonry. The military had gouged random paths through the ruins of people's homes and I'd picked my way along them, clambering into the darkest patches.

How in God's name would Germany ever get out from under all the rubble?

Hanna had also muttered a name in my ear – Bruno Fuchs – at the same time as running a finger along her throat. But I had laughed.

'I lived with danger every day in Warsaw,' I told her. 'I can live with it here too.'

But neither of us was a fool. We could both recognise bravado when we heard it.

'*Noch etwas?*'

The man who placed my beer on the table had a long white apron and a long white face that looked as if it had never seen the sun.

'*Danke*,' I said and smiled pleasantly at him. 'I'm looking for someone who comes here sometimes. A man named Bruno Fuchs. Do you know him?'

His eyes flicked to a figure in the small booth at the end of the bar. I needed no more. I made to rise to my feet but Herr White Face leaned down over me, preventing it.

'This is no place for you, *gnädige Frau*.' His tired eyes were full of concern. 'Bruno Fuchs is not a man for you to be dealing with. Drink your beer and walk out of here. That's my advice.'

His kindness caught me unawares. I was a total stranger.

Not even German. Why bother with me? To my horror I had an urge to press my face against his spotless apron and cry my thanks.

I looked up at his face for a long moment, at the decency in it, and I knew he was right. I forced myself to say, 'Thank you, but I need to speak with him.'

'None of us needs a Bruno Fuchs in our life,' he answered in a quiet undertone and moved away to his bar.

I stood, picked up my beer and walked over to the booth.

I slid on to the bench opposite the man with fierce ginger hair and one lazy eye. His cheeks were so fat they were obscene in this world of fleshless wraiths, but I took it as a positive sign. It meant he was good at what he did. Filling his pockets with money.

'*Guten Abend*, Herr Fuchs.'

His pale honey-coloured eyes regarded me in their lop-sided way over a forkful of cheese that paused on its way to his mouth.

'And who are you?'

'Someone who wants to do business.'

'I don't do business over dinner. It spoils my digestion.'

In front of him on a platter lay a hefty slab of Tilsiter cheese, thick and creamy and tempting. The tangy smell of it made my stomach churn with hunger. Herr Fuchs continued to shave strips off it and fork them into his full mouth with the relentless rhythm of a machine.

'I'll wait,' I said.

He gave the thinnest of smiles but his eyes invited no discussion. He shrugged, straining the buttons of his shirt across his chest, indifferent to the food stains down the front of his black jacket. A dusting of cheese crumbs fell from his lips, which glistened with brandy, as I sat there and watched in silence. After about twenty minutes he pushed his plate aside and lit a black cheroot. He leaned forward as far as his bloated belly would allow and blew smoke into my face. It stank like cat shit.

'Talk,' he said lazily.

I picked up his cheese knife. 'Maybe this blade can talk for me.' I said it pleasantly enough.

A big meaty bodyguard reared up from the nearest table and was reaching for me, but Fuchs waved him aside. I had his attention now.

I would be lying if I said I wasn't frightened. I was. The kind of fear that drains every instinct out of you except the instinct to run. There was something about this obscene bastard of a man that was evil. Just the smell of his sweat chilled my blood. I wanted this over quickly.

'I am here to do business,' I announced once more.

'What business is that?'

'This business.'

From my shoulder bag I removed an object and placed it on the table. It was a clock no higher than my hand, but in an exquisite hand-chased silver casing. It seemed to raise not a flicker of interest in him and I felt my hopes teeter on the edge.

'Nothing else?' He sat back against the bench rest and it creaked in protest.

Was he bluffing?

The timepiece had been discovered by Alicja, hidden under a sack of potatoes in a dingy garden shed. It was fine work. Very fine. A valuable piece. I didn't let my disappointment show, but instead gave the kind of shrug he'd given me.

'Do you know,' he sighed with exaggeration, 'how many silver watches and clocks and jewellery boxes and bracelets I am offered each day? Do you? Can you guess?'

I said nothing.

'So many that they are more worthless than shit. A bag of flour is all your clock will get you now.'

'I do not want a bag of flour. I want money.'

His puffy nose puckered up in a sneer. 'Bring me diamonds and then we talk real American dollars. Do you honestly think the people of Hanover want a clock?'

He turned his gaze from me to the men in the bar. They wisely kept their eyes on their own business, careful to keep their nose out of his.

'What about this, Fuchs? Do they want this?'

His heavy head jerked round sharply. In my hand sat a small brown-glass container. I shook it. It rattled. The unmistakable sound of tablets.

I had him.

This is how it worked.

Tablets came top of the list.

Tools came second.

Cigarettes came third.

Blankets and clothing came fourth.

Pretty things came last.

Exceptions were lipstick and hairbrushes, which were always in demand. Unfortunately there were no lipsticks or hairbrushes in my sack, but everything else was there.

Any fool should know that the last thing the people of Hanover needed right now would be something to tell the time. You can't eat a clock.

Fuchs and I faced each other in a stand-off among the ruins of Aegidien Church. A stiff wind rattled the loose timbers and skimmed the sharp edges of the ruin, while the moon threw soulless shadows across our faces.

'Two hundred marks,' he said flatly.

'Dollars,' I said. My head was pounding. 'I don't want worthless Reichsmarks. And no Allied Occupation Marks either. I need hard currency.'

He uttered a sour laugh. We both knew I was in a corner.

'The tools alone are worth more than two hundred marks,' I pointed out.

'So find someone else to sell your sack to.'

I looked around me. As though another more amenable black marketeer would step out of the night to make me an offer. I was desperate and Fuchs knew it. Sweat trickled down my spine despite the chill wind.

'A hundred dollars,' I said. 'No lower.'

He let his eyes linger on the sack at my feet. He'd

examined the objects and knew exactly what was on offer. It was worth at least one thousand marks. Probably more. His thick-necked bodyguard was prowling around us in a restless circle, his boots crunching down on the masonry underfoot. He was supposedly searching for intruders but it didn't feel like that. Not to me. I kept an eye on the brick wall of his shoulders as he moved in and out of the darkness and every time he passed behind me the hairs on my neck prickled and the muscles in my back twitched.

'Two hundred marks,' Fuchs repeated.

'Ninety dollars or I walk away.'

'You can walk away anytime you like, but leave the sack here.'

'Two hundred marks is robbery.'

'*Scheisse!* Because you are pretty and because I am soft-hearted, I will make it thirty dollars.' He put a pudgy hand into his pocket, pulled out a fold of banknotes and started to count them out.

'Eighty,' I demanded.

'Thirty is my final offer. Take it, you bitch!'

I'd always known this could happen. It was why I carried a knife in my shoulder bag. But fear does odd things to your mind, it blurs the boundaries between thoughts and pulls the rug out from under your decisions. Instead of reaching for my knife, as I should have done, I reached for my sack and broke into a run, haring over the rubble.

Before I had gone a dozen paces the brutal hand of his bodyguard seized my short hair from behind and yanked back my head, so hard I thought my throat would snap. A razor-sharp blade bit into the soft skin of my exposed throat and I froze.

I couldn't swallow. Couldn't speak. Could think of nothing except my promise to Alicja to return to Graufeld. And the certainty that I would not be keeping that promise.

The lumbering figure of Bruno Fuchs loomed up in front of me. He snatched the sack. Punched me in the stomach. My body convulsed instinctively and my throat pressed down on the blade. I felt a sharp sting. My skin split open and I felt blood flow down between my breasts.

'Alicja!' I screamed my daughter's name.

Death put out its hand to me. But instead of seizing it, I arched my neck back from the knife blade so that all I could see was the vast black pall of the sky, stabbed with the pin-pricks of stars.

'Wait!' I shouted. But the shout sounded faint to my ears.

'Finish her,' Fuchs ordered.

'No, wait. You need me.'

'I don't need *you*. I have your sack of stolen goods.' A guttural sound came from him and it took a moment for me to realise it was a laugh. 'You should have taken the thirty dollars when they were offered.'

He would have killed me and dumped my body under the rubble, whatever price we'd agreed. Abruptly my heartbeat ceased. No sound at all. No thunder in my ears. Just silence. As though my body realised before I did that my next breath would be my last.

'I can help you,' I said.

But the tendons in my throat braced themselves for the final cut.

'Help me?' His tone was scornful. 'How?'

'Tell your gorilla to remove the knife first.'

Fuchs grunted. The blade vanished.

I tried to press the palm of my hand to the wound to stem the blood, but I was shaking too badly.

'Graufeld Camp has food,' I said in a raw whisper. 'Thousands of tins of it in store. And medicines. Why kill your golden goose?'

CHAPTER TWENTY-FOUR

DAVIDE BOUVIER

'Goodnight, gentlemen.'

'Goodnight, Colonel.' Captain Percy Jeavons saluted smartly.

'Have a good evening, sir,' Davide said as Colonel Whitmore headed for the door. 'Enjoy the party.'

'I'll do my best.' He laughed, his long face lighting up for the first time that day.

Davide was aware that the evening would still be work for the colonel. It was a drinks party organised by a local member of the CCG – that is the Control Commission Germany, which was now governing the country – to bring together the various bodies involved in keeping Graufeld Camp running. These included the newly established UNRRA, as well as the Red Cross, the Salvation Army and even the Quaker Society, all of which provided the camp with desperately needed weekly handouts of food and clothes for the inmates. The trouble was that there were too many people wanting to have the final word, and resources were stretched beyond breaking point. Tempers ran high.

But Colonel Whitmore didn't shirk his duty and left the office with a ramrod straight back. Davide hoped he would at least enjoy a decent whisky. Instantly Captain Jeavons was packing away the files on his desk.

'C'mon, Davide, let's go to our own party.'

'Pardon?'

'In the rec room, I hear. Music and a splash of dancing.' His boyish eyes opened clownishly wide and he whirled an imaginary dance partner around the room, swaying his hips. 'Leave those endless piles of paper of yours, mate, and let's get dancing cheek to cheek with the nurses.'

'Nurses?'

'Yes, a bunch of them are turning up to get everyone on the dance floor.' In the air he sketched with both hands the curves of a woman's figure. 'The delectable Nurse McKinley awaits,' he laughed.

'No, not for me, thanks.'

'Invite that blond friend of yours, the one with the beautiful blue eyes that crawl right inside your head. Carla, isn't it?'

'Klara.'

'That's her. Bring her along for a spot of jitterbugging.'

Davide could not stop a smile. Just the thought of Klara bopping and kicking up her heels on a dance floor, instead of laying life and limb on the line in a burnt-out city, made his heart twist.

'No. Her daughter is sick.'

'So come anyway. There'll be a piano to get us in the mood.' As he pulled on his jacket he started to hum the first bars of Glenn Miller's *In the Mood*.

Something made Davide hesitate. It was the mention of the piano. His daughter used to play the piano every evening before bed.

He closed the file of *Fragebogen* on his desk.

The moment he walked into the smoke-filled rec room he regretted it. It wasn't just the fumes. It was the fact that Klara wasn't there. The room full of people was dreary without Klara to share it. Her teasing cool-eyed comments on her fellow inmates always amused him and he was aware that she liked to make him laugh.

But he wasn't laughing now. He should not have let her leave Graufeld Camp on her own in the ambulance, but she wasn't someone who would back down easily once she'd made up her mind. She relied on herself. She didn't trust others. Not even him. Not completely.

Davide submitted to one slow dance and two quick drinks, just to keep Percy Jeavons happy, but by then not even the piano playing could hold him. He started to weave his way through the pairs of hopeful women and huddles of raw-boned men all looking for an hour's colourful escape from the grey reality of the camp.

'Where you off to, mate?' Percy called after him.

'To Hut W.'

'What for? They play rough down that end of the camp.'

'Percy, *mon ami*, have you ever lived in an underground cave for month after month with ribs sticking through your skin and friends dropping dead at your feet?'

'Bloody hell, mate, no.' Jeavons' brow creased into deep furrows and Davide could see what his cheery friend would look like in years to come with his pipe and slippers. 'Of course not,' Jeavons muttered uneasily.

'It teaches you how to deal with rough.'

'Got any smokes to spare, *mein Herr*?'

The voice was polite and well spoken. Davide had only just stepped outside the Recreation block into the chill night air, where light from the windows cast two large amber rectangles on to the black roadway. In the middle of one stood the figure of the man who had addressed him. He was tall despite being hunched in on himself and he was standing sideways, as if to present the thinnest possible target.

Sideways also meant he was no threat. It was important that, in this camp. To offer no threat in the dark.

'I don't smoke,' Davide informed him.

'But you carry them in your pocket.'

Cigarettes were the currency of the camp. Most people carried a few stubs in their pocket. Normally Davide would not give one away but this evening did not feel normal. So he drew a small flat tin from his pocket, extracted half an army-ration Players cigarette and approached the stranger, who accepted the offering with a grateful smile.

'*Danke.*' He struck a match, watched the flame burn a hole

in the darkness and took a long drag with satisfaction. 'Where would we be,' he laughed softly, 'without the British Army?'

It was said without irony.

'Well, that's not something I care to think about too often.'

'You're French, aren't you? So you'd be at the Moulin Rouge in Paris with the dancing girls, *n'est-ce pas*?' That soft laugh again.

'No, I'd still be in Peenemünde, or Mittelwerk.'

Davide regretted it the moment the words were out of his mouth. He rarely mentioned those places. *Peenemünde* and *Mittelwerk*. A death hole underground. The words slipped out because he was not thinking straight tonight, too busy trying not to think about what the hell Klara was doing right now.

'You were at Peenemünde?' the German queried.

'I was.'

'And in the Mittelwerk underground facility?'

Davide gave a reluctant nod. In the sulphurous yellow light that spilled over them, the German studied him for a long moment.

'Yet you survived,' he commented with respect.

'As you see.'

Peenemünde and Mittelwerk were the sites of the Third Reich's infamous rocket weaponry – the V-1 flying bombs and the lethal A-4 that terrorised London, later termed the V-2. These were the ambitious brainchild of Hitler and the visionary scientist Wernher von Braun. It was put into research and production by the dedication of the Armaments Minister, Albert Speer, and by the excessive zeal of SS

Brigadier General Kammler. He ran the whole programme on the bones and blood of slave labour gleaned from concentration camps like Buchenwald.

There was an extended silence that neither man felt inclined to break. Just the seductive notes of *Take the A-Train* trickling into the night, liquid as moonlight.

'I survived,' Davide murmured. 'Survived that place of terror. I was not one of the thousands of bodies that ended up stacked into stinking heaps. You cannot imagine the stench. Corpses of nothing more than skin and bone. We were randomly beaten and clubbed. Starved, hanged and shot. Our lives hung on the slightest whim of our SS Nazi overseers. They regarded us as worse than cockroaches.'

'So tell me. How did you survive?'

Davide gave him a slow smile. 'I guess God owed me. He had already taken my family.'

The German leaned back against the wall into deeper shadow. 'That's tough on a man.'

'And on a woman.'

Their gaze hardened on each other, their outlines growing sharper, more stiff-legged.

'We cannot help but hate each other,' the German said sadly, 'for years to come. You Allies march in here as victorious conquerors of Germany and carve our country up between you, so of course we hate you. But you have every right to hate Germans in return for the evil that Hitler did in our name. The terrible crimes against humanity that he committed. I do not blame you.'

The honesty of the German took Davide by surprise. But when the friend working beside you in the gigantic underground rocket-complex gets a bullet in the brain just for going to the lavatory once too often, it's hard not to take those crimes against humanity personally.

'Do you realise,' Davide said, 'that more men died building the V-2 rockets in Peenemünde and in the Mittelwerk caves than were killed by them as a weapon? Ironic, isn't it?' He paused and his voice seemed to sink deeper into the shadows. 'Twenty-thousand workers died there.'

'So you were lucky.'

'That's a matter of opinion.'

He heard the German's intake of breath. 'I'm sorry. You will carry your own survival guilt to your grave. Just as we in Germany will carry our nation's collective guilt on our backs for the next fifty years. It is our tragedy, Herr Bouvier.'

'You know my name?'

'I do.'

'How?'

'I see things that go on around me. I see who your friends are and what they do.' He spoke in a quiet undertone.

'What are you talking about? Which friends?' But a chill gripped Davide's spine. 'What is your name?'

'Jan Blach.'

It was a blow. He stepped forward. To examine this man who knew too much. He scrutinised him closely in the gloom. A strong face. No spectacles. Large features, intelligent grey eyes and a calm controlled manner. A firm but respectful way of speaking. A man who, in other circumstances, Davide would choose to trust. But these weren't other circumstances.

'Oskar Scholz, you mean,' Davide said.

The German continued to smoke. He paused. 'So she has told you about me.'

'Klara mentioned your name, yes.'

Scholz nodded. Sharp and brisk. 'It saddens me. Klara Janowska is a fine woman. But I can guess that she will have told you that I am a danger to her here in Graufeld Camp.' He drew on the last of the cigarette and the glow of its tip highlighted the sincerity in his grey eyes. 'But she is wrong. Completely wrong. I am her friend.'

CHAPTER TWENTY-FIVE

Hatred is something that can eat you alive.

I know. I've felt its teeth. Tonight in Hanover it had taken a bite out of me by the time I scratched on the ancient oak door. Bruno Fuchs had made his Rottweiler release me and whispered an address in my ear.

No answer.

I thumped with my fist but no one came. It was well defended. Long metal strap hinges, as well as iron bars for reinforcement. No one would be opening this in a hurry from the outside, that was certain. It was part of a three-storey terrace of houses in the city on the edge of the Jewish quarter, though Hanover's Jews had long since been shipped off to Buchenwald and Auschwitz concentration camps. Around me the shops were black and roofless from when they were burned out in the destructive fever of Kristallnacht. The only movement in the street was from a clutch of urchins scavenging among the ruins and they scattered into the night like rats at the sight of me.

I stood back from the door and stared hard at the upstairs

windows, which were heavily shuttered. But was that the faintest hairline of light along a crack? I cupped my hands to my mouth and shouted.

'Hello! *Ist jemand da?* Is anyone there?'

Except it didn't come out as a shout, more a croak. Pain shot across my damaged throat and I tied my scarf tighter around it before going back to thumping the oak door, but I had only raised my fist a couple of times when I heard a bolt shoot back on the inside. The door opened no more than the width of an eye.

I could see no one. The interior was pitch black.

'Hello?' I said again. 'I'm looking for—'

A long pale arm reached out and dragged me inside.

'Sit still.'

I sat still and allowed the wound on my throat to be bathed. Small olive-skinned hands dabbed iodine on the wound and bound it with strips torn off a clean white pillowcase.

'Why?' I asked. 'Why do this for me? You don't know me.'

The young woman tending to my cut crouched down on her heels in front of me. She was as tiny as a bird. Her large black eyes widened and her huge smile went some way towards easing the pain in my throat.

'Because you need help,' she said simply. 'We can't go on hating each other forever. The fighting is finished. It is time to start helping each other. It doesn't matter what happened before. It is time to embrace each other, to forgive and forget, and plan for the future.'

I looked at her, baffled by her words.

I could not forget. And I certainly couldn't forgive.

She came to me as if she could see my thoughts like knives in my hands, and wrapped her arms around me, embracing me. As good as her word. I could feel this woman's genuine warmth seep into me, but it was not nearly enough to melt the ice that sat like a rock in my chest. Just a trickle of it reached my eyes.

She kissed my cheek and drew back. The room was excessively purple – purple curtains, purple rug, purple cushions, a purple-painted cabinet and her purple dress.

'Why purple?' I asked.

'It is the colour I see in my head when I have my happy dreams. What colour do you see?'

'I don't have happy dreams.'

'You will.' She ran both hands through her dense thatch of black hair so that it stuck out at odd angles as through trying to escape. 'So,' she said, 'you want a passport.' Her name was Salomea Kohn.

She was probably the last surviving Jew in Hanover and was an expert at forging documents. I didn't ask how or why she became one, but I did wonder. It was the greedy Bruno Fuchs who gave me her name and address and for that I was thankful, though it meant agreeing to hand over to him a carton of two hundred Players cigarettes. The passports were so close I could smell the chemicals Salomea used. It was like alcohol fizzing through my blood, making me giddy with excitement, my ears popping as tensions were released.

Hope, that faithless whore, started to lure me to her.

'Choose,' Salomea instructed as she laid out on the pine kitchen table about a hundred small photographs and arranged them in neat rows. All were of girls of around ten years old. Some with short hair, some with long; curls, waves, straight or spiky. Faces that were pretty or plain, freckled or scrubbed. Eyes that shone out at you or were dull and thoughtless. Mouths that were mean or generous. Whole worlds contained within every photograph.

I examined each one minutely. And then I chose.

From the kitchen Salomea led me through a door hidden behind a dresser and down a flight of stone stairs to a basement. The first thing that struck me was the smell. Not damp and fetid. But warm and musty and leathery, like my husband's riding boots used to smell. I felt the ends of some tight knots start to fray inside me.

It was a beautiful room that sent a shiver of pleasure through me. It was a long time since I'd seen anything beautiful. From floor to ceiling books lined all four walls, books with embossed leather covers that glowed richly in the lamplight. A huge Persian carpet softened the flagstone floor and tasselled lampshades cast odd shadows over two cushioned sofas in maroon leather. I could imagine this unusual woman living in this unusual room. As if the outside world didn't exist.

'I collect rare books,' she explained and gave the antiquarian volumes the kind of smile you give your children.

'May I look at one?'

'No.' She shook her head to emphasise the point. 'Come,' she said.

I followed her. She swung open a section of the shelving and vanished into a small white-tiled room behind it. Photographs of faces were everywhere. Pegged on lines across the room, on the walls, in racks, in piles. It was clearly her workroom. Two developing baths stood on a shelf.

She inspected the photograph in her hand, the one I had picked out in the kitchen. 'So this is like your daughter?'

'No.' I smiled at the small black and white face with shoulder-length hair and wide-set eyes. She was a pretty child. 'Alicja is far prettier but it is the closest.'

'Good. Let us begin.'

Salomea became brisk and businesslike. First she took a flash photograph of me with a very complicated-looking Zeiss folding plate camera, then she measured my height.

'Now,' she said, pen in hand, 'personal details.'

I nodded.

'Name?' she asked.

'Mrs Klara Jones.'

She raised one black eyebrow but passed no comment. 'Maiden name?'

'Parker. It was my grandmother's surname.'

'Number of children?'

'One.'

'National status?'

'British.'

A small puff of laughter escaped her. 'Profession?'

'Engineer.'

'Really?'

'Yes. I was working as an engineer on the tunnels of the new underground railway in Warsaw when war broke out.'

She looked at me with a bright fixed stare, smiling broadly as if I had just given her a gift.

'We need people like you,' she said earnestly, 'to show us what to do. Engineers will be at the forefront of creating our new world. Whereas I'll be trailing behind, dragging my books and my nettle tea along with me.'

I smiled back at her. 'No, you will be right at the very front, lighting the way with your books.'

It pleased the woman in the purple dress, that thought. I could see it.

'Is your daughter like you?' she asked suddenly.

The question shocked me. 'I don't want her to be like me.'

We left it at that and went back to the standard questions – date of birth, height, eye and hair colour. When it was finished, she hesitated, as though arguing with herself about something, but in the end came out with it.

'Your daughter does not need a passport of her own, you know. As she is under sixteen she can travel on yours. It would be cheaper for you.'

'No.' It came out too quickly. 'No, I want her to have her own passport. In case . . .' I halted. I did not want to voice my fear.

'In case you don't make it?' she said softly.

The words hung in the white-tiled room, refusing to go away.

Have you ever touched an object and known in that instant that it would change your life?

That was the sensation that flooded through me when my fingertips brushed the two small innocuous navy blue booklets.

This will change my life.

With its gold lettering. Its *United Kingdom of Great Britain and Northern Ireland*. Its royal crowned lion and unicorn. And then at the bottom in the white bar: my name. Neatly written in a copperplate hand.

My passport. Alicja's passport.

My eyes could not leave the dark blue covers. I wanted to take this young woman with her magical skills in my arms and hold her tight to me, to tell her she had saved my daughter's life.

But she knew. She knew all this. Just by looking at me.

She smiled, a tired smile. The passports had taken three hours. It was already gone midnight.

'Twenty American dollars,' she said.

'Twenty-five,' I responded. 'I wish it were more but it's all I have.'

I placed the banknotes on the antique rosewood table in her room of books and beside them I placed the beautiful clock in hand-chased silver that I had offered for sale to Fuchs in the bar. The one my clever daughter had unearthed in a garden shed.

'I want you to have this, Salomea.'

Her eyes shone like stars as her finger traced the workmanship on the clock's casing. It was perfect. She rose and walked over to one of the laden bookshelves, her purple skirts swirling around her, and removed a slim volume from it. She returned and placed it in my hands.

'For your daughter,' she said.

CHAPTER TWENTY-SIX

The moon slipped behind the clouds, making the light uncertain. The night felt thicker. But I found the house. The wind had strengthened and thrown an icy blast right into my face for the last ten kilometres of my trek back to Graufeld Camp. But first, the village. Here the wind gave me an advantage. It rocked the tree branches, tugged at pipes and shutters, and rattled the windows in their sockets.

So who would hear me?

No one.

I moved fast across the grass, avoiding the gravel drive. It was exactly as my daughter had described, set back from the road, separating itself from the more humble workers' cottages. This was a rich man's house.

He would pay a rich man's price.

'*Aufwachen!*' I spoke loudly. 'Wake up!'

I shone a torch on the bed.

The two sleeping figures jerked upright, shielding their

eyes, blinded by the sudden light in the darkness. Confused and terrified, they were vulnerable and they knew it.

'Thief!' the man in the bed bellowed. 'Get out of my—'

'Shut up,' I cut him off.

'Who the fuck are you?' he demanded but the woman clenched her hand on his naked arm to silence him. She had seen what I was carrying.

She had sense, that woman. Because I was carrying a shotgun, one I had removed from the rack on their dining-room wall. It was pointed straight at them.

'Light the lamp,' I instructed calmly, now that I had their attention.

The man was all bluster but he struck a match at his bedside. His hand was shaking so badly it took several attempts before the lamp's wick caught. It threw its burst of light directly up at him. He was dangerously red in the face, hair askew, and I could see, sharp as pinpricks in his eyes, how much he wanted to break my neck.

His wife swept her long plait of dark hair behind her and sat still, very still. One of her eyes was milky white, but the gaze of her good eye kept straying to the door behind me. I knew that she was thinking of what lay beyond that door. But I had already dealt with it.

The man had his bare feet on the floor now. He was wearing pyjama bottoms but his chest was naked, muscular and he was breathing hard. A warning of how close he was to the edge. I nudged the shotgun barrel over to the right a fraction, aimed at that broad threatening chest. He stood up.

'No, Gerhard, don't.'

She didn't trust me. She was right.

'Take what you want and leave,' she said. No panic. Quiet and precise.

I liked her. I didn't like him.

'You have a daughter,' I said.

It was as if I had thrown a switch. I saw the blood drain from her cheeks and heard the shrillness of her scream. It tore through me. For the first time I wondered whether what I was doing was right. An eye for an eye. A tooth for a tooth.

It was not the woman I was here to hurt.

She leaped from the bed, her cotton nightdress hanging from slender bones and rushed for the door. I shouted, 'Stop.'

The shotgun was loaded and cocked in my hands.

But the woman did not hesitate. She was out the door and racing down the dark corridor and one word echoed back to us in the bedroom.

'Johanna! Johanna!'

'Move,' I said sharply to the man.

'If you've hurt my daughter, I'll—'

'Move!'

I pointed the gun barrel at the door and he hurried after his wife with the lantern shaking in his hands.

'What have you done with my daughter? She's gone. Give Johanna back to me.'

The woman came for me on the landing, eyes flat and fierce.

'Your husband shot my daughter in the back.'

That stopped her in her tracks. 'What?'

'Ask your husband why I have removed your daughter. Ask him what reason I have to come for your Johanna. Ask how he would feel if I blasted a gun at her.'

'No, Irmgard, she's lying. I didn't shoot the girl. This is a mad woman, you can't believe her.'

I nodded. 'Yes, I am mad. Mad with anger, mad enough to blow your savage heart right out of your chest. So you know how it feels.'

His wife had jerked her head round, staring at him wild-eyed. 'You said you shot up in the air that night, Gerhard. To warn her.'

'I did, Irmgard. Believe me, I—' He reached for her.

'No, no, no.' She raised the flat of her hand to ward him off.

'I would not be here,' I said to him, my voice barbed with hatred, 'if you had not shot my child. In the back. When she was running *away* from you, offering no threat. I would not have taken your Johanna.'

'You swore,' the woman said, words ice cold. 'You swore to me you had discharged the gun into the air.'

'I did.'

'Liar.' I wanted to rip out his tongue. Instead I scooped from my pocket a handful of pellets and hurled them at his cowardly face. 'Here, take these. They are the ones I took from my daughter's flesh.' They fell to the floor like lead confetti, bouncing around his ankles. 'You shot her.'

He looked sick, eyes darting from his wife to me. 'Where is Johanna? I'm sorry, I was angry with your daughter. Please. Give us our child back.'

'Please,' the woman echoed.

'Why don't you ask if my daughter is dead?'

They looked at each other in the shifting light, both guilty.

'Is she alive?' the woman asked.

I made them wait. A whole minute of silence in which the only sound was the knocking of the wind and the rasping of the man's breath.

'Yes,' I said.

'Thank God.'

'But scarred for life.'

'I'm sorry,' he said.

I didn't believe him. He would do it again. He had to learn.

'An eye for an eye,' I said.

'Don't hurt her.' The woman began to weep. 'Don't hurt Johanna.'

Abruptly the big man dropped to his knees, tears rolling down his cheeks. 'I'm sorry.' His voice broke. 'The war has ruined our lives. I have no job, no money, no future. I am at the end of my tether and when I saw your daughter had come to take even more from me, my anger trampled over all else.' He pressed his hands together as though in prayer. 'I'm begging you, let our child come home to us. If she is alive still, she must be frightened and—'

I tightened the stock of the gun against my shoulder. 'The guilt is yours,' I pointed out.

'Please,' the woman pleaded. 'For Alicja's sake. For your love of your own child.'

A thousand thoughts clamoured in my head. This was not the revenge I wanted. It felt rotten and wretched. The taste of it was not sweet in my mouth. Seeing this trigger-happy man grovelling at my feet did nothing to assuage the rage that shook me each time I bathed my daughter's back. Hadn't she been through enough for a ten-year-old?

I could not bear to look at him. I turned to the woman and regretted the pain that was so sharp, she could barely stand upright. I knew what it was like, that pain. To have a child taken.

'Your daughter is still asleep. Wrapped in her quilt. Inside your pantry.'

The words were scarcely out of my mouth before the woman was flying downstairs. The man rose heavily to his feet, stared hard at me, then at the gun. I didn't want to shoot him, but I would if I had to. Maybe he saw that in me, because he turned to the stairs with a noise like a bull and was gone.

I raced down. Snatched the two silver candlesticks from the dining table and thrust them into my bag. The child was whimpering in the kitchen, the parents' voices soothing her. I slid out of the window through which I'd entered, the shotgun still tucked under my arm. I did not want a blast of lead in my back. I would discard it in the woods. Without a backward glance I set off into the night.

CHAPTER TWENTY-SEVEN

'Halt!'

The business end of a rifle was pointed towards me. I halted. The guard's face behind it looked more than happy to amuse himself with a break from his boredom.

'Who are you?' a second guard in blue uniform demanded. They came in pairs. They looked snug and warm in their heavy dark blue greatcoats and thick leather gloves. I was tired, footsore and chilled to the bone. I'd walked over twenty kilometres in the dark and cold to get back here to Graufeld, wearing a threadbare coat that deserved to be tossed in the bin and shoes with holes in their thin soles. The soldiers were seeking trouble to enliven their watch of the camp's gates, whereas all I was seeking was my bed. Dawn was not far off, a hairline crack of gold on the horizon.

I stepped forward, out of the night shadows into the glare of the gate searchlight.

'Hello, boys,' I said.

They were young, their faces fresh, their eyes brightened

by the unexpected appearance of a female on their doorstep.

'I know you,' I said to one of them.

I had spoken to him several times in anticipation of this occasion.

'Where have you been?' he frowned.

I grinned at them. 'Out for a walk. Look, I brought you back a present each.'

From my bag I whisked out the two heavy silver candlesticks and held one out to each. These weren't British soldiers. We understood each other.

The friendlier guard accepted one and it vanished from sight into his greatcoat. The other guard was less certain. I placed the remaining candlestick into his hands. He stared at it uneasily and I could see the moral battle taking place. Before he could object, the gates had swung open and I slipped through.

I have passports.

It was as unbelievable as saying *I'm on the moon.* Yet there they were. Two embossed British passports. Safe in my hand. Blue and beautiful.

When I reached my hut it lay in complete darkness and I found Alicja sprawled fast asleep on my bunk, so I didn't bother to undress, just kicked off my shoes and curled myself around her. I felt the warmth of her young body seep into mine as I inhaled the sleep-scent of her hair and wrapped my arm around her small waist.

Lying there in the dark with my daughter. The passport

still clutched in one hand. My heart fizzing with a bubble of excitement. I closed my eyes and let myself accept what this was.

It was a moment of happiness.

I would sleep now. Surely I would sleep. Just for an hour or two. My body was limp with exhaustion.

But the image of Salomea's beautiful room in her Hanover basement kept nudging its way into my head. With its rich glow of books, its exotic rugs, its fine antique furniture and its sense of the human spirit rising above the horrors that lay outside its walls. It took me to another place. Another time. Another apartment. Another voice murmuring in my ear.

'So. Do you like it? Is it beautiful?'

'Yes, it is.'

'I knew you'd love it.'

Oberführer Axel Fleischer was referring to the apartment he had just requisitioned for me in what was left of Warsaw's smartest street. It was indeed beautiful, with high ceilings, intricate baroque cornices and a row of tall elegant windows through which the sunlight streamed, gilding the polished floor.

'It's all yours, Schatzi,' Axel said expansively, waving a hand around the beautiful room as though he had produced it from a hat for my benefit.

All mine.

The heavy dark furniture gleaming with generations of tender care. The family portraits on the wall. The collection of Meissen shepherdesses. The gold menorah on the table. The weighty copy of the Torah in pride of place.

I walked over to it. But I didn't touch.

'When did the last owners leave?' I asked.

'Only yesterday.'

'Did you have them removed specially for me?'

'No, don't give them a thought. They were leaving anyway.'

I bet they were.

The Jewish ghetto had a single room with their name on it.

'What was their name?'

'I have no idea. Forget them. They are nobody. I didn't bring you here to talk about them.'

'What did you bring me here for?'

'To see if you like the apartment, of course.' I heard Axel's footsteps cross the room till he was standing behind me. 'And for this.'

He scooped up a swathe of my long blond hair and kissed the naked back of my neck. Not a light-hearted peck. His lips were so hungry and hot they burned right through me. A branding iron. His other hand circled round and caressed my breast through my blouse. As if the soft delicate flesh was his, not mine.

I dragged up a smile and twisted out of his grip. 'Let me look at the rest of the apartment, Axel. I want to see the kitchen.'

As if I had any interest in a stove and cupboards.

He laughed, pleased by my enthusiasm, but caught my wrist and lifted its soft underside to his mouth. His strong white teeth gave my skin a gentle nip, which he then kissed better. When he looked at me his blue eyes were so intense I knew I didn't stand a chance of seeing the kitchen.

'Let's inspect this room first,' he said as he directed me towards a different door.

It was the bedroom.

I knocked on the door of my neighbour. It was Apartment 3 on the floor below mine and the door was opened by a glamorous redhead in a chiffon eau de Nil negligee, though it was mid-afternoon. I couldn't decide whether she was getting up or going to bed. Or maybe she drifted around in her negligee all day waiting for her SS officer lover to turn up. That's what this apartment block seemed to me to be used for now, somewhere for certain select Waffen SS officers to come and rest their shiny jackboots. It sent a shiver through me.

'I'm Klara Janowska. I live upstairs.'

Her eyelids flicked like a lizard's. They registered no interest. She was probably in her early forties with a carefully constructed Rita Hayworth glamour, her vivid hair rippling in loose waves to her shoulders. She held an empty ivory cigarette holder in her hand.

'Oh?' was all she said. She didn't offer her name.

'I have only just moved in. Apartment Five upstairs.' I smiled at her.

Look friendly. As if you are the kind of person who would happily fritter away your afternoons in a semi-transparent negligee too.

'I have a few personal items I want to send on to the people who were in Apartment Five before me. Do you know their name, by any chance?'

Her eyes came alive. She suddenly stepped out into the hallway with me and half-closed the door behind her. Belatedly it occurred to me she might have someone in there with her. She lowered her voice.

'Listen, Miss Apartment Five, keep away from the couple who used to live there. You must have no contact with them if you want to hang on to your fingernails.' She raised her pencilled eyebrows in shock when she glanced at my hands. 'Their name was Rosenberg, if you must know. If you get my meaning. A nice couple – Samuel and Elke Rosenberg. He was a dentist.'

'Was a dentist?'

A flush of colour touched her cheek. 'Is a dentist.'

'Where did they move to?'

'Where do you think?'

'The Jewish ghetto?'

'Forget them,' the woman hissed. 'It's too late.' She stuck her empty cigarette holder between her lips. 'Too late for any of us.'

The envelope was warm in my hand. It had been tucked inside my blouse next to my skin. I wanted it to smell of me.

'Please,' I said. 'Please give it to her.'

I held out the letter. I didn't think he'd take it, but he did.

'Thank you, Oskar.'

He opened his desk drawer and slipped it inside with a glance at the name on the envelope. Alicja Janowska. It was the only thread tying me to her, gossamer thin and one that SS Sturmbannführer Oskar Scholz could break with one snap of his fingers. We were standing in his office, a freshly painted utilitarian room where I had to report once a week. Once a month I handed him a letter for my daughter. In the beginning I used to press him.

'Where is she? Tell me, please.'

But he grew tired of it. Became irritated. To the point where I *feared for her and I looped my fingers together behind my back to prevent them reaching for his throat. Whenever he was wearing his smart grey officer's cap, the urge to rip off its metal SS death's head and insert it into the parts of his anatomy where it would do most harm was overwhelming.*

But I learned to be polite. I no longer screamed at him. If I was polite he told me things. I couldn't smile or find any warmth in the coldness of my heart, but I could manufacture something that passed as polite.

'I've told you before, Klara. Don't pester me. Your daughter is in a convent. She is safe.'

'Then why can't I have a letter from her?'

He threw himself into his desk chair with a moan of impatience. I was pushing him close to the line and my fear was always that Alicja would be the one made to pay if I did. He sighed heavily and lit one of his small black cigars that smelt as evil as his soul.

'I will spell it out one more time, Klara, and after that I don't want to hear anything about it again. You understand?'

I understood.

He rapped his knuckles on his desk. I think he wanted to rap them on my head. 'I have placed you in this crucial position in Oberführer Fleischer's life so that you can feed me information on everything he does outside his office. Who he sees, who he talks to on the telephone, where he goes, what letters he receives, who comes to the apartment. What he thinks and what he hates. What he dreams about at night. I want you inside his head and reporting everything – I mean everything – to me.'

'Why?'

A frown crowded his face but he made a visible effort to push it away. 'Because I don't trust him. Though he is my senior officer, I and certain of my fellow officers have reason to believe he is not loyal to the Führer.'

'But a letter from Alicja? What harm in that?'

'Dummkopf!'

I looked down at my feet to hide my eyes from him.

'Oberführer Fleischer wants you to himself, Klara, don't you understand that? Cut free from all your ties to the past. So no, he will not tolerate any reminder that you once belonged to another man in marriage and produced a Polish child.'

'I have never belonged to any man, Oskar. The Oberführer is not stupid. Look at me. I'm thirty-four. He knows I have a history.'

'You are right that he is not stupid. He is a respected German officer. But all men are stupid when it comes to women. I told you before, he will be having you watched, every move you make. If you make contact with any of your treacherous comrades in the Polish Resistance here in Warsaw—' he paused and stubbed out his cigar. As if he were stubbing it out in someone's eye. 'You will be signing their death warrant.'

'I am no fool, Oskar. I know too well what happens in a Nazi-occupied country. But why should I believe you that he is having me watched.'

'For Christ's sake, Klara! He may be besotted by you and bring you flowers, take you dancing and fuck the hell out of you. But he does not trust you.'

'Any more than he trusts you.'

It was like a slap. He rose swiftly to his feet. Tall and commanding, arrogance etched into every bone in his body. He walked over to me and fixed his steel-grey eyes on mine. I did not look down at my feet to hide my rage. Not this time.

'Klara, think!' His voice was low and without threat. As if we were disagreeing about a book we'd read. It made his words more dangerous. 'Don't for one minute think you can run to him and tell him I have forced you to be his lover to spy on him. Yes, of course he would have me shot.' He used his hand to imitate a gun to his head. 'But he would have you shot at the same time.'

He smiled. As though he were being kind. Warning me.

'And after our corpses are tipped into the cold earth,' he said leaning close, 'who would look after Alicja? Answer me that, Klara.'

CHAPTER TWENTY-EIGHT

ALICJA

'Wake up, Mama. Wake up!'

Alicja shook her mother. Instantly she regretted it. It made her mother sit bolt upright in bed, her eyes huge with alarm and her hands groping for something inside her pillowcase. Alicja wrapped an arm around her lean shoulders to hold her still.

'It's all right, Mama. You're safe.'

Her mother's eyes came back from somewhere dark and far away and focused on her daughter with relief. 'Alicja,' she said softly.

The sunken hollows of her cheeks were grey and bruised-looking, but at the sight of Alicja the tiny muscles under her skin let go. She smiled reassuringly. 'I'm back.'

'Look!' Alicja grinned. 'You did it.'

In each hand Alicja held up a passport. The curtain around their bunk beds was drawn closed, so she lifted the small blue documents to her lips and kissed them.

'You did it, Mama,' she said again, her breath coming with great whoops of excitement. 'You are so—'

Her mother's lips touched her cheek, silencing her, and she swung her bare feet to the floor. They sat side by side on the edge of the thin mattress, her mother still in her crumpled dress and with a scarf tied around her neck. Alicja again wrapped her arm around her, pulling her close.

'Was it hard, Mama? Did you have much trouble in Hanover?'

'No, my sweetheart, no trouble. It was simple. I went to the bar that Hanna told me about where a man gave me the address of a woman who . . .' her voice fell to almost nothing, 'did the work for me, and that was it. The hardest part was the twenty kilometre trudge back to camp in the dark.'

Mama laughed. The way she laughed that time she was almost run down by a Krupp searchlight truck driven by a German soldier in Warsaw. Alicja leaned her weight against her mother's arm to tether them together.

'How much did they cost, Mama?'

'Everything.'

'No money left for—?'

'No. It's all gone.'

'We'll get more.'

Her mother's hand encircled Alicja's. 'How?'

'I will go out again through the drain tonight.'

'No.'

'I'll be careful, I promise.'

'No, Alicja. No.'

Her mother's hand gripped hard and didn't let go.

'I thought you were dead, Klara.'

The words came from Mama's friend Davide, the Frenchman who worked in Administration. He was the one who'd kept Alicja out of hospital, so she gave him a smile. He was leaning against the outside of their hut with the kind of bonelessness that meant he'd been there a long time.

'I thought you were dead, Klara,' he said again as they emerged from the hut to head over to the Washroom block.

Something in his voice sounded like pain and his face could not summon up his usual easy smile. He was a good-looking man, even Alicja could see that, with lovely dense wavy hair that moved as much as his hands when he talked. But if he'd thought her mother was dead, he didn't know her mother.

'Klara,' he said as he approached, 'don't do that to me again.'

But instead of laughing at him the way Alicja expected her mother to do, her mother stood very still and her eyes glistened with sudden unshed tears.

No. No. Her mother never cried.

No, Mama. Please.

She watched, dumbstruck, as Davide reached out and pulled her mother into his arms. He held her firmly, her forehead slumped on his shoulder. Alicja stared. Frightened her mother would never lift it up. But then he stepped back and gently unwound the scarf from her neck, revealing a blood-stained bandage underneath. Only then did Alicja see the dark telltale marks on the front of her clothes.

How had she not seen them before?

How could she be so blind?

It was the passports with their gold emblem on the front. They had dazzled her.

'Alicja,' Davide said quietly, 'take your mother to the washroom, bathe her wound and bring her to me. That's a nasty gash. I have a first-aid kit with bandages in my office. Alicja! Are you listening to me?'

'Yes.'

She took her mother's hand.

'It's nothing,' Mama insisted.

Alicja didn't know which one to believe.

Alicja stood just inside the doorway of the Administration office, shifting from foot to foot. She was uneasy. Confined in this all-male world of uniforms and hair oil, of boot polish and metal cabinets. It smelled of order and discipline.

Her mother was seated on a chair in front of one of the two desks while Davide Bouvier tended her. On the corner of the other desk a British soldier had perched himself, smoking and making sympathetic noises. Alicja watched Davide closely. She didn't trust anyone. She wanted to elbow him away and take his place.

But he handled her mother as delicately as if she were a newborn kitten. At the convent one winter a stray cat had crept into one of the dormitories and produced a litter of five kittens under one of the beds. Alicja was given the task of transferring the tiny bundles of black fur to the gardener's shed and she had carried each fragile little kitten in the palm of her hand, protecting it from the rain, as though it were made of dandelion fluff. That's how Davide handled her mother's throat.

He gently dabbed ointment on the nasty gash and covered it with a rectangle of lint, his fingers barely touching the skin of her long pale throat. He murmured softly, words Alicja didn't catch, and bandaged her neck with concentrated care.

All the time, her mother sat in silence. Her gaze was fixed on his face. Her blue eyes half-closed. Alicja felt her own throat grow tight. When Davide had finished and stood back to admire his handiwork, her mother had smiled warmly.

'Thank you, Dr Bouvier.'

But he wasn't a doctor. He was a Frenchman.

'Can you walk?'

'Of course I can walk,' Alicja said loftily.

But Rafal was right to be concerned. Her back still felt as if a swarm of bees had burrowed just under her skin.

'What did Jan Blach say when you gave him my note?' she asked.

'He said to tell you yes.'

'Did he look annoyed? Or pleased?'

'Pleased. Definitely pleased. He smiled to himself.'

'That's good.' She nudged an elbow into her friend's arm. '*Dziękuję,* Rafal. Thank you.'

They were heading over to the sports field. That was a rather glorified name for it. It was no more than a scrubby patch of land used for any kind of sporting activity, with goalposts at each end made from scrounged timber and cargo netting. It was right at the back of the camp and exerted a pull on young boys who should be in lessons and men more than ready to kick the hell out of a ball. Empty beer bottles and cigarette butts littered its edge.

'I'll stay,' Rafal offered. 'Nearby.' He patted his pocket. 'With my slingshot.'

For six paces Alicja said nothing. 'All right,' she muttered awkwardly. And because she couldn't find the right words to say thank you, she slid her hand in his.

CHAPTER TWENTY-NINE

ALICJA

It was Oskar Scholz's tallness that made Alicja uneasy. Sitting down, it would not have mattered. His long legs would have been tucked away. But here in the open, striding around the perimeter of the sports field, she was forced to tip her head back to look up at him. She could see the blond fur inside his nostrils. The scar under his chin. The way his Adam's apple moved like an animal trapped under his skin. He was already waiting there on the side of the pitch, hands in his pockets, when she arrived. The sky loomed in a brilliant blue arc above him and it seemed to her that if he reached up he could touch it.

'Hello, I'm Alicja.'

She held out her hand to show she intended no harm – that's what a handshake was for, wasn't it? – and he shook it firmly and politely. He gave her a warm smile. She was used to that. People took one look at her face and always smiled at her.

'It's because you look like a golden angel,' her mother would laugh.

But it struck Alicja as a good thing that when they gazed into her wide blue eyes they couldn't see right the way through to what was going on inside her head. It taught her not to trust people's faces.

'Good morning, Alicja. This is an unexpected pleasure.'

'I wanted to speak to you.'

'That's good. Because I would like to speak to you too.'

'It's important.'

He inclined his head down towards her, the sunlight catching the broken lens of his spectacles. 'Does your mother know we are *speaking*?'

The conversation ended. Right there.

All Alicja's words seemed to freeze in her head. Other sounds usurped their place. Shouts from the group of men kicking a football on the pitch; the noise of a home-made drum being beaten nearby; the rusty caw of a crow circling on ragged wings overhead. They all felt more real than the blurred ideas in her mind that had brought her here in the first place.

'No, my mother doesn't know.'

'I thought not.' He rubbed a hand across the back of his neck. 'Unless she sent you here.'

'She didn't.'

'I believe you, Alicja.'

Again the conversation stumbled to a halt. This was far harder than she had imagined. Her eyes suddenly sought

Rafal and found him on the opposite side of the pitch among a group of boys cheering on the striker who was racing for goal. Rafal's gaze was on her, not on the ball.

'Come, Alicja, let's walk.'

Walk? Walk where?

Scholz set off with an easy stride in a circuit of the football pitch and she had to hurry to keep up.

'Sometimes,' he said pleasantly, 'it is easier to talk when you're walking alongside someone, don't you find?'

'No.'

He smiled. 'Your mother mentioned you were sick. Are you better now?'

'Yes.'

'Excellent. What was the problem?'

'Herr Scholz, I—'

'Call me Herr Blach.'

She heard a slight roughness in his voice that time. Like sandpaper on her skin.

'Herr Blach, I didn't come here to talk about me.'

He stopped walking abruptly. 'So why did you come here, Alicja?'

'To talk about Mama.'

They walked for several minutes in silence with the breeze in their face, bringing the odours of freshly cut timber from the construction of a new hut and of cabbage soup from the kitchens. Alicja didn't care what kind of soup was churned out each day, as long as it was hot and in her stomach.

Scholz had slowed his pace to make it easier for her. They both ignored the men chasing up the pitch, but halfway around the circuit they passed behind the group of scruffy boys spectating and she saw Rafal turn his head to inspect her companion. He gave no sign of acknowledgement to her, for which she was grateful, but he patted the pocket of his trousers where his slingshot lay.

Scholz did something Alicja had not expected. He rested a hand on her shoulder as they walked. She didn't know why. Nor what it meant. But a great ache of longing opened up inside her. Papa used to do that, rest the palm of his hand on her shoulder, her head, her back, so that they were joined together. One person. It was five years since the German Messerschmidt shot him out of the sky and she grieved that she could recall so little about him now, even his laughing face fading from her grasp. But that, she did remember. The feel of his strong hand on her shoulder. Bound together, bone to bone.

'Tell me, Alicja, what it is you want to know about your mother?'

Now. Spit out the words.

'I want to know what happened to Mama in Warsaw. When I was in the convent.'

'What makes you think anything happened?'

'I know my mother.'

'Of course.' His voice was oddly gentle.

'When she took me away from the convent three years later, she was ... different.'

'Different in what way?'

She closed her lips tight. She had said enough. She felt his eyes on her as she walked but she wouldn't look at him.

'We were friends in Warsaw, your mother and I.'

'Liar!' The word slid out before she could stop it. 'She hates you.'

His hand grew heavier on her shoulder. 'Maybe now. But not then.'

'You are German. You were her enemy.'

'That's true. But friendships can cross barriers, Alicja. Don't judge me through the wrong end of a telescope. It distorts reality.'

Alicja blinked and stared down at her torn canvas shoes as they scuffed over the scrubby grass. What did he mean?

His hand abandoned her shoulder. She felt the loss of it but gave no sign.

'I'll tell you, Alicja, short and simple. I placed your mother in a job as Polish translator to a senior SS officer in Warsaw. They started an affair. She lived with him for the three years you were in the convent.'

'Liar, liar liar! Mama would never have abandoned me for a German.' Alicja spat not once, but twice in the dirt. 'She loved Papa.'

'He was dead.'

'But *I* was alive. I was still in Warsaw.'

Alicja's voice had risen. Snatched by the wind. A sickness seemed to sweep up from her stomach and lodge in her throat.

'You ask her. Whether she took an SS officer for a lover.'

Alicja clamped her teeth on her tongue to prevent any more words escaping. The more she said, the worse it got. She turned her face away.

'Very well, Alicja. Let us put this conversation behind us. It never took place. I am Jan Blach. Oskar Scholz does not exist. I can see you are upset, but you are a sensible girl. Forget the past. Go forward into the future. Tell your Mama to do the same.'

Alicja tried to nod but nothing was working right. She dragged air into her lungs by the scruff and made herself ask the question, 'Is that why Mama is afraid of you? Because you might tell Colonel Whitmore that she was a collaborator?'

He lifted his hand and stroked the back of her head comfortingly. The sun hung overhead, like a spotlight picking out just the two of them. He glanced down at her and paused in his stride, a look of sadness darkening his eyes.

'Listen to me, Alicja. Go to your mother. Tell her I say it's over between us. She has no reason to fear me. But . . .' He placed a hand under Alicja's chin and lifted it gently, so that she was forced to fix her gaze on his, 'I think you should be careful. Your mother takes risks.'

A memory slid to the surface of Alicja's mind. Of two diamonds hidden in her mother's lapels in the forest and the gang of feral women ready to cut her guts open to find them. But still Mama had denied their existence.

'Alicja,' Scholz murmured, 'take care. She could be a danger to you.'

*

'Well?' Rafal asked. 'What did he say?'

'Nothing.'

'He took a long time to say nothing.' He peered at Alicja's face. 'Are you all right?'

'Yes.'

'You don't look it. Your face is all—'

'Shut up, Rafal.'

He shut up. They walked back to Hut C without a word, their shadows racing ahead of them, heads turned away from each other. But when they reached the doorway Alicja hesitated. She touched his arm where his sleeves were rolled up. His skin always had an inner furnace.

'I'm sorry, Rafal. I don't mean to be horrid. It's just . . .'

'I know.' His smile was back.

'Go and help your mother at the laundry,' she urged.

'No. I have to stay here to keep you safe.'

'I don't need keeping safe.' It came out sharper than she intended. 'Thank you, Rafal,' she added gratefully. 'Leave me alone now.'

She walked into Hut C, into its noise and bustle and over-crowded beds. Rafal followed her.

'No, Rafal, please. I need to be alone. I need to think.'

Rafal shifted awkwardly on his big feet. 'But your mother said I had to stay with you until she gets back.'

A flash of anger cut through Alicja's patience. 'To hell with my mother.'

CHAPTER THIRTY

I was teaching a class in mathematics. I needed the pittance of money that my lessons earned me and I knew Alicja was being watched over by Rafal. I had faith in young Rafal. And in his slingshot. The class was of mixed ability, both adults and children, so I had divided them into groups and was just about to start teaching when the door opened and one final pupil walked in. It was Oskar Scholz. He took a seat at the back. He cleaned his spectacles.

For a full minute my brain shut down. Then I persuaded my legs to carry me over to stand in front of his desk. 'What are you doing here?' I spoke calmly. The children all listened.

'I'm here to learn maths of course. This is a mathematics lesson, isn't it?' His eyes challenged me.

'Yes, it is. But there is nothing wrong with your ability with numbers.'

He pulled a mock grimace. 'That's where you are mistaken. Sometimes I look at things and I fail to see what's right under my nose. I have to improve my ability to find the right answer.'

My mouth was dry. This was wrong. All wrong.

I gave him a nod of warning and returned to the front of the class. The room was bare and rudimentary, only a couple of number charts on the wall, the equipment sparse, but the twenty-three pupils turned up regularly and worked hard. They covered a range of ages from five to fifty, including adults who had never done maths before and it gave me immense pleasure normally to be teaching them the basics of arithmetic. It was a skill that could seriously enhance their future chances in life. Numbers had magic properties.

But not today. Today was not normal. Each time I wrote an addition or a multiplication sum on the board, the hair on the back of my head prickled. I expected to turn around to find an axe in my face.

It was a relief when eventually they all trooped out of class, all except Oskar Scholz. He stood by the window observing me as I gathered up the pencils and paper. I came over and stood right in front of him, too close for comfort.

'I thought we had a deal to have nothing to do with each other,' I reminded him.

'We do. You're right. But I was concerned. I heard you'd had some kind of accident.'

His gaze travelled to my throat. It was neatly wrapped up in a clean scarf, no bandage visible. Even so, I felt the blood pump to the wound, making it feel raw all over again.

'You hear wrong,' I said flatly.

He held my gaze. I remembered how adept he was at it. Not blinking. Boring into you.

'I was concerned,' he said again.

He stepped away from me. How the hell did he find out about my throat? In Warsaw he had always had eyes and ears on every street corner and at every window, and it seemed he was just as well informed here in the camp.

Never underestimate him.

I picked up the board rubber and started to clean my chalk numbers off the blackboard.

'You are a talented teacher, Klara.'

'Don't waste your flattery on me, Oskar.'

'Ah, of course, you are only interested in flattery from the Frenchman these days.'

'The Frenchman, as you call him, is a friend, nothing more.'

Oskar Scholz smiled and looked around the classroom at the benches and desks. He nodded to himself. 'You are always good at getting people to like you, Klara.'

He seemed to swell, to fill out his body and his clothes, taking up more space in the room, stealing all the air for himself. More like the SS Sturmbannführer Scholz of Warsaw. I could feel my heart trip over itself in my chest.

'Maybe,' he said, expanding his smile, 'you should work on getting your daughter to like you.'

I stalked over to the door and pulled it open. 'Get out.'

He walked out without another word.

What was the reason for it?

Why did Scholz say that?

What did he mean?

He knows nothing about my daughter.

Nothing.

He is twisting my thoughts. Panicking me. Making me question not only him, but myself. I can see cracks opening up under my feet, the way they did on the Vistula River in Warsaw when the ice was thin and the black icy waters waited to suck you down.

He can take love and upend it into hate. I've seen him do it.

But I will not let it happen here. Not now. Not with my daughter.

If that man comes anywhere near my daughter, I will kill him.

No warning.

Oskar Scholz, start saying your prayers.

I ran to Hut C.

When I saw that our bunks were empty and that neither Alicja nor Rafal were anywhere in sight, I turned quickly to Matylda on the next bed. She was sitting in just a camisole, sewing up a hole in her cream blouse with blue cotton. We all did it. Used whatever colour thread we could lay our hands on.

'Have you seen Alicja?'

She smiled obligingly, her fingers still busy. 'Yes, she went down the side of the hut outside. She was with that boyfriend of hers.'

'He's not her boyfriend.'

She chuckled. 'He soon will be.'

'She's only ten,' I pointed out.

She must have heard the alarm in my voice because she paused and studied my face. 'Of course. I was only joking.'

'They're just friends,' I said firmly. 'Thanks, Matylda.'

Graufeld Camp was a hotbed of romance. Every week yet more couples, who'd met in the camp, fell into each other's arms and got married. All desperate for love when they have nothing else. Finding someone to cling on to in order to stop themselves drowning. Matylda was just seeing things that weren't there, I told myself.

I found them sitting outside on the ground on the far side of the hut in a patch of sunlight. Alzbeta and Izak had joined them. They were all playing a game of five stones with a tiny India rubber ball and a handful of small stones. I sat down on a nearby tuft of yellow grass and watched. Rafal was winning because he had the largest hands for scooping up the five stones, but Izak was doing well too. I could see he was desperate to win and Alicja was trying to help him. I could not take my eyes off her.

Something was wrong.

Even in the sunshine her cheeks were colourless, her eyes the colour of ash. She wore Nik's scarlet ribbon looped around her small wrist like a bracelet and her fingers kept picking the end of it into fraying strands, like threads of blood on her white skin.

'Are you all right, Alicja?' I asked casually. 'Is your back hurting?'

She shook her head. Did not lift her eyes from the ribbon.

Did not look at me. I wanted to reach out across the game and pull her to me. I wanted to hold her tight till she told me what was wrong.

You should work on getting your daughter to like you.

Scholz's words dropped like slivers of ice into my ear.

Don't, I told myself. *Don't listen to him.*

'Go to bed,' Davide admonished.

'I can't. It's only the middle of the afternoon,' I objected.

'That's not the point, Klara. You don't look good. And you had almost no sleep last night.'

I smiled at his solemn expression. 'I'm fine.'

'You're not fine.' He put out a hand and placed his cool palm on my forehead. 'You're hot. Burning up. That settles it. I brought you some more aspirin.' He rattled a brown glass bottle and instantly I wondered how much Bruno Fuchs would pay me for it. 'Let's look at the cut on your throat.'

The hardest thing to find in this camp was privacy.

We found ourselves a nook at the back of the hut where a section jutted out to accommodate the stove inside. It meant we weren't overlooked. Gently Davide untied my scarf and then unwound the bandage.

His movements were light and swift. But I was conscious of the side of his hand brushing against my collarbone and his thumb sidling along the soft skin under my jaw. My instinct was to draw back. To flee from being so vulnerable. But I didn't, I stayed, chin up to make it easier for him.

As he worked, silhouetted against the sheet of pristine

blue sky behind him, I studied his features. His fine bones and unruly eyebrows. It was a good face. Not just good-looking, but good inside. Decent, where it matters. There was no harshness to it, no desire to hurt hiding behind the easy warmth in his chestnut-brown eyes. Yet there was something about the boot-black flecks within them. About the tight lines that flared prematurely around his eyes. And about the way the corners of his mouth tended to dip down in moments of repose.

It was something that spoke of the depth of his sadness. I knew Davide had suffered cruelly as part of the slave labour programme in the V-2 rocket caves and I knew he had lost his family in the war. That much he'd revealed. But the details he kept locked away.

We all kept our secrets.

It's what we carried around inside us now. All of us survivors. Sorrow. Sadness. Heartache. Secrets. You cannot go through a war without being branded.

Davide smoothed fresh ointment over the wound on my throat. As he did so, I placed the flat of my hand on his shirt front and could feel the vibration of his damaged lungs behind his ribs, a low rumble with each breath.

My head was throbbing and I thought I heard a whisper that said, *Sleep now.* But whether it came from him or from me, I couldn't say.

'There,' he said finally, 'all done. Bandaged up again. But Klara, you have a touch of fever. God only knows what that bastard had been cutting open with his knife before he cut you.'

'Skinning a cat, I expect.'

He smiled and kindly took the weight of my head between his broad hands, drawing me to him.

'Thank you,' I muttered.

But when he took away his hands, my head drooped forward. My neck too flimsy to hold it. My forehead came to rest on his shoulder and he stroked my hair. It seemed to me that his fingers were holding my thoughts and stopping them from falling out.

'I want you to listen to me, Klara. I've had an idea. I know you are desperate to get yourself out of here as soon as possible. To England. Especially now that Oskar Scholz is here in Graufeld. But we both know that the wheels of bureaucracy grind exceedingly slow around here and that it could be quite some time yet. So I've come up with an alternative strategy to keep you and Alicja safe.'

I let my head loll against his cheekbone. It felt comforting. I wanted to ask what his strategy was but the words didn't quite make it from my brain to my mouth.

'It's this,' he said, as if he had read my thoughts anyway. 'To get Oskar Scholz out of Graufeld.'

I blinked slowly as his words trickled into my brain. 'How?' I whispered against his skin.

'By getting him a *Fragebogen* Certificate of Clearance.'

CHAPTER THIRTY-ONE

ALICJA

Was it true?

Did Mama really live in Warsaw with a Nazi SS officer as her lover? Or was Oskar Scholz lying?

Alicja was curled up on her bed. Her hand lay across her eyes, blocking out the world that was spinning around her. The fingers of her other hand couldn't stop fretting at the scarlet ribbon on her wrist. She knew about collaborators. About the women who became the toys of the powerful Nazi occupiers of Poland. The older girls in the convent would whisper in corners about them. *Whores.* That's what they called them.

Mama was not a whore.

Was she?

But into Alicja's mind, like a drip of cold water, seeped the memory of their flight through the forests of Poland and the unexpected appearance of food in her mother's pocket when they were starving. And that smell on her skin. The sour smell. The farmer smell.

Alicja shuddered and buried her face in the meagre pillow, buried it so hard she couldn't breathe. Only when the violent spikes of lightning behind her eyelids threatened to brand *whore* deep into her brain did she raise her head and let air rush into her lungs.

She sat up, ignoring the raised voices in the hut. She had gone to see Oskar Scholz to find out what had happened to make her mother so different when she snatched her from the convent. Alicja had thought that she could smooth over their hatred, make them friends. She'd believed that she could chase away her mother's fear.

Scholz had been friendly. And he'd been kind. Like her father. Almost. But now it didn't matter because she no longer cared whether or not he was lying. She'd wanted to help. But she saw now. There was no helping them.

She had to be ready.

CHAPTER THIRTY-TWO

I was lying in bed, staring up at the webbing under my daughter's mattress. It was still broad daylight outside but I was dead to it. My limbs ached and the cut on my throat pulsed gently. Nothing I couldn't handle.

But there seemed to be a fire burning somewhere inside me, though I couldn't work out where. Davide had stood over me while I took a couple of aspirins. Reluctantly. The more I swallowed, the fewer I had to sell. Alicja had retreated in silence to her bunk above me, her nose stuck in the ancient book of folk tales that Salomea had presented to me in Hanover.

A *Fragebogen*.

Davide was baying at the moon. How could Oskar Scholz risk filling out a *Fragebogen*?

The *Fragebogen* was an official questionnaire – 131 questions – distributed by the four Allied military governments to millions of Germans for the denazification of Germany. The questions demanded to know every single detail of your association with National Socialism – whether you'd belonged to

201

Hitler Youth; how you voted in the 1932 election; if you'd hoped for a German victory during the war – intending to purge the country of Nazis. To root out all those who were trying to conceal their political past.

Conviction meant prison or worse. It was exactly what Oskar Scholz was terrified of. In the chaos that had swept through Germany since the war ended, the temptation to slough off his old Nazi identity and reappear as whiter-than-white Jan Blach must have been overwhelming. I can see that. Already thousands of Germans had been interrogated after filling out the *Fragebogen* and chucked in prison. Scholz had no intention of becoming one of their number.

That's what David meant.

If we could get hold of one of the white Certificates of Clearance with Jan Blach's name stamped on it, Scholz would leave Graufeld.

But what about the four thousand Jewish children I saw him help march to the cattle yard in Warsaw? The ones who were packed in trains bound for the gas chambers of Treblinka, terrified and trembling.

What about them?

It was winter in Warsaw, the kind of winter that cracks your bones. The kind that feels it is never going to end. Breath froze into pearls of ice the moment it left your lungs and the wide Vistula River had turned as hard as iron. At night the moon carved its own secret patterns in the blanket of snow that silenced the once-elegant length of Marszalkowska Avenue.

I grieved for my beautiful city, so much of it scarred and in ruins now, and I grieved for the spectral beggars who haunted the streets and who were frequently shot at random just for being an eyesore. If the cold and the hunger didn't do for them, the bullet would.

Nazi jackboots might have been marching through Poland's capital for the last two years, but don't think the war was over for the Polish people. It wasn't. Poland refused to roll itself in the swastika flag and die.

Tonight was special. Tonight Poland was fighting back. The grey Nazi uniforms and the death's head emblems had gathered together like vultures to peck carelessly at Poland's bones in an evening of drinking and laughter. Their hands on the soft flesh of Poland's women.

But like I said about a chess game. The queen is the dangerous one. The one to fear.

'What about that?'

SS Sturmbannführer Oskar Scholz placed a glass of amber brandy punch before me and raised his own whisky glass in celebration. I left my drink untouched. Beside me, SS Oberführer Axel Fleischer threw an affectionate arm around my naked shoulder and kissed my cheek, his full lips warm and moist against my skin. He liked to do that in public. To stamp ownership.

'Drink, Liebchen.' Axel laughed. 'It's my birthday. I want you to be happy.' He nuzzled my neck then drew back and studied my expression. 'Are you happy, Klara?'

'Yes, I'm happy.'

'Sometimes I wonder.'

I smiled at him and waved a hand around the sparkling nightclub that he had taken over for the occasion. It throbbed with heat and music and desire. Diamonds flashed around slender young throats, the spoils of war, while men strutted in their fine uniforms, flaunting their power and their victor's sense of entitlement. The band played good German songs with the kind of relentless beat that made your brain shake, as trays of birthday brandy punch in glittering stemmed glasses circulated every table.

'How could I not be happy here?' I laughed.

Axel Fleischer relaxed and leaned his elbows on the table to speak to a tense-looking officer seated opposite. His name was Oberführer Sammern-Frankenegg. He possessed a huge domed bald head and uneasy eyes hiding behind round spectacles. His moustache was absurd, an imitation of Hitler's, and he had a cleft in his chin you could hide a tank in. His face would sit better on a bureaucrat than on a soldier. Every time he and Fleischer spoke to each other they lowered their voices. Oberführer Ferdinand von Sammern-Frankenegg was a man I could barely look at. Or share the same air with. Because I knew what was in his head.

He had every right to be tense.

Yes, Oberführer Sammern-Frankenegg, I know.

Whenever he addressed a remark to me, I replied to the showy bar of medals on his chest, so that my eyes did not have to look at his.

'Would you care to dance, Klara?'

It was Oskar Scholz inviting me so politely, his voice a soft purr in my ear. I opened my mouth to decline, but then I looked at his face, and shut it again. I knew those silvery grey eyes of his. They wanted something from me.

*

I had learned not to grind my teeth when a Nazi touched me. My skin did not burst into flames. Or turn black. That was just inside my head.

I was wearing a long silver gown, made from the finest Parisian silk that knew exactly how to skim my hips and left my arms and shoulders bare, shimmering in the glow from the crystal chandelier. When Oskar Scholz took me in his arms with only the lightest of touches, I did not hesitate to rest my hand on the uniformed ridge of his shoulder. Without spitting. I looked him directly in the eye.

'What do you want, Oskar?'

He smiled. 'Always to the point, Klara.'

The dance floor was crowded and noisy. He leaned close.

'I hear that Fleischer called a meeting yesterday.' I felt his breath hot on my cheek. 'With a number of the Polish factory owners in Warsaw.'

'You are well informed.'

'You must have attended the meeting as his interpreter.'

'I did.'

'Who was there?'

'Six of them. Manufacturers of metal hinges, ball bearings, shell cases, flour, cloth for army shirts and light bulbs. All supply the German army.' I stared over his shoulder at the drinks table where a mammoth silver punchbowl was being refilled. 'They are demanding higher prices for their goods.'

He laughed softly. 'Of course they are. What was Fleischer's reaction?'

I switched my gaze back to Oskar. 'How is she?'

'Who?'

'You know who.'

'If you mean your daughter, she is well. The nuns send me a weekly report on her.'

'May I see it?'

'No.'

I halted. My feet didn't move. I didn't take my eyes off his.

'Klara,' he said impatiently, 'we're causing a blockage on the dance floor.'

I remained still and silent. Waiting.

He sighed. 'The nuns say that Alicja is good at her lessons, especially mathematics. This week they mentioned that she has her first adult tooth coming through and that she has a chest cold at the moment, so disturbs the whole dormitory at night.'

I realised I was breathing fast, pulling in extra air for my daughter's lungs.

'They ended,' he continued in a rush, 'by saying she can be difficult at times. She has escaped from the convent. Twice.'

I was picturing my seven-year-old daughter at night. Coughing. Alone. Awake. In darkness. Plotting a way out.

'Listen to me, Klara.' He shook me lightly but I barely noticed. 'She is looked after. She is safe.'

'Why can't I receive a letter from her through you?'

'Leave her alone. She is better off there, happy in her new life. Not thinking of you.'

'You don't run away if you're happy.'

'Now,' he said curtly, 'you have your answers. Time to give me mine.'

I nodded. I danced. I gave him his answers. Fleischer had given the factory owners an angry response and refused to pay even one zloty more than the price he was already paying for their goods. The exchange was heated but the Oberführer was adamant. Not one zloty more. He accused them of being traitors to the Nazi General Government of Poland.

Oskar Scholz steered a neat path through the throng of dancers but I could tell he was shaken.

'What is Fleischer trying to do?' he murmured close to my ear. 'Sabotage Polish supplies to the German army by forcing these factories into bankruptcy? Is that it?' I could feel the tension in the muscles under my fingers. 'To weaken the army of the Third Reich?'

'Do you want to know what I think?'

He pulled his head back. 'What?'

'I think he is taking a rake-off for himself. As simple as that.' I withdrew my hand from his. 'I think we are done for today, Oskar.'

I walked away and left him on the dance floor.

My first stop was the table with the punchbowl. The drinks waiter was busy piling full glasses on to a tray, so I had no problem helping myself with the ladle and a glass of my own. As I moved away I passed the birthday cake in the design of a gigantic castle.

'Cake, madam?'

A young woman in a waitress uniform was standing in front of me, offering me a plate with a slice of cake.

'No, thank you.'

'Are you sure?'

'Yes, I'm sure.'

She was small and sinewy with brown hair pulled back harshly and a thin face that was all sharp angles. She gave me a polite smile, but her eyes were jumpy as they flicked around the room crowded with grey uniforms and boisterous laughter. I could see that Axel Fleischer revelled in being the centre of all the attention.

'So many of them,' the waitress murmured under her breath. 'Like snakes in a pit.'

I flashed her a warning look and headed straight for the powder room.

The nightclub's powder room was stylish. Elegant black and white tiles in geometric patterns and a wall of mirrors that threw my face back at me at different angles. I kept my eyes off the mirrors and checked each of the six stalls, pushing each door open with my foot just to make sure. All were empty.

I tipped my punch away, ran hot water into one of the basins and used an excessive amount of fragrant soap to wash Oskar Scholz off my hands. Almost immediately the main door swung open and the waitress walked in. She didn't hesitate but hurried across the tiles to me and wrapped her arms around me. I hugged her tight. For a moment neither of us could speak.

'Klara,' she whispered, 'I've been worried sick about you.'

'Don't be, Irenka.' I kissed her thin cheek. 'What are you living on? You are just skin and bone.'

'We get by. How does he treat you?'

'We get by,' I smiled. Because what else could I do?

She looked at my Paris dress, smelled my Paris perfume, and her eyes filled with tears.

'Don't,' I said. 'I'm not worth your tears.'

Irenka was my friend. I trusted her. For the past two years we had fought side by side in the Polish Resistance, covered each other's back, saved each other's life. She was a radio expert and a talented codebreaker, but I hadn't expected her to be here tonight. I'd dropped a note, unobserved, into the hand of the man who sold me my newspaper in the kiosk to state that I'd be at this party tonight and to request an urgent meeting.

'I didn't think it would be you here,' I said.

'I insisted.'

'It's too dangerous.'

She kissed my cheek. 'But worth it to see you again.'

'I'll be quick. Anyone might walk in.' I went over and stood with my back against the door. 'The troops are going into the Jewish Ghetto tomorrow. To sweep out at least five thousand people. Adults and children.'

'No.' It came out of her as if she'd been kicked.

'It's true. Fleischer has been holding meetings with Oberführer Sammern-Frankenegg all week to make the final arrangements. Sammern-Frankenegg is going in with troops tomorrow, January the eighteenth, for a major action to transport thousands more of them to Treblinka concentration camp.'

Irenka's lips were white. 'God help them.'

'No, my friend, we have to help them.'

The Jewish Ghetto was a terrible place. An inhuman cage. Four hundred thousand Jews imprisoned in three miserable square kilometres by a three-metre perimeter brick wall. That's seven people to each room. Imagine it. Inhaling each other's fear with every breath, jammed so tight you hear every heartbeat. Slowly starving to death and no wood for fires in this brutal winter. Yet tales leaked out each day of extraordinary feats of love and courage by the inhabitants to smuggle in the tiniest scraps of food and fuel to keep the children alive. Escapees were shot on sight.

This was only the start. Oberführer Sammern-Frankenegg had orders to destroy the whole Ghetto and all its inhabitants. I'd heard him discussing it with Fleischer. Four hundred thousand Jews.

Four hundred thousand.

'You have to warn them, Irenka. To be prepared. Hide the children. In cupboards. Inside suitcases. It's time to take out the guns from under the floorboards. To make the petrol bombs to—'

The door to the powder room slammed against my back as two women in evening gowns forced their way in and made a rush for two of the cubicles. The sound of them being violently sick filled the small space.

My mouth was dry, my heart pumping. I exchanged a look with Irenka and she vanished from the room. I returned to my washbasin, ran scalding hot water and began to scrub my hands.

CHAPTER THIRTY-THREE

I woke. Forced my eyes open. A pulse throbbed behind them. To my surprise it was still daylight in Hut C. The steady hum of conversation elbowed out the violent sound of the gunfire that followed that evening in the nightclub. The carnage. The cries. The rumble of tanks. The reek of cordite. I could smell it now.

The way I could still smell Axel Fleischer's cologne, if ever I let my guard slip.

I lay immobile on my bunk bed in this bleak No Man's Land that I was trapped in and without warning something broke in me. Something snapped. I heard it. Such intimate knowledge of man's capacity for inhumanity was too much. It was crushing me. I fought to push it away but it was closing over my head, black as oil. I jerked upright to gasp for air and that was when I froze.

I'd felt something move. Inside my bed.

Something brushing against my calf.

I threw myself on to the floor and dragged back the bedding.

A snake.

It lay in the centre of the white sheet. Its muddy brown body was almost as long as my arm. What looked like darker paint splodges zigzagged down its back. Its long head was raised, scenting me, its chestnut-brown eyes gleaming like glass. We stared at each other. Both in shock.

'Alicja,' I whispered softly, 'give me your pillowcase.'

Whatever it was that my daughter heard in my voice, it made her act without question. She pulled the cover from her pillow on the top bunk and held it out to me, her eyes fixed on my face. Very slowly, I took it. But even that small movement was enough. The frightened creature shot under my pillow and I jumped back, every pulse racing.

Alicja leaped from her bunk to stand beside me. 'What is it?'

'A snake.'

'Where?'

'In my bed. It's under my pillow now.'

'Hold the pillowcase open.'

She moved, fast and calm. She stripped the sheet from her own bunk, flicked its layers around her arm and hand, and pressed down hard on my pillow to trap the snake. In one swift sweep of her sheeted hand, she scooped out its long twisting body by the tail and dropped it into the pillowcase that I was holding open. It was surprisingly heavy.

I stood there, aghast.

She unwound the scarlet ribbon from her wrist and tied it tight around the neck of the pillowcase. It was that simple.

She turned her sweet smile on me. 'You're safe now.'

'Where did you learn to handle snakes?' I was still trembling.

'There were lots of them around the convent. This one is an adder. We used to catch them for fun.'

There was so much I didn't know about my daughter.

We both stared at the pillowcase and then at my bed.

'Who put it there, Mama?'

As if we didn't know.

The doorkeeper of Hut W was snoozing in the sunshine. He was seated in a home-made chair, his chin nestled on his chest, a faint snore rumbling out of him. I stepped around his legs and marched right into the hut. It smelled of men's sweat and boredom and cigarettes. Heads turned. Voices called out, suggestive comments trailed alongside me. A hand gripped my shoulder. I shook it off and walked down to Oskar Scholz's bed.

The pillowcase sack was in my hand, held out in front of me at arm's length and the scarlet ribbon looked like a rivulet of blood around it. I wanted to shout at these men to get outside and dig a vegetable patch or learn how to mend a burst pipe. Do something. Instead of crowding around me, smelling my hair, touching my neck.

I saw Scholz ahead of me, stretched out on top of his bed and reading a book. He wore no spectacles and was engrossed, blocking out the rowdy noise in the hut. He was always good at that. He had the ability to ignore distractions, to focus on what he wanted. I'd seen it a thousand times, the pupils in his grey eyes like bore holes that sucked in the information he needed. I'd once watched him sitting on the floor writing a report in my Warsaw apartment at one of Axel Fleischer's wild parties, while half-naked girls pawed at him and a euphoric cocaine-snorting general blasted away on a trombone.

'You!' I called from the end of his bed in the hut.

I could not bear to call him Jan Blach. That name belonged to my brother.

Scholz lowered the book. At the sight of me he was startled. I saw him jump, saw his mouth drop open. He was not expecting me. But the unguarded moment was gone as quickly as it came and he rose to his feet.

'Klara, what are you doing here?'

'Did you imagine I would be in hospital now, writhing in pain?'

I held up the pillowcase, slipped off the ribbon and up-ended the pillowcase over his bed. The snake slithered out and dropped on to the sheet, a sleek brown blur of movement with venom in its fangs. A gasp went up around me and men scattered in all directions.

But the snake had learned that beds were not a safe refuge, so shot on to the floor. Shouts and curses burst through the hut as grown men jumped up on to beds in panic.

'You fucking bitch,' one yelled at me.

I did not wait for more. I turned and walked out.

*

I wound the ribbon around Alicja's wrist once more and tickled the palm of her hand. She smiled, refusing to laugh for me, and took her hand away, but lay down on my bed, her blond head in my lap. It was a long time since she'd done that.

'Mama, the snake could have bitten you.'

'I was lucky, sweetheart. All it wanted was my warmth.'

'A snake bite can be bad.'

'Well, let's hope it finds someone tasty in Hut W.'

Again a faint smile. Nothing more.

'Does your back still hurt, Alicja?'

A shake of her head. She wouldn't tell me if it did. I tenderly stroked her curls, winding one around my finger. She closed her eyes, her golden lashes lying like silk threads on her cheekbones, and for a moment I shut out all else. Just us. In the world. My beautiful brave daughter and me. I leaned down and kissed her forehead.

'Mama, tell me about Papa.'

The shock of the question rippled through me. She had not mentioned him since we entered Graufeld Camp.

'What do you want to know?'

'Tell me what he looked like.'

She was forgetting. Just like I was forgetting. But she had an excuse, she was only five when he was killed. I had no excuse.

'Your father was handsome and strong with wavy brown hair that curled over his ears. He loved engines.' I laughed at a memory of his tanned cheek streaked with oil. 'More than he loved me, I suspected sometimes. But never more than he loved you.' I stroked a curl back from her ice-cream smooth skin. 'He loved you more than anything else in the world.'

The corner of Alicja's mouth lifted. 'Tell me more.'

'He would have been proud of you today, protecting me from the adder. He would have sat you on his shoulders and jumped into the river with you.'

She laughed. At last she laughed.

'One day before you were born,' I told her, 'your papa and I went for a picnic in the forest.'

It was actually for something infinitely more fun than a picnic, but that was not part of the story.

'A massive hairy boar came snuffling out of the under-growth, took one look at me, snorted like a car backfiring, then dropped its head and charged straight at me. Its tusks were huge and vicious. But do you know what your papa did?'

She was holding her breath.

'He snatched up the picnic rug,' I continued urgently, 'and waved it in front of the animal like a matador with a bull. It charged at him instead.'

I heard her small gasp.

'He sidestepped it a few times and in the end it gave up and snuffled off into the forest. Your papa saved my life that day. He was my hero.'

Alicja buried her face in my thigh. I ran a hand over her bony young hip, but I was careful where I touched. I didn't want to hurt her back. She clung to my leg the way she used to cling to her father's.

'Papa is my hero too,' she whispered.

'He would have been so proud.'

There was a long silence that sat soft and comfortable between us. Her muscles were relaxing and melting back into me.

'Mama,' she said in a tight voice, 'you won't marry someone else, will you?'

I wasn't going to lie to her. From a pouch hanging around my neck but hidden inside my blouse, I extracted the two dark blue booklets that had cost me so dear. I held them in front of my daughter's face.

'Who needs a husband when we have passports?'

CHAPTER THIRTY-FOUR

ALICJA

'Herr Blach?'

Alicja had startled him. That was good. He would be off balance. She had a sense that she could knock him to the ground despite his height. He was coming out of the canteen after breakfast, his eyes foggy, as if he hadn't slept well. It took several heartbeats for Scholz to remember that Blach was his name in the camp, Jan Blach. He glanced at her and raised a hostile eyebrow.

'I've had enough of your family,' he said sharply.

He tried to brush past her but she stepped into his path. He did not disguise his irritation when she stood her ground.

'What is it this time?' he demanded.

She had the words ready. 'I forgot to say something to you. When we talked on the football field.'

'If you forgot it, it can't be important, can it?'

'I think it is.'

She could feel his annoyance crawling over her. The snake tossed on his bed was something he had no intention of forgiving.

'So spit it out,' he snapped.

'I want you to know, Herr Blach.'

'Know what?'

'That what my mother did in the past in Warsaw. Or didn't do. It doesn't matter. Not now.'

He burst out laughing. Except it didn't sound like laughter. It sounded like hot oil spitting when you splash water into it. 'Is that what you think?'

'Yes.'

'Well, little girl, you are mistaken. Everything that we do in the past matters. You will learn that. The past is like your shadow, it never leaves you.'

'When there is no sun, there is no shadow.'

His gaze didn't leave her face. 'Do you know, Alicja, that a British soldier from this camp was suffering from toothache and went to a highly qualified German dentist in Hanover for an extraction. The dentist injected him with something that almost killed him. A deliberate murder attempt. The soldier is now seriously ill in hospital and the dentist is locked up in prison.'

Alicja said nothing. Why was he telling her about a dentist?

'You see,' he pushed his face towards hers, 'hatred is all-consuming. Do you know what that means? It means it eats you up inside. That dentist threw away everything he had achieved in life for one moment of hatred. The war is still going on. Hatred doesn't listen to reason. I advise you to tell your mother to make certain she listens to reason. Otherwise . . .' He shrugged.

Alicja stepped so close she could smell fried bacon on his breath. 'What I came to tell you this morning is this,' she said. 'Stay away from my mother.'

'So fierce!'

She reached out with sudden fury and gripped the front of his shirt tight in her fist. Twisted it hard. 'I am telling you that if you hurt my mother, I will defend her.'

For the first time, he smiled. 'Ah, so the lion cub has claws. You think love is a match for hatred?' He detached her fingers from his shirt one at a time.

'I mean it. If you hurt her, I will . . .' The words jammed in her throat.

'You will what?'

'I will . . .'

'What?'

'I will kill you.'

Muscle by muscle the smile slid off his face. The silence between them was raw. After a long moment Scholz nodded.

'I believe you, Alicja Janowska.'

CHAPTER THIRTY-FIVE

DAVIDE BOUVIER

'You're not listening.'

'I am.'

'No you're not, Klara.'

'I'm listening to every word you say. Really I am.'

Davide placed a hand on her arm to slow down her pace. He had come to fetch her immediately after breakfast to escort her to the Administration block and wanted to make certain she understood the seriousness of her situation before she entered the lion's den.

'You must be penitent,' he told her.

She lowered her eyes. She was oddly subdued today. That surprised him. He had expected her to be bristling with anger.

'Be careful with your tongue, Klara. That's what I'm saying.'

She looked up at him and the tension in her face softened.

Her fingers brushed over the back of his hand. 'Thank you, Davide. I am grateful.'

'Don't, for heaven's sake, go around accusing Scholz when you have no proof he was responsible for the snake. Promise me. No one saw him enter your hut.'

His words seemed to stun her. She answered with sudden passion. 'One day, Davide, when my head is turned the other way, that man will come up behind my daughter and slit her throat.'

'What makes you think that, Klara? That he would be so violent.'

'Because I know him.'

'Have you ever seen him do such a monstrous act?'

'No.'

'Then how can you be sure?'

'There were always others to do it for him before. He didn't need to get his own hands dirty.'

'Listen to me, Klara. You could be mistaken. He might have changed. You know, people do change when their life is torn apart. We both know that.'

Klara removed her hand from Davide's.

It felt as if she'd peeled the skin off it. Of course he understood that she would struggle with the idea of Scholz experiencing a change of heart, but Davide's own heart sank when he saw her look at him as though he'd grown two heads. Without a word she entered the Administration block.

*

When they had settled in the stiff army-issue chairs inside the office, Colonel Whitmore gathered together the papers on his desk, shifting them from place to place. Building a fortress for himself.

Davide was aware of how acutely embarrassed the colonel was to find himself in this situation. It baffled Davide why Englishmen were so bad at dealing with women. As if they might explode at any moment like a hand grenade. The fear of an emotional outburst was tangible in the room and even worse, God forbid, the ever-present terror of tears. Davide had requested permission to be present at the questioning of Klara and Colonel Whitmore had more than readily agreed.

'Mrs Janowska,' the colonel said solemnly, 'I have summoned you here this morning because it has been brought to my attention that you have committed an extremely serious offence.'

Klara sat quietly. It gave Davide hope. The quickest way to an Englishman's heart was docility in a woman. She sat there, watching the colonel closely, her wide blue eyes unblinking. The only indication of her stress was one hand straying to the scarf over the bandage on her neck. Her fingers kept picking at it as if there was something inside her she wanted to pluck out.

'Mrs Janowska, you released a poisonous snake on Mr Blach's bed in Hut W. There were more than twenty witnesses, so please do not waste our time by trying to deny it. Do you have anything to say about the incident?'

Incident. A word that reduced an act of passion to manageable military terms.

Just apologise, Klara. Please. Just give him an easy way out and we can all get on with our jobs.

But even as the thought rose in Davide's mind, he knew it was not possible. Klara would no more apologise for causing Oskar Scholz distress than she would wash his bed sheets.

'I apologise,' Klara said.

Davide blinked.

Klara cast him a look. *See*, it said. *I listened to you. I can do penitence. If that's what it takes.*

Davide gave a snort of surprise and turned it into a cough. She never failed to surprise him. Clearly she had surprised Colonel Whitmore too because he visibly relaxed, confident the worst danger had passed.

Klara took her hands from her neck scarf and placed them folded demurely on her lap. 'I'm sorry, Colonel. It was foolish of me. It was just that a snake in my bed was too much.'

Whitmore leaned forward on his desk. 'In your bed?'

'Yes. I thought one of the men had somehow put it there. You know, to make a point. Like the serpent with Adam and Eve in Eden. I regarded it as a sexual threat and something in me snapped.' She laid a hand on her heart as though to still its fluttering. 'Some of the men in Graufeld can be very intimidating, Colonel.'

He frowned. 'I am aware of the problem, Mrs Janowska. Which is why we have strict rules of behaviour in place.'

'Which we are grateful for.'

'Has Jan Blach caused you problems?'

'Jan Blach?'

'The man on whose bed you threw the snake.'

'I was upset. And angry. I marched on down to the single men's huts and chucked the snake on whichever bed came to hand. It was not intended for a particular man, I assure you.'

The colonel sat back and tapped his teeth uneasily. 'It was probably one of the children trying to scare you for a prank.'

Even Davide had difficulty swallowing that one.

'But for you to throw a venomous snake at someone is a serious matter, as I'm sure you understand. It should be a matter for the German police.'

Her gasp caught them both by surprise. Her eyes widened and her hand flew to her mouth. 'Venomous?'

'Yes, the snake was an adder. A damn large one, I gather.'

'I thought it was a grass snake! I'd never have handled it if I'd realised it was poisonous.' She slumped back in her chair with a mix of shock and relief. 'I meant no harm.'

She was good. Very good. Davide wanted to applaud.

Instead he nodded sagely. 'Well, Colonel, it looks like it was more an error of judgement rather than a malicious act.'

Whitmore studied the piles of paperwork like the Atlas Mountains on his desk. Was it worth adding to it with even more paperwork about a trivial incident? Probably not. Davide watched him come to the decision and breathed a silent sigh of relief.

'Very well,' Whitmore announced, 'we will take it no further, as no one was hurt.'

'Thank you.'

The colonel rose to his feet. The discussion was at an end.

Davide had the door open and Klara was about to exit, when Whitmore added, 'You will of course apologise.'

'Apologise?'

'To Jan Blach.'

Davide saw her swallow. So hard he thought she would choke.

'Of course, Colonel.'

CHAPTER THIRTY-SIX

DAVIDE BOUVIER

Clouds had blown in from the north. A dirty grey sky clamped down over the camp, trapping the homeless beneath it, while a cold wind searched out any naked ankles or threadbare shirts.

After leaving the Administration block Davide walked Klara briskly to the Recreation hall. In silence. Neither spoke. At this time of the morning the hall was usually little used, just a few die-hards at the card tables and one old Slovak with milky eyes who sat all day at the window, gazing to the east because he feared that the bloody boots of the Soviet Army would come marching in any day now.

At the door Davide halted. There was much he wanted to say to Klara, too many words, but he held them back. He gave her a warm smile instead. 'You were very convincing in there. Remind me never to believe any-thing you say.'

She laughed. Not much of a laugh, admittedly, but he was thankful for the effort she made.

'You wait in the hall,' he told her. 'I'll go and fetch Scholz.'

'Do you have to?'

'Yes, I do. You know I do. It's the only way to keep you out of a German police cell. Let's get it over with immediately.'

He noticed the way she tightened. Elbows tucked in, shoulders narrowing. He had no wish to inflict this on her but the sooner it was done the better. He wouldn't let her go through it alone. He moved off sharply to head down Churchill Way, but she didn't let him. Her hand wrapped itself around his forearm and drew him through the doorway into a corridor that separated the main recreation hall from the smaller room reserved for mothers with children.

She halted in the corridor, a dimly lit passage that still smelled of army distemper paint.

'A moment of privacy,' she said with relief.

She'd chosen well. The camp was riddled with eyes everywhere, bored eyes, interested eyes, curious eyes, suspicious eyes. Everywhere you went. Observing everything you did. But not here. This gloomy little patch of corridor for a few minutes was theirs.

Klara took both his hand in hers. 'Thank you, Davide.'

Only three small words, yet they carried such a depth of emotion. Everyone in Graufeld Camp got through each day by being always guarded and self-protective. It was the only way to survive in the hostile environment. But it made for a lonely and isolated existence, one that Davide had taught himself to adapt to. Now suddenly with the emotion of those simple words Klara was laying herself open. Though she was wearing her usual washed-out blue dress and her ragged scarf at her throat, she had always been clad in armour. And behind each sheet of iron lay another sheet of iron. Another suit of armour.

But now he could sense the soft body beneath, the sweetness and the freshness of it. He felt a rush of love for this extraordinary, pig-headed and courageous young woman and he lifted one of her hands. Turned it over, kissed its palm and breathed in the intimate scent of her.

Instantly Klara's other hand buried itself in his hair. Gripping hard, trying to climb deep inside him. He could feel the force of it, the need in the damaged tips of her fingers. He raised his head and her slender arm curled around his neck, not soft and gentle, but lean and urgent. His skin seemed to catch fire at her touch and he drew her into his arms, her body taut against his.

He kissed her mouth. Instead of armour, her lips were soft and warm, opening to him, inviting him to be a part of her. For so long he had believed that these emotions had been flayed out of him by the war, that love was something that lay dead and cold in the past behind him. But there was a passion in Klara that brought the broken parts of him together with its heat. A furnace within her that created a new flame inside him.

He wanted to lift her in his arms. To run. To carry her away from here to wide open spaces. To tear her out of the grip of whatever it was that Scholz had over her. To see her smile, to hear her laugh.

To watch her live.

He had imprinted in his mind every line of her face and each delicate contour of her cheek, but now his fingers touched them. Traced the strong bones under the pale skin. He kissed her short hair. Silk on his lips. He discovered that the heat in her flowed even through the sunshine curls. She laid her hand on his shoulder, brushed her hot cheek back and forth over his. They stood there together in the gloom, hearts pounding. Her breasts pressed tight to his chest. Both aware that time was running out.

'Davide,' she murmured, 'what happened to your wife and child?'

He waited. Till the shock had passed.

'It's all locked away, Klara. I threw away that key.' He let his breathing steady. 'I've never told anyone.'

'I'm not anyone.'

Her face, so close to his, was gentle in the shadows. It was time. She wasn't *anyone*.

'I used to live in a beautiful village called Oradour-sur-Glane near Limoges in France,' he said in a toneless voice. 'On the tenth of June 1944 the village was wiped out. My parents, my wife, my daughter, my friends. They all were happy there. I was held captive in Nordhausen, so I wasn't present when the First Battalion of the Fourth SS Panzer Division rolled in under the command of SS-Sturmbannführer Diekemann.'

'What happened?'

'The Nazi Battalion was there to make reprisals. To avenge actions taken by members of the French Resistance. The SS Battalion shot and burned the men of the village. They herded the women and children into the church and set fire to it. Any who managed to escape were shot.'

'Dear God!' Her arms circled him.

He felt the warmth of her banishing the chill that was grinding its way through him. He could hear the sounds. Of flames. Roaring like a train. Of screams. Shrill shrieks of agony. They wouldn't stop.

Lightly Klara brushed her thumbs under Davide's eyes as if to brush aside tears, but there were no tears.

'Your wife?'

'Annette. In the church. Burned to death.'

'Your daughter?'

Silence.

He stared down at the floor for a full minute.

'Giselle was in the church. Burned to death. She was six years old. Long chestnut hair that she loved to wear in plaits.'

Klara leaned her weight against him, dragging him back to the gloomy narrow corridor.

'They were massacred,' he continued, 'along with all the rest of them. Six hundred and forty-two people died that day in my village. Oradour-sur-Glane was razed.'

Over a year now. It felt like a lifetime.

The stillness between them held them together.

'I'm sorry,' she breathed.

At that moment the outer door burst open and they stepped apart. Two women with five children in tow bustled past them to the smaller room, filling the space with noise and chatter. The stillness faded along with the screams in his head and the stench of burned flesh.

Davide kissed Klara's forehead. 'Wait here,' he said. 'I will be back.' He gave a regretful shrug. 'With Scholz.'

'How can you even bear to speak to him after what the Nazis did to your family? How can you be so forgiving?'

She asked the question quietly, wanting to understand.

'It was a moral sickness, Klara, that infected the herd mentality. They are being made to pay for it now. But it does not mean that the individuals within the herd were all bad.' He pushed open the outer door, letting in a shaft of light that sought out Klara and revealed a brightness in her blue eyes that had not been there before.

'You are right about the herd, Davide. You and I both know that we all carry a shadow within us. So who knows what we are each capable of?'

CHAPTER THIRTY-SEVEN

Davide, what have you done to me?

What is this warmth flowing through my veins, this looseness in my limbs? The muscles in my neck have grown soft and pliant. There is a lightness inside me, as if you have removed the stones that have lived in my vital organs since the day my husband hurtled to the ground in flames.

I had forgotten that I could feel like this. That it was possible. To breathe without pain. To think without metal bands tightening around my head. To see thoughts emerge that are not dipped in rage.

I step outside the Recreation building and watch Davide walk down the long straight road through the camp. The wind snatches at his jacket and he pulls it tight around him. The exertion of the walk is making him cough. I fear for his lungs. Though of reasonable height, he is not a man who takes up space. He gives space to others.

He gives space to me.

I want to run up behind him and wrap my arms around his tortured chest. To hold him close.

I waited in the road. I had no intention of spending time under the same roof as Scholz, not even if it was the Recreation hall roof. Outside I did not have to breathe his air. The clouds were racing across the sky trying to outpace each other and the wind was blowing up a dust storm in the flat barren fields that encircled the camp. Crows cruised on motionless black wings. I watched them and thought about being free.

I watched the two men in the distance, Scholz and Davide. They were heading up from the far end of Churchill Way. Chalk and cheese. Scholz the taller and broader of the two, with a chest that threatened to rush ahead of him unless he remembered to drag it back. Davide was slight but moved with a Gallic smoothness, his hands tracing worlds in the air when he spoke. As I observed him approach, I realised I was smiling.

The smile vanished as Scholz drew near. I stood, stiff and uneasy outside the hall. I was preparing words for him but they wouldn't fit in my mouth. I wanted to run, but my feet stayed nailed to the spot.

'So?' Scholz said when he stood in front of me.

He knew only too well what this would cost me.

'I apologise.'

There. It was said. *Happy now, Colonel Whitmore?*

Davide took up a position beside me, seeing me through it, as he'd promised. Scholz stared at me. Waiting for more.

'I apologise for throwing a snake on your bed.'

'A poisonous snake. An adder,' he reminded me.

'I didn't know it was an adder.'

'What prompted you to turn so vicious?'

'I believed you'd arranged to have someone place it in my bed.' My voice was cold.

'You were mistaken, Klara.'

'If my child had climbed into that bed and received a bite from the snake, she could have died.'

'But she didn't.'

'No.'

'And you have no proof it was me.'

'No.'

He let a dozen heartbeats pass.

'Klara, you are deluded.'

I walked away.

Scholz had said the same words to me before.

'Klara, you are deluded.'

I held out my hand for him to see what lay in it. 'This is not a delusion.'

It was a diamond. It winked a violet flash of light at me.

'I tell you, Oberführer Fleischer is acquiring diamonds from somewhere.'

Scholz's mouth was a tight line. 'You stole this from him?'

'No. He gave it to me.'

'Why would he do that?'

'Ask him.'

'No, I'm asking you, Klara.'

'Because he has others. He says he has lots of others.'

'If the diamonds are the spoils from Jewish jewellery businesses here in Warsaw, he should have handed them over to the Reich. Failure to do so amounts to treachery.' He was pacing his office, the diamond concealed in his fist.

If Fleischer were arrested, I'd be free.

'Find out more,' he ordered.

'My diamond, please.' I held out my hand.

'I'll keep it. As evidence.'

'Like hell you will.'

The time had come. I could delay it no longer.

Oddly, I felt a reluctance. Which was foolish. Because I knew from that very first moment that I saw Oskar Scholz sunning himself in the doorway of Hut J that I would have to kill him.

Before he killed me.

Before he killed Alicja.

And now I'd seen the way he'd looked at Davide. It had sent a chill through me. Does he see Davide as a threat to him? Or does he feel Davide has too great an interest in me? Whichever it is, I won't let him turn his venom on him. The snake was just the start.

There will be more to come.

It was raining diamonds.

They came tumbling down on me as I lay naked on the bed. A

rainbow painted my skin with splashes of orange and lilac and indigo as the light streamed off their thousand faces. I didn't move.

Standing over me was Axel Fleischer, his cheeks flushed, his eyes gleaming at the sight of the jewels. He was naked except for the SS officer cap on his head, tilted at an angle so that the empty eye sockets of its skull and crossbones badge were staring down at me. And his gun. He wore his gun. This was a man who loved his gun. A Walther P38 in its holster on a black leather belt slung around his hips.

He liked me to look at his body. It was lean and athletic with bands of muscle visible across his stomach and a smattering of pale blond chest hair that added a surprising touch of innocence. But chest hair can lie. A man in possession of hundreds of diamonds was not innocent.

He held aloft, at arm's length above his head, a black velvet pouch and it was from inside it that the flow of diamonds came. Stars falling from a night sky. They nipped at my flesh, took bites out of my skin, grazed a nipple. They bounced on my face and slid into a pool of ice between my breasts, and his excitement was plain to see.

'You believe me now, my Klara? When I say I have diamonds.'

I raised a hand and with the flat of my palm rolled a shimmering of the diamonds slowly up over my breasts and into the hollow of my throat.

'I believe you, Axel.' I trailed a few of the gems from my fingertips like a trickle of ice water. 'They are exquisite.'

'So are you.'

I laughed, soft in my throat, and he lowered his strong body on top of mine trapping the diamonds and the gun belt between us. They dug into my flesh.

'Where did they come from?' I asked as his full lips came down on mine.

'You ask too many questions, I'm always telling you that. It's not where they came from that matters, it's where they're going that counts.'

He was in me now, breathing hard. His hands stretched out my arms above my head, pinning me there, and I wondered whether he was pleasured by my total vulnerability in his power. Or if he was checking whether I was concealing a few stray diamonds under my armpits.

I swept my legs up around his hips and our bodies grew slick with sweat, the diamonds grinding into my skin.

'Is it from the station?' I murmured in his ear. 'Is that where you get them? From the suitcases? The ones stripped from the Jews on the trains to Treblinka?'

I ran fingers down his back, zigzagging between each rib with my fingernails, and bucked my hips, driving him deeper. He convulsed with pleasure.

'Is it?' I whispered.

'Forget where they come from,' he grunted.

I took his face between my hands and forced it back so that I could look directly into his eyes, so fogged with passion right now. I kissed the corners of his mouth that tasted of brandy and lies.

'Axel, I do not want you arrested. Take care. There are eyes everywhere around us. You must hide the diamonds.' I nestled my cheek against his. 'Somewhere safe.'

The Survivors

His eyes came into focus. Fixed on me.
'Trust me,' he said.
From his hair I plucked one stray diamond.
'Trust me,' I echoed.

CHAPTER THIRTY-EIGHT

ALICJA

Some days were better than others.

Alicja liked to look at it that way. Instead of thinking some days were worse than others. It was a decision she made each morning, whether to go with *better* or with *worse* and she made the choice by writing lists in her head. Today's list started well.

1. Her back was not so sore.
2. There were no snakes in the bed.
3. Alzbeta and Izak were sitting each side of her on the bed like bookends.
4. She was reading to them the beautiful book that Mama brought back from the passport woman.
5. Bella was on her lap – the doll from the village.
6. She was wearing her scarlet ribbon.
7. She had porridge oats for breakfast.

8. She'd seen a butterfly in camp. A silver-studded blue, veins like cobwebs on its wings. Searching for a flower.

BUT.

In the *worse* column, there was this:

1. Davide Bouvier took Mama away to Colonel Whitmore this morning.

That was it. Nothing else. But that was so huge it made the other things on her list look like ants.

Why Mama? What did the colonel want?

Has he locked you up? Has he? Has he?

Alicja could still remember the day when she was seven years old and her mother never came back. It was burned into her brain. A German soldier had marched into their tiny Warsaw apartment and told her that her mother had been locked up. She had stared at the eagle and swastika on his sleeve because she could not bear to look at his face. His uniform had smelled of rain and tobacco. His voice was brimming with kindness that meant nothing because he threw her into a harsh convent and left her there.

If Mama didn't come back this time, it would happen again. One of Colonel Whitmore's soldiers would come with the kind smiles they always gave her and throw her into a Soviet orphanage back in Poland.

Alicja knew this. So it was hard to tell herself it was one of the better days.

'Come and see.'

It was Rafal. He was grinning at her. Alicja put the book down, hid it under her pillow and followed his grin out of the hut. Alzbeta and Izak trotted behind.

'Look. What do you think?'

Alicja looked but could see nothing. Rafal had led them to a patch of wasteland behind the workshops – the metal workshop, the wood workshop and the smithy. Alicja always loved the sounds that came from them. Sawing. Banging. Welding. The shriek of metal. The hammering of nails. The curses and laughter. The smells of raw timber and molten iron. Things were made in there. Not destroyed.

Sometimes at night she feared the whole of Europe had been destroyed.

'There,' Rafal urged.

He had drawn a target on the back of one of the workshops. A bullseye drawn in chalk on the wooden planking.

'What's that for?' Alzbeta asked.

'You haven't got a gun, have you?' Izak's voice was nervous. The damaged side of his face twitched and he put up a hand to stop it.

Alicja's eyes grew huge. 'You've done it,' she said with the hushed awe used within a church. 'You've made it.'

'Made what?' Alzbeta asked.

'A crossbow,' Alicja guessed.

Rafal nodded. The grin resurfaced. His chin came up, his pitch-dark eyes shone with pride.

'Show me,' she said.

He dived into one of the rambling bushes on the wasteland and emerged with a sacking bundle in his arms. Slowly, when they had gathered around him, he unwrapped the sacking to reveal a crossbow.

All four gazed at it with reverential respect.

'It's beautiful,' Alicja said softly.

She ran her hand over its curves and taut lines, sleek under her palm. The weapon was constructed of pale wood, sanded to the smoothness of silk. It looked a bit like a wide wooden rifle with a bow attached crosswise to its barrel.

'This is the stock,' Rafal explained carefully. 'You put that part against your shoulder and your cheek against that bit. You pull back the bowstring with these two hooks and pulley. Then take aim. Release the trigger. And holy shit, watch it go! Getting the trigger mechanism to work was the hardest part.' He rested his finger lightly on the wooden trigger and for a moment was silent. 'But I managed it.'

'That could kill someone,' Izak muttered. He was the only one not to touch it.

'It could.'

'Why do you want a crossbow, Rafal? You have your slingshot,' Izak pointed out.

Rafal draped an affectionate arm around his younger friend's shoulders. 'To look after you all, of course.'

'Show us, Rafal,' Alicja urged. 'Shoot it.'

It was what Rafal had been waiting for. Smoothly and efficiently he drew back the bowstring, muscles straining, and notched it into place. The bolt that he slotted into the groove on top of the stock gave her a ripple of shock. It was a length of wooden dowel, over half a metre long with a pointed metal tip of about six centimetres. It looked lethal. Rafal raised the crossbow to his shoulder and eyed the target on the wall fifteen metres away.

'It doesn't have sights,' he said. 'Yet. So it's not as accurate as I want it to be.'

He took his time, then pressed the trigger. The bolt shot smoothly from its groove and ripped through the air. It hit smack in the middle of the target fifteen metres away with a solid thud that startled a pigeon from its perch on the roof.

'Your turn.'

Rafal held the crossbow out to her.

She took it. It was heavier than she'd expected. He had drawn the bowstring and the bolt was in place. She settled the weapon against her shoulder and pressed her cheek to the warm wood. She did what she'd seen Rafal do, shut out the noise of the camp and the hammering in the workshop. From fifteen metres away the target looked impossibly small. Above her the sky was heavy as stone and the ash-grey clouds sucked all colour from the world.

She exhaled. And pulled the trigger. The bolt flew.

It missed.

Rafal drew the bow again for her. She fired.

It missed.

Rafal notched the bowstring once more. She put her cheek to the wood. She tried to quieten her heartbeat but it was racing. So instead she pictured the wild-eyed woman in the forest who would have cut open her mother for the sake of a diamond. Her finger tightened on the trigger. The bolt cut through the air.

It hit the target.

CHAPTER THIRTY-NINE

It started to rain.

I had rounded up the four children and marched them into school, despite Rafal's insistence that he was supposed to be working in the laundry today. I assured him that his mother would not be hanging sheets out in the rain, so he would not be needed. All four children were keyed up and nervy, though I couldn't work out why. I left them at the classroom door with strict instructions to stay together, and hurried first to the laundry.

Hanna was whistling. Not a good sign. She was an avid whistler when annoyed. And she was always annoyed when it rained. The air in the laundry was the usual steamy stick-in-your-lungs soup, as workers toiled over their vats of hot water. Hanna was overseeing the heavy-duty mangles as they clanked and squeezed the life out of the sheets in preparation for the drying room. At the sight of me she abandoned them.

'Shouldn't you be teaching today?' she asked.

'This afternoon.'

'You've time for a cup of tea then.'

I laughed. Hanna's version of what she called a cup of tea came out of a bottle. She whisked us away to her cubby hole office, poured two shots of a liquid that look suspiciously like it might have come out of a ditch and we drank them straight down. It was ten o'clock in the morning.

After two shots of her *tea* my guts were on fire but the tight knot of barbed wire in my head had started to unravel.

'Bad day?' I asked.

'Rem Marek was in earlier.'

'Ah. That explains it.'

Rem Marek was the self-important chairman of the Camp Committee. He was a man with a knack for doing harm while convinced he was doing good.

'What did he want?'

'To inform me that now that UNRRA will be taking over the running of the camp next month, they have a consignment of industrial washing machines they want to install.'

'That's wonderful, Hanna. It will make your job so much easier.'

Her red cheeks grew redder. 'What the fuck do I know about washing machines? They'll put someone else in to do my job.'

'Oh, Hanna.' I wanted to throw my arms around my friend's big broad body in its ridiculous white sheet-tunic and kiss her angry cheek. 'You need to be thinking of the future out there in the big wide world. Maybe you could set up a laundry. In which case knowing how to use washing machines would be invaluable.'

She blinked at me. I could see she had forgotten that a world existed outside Graufeld Camp.

'What about your day?' She'd changed the subject. 'Bad too?'

'I came over to tell you I have sent Rafal to school.'

She shrugged. 'What is the point?'

'An education will help him, Hanna. Once he's out of here. He's a bright kid.'

She rolled her eyes at me. 'When will you learn? It's his hands he's good with. He's not brainy like your Alicja. What good will knowing the name of the kings of England do him when he's shoeing a horse?'

I let it pass. For now.

'Hanna, did you see anyone going in and out of my hut yesterday when I wasn't there? When you were keeping an eye on Alicja. Someone who shouldn't be there. I've asked the other women in the hut but no one noticed anything unusual.'

Hanna chuckled. Her bosom bobbed. 'Yeah, I heard about the snake.' The chuckle broke into a full-throated laugh. 'I bet you scared that bastard something rotten. Throwing it on his bed.'

'He scared me something rotten, I can tell you.'

She frowned, trying to remember. 'No, I didn't see anyone out of the ordinary there. It was probably just one of your kids having a joke at your expense.'

My eyes popped wide. 'What?'

She saw my dismay and backtracked fast. 'Little bastards wouldn't dare though.'

I held out my glass. She refilled it and I drank it down. 'No,' I said firmly. 'They wouldn't dare.'

But in my head I could see again my daughter handling the snake with ease. Her calmness. As if she already knew it was there.

Why?

Why would my daughter place a poisonous snake in my bed? A spike of pain twisted through me at the thought. To make me ill? To make me sick from an adder bite, not lethal, but enough to keep me in bed. For a week. Maybe two. To force me to stay away from Scholz.

Was that possible? Was Alicja trying to save me? If so, she was going about it all wrong.

I ran through the rain. It felt fresh on my skin. It tasted clean on my tongue. It was what this camp needed, a good cleaning, but on the inside where the stains didn't show. There was nobody about in the sheeting rain and I welcomed the solitude, as I swung down a side alley. It led to the western edge of the camp.

The roads were all straight as a poker, designed with military precision. This alley came to a halt at a blank two-metre-high concrete wall, fringed with barbed wire. Set into it was an oak door. It looked as if it had been looted from a castle, its carvings were so elaborate. To the side of it hung a heavy brass bell with a rope pull.

I lifted my hand to ring it, but my hand paused against my will. It floated in mid-air, its ugly stumps of fingernails hovering in front of my face.

Could I do it? In cold blood?

Now was the time to find out.

'Hello, Niks.'

The big broad Latvian from the rough-end of camp threw wide his arms. He enveloped me in a bear hug that knocked the breath clean out of me. When he'd deposited me back on the ground, he propelled me through the downpour along a slippery path that dissected a huge vegetable garden to a sturdy shed. Nicks booted open its door and launched me inside as if I were a bedraggled kitten.

'Welcome to my palace, Klara,' he boomed. His laughter shook the wooden walls.

'Thank you, Niks. This is very cosy.'

I looked around me. To be honest it looked a mess, garden equipment – spades, hoes, rakes, a muddy barrow – all jumbled together with lengths of wire and string and bits of God knows what. Odd newspapers and broken flowerpots sprawled in one corner, a rusty bicycle wheel and a box of nails in another. The light inside the shed had a fuzzy out-of-focus feel because the small window was curtained with cobwebs.

I'd have given my eye teeth for it.

The roof was sound, no leaks. And in the centre stood a beautiful handmade wooden chair with arms carved in the shape of turtles.

'It really is a palace,' I said, impressed.

The rattle of the rain on the corrugated iron roof meant I had to raise my voice.

'I've brought you a gift, Niks.'

From the pocket of my sodden coat I drew an earthenware bottle with a cork stopper. His dark fiery eyes gleamed. A grin leaped across his heavy features, puckering the five tears tattooed on his cheek and I found myself wanting to ask him about those five men he'd killed. Whether they walked through his dreams at night.

'Sit.' He waved me to the chair.

I slipped out of my coat, hung it on the hook on the back of the door to drip beside his greasy oilskin and accepted his offer. I sat down, hands resting on the turtles with a view out the window of rows of earthy cabbages bigger than my head, splashes of vivid green spinach and feathery carrot tops. And in the middle of them all sat a long colourful row of peachy pumpkins, obscene in their glossy nakedness in the rain.

'It's nice here,' I smiled.

'I don't suppose you came here to admire the view.'

He was rummaging among the flowerpots, rumbling like a giant in a doll's house, and produced two glasses from under one. He gave them a quick wipe on his shirt front. He popped the cork on the bottle and filled both glasses to the brim. He stretched out his big paw with its soiled fingernails and handed me one.

'*Na Zdorovie*,' I said, raising my glass. I swallowed a slug of the murky liquid and felt the top of my head fly off. Hanna had outdone herself.

'My friend Hanna is still waiting.'

'For what?'

'For you to turn up at her laundry one of these days.'

'You mean it?'

'Yes.'

The big man laughed again. Embarrassment made him run a hand over the black stubble on his head. 'Good.' He nodded to himself. Knocked back his drink. 'Very good.'

He leaned his bull shoulder against the wall by the window. He needed to keep one eye on his drenched domain outside.

'How is Alicja?' he asked.

'Much better, thank you. She loves her ribbon.'

He grinned at me. 'I heard about your snake.'

'It wasn't *my* snake.'

'There's only one kind of snake a man wants to put in a woman's bed.'

'No, Niks, it's not like that. Not with him.'

'It's like that with all men, my friend.'

'All the more reason for you to go visit the laundry,' I smiled.

But this time he didn't laugh. He folded his arms across his massive chest and thrust his jaw forward at me. For a moment I thought he might take a bite.

'What do you want, Klara Janowska? Why have you come here in the pouring rain?'

We stared eye to eye for a long moment. His expression

was fierce. I inhaled sharply, suddenly fearing I'd got him all wrong. The alcohol blurred the edges of my thoughts.

He leaned forward, his massive chest coming for me. 'You want me to kill the bastard?' he asked softly. 'Is that why you're here?'

'No, Niks. Of course not.'

For a moment there was just the sound of our breathing and the rain hammering on the roof.

'What then?' he demanded.

I finished off my drink. Made the muscles in my neck relax before they snapped.

'I've been thinking about what you said before.'

He screwed up his black eyes. 'What was that?' He was wary now.

'About killing rats in the camp. With rat powder.'

I heard him stop breathing. 'What about it?'

'What do you make rat poison out of?'

'Flour. Honey.' The grin came back. 'And arsenic powder.'

'Well, Niks.' I held up my glass for a refill. 'I think I have a rat under my bed.'

CHAPTER FORTY

I drew the curtain around my bed, shutting out the world. From my pocket I took out a small twist of old newspaper and just the soft touch of it on my palm made me edgy. With extreme care I untwisted it.

A white powder stared up at me, a teaspoon of it at most. It looked like flour. White. Virginal. Innocent. It was none of these things. It was lethal. As I bent over to study it, it started to rustle in its paper.

It scared the life out of me. I almost dropped it.

But it was my hand shaking.

Something in my brain was racing overtime and I struggled to slow it down. I sniffed the powder. No odour. No taste either, I'd been told.

White arsenic, it is called. The silent murderer's weapon of choice. Emperor Nero used it to kill his brother centuries ago and seize the empire. I didn't need an empire. Just a future for my daughter. Its full name is Arsenic Trioxide. As_2O_3 is its symbol. It has been a beneficial part of Chinese medicine for centuries and was a tool of the Borgias.

A ball of it the size of a pea will kill you.

It was hurting my eyes, just to look at it. I twisted the paper around it again, hiding it from my sight. But it was there. In my mind. I thrust the tiny packet under my mattress and my lungs drew in breath as if they were starved.

Could I do it? Kill in cold blood? Like a reptile.

Like a snake.

'You're jumpy, Klara.' Davide stroked my cheek. 'What's the matter?'

His eyes shone dark with concern and I leaned my face against his, so that he could not inspect my own eyes so intently. This man knew instinctively how to see behind my hardened-steel shutters. I was not used to it. To being so visible. It made me nervous. If Davide saw what lay behind. If he caught a glimpse of me. What then?

Would he still desire to hold my hand in his like this? Warm and tender. Or would he see it for the snake it is?

'Lift your shirt,' I said.

He laughed with surprise, which set him coughing. 'You don't waste time, do you?'

'I have something for you. If you roll up your shirt.'

'That sounds like an offer I'd be extremely foolish to refuse.'

He started to raise his shirt. We were alone standing in Hanna's cubbyhole of an office in the laundry, sneaking a moment of privacy. Davide had come to find me in his lunch break from Administration and I had brought him here where the air was heavy with steam. I'd peeled his jacket off his shoulders. Our bodies so close, so drawn to each other, it took an effort of will to step back.

'Look,' I said and held up a small blue bottle.

He smiled at me, ignoring the bottle. 'I'm looking.'

I dropped a light kiss on his lips. 'I happened to be at the hospital this morning and this happened to fall into my pocket.'

I popped the cork and tipped out on to my palm a small pool of nut-brown oil. Its aroma was sharp and clean and strong.

'Come here,' I smiled and moved closer.

'What is it?' He looked mildly alarmed.

'Eucalyptus embrocation. Good for lungs.'

He raised his shirt higher. It was the first time I'd seen any part of Davide naked and I felt such a stirring in my body that for a moment my resolve weakened.

Could I really hold back the truth from this man?

I had an overwhelming desire to lay my cheek against his flesh and let the words flow out that were choking me. *Please*, I wanted to say, *please listen. Please hold my head above the rising waves.*

Instead I put down the blue bottle, smiled at him in a way to make him laugh and rubbed my hands together with exaggerated glee. His chest was pale and narrow, but sinewy like a long-distance athlete's. I could see the elongated bands of muscle and sense the energy locked within them. I wanted to touch. To rub. To squeeze. To find out what Davide was constructed of.

I placed my oiled hands on his bare chest. We both felt the impact though it was a gentle touch. A jolt shot through us. He exhaled with a rush of air that brushed the side of my neck. Intimate. Erotic. An invitation. Though no words were uttered.

My hands started to massage his chest. Slowly at first, small circles with my fingertips below his collarbones. Then with the palm of my hand. Bigger. Wider. Long strokes down over his ribcage till his whole chest glistened and heat surged between our skin. I let my thumb trail along the strong ridge of each rib and I could sense the grit buried deep in there, the grit and the courage.

His gaze was on my face. Never leaving it. I bent my head forward, kissed the hollow at the base of his throat and spun him around to work on his back.

'Feel good?' I asked.

There was a long pause. 'Very good.' His voice was languid.

'Is it easing your lungs?'

'They feel brand new. Fresh off the shelf.'

I laughed. How easily Davide could do that. Reach in and pull up my laughter from wherever it was hiding. I thought I had lost it in Warsaw. My hands skimmed across his shoulder blades and over a series of ragged scars on one side of his spine. I didn't ask. He'd tell me about them when he was ready. His muscles were unknotting, his skin relaxing. As I wove patterns in the oil, something was unknotting and relaxing in me too. I didn't know what. I didn't want to know what.

'Klara, what were you doing at the hospital? I thought you stayed away from that place.'

My hands did not stall. Not for one second.

'I needed to go there.'

'Oh, is your throat—?'

'No, no, it's fine. I wanted more ointment to soothe Alicja's back.'

'I thought it was better.'

'Not quite.'

There. It was said. The moment fraying at its edges.

'So I decided,' I added, 'that it was time we did something about those lungs of yours.'

'They just handed out spare ointment?'

I couldn't see his face, but I could hear the suspicion in his voice.

'Not exactly,' I admitted.

I pressed the heel of my hand hard into a tight muscle under one shoulder blade.

'Did it jump off the shelf into your hands?'

'Something like that.'

'Klara!'

'I wanted to help. To make your lungs stop hurting.'

Slowly he turned. My hands moving from his back to his front once more. I could feel his heart thudding. He drew me into his arms, my blouse nestled tight against his oiled chest, his lips in my hair.

'Thank you, Klara.'

It was the tenderness that undid me. The loving, naked tenderness. It stripped the last layer of my defences. I buried my face in the eucalyptus-scented skin of his shoulder and the words that had been choking me came flowing out.

'In Warsaw there was an SS-Waffen officer. His name was . . .' I forced myself to let the words sour my lips, 'Axel Fleischer.'

Davide's hand cradled the back of my head. 'You don't have to tell me.'

'I do.'

Standing there in the dour little room, with steam clinging like dew to our hair and noise from the laundry rattling the flimsy door, I let the words spill out of me. I told him fast and straight. About my capture one summer night on the streets of Warsaw. The cold-blooded shooting of my friend Tomasz Chlebek. The interrogation in the basement of Gestapo headquarters in Szucha Avenue where no one could hear my screams. The beatings. The torture. The loss of my daughter.

'And who was responsible? Who do you think, Davide?'

'Oskar Scholz.'

'Let's give him his full title. SS-Waffen Sturmbannführer Oskar Scholz. He stole my child.'

I told him how I had grovelled to him. Begged. Pleaded. Never knowing whether Alicja was dead or alive.

No tears from me now, no sobs, but Davide had

murmured sounds. Of despair. Of comfort. He held me so tight I thought I would snap.

'There is more,' I whispered, lips pressed into his shoulder.

I told him about Oberführer Axel Fleischer. I mentioned nothing of his debauched tastes in bed, just that I had orders from Scholz to spy on him. And always Alicja's name hung between us, unspoken.

'Why did they let you live, Klara? Why didn't they silence you?'

I lifted my head and ran both my hands down his cheeks, under his jaw, along his taut neck.

'I was too quick for them, Davide. I escaped. But now he wants revenge.'

CHAPTER FORTY-ONE

I waited. I am not good at waiting. I waited for the sun. I needed it to come and burn away the rain that was pinning everyone inside their huts.

I needed people to be busy in the streets of Graufeld Camp, doing their living outdoors, tempted by the sunshine into letting it all happen in the open. Their whittling and their knitting. Their jawing and their laughing. Their lying and their fighting. Their strumming and their card playing.

Their card playing.

That's what I was waiting for.

Five days I had to wait. Long nervy days. Yes, I did my teaching. Yes, I kept up my reading to my four kids. Yes, I spent precious time with Davide. But always I was conscious of the twist of paper under my mattress. As if it might catch fire.

At night I lay on top of it. Eyes wide open, picturing the plain white powder. And what it could do.

*

To my surprise it was Izak I chose to help me. Not Rafal. Izak – with his burnt face and the bubble of fear he carried round with him – was easy to overlook. Downcast eyes and small apologetic frame. No threat to anybody. That's what people assumed.

But people can be wrong.

He came to me on what turned out to be the final day of rain. He clambered up beside me on the top bunk – I avoided sitting on the white powder when I could – and tucked in close. Alicja was safe with Rafal at school.

'Look at me, Izak.'

He didn't look. Gently I lifted his chin. His lip was split, a swollen bruise, as moist as an over-ripe plum, pulled his cheekbone out of shape. I drew him closer and kissed the top of his dark bushy hair to hide my dark bushy anger. In the beginning Izak had been bullied in the classroom but Alicja and Rafal had put a stop to it between them.

'Who did it, Izak?'

He took a long time to reply. 'Bolek's father.'

'Wait here.'

I ran through the rain all the way to Hut N and strode in. The family huts were always noisy, crowded with chatter and scolding, laughter and young voices. Arguments were frequent, but so was singing. I spotted the Vrubel family and headed over.

'Vrubel, you hit Izak,' I said in a raised voice.

A hush fell in the immediate area, heads turned, sensing entertainment. The Vrubel family consisted of the two parents, a grandfather and seven children. They took up a lot of space. Igorek Vrubel was playing cards with his two eldest sons but at my accusation he rose to his feet, cheeks florid, eyes brimming with discontent, bristling for a fight. He stood a head taller than I did.

'What's it to you?' he demanded. 'The kid deserved it.'

His gaze flicked behind me and I glanced round. Izak was rooted to the spot right at my heels.

'Do you know what it feels like to be hit, Vrubel?'

His children were always hiding bruises.

Without warning I slapped his sneering face. His head shot back from the impact and his fist bunched. He was about to hammer me but just in time he became aware of the onlookers. Even he knew you don't hit a woman in public.

'Stay away from Izak,' I said. 'Stay away from all my kids.'

'You bitch!'

He punched the air where I had been standing, but I had already seized Izak's hand and was on my way out. In the street I slowed my pace to my young companion's despite the downpour.

'You didn't ask why he hit me,' Izak muttered.

'I don't need to know. It was wrong. That's enough for me.'

'He was really shocked when you smacked him one.'

'We sorted him out,' I grinned at his tense face.

'*You* sorted him out.'

'You watched my back.'

His smile was so wide it set his lip bleeding again.

*

Today I will kill Oskar Scholz.

Are you shocked?

I am. The thoughts in my head are on fire.

I stood stiff and chill at the window and watched the sun rise. It nudged its way lazily above the horizon and spilled gold all over the streets of Graufeld Camp. Its grey soulless buildings were transformed into some kind of paradise. Which of course is what it was. Without Graufeld most of us DPs would be dead. However much we loathed the place. However much we railed against the control the Allied powers exerted over our lives. They were our saviours and this was the Eden they had built for us.

I rested my forehead on the cold pane of glass. It did nothing for the heat in my brain. Nothing would rid me of that except the white powder. Rafal was to be my scout. Izak was to be my proxy. It was all arranged. The girls were not to leave each other's side on pain of . . .

I was going to say *death*. On pain of death. But today there is too much death in my head to allow for more. So instead of *death*, I say on pain of my wrath. They both stared at me big-eyed and nodded obedience.

When it was only just light and the curtain was still drawn around my bed, I set to work.

The twist of newspaper under my mattress.

A brown-glass bottle of Hanna-concocted vodka.

A tiny teaspoon.

A cork.

I scooped up a tiny portion of the powder on to the spoon

and tapped it into the bottle. I shook it, then peered inside. The powder had vanished.

'How much, Mama?'

I jumped. I'd thought Alicja was still asleep.

'I don't know,' I said honestly.

We both stared at the bottle but there was no answer to be found there.

'It's very strong,' I murmured. 'The powder.'

'Put in more, Mama,' She was leaning over the edge of the top bunk, her golden hair escaping at wild angles, her concentration intense. 'Just in case.'

I breathed in. Aware of what I was hearing from my own child, I kept very still, my gaze fixed on her.

'I could stop now. Right now.'

She slid off her bunk in her thin white nightdress with the embroidery that Alzbeta had sewn on it. She removed the bottle from my hand.

'I'll hold it. You pour more in,' she whispered.

I poured.

CHAPTER FORTY-TWO

When it happened, it happened swiftly.

Rafal came running, cheeks flushed. 'He's there!'

'How many with him?' I asked.

'Three men.'

I expected the shakes. A dry mouth. Gut twisting. But I experienced none of these things. I was calm and breathing freely. I had been over and over it so many times in my head. The same way I used to run through every single move when I was laying gelignite charges under railway lines or inside the exhaust pipes of the Mercedes 170 staff cars, so beloved by Nazi officers in Warsaw.

'Izak,' I said.

He was at my elbow.

I took his damaged face between my hands. I could see the fierce determination in his jet-black eyes, feel the heat making the shiny scars throb beneath my palm.

'You don't have to do this, Izak.'

'I want to do it.'

His vehemence took us by surprise. Usually he was soft spoken. But we all knew he had lost his whole family to the gas chambers and the officer who gave that order would most likely be another from the same mould as Oskar Scholz.

I didn't kiss him. I shook his eager young hand. And I gave him the brown bottle.

'Quick, Rafal. Tell me.' I gripped his arm.

'You were right. They're sitting outside, playing poker.'

'Describe it.'

'They've found themselves stools. Four of them. Their table is a cardboard box. Scholz has his back facing this way, so he can't see me.'

'That's excellent.'

I pictured them, seated outside Hut W in a shifting patch of sunlight, dealing the cards. Smoking. Checking their hand. Placing their bets. Shoulders tense.

'What are the stakes?' I asked.

'Half-cigarettes.'

I nodded. 'Izak knows what to do. He'll be all right.'

But it was myself I was reassuring. Me who needed to believe it. Rafal and I had sat with Izak yesterday and taught him poker for six hours straight. He wasn't much good at it but he now knew how to play and what to call.

'He'll be all right,' I said again.

The other three children echoed my words. Rafal had hung around the camp's poker tables for weeks, drawn like a foolish moth to a particularly brutal flame, but Rafal was big and strong and noticeable. I couldn't take the chance that Scholz might have seen him with me. Whereas little Izak? No one noticed him. He was part of the background, part of the greyness of the camp.

Rafal became my eyes and ears. My runner. I couldn't risk going anywhere near the game myself. If Scholz spotted me, he'd know immediately that something was up, and the same was true of Alicja. We had taken up position on the dirt strip down the side of Hut N. I daren't go closer, so Rafal came and went. Back and forth between Hut W and Hut N, which meant I received my news in bite-size pieces.

Izak was hanging around. Scuffing his feet. Watching the poker game.

How does he look? Like a kid looking in a sweet shop window.

He has moved closer. Crouched on the ground.

Who is winning? Scholz. He wins every hand.

One player threw down his cards. Abandoned the game.

Izak is talking to them. Shows them his cigarettes.

He's in.

He's playing.

He's losing.

Scholz cleans out Izak. Pockets his winnings.

I am not breathing. I change our set-up. Rafal remains in sight of the game and Alzbeta becomes the runner, so that we miss nothing now.

I have our stories ready. They may just bury Scholz and leave it at that. But if the police get involved and come after Izak, he is to say he stole the vodka bottle from under my bed. To him it was vodka, nothing more. His stake in a poker game. If they then come after me – which they will – I will readily admit that I put arsenic in with the alcohol and kept it under my bed. Ready for the day when I couldn't go on. When the darkness opened up and swallowed me.

The *Polizei* would buy that. Suicides in Graufeld were not uncommon. Scholz's death was an unfortunate accident. Yes, I'm sorry, sir, that the bottle from under my bed caused his painful death but I could not have foreseen it. Izak is innocent. I am—

'Mama! Look.'

Alzbeta was haring towards us, arms flying in a panic at her sides. Her mouth open in a silent scream.

ALICJA

Alicja knew at once it had gone wrong. Alzbeta was shaking in Mama's arms. Her words wouldn't come out straight.

'He . . . lost.'

'It's all right, Alzbeta,' Mama soothed. 'Izak was meant to lose.'

Alzbeta's head was trembling. 'He . . . drank.'

Ice fingers crept around Alicja's heart. 'Who lost? Who drank?'

'Izak put the bottle. On the table.' Alzbeta's teeth started to chatter. 'They all played poker. But . . .'

Mama held her gently. Waiting for more. But worse than my friend's panic was Mama's stillness. Like the statues in the convent. Her cheeks as white as marble.

'But he lost.' Alzbeta forced it out.

'Izak lost?' Mama asked.

'No. Scholz. Lost.'

The moan that escaped Mama was like a cry from the grave. 'Tell me what happened.'

'Scholz didn't win. It was the first game he lost. The man who won was old. He snatched the bottle.'

'Did he drink any of the vodka?'

But Alicja knew. They all knew.

Alzbeta was nodding over and over again. Alicja put her hand on her friend's cheek to make her stop.

'What happened? Quickly.'

'He opened the bottle really fast. Started to drink. His old eyes were huge. Like they were going to pop. But,' she dragged in a whooping breath, 'Izak threw himself at him and knocked the bottle.'

'Did he get it?'

'It smashed. On the ground.'

Mama was uncurling her arms from around Alzbeta, but she pressed bloodless lips to her forehead. 'Stay here. With Alicja.'

Alicja took Alzbeta's hand. It was as boneless as jelly.

'Where's Izak?' Mama whispered.

'He ran.'

'And Rafal?'

'He's still hanging around there. To see what ...'

Mama was leaving. But her limbs were moving in a different way, the same way she moved in the forest when they were fleeing from the Soviets in Poland. Head forward, alert, tense. A wolf on the hunt. Alicja felt the hairs on her head rise and she wanted to cling to her, to hold her back. Mama turned her head to look, and Alicja saw something in her eyes she'd never seen before. A darkness. A night shadow. She started to shiver.

But when she blinked Mama was smiling. Her eyes were sky blue again.

'Take Alzbeta back to our hut,' she called. 'Don't worry. I'll be back.'

Alicja believed her.

CHAPTER FORTY-THREE

'No, Klara. Stay away.'

It was Rafal who had stepped into my path, arms out-stretched, barring my way.

'Don't go down there. You mustn't be seen.'

I was going to push past him but something stopped me. Rafal was different. He seemed larger, more solid. He'd grown older, not just his body, but his mind too. This was not the Rafal of an hour ago. Murder does that to you. It changes you.

'What happened to Izak?' I asked quickly.

'He's gone. Back to your hut. That's where you should go.'

'And the man who drank some of the vodka?'

'He's on the ground. Sick as a dog.'

'Alive?'

He nodded. 'So far.'

'Have the medics been alerted?'

'Yes. They'll take him to hospital.'

We looked at each other. There was a connection, an

understanding between us that hadn't been there before. We both knew what the other was going through, and I rested a hand on his broad shoulders. I couldn't help wondering if they were strong enough for this. I had asked so much of him.

'Come with me, Rafal. Thank you for what you did today. I told Izak to break the bottle if it fell into anyone else's hands, but he will need our help now. He respects you.'

He could not resist a faint smile and we turned to retrace our steps, when two large British Army soldiers suddenly materialised on each side of me.

'Mrs Klara Janowska?'

'Yes.'

'Come with us, please.'

How did Colonel Whitmore know that it was me?

I had expected this. But not this fast. The poisoned man was not even in hospital yet.

Had Scholz pointed a finger at me?

I prepared my face as I was marched towards the Administration building. Shock. Innocence. Distress. All on view for Whitmore to see. The distress was all too real. How could it have gone wrong? How could that poor man have won the vodka bottle and poured poison into himself by mistake?

How?

Unless Scholz knew. Unless he lost on purpose. No, he couldn't know. He couldn't. It wasn't possible.

Guilt gnawed at me. I wanted to rush to the sick man's

side, to hold his hand and cry 'I'm sorry'. All I could hope
for was that Izak smashed the bottle before it had done more
than touch the victim's lips. My own lips were dry and numb.
Scholz, if you are—

Wait.

The soldier had marched me past the entrance to
Administration and round towards the rear of the building.

'Wait!' I dug in my heels and came to a halt.
'Where are we—?'

But they were skilled at their job, well practised in the
art of control. Without breaking stride they each took an
arm and propelled me forward, my feet barely touching
the ground.

'Stop! I thought Colonel Whitmore wanted—'

My words died in my throat. In front of me parked at the
back of the building was an army truck. I wouldn't have
taken any notice of it, just another of the military vehicles
that buzzed in and out of the camp. This one was the usual
khaki green. A canvas cover. A wooden door on the driver's
side of the cab.

A wooden door?

I blinked. Since when did British Army trucks have
wooden doors? Then I saw the emblem on it and that was
when the fear hit. Like a grenade in my chest. I struggled
to free myself but the soldiers' grip on my arm was an
unbreakable one.

'No,' I shouted, trying to tear my arms loose. 'There's
been a mistake.'

They ignored me.

'Let me talk to Colonel Whitmore at once.'

The driver in the cab of the truck leaned out and nodded to two uniformed men who were leaning against the truck, watching me with interest. But their uniform was not a British Army one, any more than the truck door was a British Army one. My eyes travelled once more to the emblem on its side, drawn to it irresistibly the way a person is drawn to the edge of a cliff. It was a red star. The symbol of the Soviet Army.

They had come for me.

The Russians took over.

It was short and sharp. I was seized by fists that were not shy of inflicting pain. They bundled me towards the back of the truck and I fought to breathe.

'Sergeant!' I screamed at the retreating back of the British soldier. 'Sergeant, fetch Colonel Whitmore quickly.'

The one with Brylcreemed hair glanced over his shoulder at me and pulled a sympathetic face. 'Sorry, love, but he's the one who signed the transfer form. It's the colonel's decision.'

'No!'

'Yes.'

'Fetch my daughter. In ...' My mind went blank. I couldn't think. Didn't know my own hut. My own name.

The Russians hoisted me into the back of the truck.

'Alicja.' I dragged her precious name out of the blackness swirling inside my head. 'In Hut C. Let me say goodbye to her, please, please, let me—'

The Russian soldier, the one with a face like granite, elbowed me in the throat and I went tumbling to the floor of the truck. He leaped in behind me, agile as a mountain goat despite his Tokarev rifle. He yelled something at me in Russian, something I didn't understand, and the engine started. We were driven at speed to the camp gates and waved straight through.

'Alicja!' I screamed as the huts dwindled to nothing behind us.

'Fucking hell, Klara, you too? The Russian shitheads have us both.'

I wheeled round. It was Hanna.

Why?

Over and over in my head. The same question. Jerking and crashing. Why did Colonel Whitmore hand me over to the Russians? It could only be because Scholz had betrayed me – despite our deal. I'd always known he would.

Bastard. Stinking lying Nazi bastard son of a whore. I should have killed him earlier. Much earlier. But I tell you, it is not easy to kill someone in cold blood, not someone you know.

The truck jolted us. Shook our bones and rattled our teeth. The road – wherever it was heading – was rough and potholed. Cratered by bombs, torn up by tanks. Only our Russian guard with his granite face appeared not to notice. He sat on the bench opposite us, shoulders hunched, picking his teeth. His rifle slung across his knees, his eyes barely blinking and focused on us.

Hanna sat slumped beside me on a bench, handcuffed to my wrist. Our bodies touched wherever they could, our arms, our hips, our thighs, her foot hooked around mine. Seeking comfort from each other. Her white sheet tunic was slick with sweat. We spoke little after our first cries of surprise and bafflement. Neither of us had been prepared for this abrupt banishment.

'Alicja and Rafal won't be alone. Davide will take care of them,' I assured Hanna. 'Until we come back.'

But she scowled. 'And who will take care of us?'

I took her hand in mine. We didn't discuss the skin-crawling horror that lay ahead. Or the fact that we would not be coming back.

CHAPTER FORTY-FOUR

Graufeld Camp

DAVIDE BOUVIER

'Davide! Davide!'

The scream hurtled into the office. Davide leaped from his chair and Captain Jeavons abandoned his telephone call. Klara's daughter came racing through the door, arms flailing, tears streaking down her cheeks. Something molten erupted inside Davide's chest as he went to her and placed his hands on her small shoulders to calm her.

'Alicja, what is it?'

'Taken . . . they've taken . . .'

She was gasping and sobbing. The words jammed in her throat. Her whole body was shaking so hard he feared her birdlike bones would crack.

'Taken what, Alicja?'

He said *what* not *who*. Willing it to be a *what*.

'Taken her.'

There was only one *her*.

He lowered his face to hers and spoke in a quiet voice. 'Do you mean someone has taken your mother?'

She nodded. Violently.

His first thought was Oskar Scholz. Dear God, what was he doing to her?

'Where has he taken her? Did you see? Where? Tell me, Alicja. Be quick.'

'Away. Out. There.'

Her hand shot out towards the window, her fingers stabbing at the air. The impact of what she had seen seemed to kick suddenly in her stomach and she lurched forward, bent double. Her tears streamed straight down to the floor, darkening the boards. It was heart-rending to watch. Davide gathered her into his arms and she buried her face in his shirt, the way his daughter used to.

'Bring her back. Bring her—'

'Who took her, Alicja? Was it Scholz?'

'No.'

'Who then?'

'Soldiers.'

'Where did they take her?'

'To a lorry.'

He stroked her soft curls, soothed her, held her close.

'It's all right, Alicja. Shush, no need for panic. I'll find out where the lorry—'

She snapped back her head to look up at him, her face

stricken with horror. 'It was a Russian lorry. It had a red star.'

'No, you must be mistaken. There is no Russian lorry in Graufeld today.'

Captain Jeavons intervened for the first time. 'Yes, there is. I saw it out in the yard behind us earlier.'

Fear – bleak and gut-curdling – snatched at Davide. He released the child and ran for the door.

'No,' Alicja seized his sleeve. 'It is too late. She's gone. The Russians drove her away.' Her eyes were dark blue pools of terror.

The Russians drove her away.

Davide reacted by pushing Alicja down into his seat.

'Wait here,' he told her. 'Don't move. I'll be back.'

Davide knocked on the door of Colonel Whitmore's office.

'Not now,' came the response from within.

Davide knocked again. This time he walked straight in. Colonel Whitmore was seated at his desk drafting a report on the inadequacy of camp food supplies from the Niedersachsen depot in Bremen. He looked up with annoyance at the interruption.

'What is it Bouvier? I'm busy.'

'Sir, it's urgent.'

Whitmore put down his fountain pen and folded his arms across his chest. 'Go on.'

'A serious mistake has been made, sir. A Russian truck has just removed Mrs Klara Janowska from camp. I believe it is in error. I request permission for a vehicle to be despatched to retrieve her from—'

'There is no error, Bouvier.'

'What do you mean, sir?'

'I signed the transfer. To Soviet Intelligence.'

'Of Klara Janowska?'

'That is correct.'

The Colonel unfolded and refolded his arms. He looked uncomfortable. 'I'm sorry, Davide,' he said less formally. 'Really sorry. I know she was a friend of yours. But it was unavoidable.'

The silence in the room spread like water. Neither man wanted to cross it.

'Why?' Davide asked. 'Why was it unavoidable?'

'They had a warrant for her arrest.'

'On what charge?'

'For murder.'

CHAPTER FORTY-FIVE

Berlin

Have you ever felt Death hold your hand? It is the coldest thing on this earth.

I could feel it touch my fingers as the truck rattled into a cobbled courtyard. I tried to work out where we were. Clearly within a city. We had seen nothing of it from inside the truck, but there had been the noise of traffic and once I heard a church bell. We had spent at least five or six hours on the road, maybe more, so the obvious choice was Berlin. The Soviet Zone. It made sense. There would be no British protocols here. No Colonel Whitmores with their cups of tea. This was the world of the Russian bear and its claws could tear you to shreds.

The enclosed courtyard lay at the rear of a nondescript building that bore no signs of what its purpose might be, but the bland anonymity of it just made it worse. A rifle butt between the shoulder blades urged us out of the truck. We stood on the cobbles, stiff and silent. A chill wind whipped around the enclosed area and I was thankful for my coat, thin though it was. Hanna wore nothing but her ridiculous white-sheet tunic. The soldiers stared openly at her abundant breasts under the light material. Rage rose in my throat.

'Tell them everything,' I said in a low voice to Hanna. 'Tell them whatever they want to hear. Hold nothing back.'

'You too.'

Hanna's teeth were chattering so hard she could barely speak. I looked at my own hands. They were trembling. I hid them in my pockets.

'I intend to.' I gave her some kind of smile. 'You'll be out of here within an hour. They have nothing on you. This is a mistake, you'll see. You've got a laundry to tend to back in Graufeld.'

A single tear spilled from her and ran down her cheek. She nodded.

'Fuck them,' she said.

'Name?'

'Klara Janowska.'

'Nationality?'

'Half Polish, half English.'

'Age?'

'Thirty-four.'

'Date of birth?'

'First of March 1911.'

'Address?'

'Graufeld Displaced Persons Camp.'

'Husband?'

'Dymek Janowska. A Polish pilot. Killed in the war.'

'Parents?'

'They lived in Warsaw. My mother was English. That's why I am trying to get to—'

'Just answer the question. Parents?'

'Killed in the war.'

'Children?'

'One.'

'Name?'

I hesitated. I could not bear to say her name.

'Name?' Sharper this time.

Don't anger him. Don't anger him.

'Alicja Janowska.'

'Where is she?'

'In Graufeld Camp.'

'Age?'

'Ten.'

The relentless questions paused for the first time. He spoke German with a thick Russian accent. I didn't breathe. I didn't want him to think about Alicja.

'I left Warsaw to find my only remaining relative,' I told him. Whether he wanted to hear it or not. 'My grandmother in England.'

'In Warsaw you knew Sturmbannführer Oskar Scholz.'

'Yes.'

There was no point denying it.

'You were lovers?'

'No.'

'Never?'

'Never.'

'Did Scholz have a female lover?'

'I don't know.'

'Did he have a male lover?'

'I don't know.'

'Tell me something about Sturmbannführer Scholz that I don't know.

I snatched with relief at the brief moment for thought. Tried not to lick my bone-dry lips.

'He's a good dancer.'

My interrogator sighed. A quiet sound. But loud in the silence of the room. He rubbed a hand over his large bald head and kept his eyes on me. They were the stone-hard eyes of a man who has much to hide. He rose from his seat and walked over to me. For a full minute he stood in front of me without a word, while I locked my gaze on his boots. Highly polished. Well-cared for. They looked loved. Without warning he smacked a hand across my face and the impact snapped my teeth into the soft inside of my cheek.

He was gone. The door slammed behind him.

I have never been raped. But that's what this felt like. Being mauled. Probed. Ripped open. Nothing left for myself. Every part of me had become the possession of this interrogator. Except what was in my mind. That was still mine.

I was seated on a hard chair now. Handcuffs dangled from the arms of it but they were not attached to me. Not yet. In theory I could stand up. In theory I could say nothing.

In theory they could beat me to death.

This time the handcuffs were on.

This time they intended to get serious. My fear was solid and heavy. It sat in the middle of my chest, burning a hole in me.

Help me, Davide. How did you survive the slave tunnels?

I summoned up his tender smile. His intelligent eyes, warm as melted honey. I held them up in front of me to block out the bleak brown walls of the interrogation room. Behind me by the door stood two Soviet Army guards, young and lanky. I could hear them shift from foot to foot, the creak of boots. It marked the passing of time as I sat handcuffed in the hard chair, hour after hour, waiting for my interrogator to return.

How do I do it? How do I keep away the blackness churning at the edge of my brain?

I divide my brain into four sections. Into the first I place Davide. Into the second I place Alicja. The third contains the person I was before the war. And the fourth section, lit up like a Christmas tree, is the future. I spend time in each. I lean my tired head on Davide's, I feel his warm lips against mine. I play with a strand of Alicja's silken hair and watch the way her flawless skin flushes rosy pink when I compliment her. I embrace the idealistic happy young woman I used to be and then I look across the English Channel towards a future for us all in a thatched cottage. With roses trailing around the door. All right. Maybe not the cottage. Maybe not the roses. But somewhere safe and secure where we can be together.

Can you blame me?

Knowing I will not come out of this alive.

CHAPTER FORTY-SIX

Graufeld Camp

DAVIDE BOUVIER

Davide was angry. The kind of angry that doesn't let up but gnaws right through you. He was sitting with his arm around Alicja's shoulders, holding her safe, calming her tremors.

They were seated on a bench that gave them a view of the entrance gates. If they watched long enough, could they conjure Klara back? Alicja stared unblinking and wide-eyed into the distance. Davide didn't know what she was seeing, but whatever it was, it wasn't good.

He was angry at Klara's Russian captors, angry at Whitmore for handing her over without a fight. Angry at the whole bloody war, at the carnage and the vile mindless stupidity of it all. But nothing came close to his anger at himself for letting go of Klara's hand. For failing her. For not keeping her safe.

But Klara was not the easiest of women to keep safe.

*

'How did they know so soon, Davide?'

'Know what, Alicja?'

'Know about the murder.'

'What do you mean?'

Her small hand was tucked in his and he felt her fingers tighten their grip.

'How,' she said it slowly so that he would understand, 'did the Soviet Russians know about the murder when it only happened today?'

With a sense of foreboding, Davide turned to look at the young girl's pale face. He could see so much of Klara in it. 'What murder are you talking about that happened today?'

She glanced quickly up at him, then down at his hand around hers. A flush crept up her cheek, all the way to the tip of her ear, and she uttered a faint mew. But she remained stubbornly silent.

'Alicja, I'm trying to help you.'

'Thank you.'

He spoke gently. 'It's not your thanks I want. It's more information.'

He wanted to sit her on his lap and rock her, the way he had with his own daughter when she needed comfort, but instead he sat quietly beside her.

'What murder?' he asked. 'You have to trust me.'

It took a long time coming. But finally three words slipped out in a whisper. 'The card player.'

The card player.

What card player?

Then it came to him. 'You mean the one that fell ill in the poker game?'

She nodded, but didn't lift her gaze.

Davide frowned, bemused. 'Your mother did that?'

Another nod.

'Why on earth would she want to try to murder him?'

Just the word sent a chill through Davide.

'Mama didn't mean to. Honestly she didn't.' At last her frantic blue eyes turned on him. 'It was an accident. She meant it for . . .'

She halted. Looked away.

He understood. For Scholz.

'Oh, Alicja.' What do you say to a child who has witnessed such a thing? 'She is strong, your mother. And she loves you. She will fight to protect you, fight to the death. She has been taken for the moment but she will find a way back to you, just as she did before.'

'She was in the Resistance in Warsaw.'

'I know.'

'The Resistance killed Germans.'

He saw what she was looking for. 'Yes, the Germans were Russia's enemy as well. So when the Soviets realise that she was fighting on their side, they should let her go.' But he knew the Soviets shot Resistance fighters as troublemakers.

'I'll help her, Alicja. I promise you.'

She leaned against him.

Stay alive, Klara. Stay alive for your daughter.

Please. Stay alive for me.

CHAPTER FORTY-SEVEN

Berlin

'Oberführer Axel Fleischer.'

The name on my interrogator's lips seemed to fill the small room. It was too big for it. Too explosive.

'You knew him in Warsaw?'

'Yes.'

'How well?'

'Well enough.'

His hard hostile eyes did not attempt to hide his contempt. He possessed the swarthy looks seen around the Crimea and the arrogance of a Soviet Intelligence officer who held the power of life and death in this building in the palm of his hand. The dark shadows under his eyes did not fool me into believing he might regret any of his decisions.

'You were Fleischer's mistress in Warsaw.' A statement, not a question.

'Yes.'

'How did you meet him?'

'Sturmbannführer Scholz introduced us.'

'Is that so?'

'Yes, it is. At first we played chess.'

'That's not all he liked to play, I hear. Word has it that he liked threesomes.'

I stared at the floor.

'Was Oskar Scholz involved in these threesomes?'

'No, Comrade Colonel.'

'Why did he introduce you to Oberführer Fleischer? What did he gain from it?'

'You'll have to ask Oskar Scholz that.'

He moved so fast, I had no time to brace myself. The slap came again, but not with his hand this time. With the gun from his holster. Sounds erupted that should not be inside my head. I could not protect myself. My wrists were handcuffed.

'You do not tell me what I have to do, Klara Janowska.'

The pulse in my throat was too strong for me to squeeze words out. I blinked my understanding. Blood trickled down my cheek with the touch of a spider.

'Take her,' he ordered.

It went on and on. Till I thought I would drown.

The two Soviet guards carried me, still handcuffed to my chair, down a long corridor and into a brightly lit room that was tiled in dazzling white. Along the centre of the floor ran a channel that ended in a drain. For blood, I thought. For blood.

But I was wrong.

I and my chair were placed in the middle of the room. From behind a screen one of the soldiers uncoiled a wide-mouthed hose and he handled it with the ease of familiarity.

I was so stupid.

Even then I believed it was to wash away the blood they were about to spill. The other soldier turned a tap and a jet of high-velocity water exploded into the room with a roar. It almost blew my head off.

The water came at me with the force of an iron bar. Hammering. Punching. Thumping. Thundering into my ears. My eyes. My nose. I fought to breathe. To steal a pocket of air within the torrent of water. It slammed into every inch of me.

Into the chair. Which shot across the tiles and crunched on to its back, taking me with it. Pain and water. Nothing else existed. I thought the torrent would stop then. But it didn't. It kept coming.

Don't think that I didn't beg.

Because I did.

Whatever had once existed inside my head had drowned. I sat slumped in the chair. Chin on my chest. Blood on the handcuffs.

I could barely open my eyes a crack. It might have been the interrogation room I was in or it might not. I no longer cared. In front of my face I could make out a patch of khaki-brown. It took a while for me to work out that it belonged to my interrogator. He was talking. But his words sounded underwater. They came nowhere near my ears.

Abruptly the patch of Soviet uniform transformed into a pair of eyes. A nose. A mouth in a hard, tight smile.

'Welcome back, Klara.' He unlocked my handcuffs.

My tongue tried to move inside my mouth. It was slow and heavy.

'Klara, can you hear me?'

My tongue was getting there.

'Klara, you are a sodden mess. We can go on engaging with the hose all night, if that's what you want. But I don't believe it *is* what you want.' The eyes seemed to climb inside my head. 'Now, Klara, let's talk about the murder.'

'I know nothing about a murder. Except the murder of the Jews in the Warsaw Ghetto.'

He released a long impatient sigh. 'More importantly, let's talk about diamonds.'

'Go fuck yourself.'

The smile dropped from his face.

I honestly think he would have killed me there and then had the door not burst open, sending waves of garbled sound washing in and out of my brain.

'Comrade Colonel,' a frightened voice said something urgent in Russian.

I heard it then. A siren.

It was panic. But an orderly panic. Russian-style. The corridor was heaving. The stink of sweat heavy in the air.

Uniformed men in a hurry, desperate to get out of the building. Pushing. Elbowing. Shouldering a pathway. Shouting orders. Young faces wide-eyed with fear.

I had no room left inside me for fear. Nor panic. I forced my mind to think.

Was it a fire? I could smell no smoke.

My guard had clamped his grip on my arm and dragged me out into the crush of bodies all struggling to reach the top of the stairs. My sluggish brain remembered now. The stairs. That's what was causing the jam. We were on the first floor. But my bruised and battered muscles rebelled against fighting my way through it, with legs limp as rags. I dug in my heels. I became a dead weight on my guard and he quickly abandoned me to make his own escape.

I groped my way to a wall. I leaned against it. Relief enveloped me and my wretched brain cells started to wake up.

Hanna.

Where the hell was Hanna in this stampede?

The crush was thinning now but those who were left were moving faster. I pushed myself off the wall and was immediately run down by a lithe young soldier.

'*Prostite*,' he said and helped me to my feet.

He had the sort of face and shoulders that looked all wrong in a city. They belonged on a farm behind a plough. He looked at me, took in my sodden hair, my drenched clothes and his wide-open face shut down with distaste. Not for me. But for what he saw. He knew where I had been.

'*Bystro!*' he said.

He took my elbow in his large calloused hand and barged a path down the stairs for me. At the bottom he pointed towards the large entrance where everyone was streaming out into the street, panic still stamped on their faces.

'*Bombit*,' he said.

I stared blankly. 'A bomb?'

'*Da*.' He nodded.

'The war is over. No more bombs.'

And then it hit me. An unexploded bomb. The lethal metal canisters lay scattered throughout the cities that had been targets during the war. Bombs that had been dropped from aircraft but failed to explode on impact. Lethal killers biding their time. Hiding in cellars, waiting to do their job.

In the basement of this building?

My new friend pointed at me and then at the corridor that led to the back of the building. He gave me a gentle push in that direction. I got the message. If I went out the front door I would be rounded up instantly and the interrogations would start all over again somewhere else.

'*Spasibo*.' My only word of Russian. 'Thank you.'

I raced as fast as my wobbly legs would carry me to the rear of the building. It proved to be a maze of doors and narrow corridors. They were already deserted. I felt the wheels slow in my head, my thoughts stopped falling over each other.

Find the back entrance.

Think. Where? Where is it?

Look for the kitchens.

I threw open doors. One turned out to be an empty

military-style canteen. Behind it lay a kitchen. I rushed in.
And stopped dead.

Hanna was leaning over the sink, a trickle of blood dripping from her nose.

'What the fuck are you doing here?' Hanna dashed the blood
away with a cloth, ran over from the sink and clasped her
arms around me. 'Oh Klara, you look a mess. But you're still
in one piece.'

The warmth of her body in its stupid scrap of white sheet,
tight against mine, slipped something loose inside me. I had
been holding everything back – the fear, the certainty I
would never see my daughter or Davide again, the rage and
throat-searing anger. The humiliation. The crippling sense
of failure. The desire to scream. The closeness of death. The
pain. The stubborn refusal to let go of my dreams.

It all came. A great tidal wave of it engulfed me and spilled
into tears pouring down my cheeks. I tried to shake them
away. Now was the wrong time. I wiped my wet sleeve across
my nose and cheeks, but the tears wouldn't stop.

'Look at you, girl.' Hanna squeezed the breath out of me.
'Let's get our backsides out of this hellhole before the bloody
bomb blows our brains into confetti.'

We found the back door. It had been left wide open from
when the kitchen staff made a run for it. Not a soul was in
sight in the narrow street, just shadows ducking out of the
wind. Everyone had fled. The building could disintegrate
in a violent hail of bricks and glass at any moment. I was

wet and sore and shaking like a dog in a storm, but I had the sense to snatch two brown coats from a row of them on hooks behind the back door.

It was that moment just before twilight. A sky of grey and ash with darkness fringing its edges. Nothing was stable, nothing stayed the same. Berlin lay before me and somewhere in it was one place I needed to find.

CHAPTER FORTY-EIGHT

Graufeld Camp

DAVIDE BOUVIER

The man looked sick. Worse than sick. He looked as though he had already slipped one foot into the grave. He lay unmoving in the Graufeld hospital bed, eyes closed, skin grey as old bones, except where a livid rash marked his cheeks and chest. The only sign of life was his laboured breathing. Davide watched the rise and fall of the man's ribcage and willed it to keep working.

If he died . . .

Merde. Klara!

Haven't we all seen enough death? Time for it to stop. To finish. Let it go, Klara. Let it go.

The man in the bed groaned as if in pain. Davide took his hand. 'It's all right, *mon ami*, you aren't alone. They are fine doctors here, they are taking good care of you.'

The hospital ward was busy, full of chatter, of comings and goings, of nurses offering professional smiles.

'How is Helmut Gessler doing?' he asked one bright young British nurse in a small starched cap who came to check the bed chart and take the patient's pulse.

'He is doing well,' she said confidently. 'Improving by the hour. He's a fighter.'

Davide studied the man again. *Improving* was not a word he'd have used to describe the limp figure between the sheets. He kept vigil for an hour at the bedside. He asked himself how he would feel if it were Oskar Scholz lying here in the sickbed, Oskar Scholz's hand looking as if it had lost its grip on life despite being a fighter.

If Oskar Scholz had threatened the life of his daughter, he'd have done the same.

As Davide left the hospital a small shadow tucked into place at his side. He glanced down. It was the slight, dark-haired boy with the disfigured face, the one that hung around Klara. The one that joined the poker game. What was his name? Izak, that was it.

Davide patted the boy's shoulder. 'You all right, Izak?'

The boy looked tense. Curled into himself. He didn't answer, but kicked a stone and slowed his pace to Davide's. 'Is he going to die?'

'Helmut Gessler?'

'Yes.'

'No, don't worry. They say he is improving.'

The dark eyes shot a look at Davide. 'I want him to die.'

'He has done nothing to deserve it, Izak.'

'He is German.'

Davide stopped walking and stood face-to-face with the boy. 'The war is over,' he said gently.

Izak put a hand to the terrible slippery burn scars that distorted one side of his face. 'This isn't over,' he said.

'There are people who can help you, Izak. Doctors. Surgeons who rebuild faces.'

The boy allowed a flash of hope to show, then smothered it. 'Where have they taken her?'

'To Berlin, I suspect. And Hanna too. How is her son?'

'Rafal? He wants to kill Scholz. He says he's the one who set the Soviets on them.'

'We have no proof of that.'

'We don't need proof.'

'If you say that, Izak, you are no better than the Nazis.'

The boy's eyes filled with tears. His narrow chest heaved.

'Izak, the hating has to stop somewhere. We can't build a future on hate.'

Davide rested an arm on the boy's shoulders, expecting him to pull away, but he didn't. Together they walked on in silence until Izak kicked at another stone.

'Berlin is far away,' he muttered.

'Yes. It's in the Soviet Zone of Germany. In the east.'

'How will she get back?'

It was Davide's turn to kick at a stone. 'She'll find a way.'

CHAPTER FORTY-NINE

Berlin

Berlin was a city in ruins. The guts had been ripped out of it. As I moved, appalled, through the rubble I grieved for the starving city. It was not Berlin's fault that it had fallen into the hands of a madman whose dream was to own the world.

Three hundred and sixty-three air raids. Think of it. Picture the skies black with bombs. I was told in Graufeld Camp that in one air raid last February 1,000 B-17 Flying Fortress bombers and nearly 600 P-51 Mustangs had decimated much of the city. Thousands killed. The injured screaming in the streets. Fires raging. Thousands more people homeless.

A city in tears.

Just as my beloved battered Warsaw lay in tears.

Hanna and I picked our way through the ruined streets. It was a ghost town, a *Geisterstadt*. Skeletons of buildings loomed around us and vast piles of masonry had changed the landscape of the city. It would be hard to navigate my way through it.

Before leaving Warsaw last spring I had studied Axel Fleischer's map of Berlin, committed it to memory so that I would know my way to the district of Prenzlauer Berg. But now? Landmarks were gone. Street names had crumbled in the dirt.

I was lost.

'Hanna, what happened? How did you end up in the kitchen?'

'I was doing the same as you, looking for a back way out of there. One of the bastard guards put a fist in my face.' She touched her swollen nose with a fingertip.

She told me she was questioned. About me. About Oskar Scholz. About what I'd told her concerning my life in Warsaw. Had I ever mentioned Axel Fleischer?

'They didn't hurt me, if that's what you want to know.' She ruffled my short hair affectionately. 'They were probably saving the thumbscrews for tomorrow.'

'I'm sorry, Hanna.'

'For what?'

'That your friendship with me put you in danger.'

'It's not you who put me in danger, Klara. It's the bastard Russians who did that. But when someone started running round yelling "unexploded bomb", my shit-faced interrogator took to his heels like a whipped dog.' She chuckled. 'So I went looking for you and an escape route.'

'Thank you, Hanna.' I felt choked with gratitude but knew

she would not welcome a fuss. I rested my shoulder against the cushion of hers. 'I'll get you out of here, I promise.'

She looked at the mess around us. 'Where the hell do you start?'

'There.'

I pointed. Two hundred metres ahead of us a string of about thirty women were crawling over a bombsite, the way ants crawl over a crushed peach. Thin grey figures in headscarves. They were the *Trümmerfrauen*. The women who sift bricks from the rubble. Moving from bombed building to bombed building. Scrabbling, finding, scraping, cleaning. Reclaiming bricks to be used in the reconstruction of Berlin.

Sixty-thousand *Trümmerfrauen* were employed by the city at the pittance rate of twelve Reichsmarks for every thousand bricks cleared. When I approached one, she straightened her bent back with a groan and a smile, welcoming the respite from the task. They were clearly hurrying to finish before darkness claimed the streets.

'*Entschuldigung,*' I said, 'could you help me, please? I'm trying to get to the Prenzlauer Berg district.'

The woman wiped her face on her sleeve. Both were covered in cement dust. She indicated back the way we had come and reeled off a list of directions involving crossroads, blockages, shortcuts and side roads. Her tired eyes inspected us with interest. I didn't like to think what we looked like.

'Be careful,' she warned, lowering her voice. 'You're not from around here, are you? If a policeman stops you, he will demand to see your identification papers. Best to avoid them.

If a Soviet soldier stops you, run like hell. He will demand far more from you ladies.'

Hanna gave a sharp laugh.

I thanked our guide. In the pocket of my stolen coat lay two hand-rolled cigarettes. I pulled one out and handed it over to the woman coated in her shroud of grey. She tucked it behind her ear.

'Thank you,' I said, 'for your help.'

She shrugged. 'We all need a bit of help these days.'

There were pockets of Berlin's streets still standing. Stretches of road still lamplit. The wide main thoroughfares had been cleared so that traffic and trams could move freely along them. But they were dangerous. Police patrolled them and armed Soviet soldiers stood on street corners looking for easy prey.

We moved fast, but warily. And we kept to the side streets. They were tough to navigate as darkness deepened and few had street lamps that worked. Twice we were challenged but each time we didn't wait to argue. We ducked into the maze of broken buildings, which offered a million places to hide, and we didn't move till our pursuer had abandoned the hunt.

'Klara?'

'Yes?'

'How much further?'

'Not long now.'

'For us? Or the journey?'

I made an effort to laugh and drew her arm through mine

to help take the weight off her feet. 'At least we're warm.'

The coats were good wool, but every swirl of the chill night wind threw rubble dust in our faces. Hanna peered at me, our noses almost touching, barely able to see each other in the blackness.

'Klara, what are you doing?'

'I'm looking for Oderberger Strasse. I'm trying to get us out.'

'Is that so? It feels to me like you're trying to get us in deeper.'

I smiled. 'You know me too well, my friend.'

By some miracle Oderberger Strasse in the Prenzlauer Berg district was still standing, spared by the Allied bombs. The sight of it brought back memories of Warsaw, sharp as arrows, memories of Axel Fleischer's lips trespassing on parts of my body that were not his. In his wallet a carefully folded photograph of his wife on horseback, her face a perfect sepia oval. Too small to make out her features clearly, however hard I looked. At the cinema his hand hot and possessive on the back of my neck.

Far worse. The smile on his face when he boasted of Hitler's plans to exterminate Warsaw's Jews and raze the city to the ground. To build a new Germanic one in its place. We did fight back hard. In the summer of 1944 the Warsaw Uprising was a titanic battle, sixty-three days of hand-to-hand street fighting to defeat our German occupiers, by the courageous Poles of Warsaw. But we lost and were made to pay the price. Sixty per cent of our population was slaughtered. Eighty per cent of our houses destroyed.

And one of our overlords, who was among those at the heart of this savage destruction, was lying in my bed. I should have stabbed him. A knife into his throat in the middle of the night. That's what you're thinking. You can't imagine how close I came. Twice I touched the blade to his skin. Twice I drew back.

Why?

Because of reprisals. Himmler would have ordered what was left of my city to bleed to death. Ten thousand inhabitants would have been shot in exchange for my one Oberführer. It was the way they did things in the Waffen-SS.

'Are you okay?' Hanna nudged me.

'Yes.'

'Sure? You look—'

'I'm sure. Let's get moving.'

Amber light from the lamps fell in pools on the cobbles at regular intervals along the street. We hurried through them, heads down, past the magnificent Oderberger public bathhouse. It seemed unfair for a bathhouse to exist, however beautiful, while people's houses lay in the dust.

I halted in front of a black oak door with a tarnished knocker. There were five doorbells. I pressed the second. Nothing happened. I was nervous, though I had no reason to be. I had run through this moment a thousand times in my head.

Hanna lost patience and banged the knocker. After a

minute it was opened by a youngish man with a neat ginger beard and crutches. He had lost a leg but still had a military bearing and a bar of medals on his jacket. He regarded us the way he must have regarded enemy snipers in the dark.

'*Guten Abend*,' I said politely. 'I am looking for Frau Fleischer.'

'She is no longer here.'

I had warned myself to expect this, but still my stomach crawled up to my throat.

'Fräulein Huber lives in the apartment now,' he added.

'Magdalena Huber? She is here?'

'She is.'

'May I speak to her, please?'

'Does she know you?'

'No.'

'Your name?'

'Frau Janowska.'

He looked from me to Hanna and back again, doubt written over his face. 'Wait here,' he said. 'In the hall.'

He swung off on his crutches and manoeuvred himself with impressive skill up the first flight of the wide staircase. We heard him knock on a door. A low murmur of voices, then his head reappeared over the handrail of the wrought-iron banister.

'Come up, Frau Janowska.'

Hanna and I ran up the stairs.

CHAPTER FIFTY

Graufeld Camp

DAVIDE BOUVIER

'I've been expecting you.'

Oskar Scholz was leaning against the corner of his hut, smoking a cigarette. He was watchful. He had obviously been waiting for Davide to turn up, a scarf wrapped around the lower half of his face. His spectacles still cracked. The wind was sharp, chasing brown dust from the barren fields and throwing it about the camp. Clouds skidded across a dull white sky that stole all colour from Graufeld, leaving it stark and bloodless.

'So she has gone,' he said.

'Thanks to you,' Davide responded. He didn't hide his anger.

'I had nothing to do with it.'

'It was what she feared. That you would report her to the authorities for what happened in Warsaw.'

'I reported her to no one.'

'You're lying. Someone contacted the Soviets. You are the one who wanted her removed before she informed on you as a war criminal.'

'Is that what you think? Is that what she told you?'

Davide was not a violent man. He used to be a scientist, a protector of life, not a taker of life, until forced to work on Wernher von Braun's death rockets. But despite everything he had said to the boy Izak about letting go of hate, he now had a desire to take hold of this man. To beat him to the ground for what he had done to Klara. Already she could be lying dead in some Soviet mass grave. To beat him till he was begging for death.

Scholz studied Davide for a long moment. 'You care for her too much,' he said at last.

They walked the inside perimeter of the camp. Side by side, they talked. Not face-to-face. Face-to-face would have sparked too many clashes, too many challenges, emotions would have spilled too fast.

'Walk with me,' Oskar Scholz had said. 'And I will tell you the truth about Warsaw, Davide Bouvier.'

'I have heard the truth from Klara. I don't need your filthy lies.'

'What makes you think her version is the truth?'

'Because I trust her.'

'You are at fault there. She has given you no reason to trust her. You know what she is capable of. Look what she tried to do to me. Klara and I had a deal that both of us would remain silent, yet she tried to poison me. And she used a child to do it, so that her hands would remain clean. Tell me, Davide, is that a woman you can trust?'

'I am reporting you to Colonel Whitmore as a Nazi war criminal. Klara is beyond your reach now, so your deal is null and void. I do not need to keep silent to protect her.'

Davide turned on his heel to head directly for Colonel Whitmore's office. He could at least do that for her.

'First,' Scholz said quietly, 'walk with me. And I will tell you the truth.'

'The murder.' Scholz said the word carefully. The way you would handle a grenade. 'Let's talk about that.'

'Which murder are we talking about?' David said sharply. 'The ones committed by you? The time you murdered her friend in the street when you arrested her? Don't look surprised. Yes, she told me about that. Or the murders committed by you and Axel Fleischer every day of the week on the streets of Warsaw because he liked the smell of blood? And because Hitler wanted the Poles destroyed. Are those the murders you want to discuss?'

They were walking fast. Too fast for Davide's comfort. His lungs tightening in the cold. They were at the distant end of the Recreation field, far from the other DPs.

'Did she tell you,' Scholz asked in a polite tone, not rising to Davide's anger, 'about the murder in the nightclub?'

'What nightclub?'

'The nightclub called the Glass Slipper. The one in which Klara Janowska murdered thirty-two people.'

'Klara liked nightclubs, Davide. She came alive in them. Sometimes she could be tight-lipped at home, but in the hot, crazy, wild world of nightclubs, she lit up. She burned so bright she put all other women in the shade. You may not think it now when you see her here. Here she is drab. No flesh on her skinny bones. Her clothes looking like shit. But in her jewels and her finery and her hair like a river of golden silk down her back—'

'Klara is never drab.'

Scholz gave a wry smile. 'Maybe not. But her appearance is not what it was. You may think she doesn't care about looking the way she does now, but I know her. She adored what she got from Fleischer, the rings and the necklaces and the fine gowns. She flaunted them.' He laughed, a happy laugh. 'I was a fool.' He halted and lit a cigarette, struggling for a flame in the wind. 'Like you are a fool, Davide,' he added, exhaling smoke. 'She played us both for fools.'

Davide had heard enough. 'I am not the kind of fool who falls for your lies, Scholz.'

'No, just for hers.'

'Go to hell, Scholz. I am informing Colonel Whitmore that—'

'Wait.' He rested his large hand on Davide's arm. Not hard. Just enough to detain him. 'Let me tell you about that night at the Glass Slipper.'

*

'She looked like a goddess.' Scholz smiled at the memory. 'Sheathed in silver. A diamond choker on her long swan neck. We all sat at a table together – Fleischer and his hangers-on. And Klara of course. It was Fleischer's birthday and he was making a big celebration of it to impress his guest of honour, Ferdinand Von Sammern-Frankenegg. One of Hitler's favourites.

'Klara likes important men. She laps up their attention. When Sammern-Frankenegg paid her scant attention, she did what she always does when ignored. She turned a cold shoulder on him and made a point of dancing with everyone else of rank in the room. She even danced with me. A rare honour.

'Halfway through the evening, people started being sick. Collapsing on the floor. I'm sure you know what is coming. The punchbowl was poisoned with arsenic. Thirty-two people died. As many again were seriously ill. Not just German officers. Their wives as well. Even Polish industrialists who were there. Screaming in agony.

'I know it was Klara. I saw her do it. It looked to everyone else like an attack against the regime by an agent of the Resistance, but I knew her better. It was an attack on the highest-ranking officer in the room who was ignoring her – Sammern-Frankenegg. But he drank whisky. As did Fleischer. As did I. We survived.

'All Polish people in the room were questioned. I saved her. I said she was with me all the time on the dance floor. I lied for her. Risked my own neck for her. I accused the waitress who was serving the cake. I had her shot that same night in front of everybody.

'Do you know what Klara did?

'She slapped my face. For saving her life.'

CHAPTER FIFTY-ONE

Berlin

'Come in, please,' said the tall woman in the doorway. 'It is chill out here on the landing.'

It was scarcely less chill in the apartment. My eyes were greedy to see it. To see the elaborate cornices, the intricate ceiling bosses. The tall elegant windows and the beautiful period furniture. The vast gilded mirror. Yes, Axel Fleischer would have liked that. I could picture him strutting in front of it, flaunting his specially tailored Oberführer uniform and highly polished jackboots.

The room smelled of him. It couldn't, I know. But it did.

'Thank you for seeing us, Fräulein. I am Frau Janowska and this is my friend, Frau Pamulska.'

Magdalena Huber's face was not accustomed to smiling much but she waved us to a pair of armchairs beside the unlit woodstove with old-world courtesy. Her manner was that of a headmistress. Which is what I knew she had once been.

315

Her mousy hair was swept up into a thick old-fashioned bun on top of her head, adding to her already exceptional height. Her skin was unusually pink and she was painfully thin, but almost everyone in Germany was painfully thin.

'I am looking for Frau Fleischer,' I said. 'I believe she used to live here. Do you know where she is now?'

She chose to stand in front of us, rather than to sit. There was no flicker on her face as she said, 'Waltraud died in an air raid. In the cinema. Early this year.'

'And Rudi, her son?'

'He was with her. She took the boy to see *Der Schneemann*. They were both killed. He was . . .' She closed her eyes and shook her head mutely.

'Nine years old,' I murmured. Almost the same age as Alicja. 'I'm sorry.'

'You knew them?'

'No. I knew her husband, Axel Fleischer, in Warsaw. He told me about them. And you. He told me about you, how much he admired you and relied on you. He called you *wunderbar*.'

It was as if I'd lit a fire inside her. Her pink cheeks burned and her hazel eyes glowed. The sadness that hung from her bony shoulders evaporated.

'He said,' I continued, 'that you were far more than just a tutor to his son Rudi. You ran the household while his wife spent her days shopping for gowns. That's what he said.'

Magdalena Huber sat down, stiff at first. 'Thank you, Frau Janowska,' she said formally.

But slowly she started to fold forward on herself till her shoulders were almost resting on her long thin thighs. Her hands covered her face. She made no sound. Her body silent and immobile. Minutes ticked past while Hanna and I waited for the wave of grief to pass. Finally I could not bear her loneliness anymore and I went over, knelt beside her and laid a comforting hand on her back. I could feel the tremors within her.

'Did Axel know you loved him?' I asked softly.

'I didn't think he even noticed me.' Abruptly she straightened up, spilling off my hand. 'Were you his mistress in Warsaw?'

'Yes, I was.'

'Did you love him?'

'No, I didn't love him.'

She nodded. 'I understand. Why would you love a German?'

She rose to her full height and smiled sadly. 'I have no food or drink to offer you, I'm sorry. I have nothing in the house.' She glanced down at her fleshless hands. 'We are all starving to death and when the winter snow comes, we will lie down and die. The cemeteries will be overflowing.'

I took her hand in mine and chafed it to bring warmth into it. Beside the cold woodstove sat a pile of chopped-up chair legs waiting to be burned, but clearly she was saving them for winter. I glanced around at the fine pieces of Axel's antique furniture. The cabinets already stood empty. The pictures had been stripped from the walls. The chairs would all be reduced to kindling before the year was past.

'Fräulein Huber,' I started, my mouth dry as I framed the words in my head, 'I have one question to—'

A sudden raucous noise – like a goose having its neck wrung – burst through the apartment and made Hanna reach for the paperknife lying on top of the desk in the corner of the room. I spun round to face the door, pulse thumping.

Magdalena Huber creased with laughter at our alarm. 'It's only Charlie,' she assured us. 'He's hungry.'

'Who the hell is Charlie?' Hanna demanded.

'He's my friend. Come and meet him.'

Hanna and I exchanged a look but followed her to what turned out to be a green-tiled bathroom. As soon as the door was opened, a fishy smell hit us and out trotted a very irate, tall but scrawny bird with feet like yellow dinner plates.

'Charlie is a pelican.' Fräulein Huber smiled fondly at the creature and patted its ruffled feathers. 'I called him Charlie after Charlie Chaplin because he has big feet and makes me laugh.'

The bird was ugly and bad-tempered, and his long beak looked like a lethal weapon. I backed away uneasily but Hanna was grinning from ear to ear.

'Roast dinner tonight!' she laughed.

Magdalena Huber gave her the kind of look she must have given Axel's young Rudi when he stepped out of line. 'Charlie came to me when they tried to move all the animals in Berlin Zoo to safety from the bombing and he escaped. I daren't take him back because there are too many

Berliners out there with the same barbaric thought as you, Frau Pamulska.'

She didn't want to lose her odd friend, I could see that. 'What do you feed him on?'

'Fish, of course.'

Hanna grunted. 'You starve, while your ugly friend here gets to dine on fish?'

The creature rubbed the side of its head against Fräulein Huber's thigh, rolling its yellow eye. 'We have a friend, don't we Charlie, a fisherman called Erich. He goes out in his rowing boat on the Hafel for us.'

I stared at Hanna. But she didn't hear what I heard. She was too busy imagining succulent pelican stew.

'Fräulein Huber, I have one more question to ask,' I said.

She must have noticed something in my voice, something that told her this is why I had come. Her head turned sharply. Her intelligent eyes studied me.

'Ask it,' she said.

'Axel Fleischer had a sister.'

She raised an eyebrow in surprise. 'That's true. Irmgard Köhler is her name.'

'I believe she lives somewhere near Hanover.'

'Yes, she did. But I have no idea whether she is still there or even if she is still alive.'

'Do you have her address?'

Our gaze fixed on each other, this proud woman and myself. What did she see when she looked at me? What did I see in her? I believe we both saw a part of ourselves, a part

319

we were terrified of losing: blind conviction that we could make life better if we worked at it hard enough.

'Come,' she said.

We followed her back into the salon, Charlie slapping along behind us. She opened the delicate rosewood desk in the corner – soon destined for the fire, no doubt. After several minutes she handed me a piece of paper with an address written on it.

'Don't harm her,' she said.

I felt blood flush to my cheeks. Is that what she'd seen in me?

'Fräulein Huber, thank you.' I offered her a grateful smile. 'Does your fisherman friend ever fish at night?'

I'll say this for Magdalena Huber, she knows how to pick her friends. Within an hour we were in a cart that reeked of fish, trundling through the city behind a broad-in-the-beam grey mare. She had an odd rolling gait with a long stride and constantly swivelled her ears, but she pulled hard and didn't hang about.

We were travelling with Erich, Magdalena's fisherman. He was small and reflective, a man who thought before he spoke. He was clearly devoted to Magdalena, regarded Charlie as a naughty child, and took to Hanna immediately with her loud-mouth cussing and mobile bosom. Of me he was cautious. I didn't blame him. I'd be cautious too.

He warned us about the city curfew. No one was allowed on the streets between eleven o'clock at night and five in the

morning. It was strictly enforced with a fine of 150 marks
if caught.

'We have to get you ladies off the streets before curfew,'
he told us.

'What about you?' I asked.

He tapped the side of his nose. 'Too slippery for them
Russkie knuckleheads.'

From Oderberger Strasse we rode seated in the back of
the cart with a stinking tarpaulin over our knees that kept
the night's chill off us. It was just before nine o'clock, so
Erich did not expect trouble, but if we were stopped, neither
of us possessed identity papers. The roads were dark, with
spasmodic street lamps and piles of rubble to catch out the
unwary. But Erich knew what he was doing. He manoeuvred
us safely on to the long straight road that would take us all
the way to the Olympic stadium.

As soon as we were passing through Tiergarten, savagely
stripped of its trees for fuel, the horse picked up its feet and
I felt hope flutter its wings inside me.

Hanna fell asleep, her head resting on my shoulder. There
was something soothing about the rhythmic clopping of the
mare's hooves in the darkness. I could so easily have forgotten
the danger and let my chin droop to my chest if it weren't for
the patrols of Soviet soldiers, which sent shivers through me.
But Erich was right. They took no notice of us. A workman
and his women on their way home. Nothing of interest.

I don't know how long we travelled. An hour? Maybe

nearer two. Time seemed to lose its meaning. The night was cold but not wet, for which I was thankful. I tried to ignore the hundreds of burned-out hulks of cars hunched on the sides of the road, grim reminders of the bombing raids and flash fires that blackened the city. I didn't smell the river but clearly the horse did. Its ears pricked forward and I saw Erich's back straighten in anticipation. I tried to thank him for what he'd done for us, but he would have none of it.

He stabled the mare in a barn, his movements swift and silent, and while I waited I could see the moonlight picking out the bulk of the Olympic stadium, built for Hitler's Berlin Games in 1936. Erich had brought us to Pichelsberg, between Charlottenburg and Spandau. We were to continue from here by boat.

'Come,' Erich hissed.

We followed on his heels, down towards Wannsee. The path was deserted and I could hear the murmur of the river. To my horror, Erich started to vent his fury loudly at the filthy state of the rivers Spree and Havel, so polluted by industry and excrement that the barbels, which used to be his main catch, had vanished. He was making do with roach and gudgeons. And eels at night. It was a good thing Charlie liked eels, he laughed.

The night was colder on the riverbank than I had expected and I pulled my coat tighter around me. His boat was blunt-nosed, moored under the overhang of a tree, and once we were all safely aboard, Erich's words dried up. There was only the water.

He rowed through the darkness in silence, just the pull of the blades through the water. Long easy strokes that carried us further downstream towards the borders of the Soviet Zone, the chill wind in our faces. Being on water does something to you. It soothes the soul. Being on water in darkness is just you and the stars.

But every minute that I was away from my daughter at Graufeld Camp, Oskar Scholz was still there. With only Davide to stand between them.

CHAPTER FIFTY-TWO

Graufeld Camp

DAVIDE BOUVIER

The light in Graufeld Camp was fading fast. The DPs withdrew from the streets into their huts and lit the stoves. Nights
were always the worst, the darkness never-ending. The
winter was coming and it could only get worse.

Davide was still on his route march outside with Scholz.
He was cold. Hearing things about Klara that he had no wish
to hear did that to him. What he realised was that Scholz
loved to talk about her, to say her name. He rolled it round
his mouth the way he would a fine wine.

'How many bloody times are you two going to circle this
wall?' A man with a pinched face stepped out in front of
them. 'You've been at it for hours. It gives me the fucking
creeps, it does.'

The man was looking for trouble, bored and in need of

324

fun. His idea of fun was to put his fist in a face. This happened somewhere in the camp every hour.

Davide neatly sidestepped the burly figure blocking their path, but Scholz took the comments personally. Or maybe he too was after some fun. It only took five seconds. He seized the man's ears and at the same time raised his own knee. The sound of kneecap splintering nasal bone and cartilage was like stepping on a bunch of snails. Wet but brittle.

Scholz moved on with no comment.

As they passed behind the laundry and felt the blast of warm air expelled from its vats of boiling water, Davide lingered, inhaling the steam into his tight lungs.

'You love her, don't you?' he said.

It caught his companion by surprise. Scholz shook his head vehemently.

'No. Klara is a clever, scheming, lying, selfish bitch who uses men to get what she wants. Including you. Why the hell would I love her?'

They walked on in uncomfortable silence for most of half a circuit along the perimeter wall, but Davide was acutely aware of an odd tenuous connection binding them together, step by step. They both loved Klara. Despite the German's adamant dismissal. But how could a man who loved a woman concoct such lies about her? And yet . . . there were whispers in Davide's head. Voices. Murmurs. They made him question the Klara he knew.

Selfish bitch.

No, no. That was not Klara. She would sacrifice everything for that daughter of hers. Even her life. Scholz had gone too far. Davide halted, in sight of the rear of the Administration building. The daylight was failing and the colonel's lamp was burning. He should walk in there and speak with him now.

'To hell with you, Scholz. Why should I believe a word you say? You executed her friend in the street the first time your paths crossed. You tore her fingernails out yourself.' Davide's voice was rising. 'You stole her child in order to force her to do your bidding. You, Scholz, are the scheming, lying, manipulative bastard, not Klara. It is no wonder she does not love you.'

Scholz swayed on his heels. His self-control splintered.

'Did she tell you the truth, Davide? That her friend in the Resistance tried to shoot me that night? He had a gun in his pocket. I didn't want the bastard dead, I wanted to question him. He forced my hand. Did she tell you that?' His cheeks were streaked with red veins. He threw off his spectacles.

'No. She did not.'

'And did she tell you,' Scholz demanded in a heated voice, 'that the other interrogator at headquarters tore not just a prisoner's nails off but their fingers as well. The interrogation had to be done, she was a Resistance fighter. So I did it myself. As gently as I could.'

'Gently? For God's sake, Scholz, there is nothing gentle about ripping out a woman's fingernails.'

Scholz groaned at the memory.

326

'And the child?' Davide demanded. 'What explanation do you have for the abduction of her child?'

A crow drifted low over the camp, skimming the darkening ground, a black smear that cast a shadow in Davide's mind.

'Have you ever heard of *Lebensborn*?' Scholz asked.

He did not wait for an answer.

'Hitler thought of everything. He thought on a grand scale. I say this quietly, Davide, to you and to no one else. Hitler had a vision, whether you agreed with it or not. And *Lebensborn* was one of his key strategies. It was initiated by the SS to purify our gene pool for the German race. A brilliant concept. To encourage the birth of Aryan children – blond hair, blue eyes – even among unmarried mothers. But this is the relevant point here – the children were removed and given up for adoption to German parents who were "racially" worthy. The SS even kidnapped suitable children from the countries we had conquered in Europe. Fifty-thousand children were taken to be *Germanised*.'

Scholz turned to Davide, face-to-face.

'And what Polish child do both you and I know who would have been ripe for kidnap? Perfect for a carefully selected Aryan family longing for a beautiful pure Aryan daughter. Who Davide? Who would you guess?'

'Alicja.' Davide felt sick at the thought.

'Exactly.'

'You hid her from the SS?'

'I did. In the convent. If she had been sent for adoption in

Germany, Klara would never have seen her daughter again.'

'Did she know this?' Davide frowned. It did not tie in with what Klara had told him.

'Of course she knew. I was trying to help her. To save her daughter.'

'So why would Klara lie about it?'

'Only she can answer that.'

CHAPTER FIFTY-THREE

Berlin

I didn't like hiding. I'd done too much of it.

On my trek with Alicja from Warsaw in Poland all the way to Graufeld Camp in Germany we had lain face down in ditches. Spent wet nights in forests. Slid into rat-infested culverts to avoid detection. It damages you. Strips you of your humanity. Turns you feral.

I didn't want that. Not again.

Erich, our fisherman, was good. He knew the river like he knew the palm of his hand. At times he let the current take us, so there was not even the whisper of the oars. There was no chance the Soviet guards could see us in the dark, but that didn't stop us holding our breath. Hanna and I buried our pale faces in our knees, hunched over like crabs in the bottom of the boat as it glided over the water.

It was choppier here. The Glienicke bridge at Potsdam lay just ahead. The Nazi army had blown up the original arched metal structure, but a temporary wooden bridge had been erected in its place. It marked the boundary. Here the British Zone of Berlin ended and the Soviet Zone of Germany began.

We heard the voice of the Soviet guards on the bridge, saw the glowing tips of their cigarettes. A truck's engine idled somewhere close. Someone laughed. And fear slid through me like a snake.

'Thank you, Erich. I am grateful to you.'

I shook the fisherman's hand warmly and gave him the second cigarette from my coat pocket. It was all I had. Hanna gave him far more. She clasped him to her bosom and growled sweet nothings in his ear. When she finally released him, he returned to his boat with a grin splitting his face. She and I stood shoulder to shoulder on the riverbank and watched the night take him back to Berlin.

What you have to understand is this. Berlin lay in the heart of Soviet territory. When the Allies carved up Germany between them at the Yalta Conference, Stalin took control of the eastern sector which included the capital city. The cherry on the cake for him. It meant Berlin was surrounded in all directions by Soviet-occupied land.

There was no way back to the British-controlled Zone in the west of Germany – which was where Graufeld Camp lay – without crossing Soviet territory. That is why we were here. In the middle of the night, well outside the city limits, stranded in Soviet Germany, with rivers to cross. The border to the British Zone still miles away.

Ninety miles, to be exact.

It was going to be a long walk.

We were trudging through a field, ridged and treacherous. Stumbling in the dark.

'Stay off the main roads,' Magdalena had urged. 'If you keep to the fields and woods, you should be safe. The Soviet guards only patrol the main roads.'

'Thank you,' I smiled, 'we'll take your advice.'

It was Erich who had jumped in with the truth. 'It's not the guards you've got to watch out for. It's the filthy brigands.'

'Brigands?' Hanna gasped.

'Oh yes. Robbers. Thieves. Preying on travellers. There are thousands of refugees fleeing to the west ahead of the Red Army with all the possessions they can carry.'

'But we have no possessions,' I pointed out. 'Nothing to steal.'

Magdalena looked me up and down. She sighed. 'Klara,' she said sternly, 'you have plenty to steal.'

The moon had risen and its darts of light skimmed the surface of the narrow river like silverfish. Beneath its skin the water looked black and solid. Its waves were churned by the night wind.

'Are you sure?'

'Yes, I'm sure, Hanna.'

'It looks too dangerous. Look at the size of me and look at the size of that boat. How do you know it won't get swept away?'

'Hanna,' I said firmly, 'just get in it.'

I propelled my friend on to the end-board of the tiny ferry boat. Erich had warned us that many of the bridges were down, blown up by the retreating German army.

'Don't let that stop you, ladies,' he had chuckled. 'You can swim, can't you?'

'No,' Hanna had slapped his knee, 'I can't.'

'I'll look after her,' I told him. 'Even if I have to carry her on my back.'

The three of us had laughed softly, clinging to the smallest of straws.

The ferry boat seated six at most. It turned out to be a hand-operated cable ferry with a rope to pull on to get yourself across. In the dark we were clumsy and the boat rocked wildly. As I stood to pull us off the bank, Hanna clutched my coat.

'Look.'

Two scrawny shadows emerged from the darkness on the riverbank, a hand raised in entreaty.

'Take us,' an elderly woman's voice begged. It was dry and rusty as an old gate.

Alongside her limped an old man, leaning heavily on a stick. Both were wrapped in black blankets, both were thin as pins.

'Of course,' I said. 'You shouldn't be out at night. Have you somewhere to go?'

'Yes, we have. We are looking forward to getting there.'

'Not far?'

The man smiled sadly. 'No, not far.'

I took a grip on each bird-like claw and helped them into our frail craft. In the shifting moonlight their faces looked drawn and gaunt, people from a lost world.

No lights flickered on either bank, so I took hold of the rope with both hands, bent into it and pulled. The boat creaked. Gave a lurch. Then we were afloat, moving unsteadily across the stretch of water, which was about eighty metres wide. I was working the rope, eyes fixed on the blackness ahead, when I heard a soft sound emerge from our two passengers. They were singing. Sweet scratchy notes whispered into the night that sent shivers of pleasure down my spine. It was a love song.

'Silence,' Hanna hissed. But it was half-hearted.

The song continued to its end, by which time we had reached the middle of the river, though it was hard to estimate distance in the dark. My eyes checked and rechecked the far bank, but I could see nothing to scare me. The work wasn't hard now, standing and hauling on the rope, my feet well braced. It kept me warm. But when the boat suddenly started to rock wildly I almost pitched head first into the swirling waters.

'Fuck!' Hanna screamed. She gripped tight to the gunwale.

The old man and woman were standing up on the bench where they'd been seated. Holding hands.

'Thank you, my dears,' the woman called solemnly. 'We go no further.'

'No!'

My arms reached out for them but they were gone. They had stepped off the boat. Scarcely a splash. The current sucked them deep.

'No,' I whispered. 'No, no.'

I started to throw off my coat, but Hanna pulled me down on top of her. The boat rocked violently.

'It's too late, my friend,' she muttered, her cheek pressed to mine. 'You'd never find them down there. The water is blacker than Stalin's heart.'

I struggled, but I knew she was right. As I seized the ferry's rope again and began to haul hand over hand, tears were pouring down my cheeks.

At times I thought the night would never end. Parts of the blackness seemed to stick in my mind and I couldn't tear them away. The sound of a splash, no louder than a pebble dropping into a pond; I heard it again and again as we trudged on.

After leaving the Brandenburg region we navigated by means of the *Autobahn*, the A2 motorway that ran from Berlin to Hanover. Not that we went anywhere near it, not even in the dark. We skulked through the woodlands that cut across the country, keeping north of the road, using the moonlight and the occasional flash of a car's headlamps to keep us on a westerly route.

'I've got to rest,' Hanna moaned. She leaned back against a tree. 'Just for a minute.'

We were exhausted. Hungry and thirsty. Cut and

scratched by undergrowth and branches. Desperate for sleep.

'We'll get cold if we stop moving,' I said.

'My feet are too bloody sore. They won't go another step.'

I wrapped my arm around Hanna's broad waist and drew her arm across my shoulders, taking some of her weight. With an effort I prised her off the tree.

'You aren't going to make me go any further, are you?' she wailed.

'Yes, I am.'

'You bastard.'

CHAPTER FIFTY-FOUR

Graufeld Camp

DAVIDE BOUVIER

Davide stood at the window of his hut and made a bargain with the moon.

Keep her safe. Give her strength. Don't let her falter. Bring her back to me.

In exchange I will wear your medallion around my neck, Diana, goddess of the moon. For the rest of my life. Diana the huntress, don't let Klara be the hunted.

It was foolish. This deal. He knew it. He was not a religious man, despite a Catholic upbringing. He had no reassuring beliefs to fall back on. No comforting scripture to ease the terror of what the Soviets could be doing to Klara right now.

So instead he stood vigil over the moon's cold light. He watched it glide, fitful and inconstant, through the camp, etching the edge of a roof, turning the dirt to silver dust. He pictured Klara's eyes watching the same moonlight. He pictured it touching her face. He dared not think of worse.

It was all he had of her.

I looked after your daughter today, Klara. I kept her safe. I stuck like a leech to Scholz's side and listened to his words dripping poison into my ear. Because every moment that he was with me meant a moment that he was nowhere near Alicja.

Is it true, what he said?

About you.

Do I know you at all?

Come back. Let me hear your voice. Let me feel your breath. Let me learn who you really are.

Come back, Klara. Come back. Until you do, I swear I will keep your daughter safe.

CHAPTER FIFTY-FIVE

There were others in the woods. I heard them. Their rust-lings. Their whispers. Their tread on a stick that snapped. The quickly stifled cry of a child.

We steered clear of them. They steered clear of us. It was safer that way.

We were all headed to the West, to the land of milk and honey. Except I'd tasted their honey. Graufeld Camp honey. It tasted bad. But the fact that they were offering us – and millions more refugees like us – any kind of honey at all was a gut-warming miracle that made me kneel in gratitude.

A flame flickered in the forest. It was small and half-hidden by the trees, but unmistakably there. Burning a hole in the darkness.

'They might have hot food,' Hanna moaned in my ear. 'I'm dying of starvation, you'll have to bury me soon.'

I squeezed the shoulder of Hanna's damp coat. 'Shush. We'll take a look.'

It was too tempting. We were consumed by the desire to approach it, drawn like moths to its bright heat. We crept from tree to tree, till we were close. Something was cooking. I put out a hand in the dark and held on to Hanna because I didn't trust her not to rush forward, snatch up the cooking pot and take off into the night with it.

The travellers turned out to be a group of ten. I counted each mound on the ground, cocooned in fallen leaves. One was sitting cross-legged by the fire, stirring the pot. An old woman with long silvery hair hanging in a plait down her back. She looked like a spirit of the forest. She waved a wooden ladle in our direction. 'I see you there. I have fox eyes.'

I was uneasy, but Hanna did not wait to be asked twice. Before I had even blinked, she was seated at the fire with a wooden bowl of soup in her hand.

'And you my friend?' the woman offered, her face kind behind the leaping shadows that twisted across it.

'I cannot take your food.' I gestured to the other figures. 'Your family need—'

'My family need to never forget how to be generous to others. In these violent, selfish times, it is all too easy to lose sight of it.' She thrust a bowl of soup into my hands.

I sat hunched over it, head lowered. Fighting back the tears that dripped into the steaming liquid.

'Thank you,' I muttered. 'Thank you,' I said again. 'For ...'

'For what?'

'For reminding me.'

'Finish your soup, and sleep. I will watch out for danger.' She threw a log into the flames.

'It would be better to let the fire die down. It would be safer. That's how we found you.'

'I know. But there are others out there,' she waved a scrawny arm towards the black secretive trees, 'who need soup in their bellies.'

I didn't argue. She was right.

With soup inside her, Hanna scooped up a mini-mountain of autumn leaves on the damp bed of earth beneath the trees and burrowed into it. Within five seconds she was asleep. I settled down next to her, comforted by her familiar bulk and the dirty white kerchief around her head.

I lay among the dead leaves, unable to sleep. I listened to the wind in the trees and the night sounds of the woodland floor, its rustlings and scurryings. I thought of Davide, so vivid, so real I could touch his hair and smell his skin. He possessed that same kindness of heart as the old woman, that same belief in the inherent goodness of humanity even when it kicked him in the teeth. I loved him for that. It took courage. More courage than I possessed. I wanted to wrap my arms around him, to bind myself to him and him to me. To shrug off the past, like the dirty shabby coat it was.

I smiled at the moon as it slid between the branches and let my eyes drift shut. But the smile that awaited me inside my head was not Davide's. It was Oberführer Axel Fleischer's.

*

'*Did you miss me, Schatzi?*'

'*Of course. You know I always do, Axel.*'

'*Tell me how much you missed me while I was gone for three days.*'

'*Better still . . . let me show you.*'

I unbelted my silk kimono and let it slip to the floor. '*I've been saving it for you.*'

Axel Fleischer's pupils turned into huge black holes of desire.

But was his desire for me? Or was it for the small packet of white powder I'd pasted between my breasts?

I leave you to guess.

Afterwards he was talkative. It was always the way. The white powder loosened his tongue. His heavy leg lay across mine on the crumpled crimson sheet, and his fingers brushed with lazy pleasure over the red bite marks he'd left on my breast.

'*How was your sister?*' I asked. In no hurry. Keeping it casual. No special interest.

'*Irmgard? She's scared. Like the rest of us. Hitler is losing this war, it's obvious for everyone to see, and the whole of Germany will be made to suffer the consequences.*'

I stroked his forehead. It was damp with sweat. '*You don't need to be frightened, Axel. You are ready for whatever comes. You have prepared for it.*'

'*Of course I have. But millions of Germans haven't.*'

'*The Allies will not catch you.*'

'*You're right, they won't. I am too clever for them, my Klara. I'm not stupid enough to think the people of Warsaw won't come for me like rabid dogs when the surrender by Hitler finally comes.*'

'Can you blame them, Axel?'

'Blame who?'

'The people of Warsaw.'

'These ignorant Polish peasants are lucky to be alive at all.'

'How many of them have you killed?'

'Me personally? Or Germany?'

'You.'

A slow satisfied smile spread across his face. 'Tens of thousands.'

'I am one of those ignorant Polish peasants, Axel. You forget that.'

His arm encircled my neck and pulled me on top of him, our naked skin clinging together, slick with his sweat.

'No, my Klara, you aren't a Pole anymore.'

'So what am I?'

'You're mine. My Klara. When I go, you go with me.'

He kissed my throat so hard I thought I would choke. Sometimes I feared he would bite right through it.

'Your wife?' I murmured.

'She will stay in Berlin. The Russians can have her.' He laughed, a strange complicated sound.

'Your son, Rudi?'

'Ach, don't mention the boy. He is as weak-minded as his mother.'

'Where will we go?'

'To Hanover first, of course. Then wherever you want. London? New York? Rio de Janeiro?'

I breathed very softly, my lips brushing his. My throat tight. The words would scarcely come.

'In Hanover,' I whispered, 'is everything safe?'

'Ja, all is safe.'

'Does your sister know where you've put it? She might be tempted.'

'I am not foolish, Schatzi. I trust no one. Not even my sister.'

'Not even me?'

He slapped my bare bottom. Hard enough to leave a bruise. He chuckled happily. The white powder always made him happy.

'Especially not you, my Klara.'

'Good. It means it is safe. As long as your sister doesn't suspect anything.'

'No, don't fret your pretty head about that. I've hidden it well. In the forest where she and I used to play when we were young. She would never go there now.' His pupils were huge black cocaine caverns and his heart was racing against mine. I could see white frosting on his nasal hairs. 'Irmgard was always frightened of it.'

He burst out laughing at the memory of his sister's fear. I rolled away from him. I could take no more.

CHAPTER FIFTY-SIX

I woke. I'd heard a sound. The night was dense black, no moonlight. I listened hard but could only catch the snores from those sleeping around me and the crackle of the fire. The soup woman's head had slumped on to her chest as she dozed. My pulse was thumping.

I rolled over and nudged Hanna awake. 'Hanna, I think we should move.'

'Later,' she groaned. 'Go away.'

'No, Hanna,' I whispered. 'Now.'

She sat up, alert. 'What is it?'

'I'm not sure.'

I brushed the leaves off her and pulled her to her feet. We crept deeper into the trees where, without the fire, a solid darkness descended like a blanket thrown over us. We could only find each other by feel.

'We can't travel through the woods until it's light,' I murmured. 'Dawn can't be far off.'

We found a fallen tree and sat down, nestled close together, trying to keep warm. The breeze was icy at this hour laden with the scent of earth and the musk of deer. Somewhere nearby, an owl hooted, startling us both, and I wondered if it was really an owl.

'You rest,' I said. 'I'll watch.'

'You don't want to leave them, do you?'

'Who?'

'The soup people.'

'It's too dark to move on yet.'

'I know you, Klara. You'd keep going day or night to get back to that daughter of yours.'

'What about Rafal?' I asked to change the subject. 'You haven't mentioned him once. Aren't you worried about your son too?'

I felt her weight grow heavier on my shoulder. 'He's not my son, Klara. We met on the road out of Poland and thought we'd do better together.' She sighed uneasily. 'But don't tell anyone in the camp. A mother with a tall son stands more chance of not being molested.'

Of course. It explained the distance between them. Everyone had their past tucked away from view.

'He is very fond of you,' I said.

'Rafal is a good boy. He'll be watching over your Alicja.'

'Rest,' I whispered again. 'I'll watch.'

Out there hidden in a fold of darkness among the looming beech trees there was someone else watching, I was certain. Someone else waiting for dawn.

*

It happened fast.

It started with a gunshot. It wasn't quite dawn. It was that finely balanced moment pre-dawn when it feels as if a coin has been flipped. The blackness switches to a cold tombstone grey, opaque and tight-lipped. A time of secrets.

A thick heavy stick was lying across my knees.

Shouts and screams rose from the group around the fire and a man's loud voice bellowing orders. The sounds ricocheted off the tall black trunks. Spinning into the darkness. Sending confusion through the camp. Panic burned through the chill air.

'Shut the fuck up or I'll shoot her,' a man yelled.

The screaming ceased abruptly. But the silence was worse. I moved fast to the other side of the small clearing where I took cover behind a cluster of birches. But I could see him. A shadowy figure wreathed in the grey mist that had slunk in on its belly. I edged forward. Still hidden. Darting between trees.

I worked my way to a spot behind him. I saw the back of a bald head and a tattered greatcoat. He seemed to be alone. But it came as a shock when I realised he was gripping the old woman's grey plait and that she was down on her knees on the ground. The barrel of a gun was pointed at her head. There was something so humiliating about her position. It angered me even more than the danger. I couldn't see her face but her body was quiet, her limbs calm. She was not one to panic.

In front of them stood the huddle of refugees, clustered

together, women, men and children. Some in tears. Others clinging to each other. The man was shouting orders to fill a sack with their food and belongings. He was jittery, his finger twitching on the trigger.

I fought to slow the racing of my pulse, then stepped out from behind my tree. The stick weighed heavy in my hand. I strode forward into the gloom and one of the refugees saw me. He had sense enough to give no sign but started begging loudly for mercy to overlay any sound of my approach.

I was quick. I picked my spot and swung the stick on to the brigand's naked scalp with a force that dropped him to the ground. He folded up as neatly as if asleep. I scooped up the gun and snapped it open. There were no bullets inside.

I knelt at his side in the morning mist and did not wish him dead. I felt for a pulse. His head was bleeding profusely but he would live. One of the men was already roping his wrists and ankles together. Other people raised the old woman to her feet and she came to me. She wrapped her hands around mine, giving me her warmth.

'Thank you,' she said simply.

'Thank *you*,' I responded and retreated back among the birches.

Hanna was waiting there. We sat off westward, our backs to the sunrise.

'Remind me,' Hanna said with a booming laugh, 'never to point a gun at you.'

CHAPTER FIFTY-SEVEN

Graufeld Camp

ALICJA

'You have to eat, Alicja.'

Alicja shook her head. 'I can't eat, Davide.'

Even a mouthful would make her sick. She was cold deep in her bones. She couldn't eat. Couldn't sleep. Couldn't see straight. But there was a firestorm inside her head, like the one she'd seen in the convent when someone threw a burning oil lamp inside the storage shed. Flames so high they seemed to lick the stars out of the night sky. They never did find out who that wicked someone was. But for nights Alicja had lain awake warming her hands on that firestorm. Hearing again the whoosh when the flame took. They should have let her write to her mother.

'You haven't eaten since . . .'

Davide stopped. They all knew what came after *since*, but

no one wanted the words in their mouth. *Since the Russians took her.* Davide had not left Alicja's side for even a heartbeat today. She'd found him waiting outside her hut at first light this morning, his jacket collar up round his ears. She had felt a rush of gratitude but at the same time she wanted him to go away.

'Don't you have to work?' she'd asked after a couple of hours of his company.

'No. Not today. Not tomorrow. Not till she comes home.' He'd smiled that warm smile of his. 'Get used to it.'

'This isn't home.'

He didn't argue.

This afternoon he had walked her with Rafal to the Recreation block, sat them down at a chessboard and watched them play. Alicja let Rafal win every game. Halfway through the third one she turned away from the board and stared hard out of the window. There was nothing out there but she continued to gaze out, letting herself picture the images she had fought off till now. She pictured how Mama would look in chains in a Soviet dungeon. Fury came blowing down her nostrils.

'You all right, Alicja?'

How could he ask that?

How could she be all right when her mother was having hot pokers pushed in her face?

But Davide wouldn't let it go. 'Have you ever spoken with Scholz yourself?'

She felt Rafal's gaze leap to her face. Should she tell? Or

keep her mouth shut? But there was something in Davide's eyes, in the way they held on to you, that made it hard to lie to him.

'Yes,' she said.

'Did you believe what he said?'

She tried to form the word 'No'. But it froze on her lips without emerging as a sound. Instead she shook her head. It was easier.

'Of course not,' she whispered. 'He lies.'

'If that is the case, he lies well.'

Did Davide know about the Nazi lover? She stared hard at his face. Did he? She couldn't tell. But suddenly she didn't want him to.

'Davide, do you love my mother?' She blurted out the question before she could stop herself.

'Yes, I do.'

No hesitation. *Yes, I do.* And the tight edges of his jaw softened.

'But,' he added, letting the word slide out quickly as if it tasted sour, 'do I trust her? That is a different matter. Tell me, Alicja, do you trust her?'

Alicja kept quiet. She wanted to shout a loud 'Yes', but it wouldn't come. Instead she asked, 'Can you love someone if you don't trust them?'

'Of course you can.' It was Rafal who answered, his dark gaze hooked on the chessboard. 'Everyone did bad things in the war. I bet you did too, Alicja.'

She made no answer.

'What do you know,' Davide asked gently, 'about what your mother did after you went to the convent?'

'Only what Oskar Scholz has told me.'

'Bad things?'

She nodded. Teeth clenched.

'Even if they are true, do they matter?' Davide said. But Alicja knew he was asking himself, not her. 'If we love your mother, surely we can trust her.'

'You are both wrong.' Rafal spoke up again. His voice was low and harsh, almost a man's voice. He was holding on to the white queen, nudging the other pieces off the chessboard with her. 'Of course we don't know who your mother was during the war.' He lifted his black eyes and scowled at them. 'But we know who she is now.' His gaze challenged them. 'Don't we?'

'Yes,' Alicja answered with sudden conviction. 'Yes, you are right, Rafal. We do know who she is. She has shown us every day. She fights for us all.'

She stood up abruptly, aware now of what she must do. But first she had to shake off her French shadow.

'I think I might eat something now, Davide,' she said.

'Good.' He jumped to his feet. 'I'll fetch you something from the canteen.' He took two steps away, then halted. 'Try not to worry, Alicja. Your mother's grip on life is strong.'

Alicja nodded.

'Make sure you stay right here while I'm gone,' Davide told her. 'And you,' he addressed Rafal sternly, 'you watch her like a hawk.'

*

'Just a minute, young lady. Where do you think you're going?'

Alicja's hand snatched away from the door to the men's ward. 'I came to see the man who is ill.'

The hospital ward sister looked to Alicja like the kind of person who would roll right over a child. She was solid and thickset with a big chest and large round bossy eyes.

'All the men in that ward are ill. Which one do you mean?'

'The poisoned one.'

The sister, in her clean white starch, came closer. She smelled of camphor. 'What do you know about the poisoning?'

Had she made a mistake? Alicja edged away from the door. 'I just want to know how he is?' she said. 'To wish him better.'

'That is very kind of you, child. He's doing as well as can be expected.'

Alicja looked at her blankly. What did that mean? Expected by who?

'Now, run along, girl. Children are not allowed on the men's wards.'

'Is he still alive?'

'Oh yes. That's our job.'

'Will he stay alive?'

The sister cracked a token smile. 'You'll have to ask God that one.'

Rafal trailed along beside Alicja, dragging his heels in the dust. Watching her like a hawk. It drove her mad, but at the same time made her feel safe. He carried his slingshot openly in his hand as a warning.

Alicja hadn't been to church since her mother stormed into the nun's chapel breathing fire, to rescue her from the convent. Graufeld Camp's chapel was a plain-faced building with an iron cross above the door, which Alicja had studiously ignored till now. She wasn't sure whether she would be chased out, so entered cautiously.

But no, no one chased her. The place was empty, and to her surprise it was light and airy with pale pine pews and no stink of incense lingering like bad breath. She'd had her fill of incense and rosaries in the convent. But she bobbed her knees. Crossed herself and scurried down to the front pew so God could hear her better. She bowed her head, pressed her hands together in prayer and whispered into the empty space.

'Please look after Mama.'

Was it the words? Was it the place? Was it the silence?

Whatever the cause, something cracked open inside her. Tears started to flood down her cheeks, dripping to the wooden floor. Her shoulders shook uncontrollably and far away in the back of her head she could hear her mother's voice, but she couldn't make out the words, however hard she tried. She began to rock back and forth.

'Can I help you, my dear?'

Alicja jumped to her feet. 'No. No. Thank you.' But her words were drowning in tears.

She looked up. A priest's white collar stared back at her. She didn't lift her eyes to the face above it.

'Shall we pray for your mother?' he asked in a gentle tone.

He knew. Of course. Everyone knew. News of an inmate being transferred to the Soviets went through the camp like a bushfire.

Alicja edged around the priest. In a black suit, not a black dress. That was better in her mind. 'No. Thank you. God won't listen to me. I asked Him every day for three years to let me be with Mama again but He didn't lift a finger to help me. But He will listen to you, won't He?'

A strong hand rested on her head. 'But He did listen to you, child. Your mother was here with you.'

'So why did He take her away again?' It came out fierce. Loud. But she wouldn't cover up her mouth.

'My child, our Holy Father knows all . . .'

But she was running. Back up the aisle. At the door she remembered what she'd come for and called out to the priest.

'And ask Him to make the poisoned man better. Please.'

God might be too busy. He had a lot to look after. But Colonel Whitmore only had Graufeld Camp.

Alicja knew Davide would not be at his desk. It would make it easier. He was probably in the Recreation building with a nice slice of toast waiting for her and she felt bad about disobeying him. But she had to keep trying.

Had to.

Colonel Whitmore had said 'No' once already. But he was an Englishman and Mama said that Englishmen were always too polite for their own good. Alicja would beg. She'd cry. She'd stand on her head, if that's what it took to make him cave in politely and issue a new transference order to the Soviets. She entered the Administration building and Captain Jeavons tried to stop her, but she was too quick for him. She had the door to Whitmore's office open before he could grab her.

'What is it, Jeavons?' The colonel looked up from his desk, forehead creased in annoyance.

'Sorry, sir. This little monkey managed to—'

'Outsmart you?' Whitmore gave a thin smile. His gaze settled on Alicja and he uttered a sigh, but didn't put down his pen.

'Two minutes, Jeavons. Then come and get her. Two minutes, no more.'

'Yessir.'

The Colonel rose to his feet. He was so tall he blotted out the window. There was something very straight about him. Not just his body, but his face too. All made up of straight lines. When he strode from behind his desk towards Alicja, she backed up fast and kept the chair between them. But he did no more than pull a clean white handkerchief from his pocket and hold it out to her.

'Wipe your face, girl. You can't go round looking like that.'

She took the handkerchief. Dried her face. She offered it back to him.

'Keep it,' he said. 'I dare say there will be more tears to come.'

She didn't like the sound of that. That wasn't what she wanted to hear. She licked her dry lips.

'Yessir,' she said. Like Jeavons.

'What's your name?'

'Alicja Janowska.'

'And what is it you want, Alicja?'

'I want you to bring my Mama back to Graufeld Camp, sir.'

The colonel sat down heavily on the front edge of his desk, put his hands on his knees and jutted his head towards her.

'I understand that you are upset, Alicja, but—'

'I am not *upset*. I am . . .' She hunted for a word that would make him understand. But while she hunted, the tears came again and she couldn't make them stop. She scrubbed at them with his handkerchief and wanted to shout a stream of cuss words the way Hanna did, but she didn't dare. Not in front of Colonel Whitmore.

She started again. 'I am . . . desperate.'

She lifted her gaze from his shiny brown shoes, up the razor-straight crease of his trousers to his face. It had changed. The straight lines had melted. He was rubbing a hand back and forth across his bushy eyebrows.

'Alicja, the Soviets have every right to request an interview with your mother about crimes committed.' His voice was heavy. As if his mouth was full of stones. 'What is it you want me to do?'

Alicja darted to the side of the desk. Snatched up the telephone receiver and held it out to him, forcing it into his hand. Startling him.

'Call them. Order them to give her back.'

CHAPTER FIFTY-EIGHT

'Is it safe?' I asked.

'Probably.'

The farmer shrugged his shoulders. The kind of shoulders you get from hauling pigs around all day. He'd stopped twenty kilometres earlier to give us a lift in his ancient wheezing truck with three rowdy black and white pigs in the back. Scharz-Wesses, he said they were. Three ugly ill-tempered sows. It was tempting to light a fire on the side of the road and roast one of the fat creatures. I could see Hanna eyeing them with the same thought.

'Safe enough,' the farmer muttered, as he shifted gear to an accompaniment of grinding metal and a bone-jarring judder.

'It doesn't look good,' I said uneasily.

The bridge looked anything but safe to me. Soldiers in Soviet uniform patrolled each end of it. The German army in retreat blew up the old bridge across the Elbe, so this one was a temporary pontoon one that the Russians had installed to keep traffic flowing.

'What are you going to do then?' the farmer asked. 'Swim across?'

He meant it as a joke. His bearded face broke into a hairy grin, revealing a black hole where his front teeth should be.

I didn't take it as a joke.

I took it as an option.

I studied the glittering silver skin of the river that lay directly ahead of us and I weighed up my chances.

'No,' Hanna snapped. I could hear fear snag in the word. 'No, no swimming. We can always wait until dark to cross the bridge.'

I couldn't wait. I couldn't. It was asking too much. It had taken us most of the day to get this far. The Elbe was one of Germany's main shipping arteries and had marked the boundary between East and West. But in July the Allies had backed off further and allowed Soviet Russia to grab even more of Germany. The border had shifted fifty kilometres to the west, from Magdeburg to Helmstedt.

'They're too lazy.' The farmer chewed on the blackened stem of his pipe. 'They won't bother us.' He nodded towards the Soviet guards who lolled against the edge of the pontoon bridge. 'You want to take the risk?'

I pulled my headscarf low over my forehead and clambered with Hanna into the back of the truck with the pigs.

I took the risk.

I am back. Do you hear me, Alicja? I am back.

Within spitting distance of Graufeld. But he will come

for you. I know he will. And when he does, you must be ready to run.

I have run, Alicja, I have run my heart out for you. I have run my feet to blisters for you because you are in every step I take. He will not be expecting me. Not yet.

If at all.

As long as he thinks I am a plaything of the Soviets in Berlin, where they are trained to dismantle a person piece by piece, he will believe he is safe.

But if he knows I am free . . .

Then run.

CHAPTER FIFTY-NINE

Graufeld Camp

ALICJA

Alicja ran. She ran like there was a wolf at her heels. She raced from the Administration building into the drizzling rain that was starting to fall. Her heart was beating so hard, it deafened her ears.

Mama was free.

The words sang in her head. *Mama was free.* Alicja had walked from the chapel, where prayers drifted from pew to pew like smoke, to Colonel Whitmore's office, and in that short time God had lifted a finger and set her mother free. He had listened to the priest. Not to her. To the priest. His prayers were powerful.

Mama was free.

The colonel had not used those words. Of course not. He had said – after speaking on the phone to three different people – your mother has gone missing. But there had been a shine to his eyes that wasn't there before. A twitch to his lips.

Your mother has gone missing. They don't know where she is.

'And Hanna Pamulska?'

Hanna Pamulska as well.

As she ran she shouted to Rafal. 'Find Davide. Go to the canteen. Find him quickly.'

She flew to the Recreation building in case he was still there, but as she hurried towards the door a hand shot out. It fixed around her arm. She looked up. It was Oskar Scholz. He was leaning against the wall beside the door, wearing a dark shirt and a scruffy old jacket that glistened in the rain. It felt like a big black spider had just latched itself on to her.

'Alicja,' he said, 'I've been looking for you.'

The heavy grey sky seemed to slam shut on the camp. She tried to pull away but he held firm.

'Let me go.'

'Stop it, Alicja.' His voice was sharp. 'I have news for you.'

She ceased struggling. 'What kind of news?'

'About your mother.'

Her scalp prickled. 'You know already?'

'Know what?'

But the cat suddenly got hold of Alicja's tongue. She shook her head.

'Come with me, Alicja. Let's go somewhere private where we can talk.'

He pulled her wrist but she dug her heels in. She could feel the strength of him, a man accustomed to having people jump to do what he said. She squirmed her wrist back and forth, burning her skin.

'No,' she shouted.

He took as much notice as he would if the dirt under his feet spoke up. He dragged her one metre, two metres, gathering speed, till Alicja was stumbling along against her will. But a sudden crack brought him to an abrupt halt. Like the sound of bone on bone. He arched his body in pain.

Alicja knew that sound. A stone had thudded against the bony spot between his shoulder blades and now lay on the ground at his feet. She whirled around, still in his grip. Rafal was there. Thirty metres away. Slingshot in hand and loading a second stone. No one else was nearby. Just when she needed the crowds, they deserted her.

'*Scheisse!*' Scholz cursed. 'I'll break that bastard's neck.'

He dragged Alicja down the side of the Recreation block to the rear where there was a lean-to shed stacked with sawn logs. He pushed her up against the wooden planking, his hands either side of her head. She was sure that he was about to crush her skull.

'What news,' she asked quickly, 'of Mama?'

'They are transferring her back to Warsaw.'

'You're lying!'

His face came closer. Filling her vision. His spectacles were spotted with rain. 'It's true, Alicja. The Soviets are taking her away to—'

'No, no, you're lying. You're lying. They don't know where she is.'

'What?'

'They've lost her. Colonel Whitmore said so.'

'You mean your mother has escaped?'

'Yes.' She flung the word at him with pride. 'She'll be coming back to—'

His hand closed around her throat. She could make no sound. The back of her head thumped against the shed and she couldn't see straight. Her hands tried to claw at his fingers. She scratched. She kicked. Her lungs begged for air. She felt sick and dizzy and the sounds in her ears were like an express train roaring through her head. She could feel the life draining out of her.

Her feet slid from under her, so that just his hand held her upright. Her lips fluttered, trying to speak, but there was no breath in her. He was saying things. She knew because his lips moved and his teeth showed, but the sound of his words was flattened by the express train. She wanted to shout 'Mama'. But it was too late. Something was unravelling inside her.

The blow came out of nowhere.

She saw it, rather than heard it. A solid thwack on the side of Scholz's head with a heavy log. A blur of movement. Scholz vanished. There in front of her one moment, gone the next. The iron band on her throat vanished with him and air swooped into her lungs with a noise that set her teeth on edge.

She would have fallen, but hands held her on her feet, gentle hands. A man's quiet voice in her ears. Davide's voice.

She laid her head on his chest. Waited for thoughts to climb back inside her brain. Davide's hand stroked the back of her head and it made her tears trickle on to his shirt.

'Rafal fetched me,' he said, holding her tight. 'Alicja, if you ever run off on me again I will throttle you myself.'

She had to laugh at that.

CHAPTER SIXTY

The odd thing was how easy it was. No questions. No rifles in our faces. No bullets in our brains. Nothing. Honestly, nothing.

The further we travelled from Berlin, the less anyone cared where we were going. Or where we'd come from. Everywhere refugees were on the move. Everything was in chaos. Grey figures in headscarves and dusty suits. Some bent double under back-breaking loads or hauling carts piled high with blankets and thin-legged children. Others walked sedately with no more than the clothes they stood up in.

All fleeing from Stalin's boot. Yes, at the border with West Germany itself there were a few flimsy checkpoints across the roads, but we all had the sense to avoid them. In the fields and forests there were no fences. No guards. Not yet anyway. They would come soon enough, I was sure of it. Just as soon as it dawned on Stalin that his territories would end up deserted and his economy in tatters, if he didn't put a stop to the haemorrhage of humanity.

It was Hanna who wangled a lift for us in a British Army truck, once we were safely in the West again. With a bunch of six bright long-limbed young men who were full of whistles and noise and laughter because they had survived the slaughter of war.

They offered to trade cigarettes and chocolate for a kiss on our cheeks. Hanna took the trade.

'Wait for me, Hanna.'

'I thought you were in an almighty rush to get back to the camp. To see your daughter.'

'I am.'

'Then why stop here? We're so close to it.'

'I have something to do first. Someone to see.'

'I'll never understand you, Klara.'

Hanna sat down to the ground on top of a crunchy heap of bright orange leaves and slumped back against a tree at the edge of the forest. She lit a Players cigarette and sank her teeth into a bar of chocolate.

'Off you go, Klara, to see your someone.' She exhaled a skein of smoke contentedly. 'No rush.'

This time I walked up the gravel drive in daylight. I knocked on the front door. Instead of creeping round the back like a thief.

The house was even more impressive than when I'd seen it at night. Half-timbered with decorative brickwork and fancy lattice windows that were speckled with the first drops of rain. I tried to picture Axel Fleischer here, striding up this same drive in his gleaming black boots. Knocking this same oak door. His sister opening it with a welcoming smile and drawing him inside with a warm embrace to the house he'd lived in as a child.

I didn't know this was her house. Not that first time. With hindsight, I might have guessed. But the last time I was here in the village of Hagendorf I had other things on my mind. I stand here now and wait. Sweat on my palms. My heartbeat rattles my ribs.

I lift the brass lion's head and knock.

The door opened sooner than I expected. The woman with an eyepatch stood in front of me, her long black hair swept back. It emphasised the likeness to her brother.

'Hello, again, Frau Köhler.'

Her polite expression crumbled. 'You,' she said. An accusation.

She slammed the door in my face.

I knocked again. And again. I kept banging down the brass knocker until the door snapped open once more.

'Stop that! You'll wake my child.'

I held out my hands, palms up. 'I am unarmed. I intend you and your daughter no harm. Please, let me—'

'Go away.'

'Please, let me have a moment of your time and then I will leave you in peace.'

She took her time making the decision. She studied my

filthy coat and damp dishevelled hair. But mostly she studied my face. I didn't like to think what she saw there, but she stepped back inside the house. With a stiff jerk of her head she indicated that I should enter.

I nipped in smartly. Before she could slam the door on me.

It was the kind of house you wanted to touch, to run a palm over the polished surfaces of the heavy furniture. To trail a finger along the elegant Meissen porcelain figurines. Axel Fleischer and his sister liked nice things around them. I was one of his nice things.

She led me into the dining room. The dining table was conspicuously bare.

'You stole my silver candlesticks,' she said without preamble.

'Yes. I was angry and I needed them to get back into the camp.'

'So what is it you need to steal from me now?' She folded her arms, pulling her primrose-yellow cardigan tight around her thin frame.

'I've come to give you something.'

Irmgard Köhler sat in her green velvet armchair, weeping into her dainty handkerchief. I felt a wave of sorrow for her. I remembered only too well what it felt like to lose a brother, but I could not join in her grief for Axel Fleischer. That was her affair. Hers alone.

She had been informed of his death two months ago, she told me. But she had clung to the desperate hope that – in the wild chaos and confusion that had turned the country on its head at the end of the war – the authorities were mistaken. That he had vanished into thin air, like a million other Nazis. To evade retribution. She told herself every morning that one day soon he would knock on her door.

This all came out of her in gasps. Raw and painful.

Then followed the question. The one I'd been dreading.

'How did he die?'

'In my arms. Shot by a Resistance fighter.'

'Was the Resistance fighter arrested?'

'No.'

'Where did it happen?'

'In my apartment.'

Irmgard wiped the tears from her face and ran her hand-kerchief behind her eyepatch. I tried not to stare at it. She lifted her chin and sat upright.

'My brother died in your apartment?'

'Yes.'

'So you were his whore?'

I swallowed back the words that leaped to my tongue. 'Yes.'

'Is your daughter his?'

My hand went to my throat. It felt like ice. 'Of course not. She is much too old.'

Her dark eyes regarded me with intense anger. I knew it was not really directed at me. It was at the damage. The havoc that war had brought to us all. But it was hard to sit and take it, when it was her husband who had shot my daughter in cold blood.

'So why are you here?' she demanded.

'I told you. To give you something.'

'All you've given me is bad news.' She turned her face away from me. 'Leave now.'

'I came here to tell you how your brother died. Which I have done because I thought you'd want to know.' I kept my voice kind. She'd been hurt enough. 'And to tell you that as he lay in my arms, his last words were of you.'

Her breath raced in and out. She cradled a hand over her eyepatch as though all this emotion was making the socket hurt.

'Tell me,' she said.

'He said he was sorry.'

'Sorry? For what?'

'For frightening you so much in the forest when you were young together.'

Her eyes widened. 'He said that?'

'Yes.'

She shook her head and for one horrible moment I thought she would say she didn't know what Axel was talking about. But no.

She shook her head again, but in amazement, not bemusement. 'We used to cycle to the Deister forest. He always liked to go and climb one special tree. A vast oak with twisted branches and bark that tore your skin off.'

'You didn't like it?'

'I hated it. But he used to make me climb. Higher and higher.' Again she wiped the eyepatch. 'It amused him. He'd make me edge further and further out on a branch and then he'd shake the branch.'

I wanted to put my arms around this woman whose whole body shook at the memory of her fear. That was Axel. That was Axel all over.

'One day ...' She was quiet now. Too quiet. 'One day he shook the branch and I fell. From high up beside a rook's nest. I fell and broke my leg.'

'I'm sorry.'

'And a twig spiked into my eye.'

Axel had done worse. Far worse. I had seen it. But this woman's story clutched at my heart. I sat in silence with her, wondering how she could grieve for a brother who had done such things to her. Irmgard gathered herself together and went into the kitchen. She made us a cup of something that tasted of acorns.

'Thank you,' she said. 'Thank you for coming to tell me Axel's last words were of me. That he was sorry.'

I didn't look away. I looked right back at her dark grateful eyes. But I hated lying to her.

'I would like to go and visit that oak tree,' I said softly. 'As it obviously meant a lot to Axel. Can you draw me a rough map to show where I'd find it in the Deister forest?'

She smiled at me for the first time. When she should have scratched her fingernails down my face.

'Of course. It's at the Wennigsen end of the Deister hills. Just off the main trail. I'll fetch some paper.

It was that easy.

As I watched her draw a map of the forest trails, I felt the muscles between my shoulder blades start to unknot. The pulse in my throat eased off.

It was done.

I had just finished my drink and pocketed the sketch, when the door opened with a rush of cold air. Irmgard Köhler's husband launched himself into the room, snatched me up like I was a pup and ordered his wife to telephone the police.

CHAPTER SIXTY-ONE

The German police wanted nothing to do with me. They filled out a form at the police station because Herr Köhler had lodged a complaint against me. For causing distress to his wife. But Irmgard would not back up his accusations, not even when he switched to kidnap and theft. So the charges were dropped and I was returned to Graufeld Camp. The German police were pleased to be rid of me.

I was instantly summoned to Colonel Whitmore's office.

Hanna was missing. She should have been standing right beside me in her white tunic. Not that it was white any more. Last time I saw her it looked as though she'd climbed up the inside of a chimney in it. My own skirt and blouse were no better, testament to the number of ditches and mud holes we had scrambled through. Full of rips and scratches. Torn seams where the pressure hose had got to work. When I looked at myself I wasn't surprised the colonel wanted to send me back.

'I am obliged to return you into Soviet custody, Mrs

Janowska, until they have finished their questioning,' Colonel Whitmore told me for the tenth time.

He used that word a lot. Obliged. 'The German police were *obliged* to hand you over to me.' As if I were a food parcel. 'I am *obliged* to return you to the Soviets for questioning. It's not that I *wish* to do so, I want you to understand that.'

I understood. I did. It was his job. If he made an exception for me, he would have to make an exception for everyone. And he was British. The British always stick to the rules. All of a sudden I was aware of silence in the room. Colonel Whitmore had stopped talking. I focused on him and saw for the first time how sad he looked. Sad and tired. He was regarding me expectantly, waiting for a reply.

'Hanna Pamulska?' he prompted. 'You have no idea where she is?'

'No, sir. She was supposed to wait for me at the edge of the wood where I left her, but she wasn't anywhere around when the police led me back there.'

'Unfortunate. If you hear any word from her, I expect you to inform me.'

'Yes, sir,' I said.

He looked relieved. He thought I would be no trouble.

I stuffed my rage and humiliation back down my throat. I tucked my ice-cold fear and my hot shame out of sight. I offered him a bland inoffensive face.

'Sir, I have one request to make.'

'What is it?'

'When the Russians took me last time, it was all so fast

that I had no chance to arrange for the care of my daughter.'

He said nothing. Shuffled some papers.

'This time, Colonel, I would like time to arrange for someone to look after her while I am gone. And I want to fill out a form to apply for her to be taken into one of the children-only camps. It would be safer for her in one of those.'

His thick eyebrows shot up, startled. 'Really?'

'Yes, Colonel. Really.'

'How long do you need for this?'

'Two days.'

He frowned. 'I believe one day would be sufficient.'

'Two days, sir. So that I can spend time with her before you hand me back to Soviet Intelligence. I may be gone some time in Berlin.'

I stared at him, unblinking. Stared hard. So hard I saw a scarlet flush start to creep up his cheek. We both knew I wouldn't be coming back.

Alicja was there. Waiting for me outside the Administration office, kicking at the puddles on the ground with impatience. She looked skinnier, thin as a thread. And there was something wilder about the movement of her limbs, more feral, that I hadn't seen before.

I called her name and she looked up from the muddy puddles. At the sight of me she froze. Her eyes were huge in her face and as grey as the rain, instead of blue. Her mouth opened but no sound came out and it was that odd silence in her, even more than her immobility, that tore at my heart.

I knew the reason for her stillness. She was afraid. Afraid to move in case I vanished. I flew to her and scooped her into my arms, holding her in the circle of my love. I knelt down in the wet dirt and she buried her face in my neck. I rocked her and rocked her the way I did when I snatched her out of the convent and she wouldn't stop shaking.

'I prayed for you, Mama,' she whispered in my ear. 'I asked God to bring you back to me. And to save the poisoned man.'

That surprised me.

'And I asked Colonel Whitmore to bring you back,' she said.

I kissed her damp cheek. Her ear. Her hair. 'Thank you, sweetheart. I will always come back to you, always. Don't you know that? But even when I am not at your side, I am in every breath you take. Don't ever think you aren't with me. Because you are. In every thought inside my head.'

I felt her small chin start to tremble. I pulled back to take a look at my daughter's face. My eyes darted over it from feature to feature, checking each one minutely.

'You need more meat on your bones, Alicja.' I smiled. She lifted her head to try to match my smile. That was when I saw the livid bruise on her neck. The sight of it brought bile to my throat.

Alicja was asleep. At last she dared to close her eyes. I set two women from the hut to watch over her and I stepped out into the wet night. It was that kind of sharp-edged rain that soaked straight through to your skin and the wind had a mean winter bite to it.

Out of the darkness Davide appeared. He was carrying a ragged umbrella – I had no idea where it came from – and leaping over puddles. He opened his arms wide as he came near and I walked straight into them. After all my wanderings it was like coming home. I pressed my wet cheek to his, my arms clasping him close. We stood like that for a long time under the umbrella. No words. Indifferent to the wind and rain. Only aware of the heat between us as we found each other again.

Then we ran through the camp, arms linked, while the wind tried to rip the spokes from the umbrella. We stopped at the carved oak door in the walled vegetable garden and I took out the big iron key that I had borrowed from Niks. We splashed our way to the Latvian's small shed and tumbled inside, shaking ourselves like wet dogs. Skin touching. Pulses racing. Never taking our eyes off each other. Wanting to devour. To taste. To grasp. To love.

We stripped off each other's sodden clothes. Peeling them off piece by piece to find the being underneath. We wrapped ourselves in a threadbare green blanket that Niks liked to huddle in when the wind rattled the window loose in its fixings. Its weave smelled of tobacco and mice, but it became our skin, binding us together.

We didn't need words. No hows. No whys. No what ifs. We just needed each other. My body ached, but not from its blisters or from its scratches and bruises. It ached with the pain of needing him. In the flickering light of the candle his skin possessed a lustre and when he whispered my name it was in a tone of voice that I'd never heard from him before.

Our lovemaking was tender at first. Lingering kisses and silky caresses that set our skin on fire. Teasing out secret places that shuddered with desire,. But I wanted more. More of him. More of what lay inside him. It became fierce in those final soul-piercing moments when we tore away the last barriers with bare nails. When we became a part of each other.

No yesterdays. No tomorrows. Just here. Just now. In Davide's arms I could breathe each breath to the full and not worry about the next.

How do you thank someone for saving your child's life? How do you say, 'I am grateful to you for not letting my child die,' without falling to the ground and kissing their feet?

So I kissed Davide's feet.

He laughed. It was the best sound. And he drew me up to curl beside him, my head nestled on his chest. I could hear each beat of his heart. He ran a hand through my hair, as if to pluck out the thoughts inside.

'Tell me, Klara,' he said quietly.

I wrapped a leg possessively around his. I planted a kiss on his collarbone. I breathed. Then I told him all that had happened since I'd left Graufeld Camp, and he uttered no words, but I could hear his heart hammering worse than a drum. I could feel his lungs pumping harder than bellows. When I finished, he lay silent, his fingers knotted in my hair.

'People were kind to me,' I said. 'I am grateful.'

'Grateful to the cruel bastard who turned a hose on you?'

I swivelled on to my stomach, so that I could look at his face. 'Tell me what happened here. In Graufeld.'

He was reluctant. It made me nervous. There was something I needed to know. Not just Scholz's attack on Alicja. Something else. Something that was making Davide sit tight on his words.

Eventually it came out, Davide's conversation with Scholz. The German's accusations against me. They made me sick inside. I rolled away from Davide's side and sat up cross-legged in the cold damp air while the noise of the rain on the metal roof sounded like the hooves of spooked horses. I lifted one of his hands and curled both of mine around it.

'Did you believe Scholz?' I asked.

He gave me a slow smile. 'Should I?'

'I wouldn't blame you if you did, Davide. I know how devious he is. He takes part of the truth and twists it into something dark and dangerous to suit his own purpose.'

Davide's thumb stroked my palm. 'He is a convincing liar, no doubt of that. But I love you, Klara. Oskar Scholtz and his lies can't alter that.'

I pressed my hand to his chest, seeking out his heart. 'You don't know what that man can do,' I whispered.

CHAPTER SIXTY-TWO

I hung one pouch around Alicja's bruised neck. The pressure point where Scholz's thumb had drilled into her was an angry purple that spread sideways like a piece of seaweed, yellowish black. Each time I looked at it I had to stop myself from screaming.

But I silenced myself by painting images in my head. Of a long thin-bladed knife, a boning knife, the kind my father used when slicing a leg of pork. Sliding neatly between Scholz's ribs.

Would you blame me?

I hung the other pouch around my own neck. They contained our passports. It meant we were ready. I had told Rafal, Izak and Alzbeta that as soon as I had set us up in an address in England I would rush back and claim them. But I hated the idea of leaving them.

'You remember everything?' I whispered in the dark of early morning.

'Yes, Mama. Don't fuss.'

'It will be a long, long day for you.'

'I know. Don't worry so much.'

'You'll be safe there. As long as you stay hidden.' I cradled her precious face between my hands, so bright and eager to start on her new life. 'Promise me you'll stay hidden, Alicja.' I tightened my hold on the delicate bones.

'I promise.'

I had no choice. I had to believe her.

'Let's go.'

She gave me an odd little smile. 'What about Davide?'

'He'll come. When we are settled in England.' But a tremor hit my hands and I released her.

'Have you asked him?'

'Not yet.'

She clasped her arms around my neck and kissed my cheek. 'Be careful, Mama.'

'Don't fuss,' I smiled in the darkness, aware of her warm breath on my ear. 'It will be easy.'

But she didn't unclasp her young arms.

I risked the curfew. I had to get Alicja into the culvert before it was light. We waited just inside the door of our hut and I held her hand. It seemed startlingly slight, as if it had shrunk while I was away. I could feel sweat on my palm but didn't know whether it was hers or mine.

As soon as the nightshift guard was safely past, we slid outside into the black shadows and scuttled along the street. I could sense my daughter's excitement. She was chasing along, so eager to play her part that it frightened me. She might forget to listen to my dull voice of reason in her head. She might go skipping straight into the arms of trouble.

We ducked down the side of the laundry and it made me wonder yet again. Where the hell are you, Hanna?

I had a blanket under my arm and a stolen apple in my hand. This will be our last day here, my daughter. Trust me.

I made a big show of scouring the camp. Calling my daughter's name. The children did too. They darted from hut to hut, adding their light cries to mine.

'Alicja! Alicja! Alicja!'

I could hear my voice rising, growing ever more frantic. Other mothers joined the search and we surged as a posse down to the rough end of camp, right into the heartland of the men's huts. The odd thing was that the men acted guilty. They didn't meet our eyes, turning their backs or shouting abuse. As if our suspicion stained their skin with the mark of Cain.

Niks lumbered up to help. The big bearded Latvian barged into huts, upturned tables, demanding to know who was hiding my daughter.

'Where is she? Which one of you fiends from hell has taken Alicja? I'll break your fucking necks if you've touched a hair of her head. You hear me?' he bellowed.

I thanked him from the bottom of my guilty heart. I hadn't meant to hurt him.

It was Niks who charged snorting and stamping into Hut

W. I had been avoiding it. I walked straight past it. I wouldn't lay my eyes even on the doorway in case Scholz was standing there, his broken spectacles watching me, assessing me, raking through my lies.

'Klara!'

I spun round. Scholz was right behind me. Anger burned in his eyes, turning them as flat and as dark as slate.

'What have you done with her?' he hissed.

His spittle touched my lips and it took all the willpower I possessed to stop myself sinking my claws in him. This man tried to kill my child. If I attacked him, if I ripped his tongue from his head, I would be locked away. What good would I be to Alicja then?

'Where are you hiding her, you lying bitch? What are you up to?'

But he didn't raise his voice. His tone was quiet. He kept it close and intimate. Between the two of us. And because my hand refused to listen to me, it hauled right back and smacked him hard across the face.

'You think your daughter has somehow left the camp?'

'Yes, Colonel, I do.'

'How on earth could she get out?'

'I don't know, sir, but it seems she has. Your men have searched for her.'

Four of the British soldiers had been through the camp with a fine toothcomb, fast and efficient. When they searched the laundry, I didn't breathe. Rafal had stood in the drying yard bouncing a ball against a wall and whistling softly. Not once did he look in the direction of the drain to the culvert.

'I need to go outside to look for Alicja,' I said with a tremble in my voice.

'She could be anywhere.' He waved a hand at the window. 'Germany is a big country.'

'She hated being cooped up in here. She has said time and time again that she wants to go to those wooded hills to the south of us.'

'The Deister hills?'

'Yes, sir. I can only suppose that's where she is heading.'

'That's a big supposition, Mrs Janowkska.'

'It's all I've got to go on.' My voice broke. I dabbed at my eyes with a handkerchief and felt a darkness tuck around me.

The colonel ventured out from behind his desk and patted my shoulder kindly. 'I have a daughter myself, you know. I wouldn't want her to be out there alone.'

I raised tearful eyes to his. 'Alicja is all I have in the world.'

CHAPTER SIXTY-THREE

When you want something so badly.

When you've planned and worked so long.

When you feel it just at your fingertips.

Then, it is hard to sit still. To talk about the weather and cricket. But the sandy-haired soldier sitting beside me in the truck was English and he loved his national pastime. He was young and proud to show off his single lance-corporal stripe. Excited at the prospect of going home next month. I asked him about England and he told me he lived in a seaside town called Torquay where he and his father played cricket on a manor house pitch at Cockington.

'Do they have thatched cottages there?'

'Yes, lots of them.'

'And roses?'

He laughed, wrinkling his freckles. 'Everywhere in England has roses. You'd love it there.'

I looked out the side window of the truck as though searching for my daughter. I didn't want him to see my face.

*

'No! What are you doing? Take it off. Stop!'

'Sorry, love. Colonel Whitmore's orders.'

'But I'm not a prisoner. I've done nothing wrong.'

I stared in horror at the metal handcuff on my wrist. I shook it hard. Felt it bite. The other end was fixed to the soldier's own wrist. He had snapped them on the moment I'd jumped down from the truck when it parked under the spread of an oak.

'No!' I said again.

'The colonel thinks you might run. With the Russkies after you and everything.'

Whitmore had out-thought me. He'd seen what was coming. So he'd whipped my dreams out from under my feet. My hand stayed still, refusing to move, but the soldier gave it a tweak.

'Come on, love. Let's get going. We've got a lot of woodland to search if we're going to find your daughter.'

'Alicja!' I screamed. 'Alicja!'

CHAPTER SIXTY-FOUR

Graufeld Camp

ALICJA

Alicja lay in the culvert pipe. She heard them search. She heard them go. She did what she had promised, she waited. The world was reduced to a circle of corrugated white light at the end of the pipe and it seemed to beckon her.

She made her eyes close to block it out and rested her head on her forearm. It felt like living inside a grey tin can. The air claustrophobic and sour. It was hard on her elbows and hip bones, and it made the scars on her back ache as she lay on her front in the mud. Last night's rain had washed soil and debris down the drain and the stink was how she imagined a tomb to be. She didn't want to die here. Please, God, don't let me die in here.

She sang one of the nuns' hymns to herself and it calmed the fluttering inside her head. Mama had pushed a blanket in with her for warmth and she wriggled it tighter around her. She also had an apple and a slice of bread. She took a bite of the apple and started counting in her head.

By the time she got to 11,864, Rafal's face appeared at the end of the pipe.

'You took so long.'

'There were too many soldiers around,' Rafal whispered. 'They are still searching for you.'

His voice echoed oddly in the pipe.

'Rafal?'

'Yes?'

'Do it quickly.'

He was stretched out on his stomach in the dirt outside, peering down into the pipe, but his face was in shadow and so she couldn't see his bright brown eyes.

'Are you all right, Alicja?'

She nodded.

Rafal pushed his arm into the pipe and her hand gripped his. She held on tight.

'I'll be quick,' he promised.

'You'd better be.'

'When you smell smoke, it'll be safe to run.'

'Rafal.' She didn't let go his fingers.

'What.'

'Thanks.'

He squeezed her hand and laughed, the sound of it rippling through her grey world.

'Give me the sack,' she said.

He pushed a sack through the opening. 'Take care,' he urged. 'Go now.'

He was as good as his word. It wasn't long before Alicja could smell the smoke as it swirled through the camp. She wasn't sure what Rafal had set on fire, but whatever it was, it must be big.

She heard voices. Shouts.

'Thank you, Rafal.' She laughed with relief, but clapped a hand over her mouth so that it wouldn't float out for the world to hear.

As fast as an eel she wriggled backwards out of the pipe into the fields on the far side of the wall. The guards would be too busy running around with buckets of water and sparks in their hair.

She dragged great waves of clean air into her lungs and slung the sack over her shoulder. With a secret little whoop under her breath, she took off across the boggy soil as if the hounds were at her heels.

CHAPTER SIXTY-FIVE

If it hadn't been so appalling, I'd have laughed. We must have looked comical. Me and my soldier, yoked together like twins. Trudging along the trails through the forest, calling out my daughter's name in an echo of each other.

I made walking hard for him. Turning this way and that, darting in the opposite direction to chase a shadow. I wanted him to be sick of me.

The going grew tougher. Not because the Deister Hills were particularly steep or high, they weren't. The land here was so pancake flat that even this small range of low-forested hills stood out as a relief to the eye. It was only a few kilometres from Graufeld Camp and – more to the point – only a few kilometres from the village of Hagendorf where Axel Fleischer had lived as a boy. It was the mud that slowed us down. From last night's rain. We slipped and slithered, yanking each other's wrist, as we followed the main hillside trails under the trees. The lance-corporal had parked at Wennigsen and we had continued on foot.

We shouted till we were hoarse.

How Alicja would have liked it here. I worried about her inside the pipe. Above our heads arched a glorious golden canopy of autumn beech leaves, with splashes of rich russet-browns and smooth silver-grey trunks. Beechnuts peppered the mud like brittle marbles under our feet.

But what good were beech trees to me now? I needed undergrowth. I needed bushes. I needed a tangle of brambles or a clump of elder. The beech canopy was so dense that it blocked out the sky in the summer and nothing grew on the forest floor. The lack of ground-level vegetation allowed us easy vision between the trees, making this a place where it would be no problem to keep someone in sight, to track their movements as they flitted from tree to tree.

'You all right?'

My lance-corporal was regarding me with mild concern. He was a big-boned soldier who was clearly enjoying being out in the woods for a change. Even if it meant running round attached to a deranged woman.

'No,' I said. 'I'm not all right.'

My soldier may be fit. He may be strong. But he was young. He didn't stand a chance.

'What's the problem? If it's your daughter that you're—'

'I need to go to the toilet.'

I watched the colour flush up his cheeks.

'Can you wait?' he muttered.

'No.'

I craned my neck around a nearby tree and pointed. 'That looks like a clearing over there. It might be better.'

He didn't argue. We struck off the trail towards an area where the flat grey sky was visible and the sentinel trunks dwindled. It had been coppiced. Trees had been chopped down and allowed to start to regrow, filling the forest floor with light and bushes. Thick abundant bushes.

Perfect.

I turned to face the lance-corporal. 'You'll have to unlock me.' I held up my wrist.

He frowned and shook his head.

'Why would I run?' I asked him. 'I have nowhere to run to. I have to find my daughter. It will only take me a minute. I'll be behind those bushes over there.' I smiled. 'Don't worry.'

An older man would have said no. An older man would not have been so acutely embarrassed by female bodily func- tions. He'd have left the handcuffs on and looked the other way. But my soldier was young. He unlocked the handcuffs.

I ran. I ran for my life.

That is the truth. The literal truth.

If I am caught, I will be shot. Not by my soldier. Not by Colonel Whitmore. But by the Soviets when I am handed back. My soldier might as well put his own Lee-Enfield rifle to my head and pull the trigger.

I ran the way a deer runs. Jinking back and forth. Diving into undergrowth. Ducking behind broad oaks. Leaping ditches. Scrambling over rocks.

I lost him. My soldier.

Twice he came close. But not close enough. I led him away from where I wanted to be, his crashing and cursing always within earshot. And just when he thought he had me cornered near the top of the ridge, I slid down a steep gully and vanished.

Farewell, soldier.

I doubled back. Tore through the forest. Skimming the mud and barrelling down slopes. Finding my bearings. My heart was thumping wildly but I am good at direction. I can put a map in my brain, the way a bird can navigate across continents. And I had Irmgard Köhler's sketch of the forest nestling in my pocket.

I wove my way to the main trail that I was looking for and set out on my search for the oak tree, the one Axel Fleischer had named *Der Mörder*. The Killer.

I heard something. A noise, a rustling. I stopped. It stopped.

Was it in my head?

Was the laboured breathing mine? Or someone else's. Or was it the wind teasing me? Stirring up the leaf litter that lay like a path of gold under my feet?

I shook my head. Emptied such fanciful notions out of it and hurried onward. With every step I thought of Alicja jammed in the culvert at the back of the laundry and I feared for her. Stuck there alone, but safely hidden from Scholz. Yet a part of her was here with me, I was convinced. She was up in the very top branches of the trees, watching me, urging me on. Her young voice was in the whisper of the wind and in the fine drops of rain that had started to fall on my skin. My daughter was here. I could feel her. Yes, it was nonsense, I know, but it was also true. Where I went, Alicja came too.

I moved faster, the trees denser here. Not just beech, but a rich mix of oak and spruce and tall elegant birch, their greens and golds blending and overlapping in ever-shifting waves of colour. I found the path where I must turn to the left, indicated by a stone marker, just as Irmgard had told me. I dragged my feet out of the mud on to the new stonier pathway and a kick of excitement caught me unawares. I uttered a sound. Inarticulate but full of the thrill that was sending shivers through me. A soft sound. Nothing more.

A sound came back to me.

The hairs on my neck rose. I spun in a circle. Eyes fighting the greens. To search out a figure tight against a tree trunk or a shadow that moved where no shadow should be. Another sound. Nearer now. My heart leaped into my throat.

I stepped off the path and tucked myself behind a tired old chestnut tree. I didn't breathe. The undergrowth was thick and tangled with a hundred dark places to hide.

Was it my soldier? Had he tracked me somehow?

I bent, picked up a pebble and tossed it into the centre of a bed of bracken that reached almost to head height. Instantly I heard the cracking of stems and saw the ferns waving wildly. A dark shape lunged at me out of the shadows.

It was a wild boar. A mammoth bristling brute with massive grey shoulders and sharp white tusks that could rip open a person's legs, leaving them in shreds. I leaped backwards. Groped for the tree behind me and slid my body to the other side of it, but my eyes never left the small malicious eyes of the boar. It was three metres from me but I could smell it, rank and earthy. It grunted and huffed. A moist skin-crawling sound. And swung its heavy snout from side to side, wet nostrils twitching obscenely. One foot scraped at the mud.

Panic plucked at the edges of my mind.

Was the creature uncertain? Impatient? I didn't know and I didn't intend to hang around to find out. We had boars back in Poland, huge black-backed forest dwellers. I'd heard they had poor eyesight but a keen sense of smell. I bent slowly and chose a hefty stick from the debris at my feet.

Retreat? Or attack?

I chose the former. Silently and slowly I crept backwards, with the tree always blocking the animal's view of me. Past one tree, then another. I heard a loud grunt of frustration and a growl deep in the cavern of its chest. I froze. I raised my stick, ready to strike. If it came.

But a pair of wood pigeons chose that moment to come clattering down into a nearby tree, rowdy and argumentative. They must have distracted my aggressor because the animal abruptly turned with a flick of its tail and charged back into the bracken.

It was over.

My breathing eased up. I slunk away.

CHAPTER SIXTY-SIX

I was jumpy now. I looked over my shoulder at every flutter of a leaf. I listened to every sound that whispered among the trees. A hundred times my heart turned over.

I heard voices. I saw faces that were not there. As the rain grew heavier, I peered through its veil and could smell the damp breath of pursuers. The gaunt women, who robbed me of my two diamonds with such violence in a forest, came into my mind and I couldn't drive them out.

Forests cut you loose from reality.

All the best stories are set in forests. Stories that scare. That make children hide under the blanket. That sink claws into your mind. All the worst things that we see only in our nightmares hide in the black and secretive corners of a forest. They come to unfasten the nuts and bolts of our mind. To steal our soul.

That is the power that forests possess. So when I stood in front of the most colossal oak tree I had ever set eyes upon, I understood. Its massive branches seemed to spread out as far as the sky, dwarfing those around it. Defying gravity. Twisting and turning as if in pain. I could believe the delicate tips of its fingers were trying to draw the life of those around it into itself.

I understood why Axel Fleischer called it The Killer.

First I circled the tree, assessing it. The way you circle an enemy. Or a new friend. I admired its massive girth and its ancient boughs, the lower ones so heavy that they had sunk to the ground, providing an easy route up. Then I looked for its secrets.

I narrowed my eyes against the spitting rain and inspected each of the long rugged branches. Some parts were so old they were blacker than the backside of that boar I had words with earlier. I inspected the trunk. A rough blackish brown and with deep fissures marking its bark, but it offered no clues. I wiped the rain from my eyes. The longer I looked, the less I could see. There was only one way to do this.

I took hold of one of the tree's limbs that had dipped right down to the forest floor and started to climb. The bark was wet. Slick underfoot. But I made easy progress, scampering up to the trunk and then clinging to the next branch and swinging myself up. I kept that going. Climbing and swinging. So that I got to see all around the trunk, peering up and down it at each level, sticking my fingers into knotholes or mossy crevices where insects lurked.

I found nothing.

But I was only halfway up. I had been so focused on the

tree itself that I had forgotten to look down. I did so now and for a moment my world spun around me. It took flight in a swirl of green and gold. The black earth and the steel-grey sky seemed to swap places. I lurched.

How high was I?

Twenty metres? Thirty metres? More?

My stomach flipped.

I pictured Irmgard Köhler as a child. Eyes wide with fear, perched on one of these branches all those years ago. Her brother laughing. Goading her. Driving her to lose her grip. A scream. A crash. A crumpled figure on the ground, down there, curled up and clutching her eye. What did Axel feel?

Quickly I started climbing again. I searched every inch of that massive trunk, cursing it now. As angry at it as if it had pushed Irmgard itself. I glanced up. The sky loomed huge just above me, so close I could have reached out and taken a piece of it if I'd wished. When I glanced down, the world looked tiny. The other trees had shrunk. A deer, no bigger than a mouse, dodged into a clearing.

I scanned the forest. I could see no one.

Yet a pulse in my throat kept throbbing. I climbed higher. Slower now, breath tight. Leaves like golden wings spread around my head. My hand reached to the next branch and as I hauled myself up, impatient now, I saw it.

A hole.

Just where the branch joined the trunk. A hole the size of a man's head. A squirrel's drey? Or the den of an owl or a pine marten, I would guess. Cautiously I inserted a hand.

I felt nothing at first, but pushed my fingers deeper. No fur or feathers. No sharp teeth. A scattering of nuts, acorns and beechnuts, a winter hoard. Then my knuckle caught on something hard. Something metallic.

I didn't move. Didn't blink. But a heat started up inside me despite the chill of the rain and spread to the tips of my fingers. I tapped a nail on the hard surface in the hole and heard it ring.

I had dreamed of this moment. Conjured it up a thousand times in a thousand different ways, and wondered what it would be like. Now I knew. I gripped the metal box that was in the hole, wriggled it out and slithered down the tree.

The Killer tree did not kill me, Axel.

You do not get your revenge.

I was safe on the ground, the box in my hand. My mind already out of control, racing ahead of me. To thatched cottages. To roses around the door. To a world where I could at last work again and Alicja could go to a proper English school in a neat school uniform. And Davide would be there, laughing with a dog at his heels and we would run on a beach and—

I stifled the images.

I sat down heavily on one of the oak tree's roots that writhed up out of the soil like a serpent. My knees were shaking and when I looked at my legs I was unnerved. They were covered in blood and mud and scratches, the legs of something feral. Something you would not allow in the house. My hands and arms were the same.

What had happened to me?

My fingers were clamped on the box, so rigid I had to prise them off. The box was a large gunmetal grey cash box, its surface embedded with animal dirt and dead insects. I should have found it unpleasant to hold. I should have wiped it first with my filthy skirt. But I did neither.

I shook the box hard but it didn't rattle the way I'd expected it to, just a muffled bump inside. I tried to force the lid open but it wouldn't budge. I'd come prepared and pulled a knife from a sheath that hung from a thong around my waist under my skirt. It wasn't hard. Half a dozen jabs and the lock sprang open.

I could feel my teeth welded together as I started to raise the lid. What if it contained photographs of his mother? A lock of hair of his first love? His pet dog's collar? What if—?

I threw back the lid and almost wept with relief. Inside the box lay a roll of black velvet material, the kind jewellers use to show off their wares. Gently I unravelled one end. A diamond winked up at me. My hands worked faster. Faster. More and more diamonds, throwing luminous sparkles and dazzling dreams in my eyes. Despite the grey drizzle, they burned with an inner fire. Hundreds of them.

Laughing softly, I lifted out a handful and let them trickle through my fingers back into the box. But instead of sparkle. Instead of glitter. What I saw was blood dripping from the diamonds. It was gone in a heartbeat. Their iridescence shone through, but it was too late.

. I threw the rest of them back in the box with distaste and told myself it was a reflection of the russet leaves above me. Or even of the crimson streaks of blood on my hand. But I slammed the lid shut.

'Hand over the box,' a voice said behind me.

The barrel of a gun bit hard into the back of my neck.

'Did you think I would let you go, Klara? Did you honestly think it was the end?'

Oskar Scholz stood before me in his mud-spattered clothes, the cash box cradled in one hand, a Mauser pistol alert in the other. I blinked hard, unconvinced by my eyes.

How could this Scholz be real? How could he be here?

'Oskar, do you know what Axel Fleischer called this tree?'

He was startled by my question.

'He called it *Der Mörder*,' I continued. 'The Killer.'

He reacted with a burst of laughter. 'A good name for it. It will be the death of you.'

'Or you.'

'Don't delude yourself, Klara. As long as you did not have these beauties,' he shook the box, making the diamonds chatter, 'in your possession, you were safe. But now,' he shrugged, 'I have no further use for you.'

Dread slid down my spine, as he levelled the gun at my chest. If a man is talking he forgets to pull the trigger. Scholz is a man who will always want you to know how clever he is before you die.

'You didn't come to Graufeld Camp by accident,' I said calmly, 'did you?'

401

'Of course not.' His eyes gleamed. 'I do nothing by accident. I scoured the Displaced Persons camps of Germany for
you, trudging from one shithole to another in my search for
you.' He gave me an odd smile. 'I know you, Klara. We both
were aware that Fleischer had the diamonds and I was certain
you would not leave without them. If you and your pretty
daughter were stuck in Graufeld, it meant you hadn't located
them yet. That's why I didn't touch you. There was no need for
you to be frightened of me.' He stepped closer. 'Not till now.'

I nodded slowly. 'It's why I came here. To be near Hanover.
I knew Axel Fleischer's sister lived somewhere near.'

That laugh again, loose and full of self-congratulation.
He was Sturmbannführer Scholz once more. 'We are
both cunning.'

'So it would seem.'

'Did you think I came because I was in love with you? Is
that what your Frenchman told you?'

'Admit it, Oskar. You were always a little in love with me.'
My throat was so tight I had to force the words out. 'As I was
with you.' I saw him blink. Saw the thought swell inside his
head. 'We could share the diamonds, Oskar,' I added softly.
'We could go together.'

The wind took my words and whispered them again in
his ear. The tip of the gun dipped.

I thought I had him.

'Ah, Klara, I always admired your spirit. But I know you
would sink a knife between my ribs the moment my back
was turned.'

I'd lost him.

I edged closer. 'How did you find me here in the forest?'

'You led me a merry dance. What you don't realise is that I'm working for the Soviets now. They have one of the Graufeld guards in their pay and he smuggled me into the back of the truck you left in. So I followed your crazy chase through the forest.'

'You are helping the Soviets?'

'That's right. They imprisoned me before I could get out of Warsaw and offered me a deal. If I found them Fleischer's secret stash of diamonds, I could walk free.'

'You believed them?'

'Don't be a fool. Of course not. They'd shoot me the minute I handed them over. No, my sweet Klara, I am off to South America with these.' He rattled the diamonds again. 'That's why they wanted to interrogate you. They didn't give a fuck who you had or hadn't killed, they just wanted the diamonds.'

My hand slid into my waistband where my knife hung hidden beneath my skirt. 'There is no need to kill me, Oskar. You can go.' My fingers touched the handle of the knife. 'I will say nothing.'

'Don't move, Klara. Don't touch the knife. You think I didn't watch you open the box with it?' He smiled at me sadly. *'Auf Wiedersehen*, my friend. This is goodbye.'

Darkness came to engulf me as the gun pointed at my head. But I would not go silently from this world, not as long as Alicja and Davide were still in it waiting for me, loving me. The bullet would strike, but so would my knife.

403

I drew a final breath. But before I could move ... Scholz screamed. A terrible bone-scraping animal sound. He collapsed face down on the ground in a paroxysm of jerking limbs.

A crossbow bolt was embedded in his back.

CHAPTER SIXTY-SEVEN

ALICJA

Alicja threw down the crossbow and ran. She raced across the small clearing around the massive oak tree where her mother stood. Her gaze fixed on the man on the ground.

'Mama,' Alicja cried out.

Her mother lifted her head. A jerky disjointed movement. But the moment she saw her daughter coming, she flung her arms wide and Alicja flew into them. They closed around her and crushed her tight against her mother's filthy clothes. She felt Mama's cheek rub hard over her own and heard the whispered words, 'Thank you, my love, thank you.'

'Is he dead?' She held her breath.

'No, Alicja, he's alive.'

Oskar Scholz uttered a groan and Mama walked over to him and knelt down. She touched the back of his jacket where Rafal's bolt had struck and he yelped like a snared rabbit.

'You'll live,' her mother said in a cold tone. 'It is in your shoulder blade not your lungs. If you start walking right now, you'll get to camp before you bleed to death.'

'Help me to get there, Klara,'

'The only place I would help you to, you murdering bastard, is hell.'

Alicja saw her pick up the gun that lay among the golden leaves, rise from her knees and move away from him. The thin rain was spreading the scarlet patch on his jacket.

'I warned you,' Alicja shouted at the wounded figure. 'I told you I would defend her.' Tears stung her eyes but she didn't know why.

'Bitch cub,' the German growled into the earth.

She turned away. She couldn't bear to look at him. Her shoulder still felt the kick from releasing the crossbow bolt and her right arm wouldn't keep still. Instead she focused her mind on the metal box that lay on the ground near him.

'What's in the box, Mama?'

'Nothing.'

The man grunted. 'Liar. Tell her the truth, Klara. Show her what's in the box.' He tried to reach out a hand to it, but the pain was too much. 'Show her what this has all been about.'

Alicja darted forward, snatched up the box and retreated.

'Open it,' her mother said.

Alicja lifted the lid. It was like looking at the inside of a rainbow. Reds and purples and dazzling indigo that came and went like the colours of the sea.

'Diamonds,' she breathed. 'So many.' She stirred them with her finger and felt their sharp edges nip her skin. 'We can buy identity papers and ration cards and travel tickets and—'

'Close the box.'

But Alicja couldn't. She scooped a dozen of the gems out and rolled them across her palm, laughing with excitement. 'Look, Mama, look how they sing in the light like—'

'Put them back.' Sharp. Stinging.

'But we can go to England now like you wanted. What is it, Mama?'

'There is blood on them.'

'No, they are bright and clean, look.'

'No. No, Alicja. They are thick with blood. Jews' blood.'

'Why?'

'Because they were stolen from Warsaw's Jews.'

Alicja felt a thud of horror in her heart.

'Listen to me, Alicja. I didn't think enough about that till now. I was wrong. I intended to share them with the sister of the man who stole them and with his friend still in his Berlin apartment, but now—'

'You fool!' It came as a roar from the wounded man on the ground.

Mama turned her back on him.

'If we kept some for ourselves, Mama, would that be wrong?'

Her mother's face softened, her hand stroked her daughter's wet hair. 'Yes, it would. But don't look upset. The diamonds have to go back to—'

Mama paused, her blue eyes widened and a smile spread across her muddy face. A figure had emerged from among the trees.

'Hanna!'

Alicja accepted the kiss from Hanna. But this was a different Hanna. A stiff and prickly Hanna who couldn't keep her eyes off the man on the ground or the blood on his back.

Mama didn't seem to see it. 'How did you find us, Hanna? I've been worried about you.'

'I was watching the camp, Klara. I saw you leave in the truck but I couldn't follow on foot.' Her eyes travelled to the box in Alicja's hands and lingered there. 'When I saw Alicja leave, I followed her. She was too quick for me at times but,' she gave Alicja a smile, 'quick enough to wing this Nazi bastard, I see.'

'I found the map of the forest trails in Mama's pocket and copied it out. That's how I knew where she was going and how to get there.' Alicja pointed towards the oak. 'Oskar Scholz was here threatening to shoot her.'

The German had eased on to his side and was eyeing Hanna the way you eye a snake. Alicja was starting to regret missing his lungs with the crossbow, but Mama walked over to him and took hold of one of his arms. He tried to pull it free but was too weak.

'Help me, Hanna,' Mama said.

Together the two women yanked him up on to his feet. Neither was gentle. His screech of pain startled a rook from its treetop perch.

'Shall I pull the bolt out, Mama?' Alicja wanted to return it to Rafal, but the thought of tugging it from the bone scared her.

Hanna didn't hesitate. She ripped it out of him.

'Bitch!' he growled with teeth bared.

Alicja saw the sweat on his brow. His lips were grey. She had a sudden fear that these three people were going to kill each other.

'Tell them, Hanna,' Scholz said in a hoarse whisper, 'why you're really here. Tell them that you work as a spy for the Soviets too. No more her friend than I am.'

Mama swayed, but uttered no sound. Waiting for her friend to deny it. The wind chased amber leaves around their feet but neither moved. Alicja went to stand next to her mother and took her hand.

'Is it true?' Mama whispered.

'God damn your putrid soul to hell, Scholz. Yes, Klara, it's true. Don't look at me like that. The fucking Russkies have thrown my elderly parents in prison and put me in the camp with you to find out about the diamonds.'

She glanced at the box. Alicja clutched it tighter.

'They ordered you to become my friend?'

'Yes.'

'So you weren't really interrogated in Berlin?'

'No. They were pleased with me and gave me vodka.'

'Your bloodied nose?'

'I did it myself when I went in search of you.'

Mama's hand shot over her mouth. 'It was you, wasn't it? You put the snake in my bed.'

'Yes, but not to hurt you, never to hurt you. I had to spur you into action. To make you so frightened of Scholz, you would go hunting for the diamonds.' Hanna shook tears from her eyes. 'I love you and your daughter, Klara. You are my dear friend, but I am frightened for my parents, so—'

The wounded German laughed, a sibilant sound that made Alicja's skin crawl.

'You blind bitch,' he said, breathing hard. 'They will be dead by now. Don't you know that? And when the Soviets come for me, demanding the diamonds, you can bet your hide that I'll be telling them that you, Hanna Pamulska, let them,' he jabbed a finger in the direction of the box in Alicja's hand, 'get away.' He was listing dramatically to one side, unable to stay upright. 'You hear that, you bitch?'

It was Mama who reacted. She removed the box from Alicja's embrace, brisk and firm. She would take no dissent. Alicja could see her mother's eyes had grown a shell over them. Hard and clear as glass.

'Alicja, run and fetch your crossbow.'

'But why do I need it?'

'Fetch it, Alicja. Be quick.'

Alicja took off so fast her heels were skidding in the mud. Why did Mama want the crossbow? Which one of them was she going to shoot?

She reached the big spruce tree where she had abandoned the bow, and was bending to pluck it up from the sack when she heard a gunshot. Her whole body lifted off the ground

410

with shock. She spun round and heard a great wail of sound come out of her own mouth.

The two women were standing shoulder to shoulder. Their backs to her. Blocking her sight of what lay sprawled on the ground. But Alicja could see enough to know.

It was Oskar Scholz.

CHAPTER SIXTY-EIGHT

We buried him in a shallow scrape. He deserved no better. You may not think so, but it's true. Hanna and I hauled his carcass deep into a tangled fortress of bushes and brambles.

With branches we dug out an indentation in the mud big enough, rolled Scholz's body into it, and offered no words of peace or forgiveness over it. In death he seemed to shrink. The strength and cruelty sucked out of him. As I gazed down on to the rain-soaked empty shell, stained with mud and streaked with wet leaves, I found it hard to remember why I had feared him so much.

Now I feared for my daughter. I kept her busy, running back and forth collecting a funeral pile of branches and leaves, but when it was done, when the body was covered and out of sight, I took her in my arms.

Her young arms clung around my neck. I felt her heart beating fast against mine. I held her in my arms, crooning softly to her, until she was ready to look me in the eye.

'Will he come back?' she whispered.

'Never. I promise.'

'I'm glad he's dead.'

'So am I.'

We would talk of this later. But for now, it was enough.

It didn't matter which of us had shot him. He was gone. In my heart I wasn't ready to believe it yet, but my mind told me it was true. Hanna wanted the diamonds, to share them between the two of us. She trickled them through her fingers, balanced them on her fingertips and held them up to my daughter's earlobes.

'Come on, Klara. Let's live a little. We can buy all our dreams. Isn't that what you want for Alicja?'

Alicja's huge blue eyes regarded me hopefully.

'Yes, of course it is,' I replied. 'But not with these.'

'What are you going to do?'

'We're going back to the camp. I am sure Colonel Whitmore will make a deal when he sees what I have to offer.'

'Well, fuck that,' Hanna snorted. 'I'm not going back. Ever. Now I'm out, I'll take my chances.'

I lifted the lid of the box that Alicja still clung to like a life raft. I lifted out around a dozen or so of the flashing gems and tipped them on to Hanna's palm. Instantly she closed her fingers over them.

'Go and kick that future of yours into shape,' I urged, giving my friend the kind of hug you give when you know it is the last. 'Go buy yourself that laundry.'

As Hanna crushed me to her bosom she whispered, 'I'm sorry, Klara.'

I stroked her wet cheek. 'I know.'

She rumpled Alicja's hair, called out, 'Take damn good care of those sparklers,' then turned and walked away.

Both of us felt the huge hole she left in the forest. Together, hand in hand, Alicja and I headed towards the track that led to Graufeld.

'I know one thing, Mama.' She was jiggling the diamonds as she walked, listening to their voices.

'What's that?'

'Davide will be happy that you are coming back.'

I smiled.

CHAPTER SIXTY-NINE

I'll say this for Colonel Whitmore. When I was marched into his office with Alicja at my side, both of us looking like something his men had dragged out of the gutter, he didn't turn and run. He didn't invite us to sit down on his nice clean seats, but he did seem genuinely pleased to have us back under his wing.

I removed the box from my daughter's arms and placed it on his desk. I raised the lid to reveal the diamonds and watched the colonel's jaw drop. His eyes popped out on stalks. The sight of all their glittering beauty made him gasp, as they sent rainbows dancing across his ceiling. Everything else in the room looked drab. But we both knew it wasn't their glitter that counted. Nor their rainbows. Nor their inner fire and beauty. That's not what made jaws hit the floor. It was their hard value in gold coin that made these beguiling nuggets of carbon so lethal.

'Where on earth did they come from?' Whitmore demanded.

He picked up one in his hand. Just one. From hundreds.

Such restraint. I still could not look at them. Even that solitary diamond was like a clot of blood on his palm.

I told him a carefully trimmed down version of the truth. That they had belonged to a Nazi officer in Warsaw who had *acquired* them from the hundreds of thousands of Jews he had transported off to Treblinka and Auschwitz. That I had learned of their existence and hiding place in the Deister hills. That Alicja and I had gone to search for it. That was all.

That was enough.

Colonel Whitmore studied me long and hard. He was an intelligent man. Nobody's fool. He knew I had just picked out the barest of bones to give him, but he had the sense not to ask for more.

'Sir, I wish the diamonds to be donated to a charity for the rehoming of the Polish Jews who are still alive.'

'Yes, that sounds like a just cause for them. I congratulate you, Mrs Janowska.'

I felt my cheeks colour fiercely. I did not want his congratulations. He weighed the jewels, locked them away in his safe and presented me with a receipt.

Now came the delicate part.

'Colonel, about the Soviets.'

His expression sharpened.

'When the Soviets interrogated me in Berlin, they weren't interested in me, only in the diamonds. But now that the diamonds are safely in your possession, there is little point in sending me back to Berlin. Is there, sir?'

As I said. He was an intelligent man.

But he held on to his answer. Made me wait. After a full minute of considering his options, like the skilled military man he was, he nodded.

'No point at all.'

He smiled at me and shook my dirty hand. Shook Alicja's hand too.

'Thank you, Mrs Janowska. The least I can do in return is to put in a request for your case to be expedited in the search for missing relatives.'

'Thank you, Colonel.'

Alicja's gaze remained firmly on the safe.

'You look like shit, my love.'

I laughed and twined my muddy arms around Davide's neck. 'Wash me.'

The washroom showers, as always, had a never-ending queue, so Davide sat me down on a stool, still in my filthy clothes, in the laundry's drying yard. The rain had eased and thin wisps of autumn sunlight drifted around my feet. There were no sheets today. Just us, alone. Except for a bold squirrel with a cheek full of nuts burying them for the winter when times grew harsh.

Davide gently washed my arms with long slow strokes. It felt like silk on my limbs. It was only an old square of flannel cloth, nothing special. But after the battering I had taken, inside and out, in the forest – after the thorns and branches and twisted briars, after men with guns and friends with lies – I felt as if parts of me had been torn off.

My body was struggling to put itself back together again, in the same way my mind was. In Davide's hands the flannel soothed the scratches. His touch helped heal the cuts. Both mental and physical. As I watched him run his strong fingers over my skin, I knew he was remembering each mark, each bruise, because every one of them told him the things I could not put into words.

'Is it over?' he murmured.

'It's over.'

'Are you free?'

Such a strange question when we were surrounded by high walls and barbed wire.

'Yes, my love, I am free.' I leaned forward and kissed his lips.

He dipped the flannel in the bowl of soapy water and with a smooth, steady rhythm he cleaned my palm. My wrist. The tip of my elbow.

'Davide, how is the man who drank the poison?'

'He is doing better every hour apparently.'

'I'm so glad. Thank you.'

He smiled thoughtfully as he dipped the flannel once more. He held my chin in one hand, studying each feature as he scrubbed it clean. He washed my forehead, my mouth, my ears. Firmer now. Wiping the dirt off me. The blood and the filth. Again and again till I could breathe.

I took hold of his face between my hands and rested my head against his.

'Davide, I will be working hard – teaching more hours

and stealing more tins from the kitchens – to save for the cost of identity papers for myself and the children. But,' I brushed my lips across his, tasted the special Frenchness of him, 'it doesn't have to be England. France is a big country. It might have a corner somewhere for us.'

'Klara,' his voice was tender, 'do you know how many people in this camp have got married to each other in the last four months?'

'No idea.'

'Forty-eight.'

'Is that so?'

'That seems to me a very awkward number. Fifty is a much neater number in the ledger.'

I laughed and twined my clean arms around Davide's neck.

'Kiss me.'

CHAPTER SEVENTY

That night sleep wouldn't come. I pushed my fingers hard against my eyelids to erase what lay behind them, but it wouldn't go.

I filled my mind with images of the good memories in my life. The strong memories. To drive out the others, the ones I fought to turn my back on. I pictured Davide's laughing brown eyes and rekindled the feel of his hands on my skin when he soothed my ragged cuts today.

I pictured my daughter's brave face, so fierce when she saved my life by the oak tree. And her secretive smile when I kissed her goodnight. She thought I didn't know about the two diamonds she had concealed in her pocket when she held the box so close. To replace the ones she gave away to the thieving women in Poland's forest.

I smiled at them all.

But as I started to finally drift into sleep, floating on its very edge, that's when it came at me. The memory that would never go.

It was the end of us.

The German army was in full retreat. They had caused the deaths of six million Poles, half of them Jewish. The Soviets were about to march on the city of rubble that had once been my beloved Warsaw. Oberführer Axel Fleischer stormed into my apartment with Sturmbannführer Oskar Scholz at his heels.

'Come, Klara,' Axel said in a hurry. 'Pack your things. We are leaving at once.'

'I am not leaving without my daughter.'

A frown of annoyance flashed across his face. 'I thought you'd have forgotten about your daughter by now.'

'I will never forget about my daughter.' I swung round to Scholz who was standing by the door, impatient to leave. 'Where is she, Oskar?'

'No,' snapped Fleischer. 'We don't need a child slowing us down.'

'I won't leave without her.'

'Very well. Scholz, where is the girl?'

'In the convent of St Mary of the Blessed Sacrament.'

Fleischer lifted the telephone. 'Get me Leutnant Hausmann at Headquarters.' He fixed his eyes on mine. 'What is your daughter's name?'

'Alicja Janowska.'

He waited and I dared to hope he would send for her.

'Hausmann? I want you to go to the convent of St Mary of the Blessed Sacrament and find a girl called Alicja Janowska. Take her outside—'

My heart leaped with joy.

'—and shoot her.'

*

421

It broke me. It robbed me of reason. I reacted without hesitation. Instinctive. Unthinking. Instant.

I ran to the bureau. Reached into my writing case and snatched out the Walther PPK I had the sense to keep hidden there. In two seconds I was back at Axel Fleischer's shoulder, the dark-metal barrel of the gun jammed against the side of his head. His ear grew crimson.

'Rescind that order,' I said fiercely.

He didn't move. The telephone receiver still in his hand.

'Rescind that order or you will die before your next heartbeat.'

His blue eyes narrowed to slits. He tried to turn his head to look at me but the gun didn't let him.

'Choose,' I said. 'Now.' My finger tightened on the trigger. 'Choose.'

'No, damn you, Klara. I will not be dictated to by you. I will not take orders from a Polish whore. Who do you think you are? If I say she dies, she dies.'

He banged down the receiver with an angry clatter. Again I reacted. Instinctive. Instant.

I pulled the trigger. The noise was deafening in the silent room. Deafening to my ears, but also deafening to something deep inside me. Oberführer Axel Fleischer dropped like a stone at my feet. I pointed the gun straight at Oskar Scholz's heart.

'Pick up the phone, Sturmbannführer Scholz. Call Leutnant Hausmann. Rescind that order. Now.'

Oskar Scholz looked ready to kill me, but his pistol remained in its holster. He made the telephone call. He rescinded the order.

When it was done, he stood in front of me, rigid with shock. 'I will be the one blamed for this, Klara Janowska.' His lip was trembling with rage. 'Wherever you run, wherever you hide, I will find you. And I will kill you. But first, I will kill your daughter.'

I forced him into Fleischer's study, locked the door and ran. I ran for Alicja's life.

CHAPTER SEVENTY-ONE

'You have a visitor.'

It was a month after Alicja and I had returned to Graufeld Camp that Colonel Whitmore greeted me in his office with the last words I'd expected and a beaming smile. He had the contented look of a parent about to bestow a Christmas gift.

'*A visitor?*' I knew no one who would visit me. This was a mistake. Or worse.

He whisked me down a corridor with long military strides. He was a man who liked to get things done.

'Who is it?' I asked warily.

He gave me the parental smile again. 'Wait and see.'

I didn't want to wait and see. I wanted to be prepared.

The colonel threw open a door with a flourish and I walked into the room quickly. To face this *visitor.*

'Surprise!' Colonel Whitmore chuckled softly.

My heart stopped. I froze. No breath. No thought. No belief in what my eyes were telling me they were seeing. I didn't hear the colonel withdraw and close the door quietly behind him. The room was a spartan office, like any other military office, but the tall male figure standing in front of the desk was not like any other figure. It was my husband.

'Dymek,' I whispered.

Tears were rolling down my cheeks. This was a phantom, I knew it was. A ghost. A spectre. A trick of the light. But I felt a rush of warm gratitude to whatever gods had decreed I should receive this *visit* from my dead husband.

'Klara.'

He started towards me. With that smile of his. That teasing one that had always known how to put my world right whenever a disaster had crept up on me. But I leaped to him and threw my arms around his strong shoulders, clutching him tight to me before he vanished again.

He may be a fantasy of my lonely mind, but I could feel the warmth of him through the navy serge of his suit, and the strength of his arms as they closed around me. Smell the scent of his aftershave where my cheek touched his.

I jerked back my head. My Dymek never wore aftershave. Yet it was my husband's face. I ran my fingertips over it but there were no scars, no burns, just his warm brown eyes gazing at me and the long straight nose I'd loved to stroke. It was still the animated face of a man who sought adventure, but in the delicate cobwebbing around his eyes there were lines that had not been there before.

'It's you,' I whispered.

'It's me.' With the gentle touch I remembered so well, he wiped my tears away with his fingers.

'You're not dead?'

'No, Klara, I'm not dead.' He kissed my cheek and I expected part of my skin to melt but it didn't. 'See?' he said.

Something was wrong. I could sense it. But I didn't know what. Something wrong with him? Something wrong with me? Vital parts of me were shaking inside.

'You didn't die? When your plane was shot down?'

I stepped back a fraction and ran my hands over his arms and his chest, feeling solid muscle and whole healthy limbs. My disbelief was washed away by a joy that knocked me off my feet. I collapsed on a chair and Dymek knelt at my side. I reached for his hand.

He was telling me things but all I could take in was the shape of his mouth and the patch on the side of his head where there was no hair. His scalp was pink and shiny underneath.

He was shot down, he said. Both legs smashed. Rescued by Resistance fighters who cared for him in a safe house.

'I'd have come to you. If you'd sent word,' I told him.

'I did. But our apartment was bombed. Your parents' place too. I was told you had all been killed in the explosions.' He paused, a deep furrow appearing between his brows. 'Including Alicja.'

'She's here,' I smiled.

'How is she?'

'Well. Strong. Brave.'

Tears welled up in his eyes. In a way they hadn't done for me.

'I was there all the time,' I told him. 'In Warsaw throughout the war.'

He raised my hand to his lips and noticed my damaged fingertips. He wound both his large capable hands around mine. Was he hiding them? Or keeping them safe?

'I was passed through the Resistance network,' he said, 'after my legs healed and I got myself to England. I joined the Polskie Siły Powietrzne, the Polish air force in Britain and flew planes against Hitler's Luftwaffe for the last years of the war.' He paused again. An awkward, uneasy suspension of time. Neither of us knew what to do with it.

'What about you?' He looked at me intently. 'In Warsaw.'

'I got by.'

'It is wonderful that you got out before the Russians marched in.'

'How did you find me? Why now? After all these years, if you believed we were dead.'

He rubbed the tip of my thumb with his own thumb and I felt a ripple of pain under the skin.

'In England I tracked down your British grandmother,' he explained. 'Her house in Exeter was bombed but after a lot of searching and paperwork, I found her in a village called Cherhill in Wiltshire.'

'You found Grandma?'

I was shivering again. I stroked the back of his neck. 'Thank you, Dymek. Thank you. You always were good at—'

He shrugged off my thanks. And my hand. 'It was terrible informing her of your family's death. She took it hard.'

'Poor, poor Grandma. But now ...' I smiled at him. 'She knows?'

'Yes. She telephoned me yesterday to say she'd received an official letter asking whether someone named Klara Janowska in a DP camp in Germany was any relation.' He laughed and I wanted to tell him how many times I had tried to conjure up that laugh in my dreams. 'She thought you must be an imposter.'

'But you came anyway.'

I felt him soften. Not just his lean muscles. His eyes, his chocolate brown eyes seemed to melt. 'Of course I came, Klara.'

He took both my hands between his and for that single moment, we became one tight unit again. And it gave me the strength to sit back from him, withdraw my hands and ask in a calm voice, 'What is wrong, Dymek?'

He exhaled hard. 'I thought you were dead, Klara. Six long years.'

I knew what was coming. I knew it before the words left my husband's lips.

'I am married, Klara.'

'What's her name?'

He looked me directly in the eye, trying to decide whether I could take this hurt.

'Her name is Nell. She is English, a teacher. She's clever,

Klara. You'd like her. And . . .' The pause again, the pause that meant I would not want to hear what was coming next. 'And we have a son. George. Named after the king of England.'

I breathed slowly. 'How old is George?'

'He's three.'

'Three years old.'

I swallowed hard. A half-brother for Alicja. In England. I rose to my feet and stood close to Dymek, placed my hands flat on his chest. His heart was racing.

I took my time studying his face. With such affection. I wanted him to know how much he meant to me. I knew I was saying goodbye for the second time to the man who used to be a part of me. Saying hello to the man who was Nell's husband.

'I am happy for you, Dymek. Truly I am.'

Did I mind?

Of course I minded. I minded like hell. That Dymek had found himself a replacement wife and child so fast. Before the varnish on our coffins was dry.

But did I blame him? Was I angry?

No, of course not. Not one bit. We all need love and we all need to give love. It's what keeps our souls warm and alive. Without love, something dies in you. I thought of Davide. I thought of Alicja. I thought of Rafal, Alzbeta and Izak. How my love for them had helped bring me back from the brink.

I slid an arm comfortably through Dymek's and led him out into the sunlight.

'Come and see Alicja,' I smiled, 'and our family.'

Dymek stared at me, surprised. 'You have more family?'

'Yes. Yes, I do.'

As we walked through the camp and he looked around him, I took to viewing Graufeld Camp through his eyes. Even in the sun, it was dilapidated. It was shabby and grey. Just as the DPs themselves were shabby and grey. Unwanted. It's true. That's what we were. Unwanted people. But I couldn't bear Dymek to see it that way. This place that had given my daughter and me a roof over our heads and food in our belly. It had given us life. When we were in the grip of death.

'We are lucky,' I said at his side, 'to be here.'

He gave me a long assessing look and said firmly, 'You are not the same person I knew, are you, Klara? Not the bright young woman who kissed me goodbye that day in August 1939.'

I stared ahead at the group of five people – Davide and the four children – playing the simple game of French boules on a patch of dirt. Davide was teaching Izak the expert grip on a *boule* and they were all laughing. Rafal of course was cheating as usual.

'No,' I said honestly. Without regret. 'Life changes us. That girl has gone, Dymek. You can't walk through the fires of war and not get burned. But now Europe will be free. That is why we fought the war, that's what so many people sacrificed their lives for. Because without freedom how can we believe in ourselves? How can we ever be happy?'

'Are you happy, Klara? Despite—' he waved a dismissive hand around my home, '—despite all this?'

'Yes, I am. Love heals so many wounds.'

'You are in love?' His surprise that love could be found in a place like Graufeld Camp was obvious.

'Yes, Dymek, I am. And even happier now that your arrival means Alicja and I will be given our nationality papers.'

'And entry to England.'

I nodded. The future, I'd learned, need not mean a cottage and roses.

'Come,' I said. 'Meet my family.'

I waved to the tight-knit group engrossed in the game. Alicja waved back. But her hand froze mid-air as she stared at the man at my side. With a small cry, she seized Davide's hand and they came racing towards us. I reached for them. At last we were no longer displaced persons. Our place was together.

Acknowledgements

I want to say a heartfelt thank you to my editor Jo Dickinson for her brilliance and for her wonderful support – it means the world. And my grateful thanks to the whole awesome team at Simon & Schuster who are the best. The very best. Thanks to you all.

Very special thanks to my agent Teresa Chris who is my rock and my guide, and who often understands what I need even before I do.

I am very grateful to Anne Menke and Horst Menke for helping me to get both my German language and my German geography right. Any errors are definitely mine alone.

I am also indebted to Chris Mason for the invaluable insight he gave me into his experience of the world of post-war Germany. It gave me the courage to be brave.

As always my love to my good friends at Brixham Writers who are generous with their support and laughter. And cakes.

Warmest thanks to my dear friend Marian for being the

biscuit-nibbling bridge between my scrawled pages and the tidy manuscript on-screen.

And then there is Norman. Ever full of creative ideas and boundless encouragement. My huge thanks and love.

Kate Furnivall

The Liberation

Italy, 1945.
A country in turmoil.
A woman with one chance to save herself.

Caterina Lombardi is desperate – her father is dead, her mother has disappeared and her brother is being drawn towards danger. One morning, among the ruins of the bombed Naples streets, Caterina is forced to go to extreme lengths to protect her own life and in doing so forges a future in which she must clear her father's name.

An Allied Army officer accuses her father of treason and Caterina discovers a plot against her family. Who can she trust and who is the real enemy now? And will the secrets of the past be her downfall?

This epic novel is an unforgettably powerful story of love, loss and the long shadow of war.

'A thrilling roller-coaster of a read, seductive, mysterious and edgy. I LOVED it'
Dinah Jefferies, author of *The Tea Planter's Wife*

AVAILABLE NOW IN PAPERBACK,
EBOOK AND AUDIOBOOK

SIMON &
SCHUSTER